RAVES FOR

THE

"[Will] have you questioning the ethics of the medical biz—and praying that you don't ever need a serious operation."—*New York Post*

"Deft plotting, sure characterization, and cutting-edge technology . . . A thriller that will extend the burning hours of your bedside reading lamp."—*Iowa City Gazette*

"Palmer's novel has all of the ingredients to ensure . . . another engrossing drama by a master of the genre. Enthusiastically recommended."—*Library Journal*

"Keep[s] readers rooting for the home team through extortion and murder, medical mayhem, and medical miracle."—*Booklist*

"Twisting, suspenseful."—*Pittsburgh Post-Gazette*

"*The Patient* is wonderful . . . Palmer is a master at mixing the medical and terrorist thriller. The drama is tense and builds to a terrifying conclusion."
—*Times Record News* (Texas)

"Suspense is maintained throughout, ending in a violent climax."—*Mystery News*

"Adrenaline-pumping action and cutting-edge medicine mesh seamlessly in *The Patient,* making it one of the most exciting medical thrillers."—*Morristown Daily Record*

"A top-notch thriller . . . filled with bits and pieces that only someone who has lived his or her life in the medical profession can convey."—*The Colony Times*

MICHAEL PALMER

THE PATIENT

BANTAM BOOKS

NEW YORK TORONTO LONDON SYDNEY AUCKLAND

THE PATIENT

A Bantam Book

PUBLISHING HISTORY
Bantam hardcover edition published April 2000
Bantam export edition published July 2000
Bantam paperback edition / August 2001

Library of Congress Catalog Card Number: 99-057838

ISBN: 0-553-58038-8

PUBLISHED SIMULTANEOUSLY IN THE UNITED STATES AND CANADA

Bantam Books are published by Bantam Books, a division of Random House,
Inc. Its trademark, consisting of the words "Bantam Books" and the portrayal
of a rooster, is Registered in U.S. Patent and Trademark Office and in other
countries. Marca Registrada. Bantam Books, 1540 Broadway, New York,
New York 10036.

PRINTED IN THE UNITED STATES OF AMERICA
OPM 10 9 8 7 6 5 4 3 2 1

For Beverly Lewis

ACKNOWLEDGMENTS

The many, often lonely and uncertain hours spent here in front of my Mac have been much more bearable because of my friends and family. This page is one of the ways I get to express my appreciation to them.

At the Jane Rotrosen Agency, Jane Berkey, Don Cleary, Stephanie Tade, and Annelise Robey have made writing easier for me in many ways.

At Bantam Dell, Beverly Lewis, Christine Brooks, Irwyn Applebaum, Nita Taublib, Susan Corcoran, and Barb Burg have done the same.

Sam Dworkis, Mimi Santini-Ritt, Sarah Elizabeth Hull, Dee Jae Jenkins, Matt Palmer, and Beverly Tricco have been invaluable as critical readers.

My deepest gratitude to Holly Isbister, Pamela Kelly, and the rest of the crew in the Brigham and Women's Hospital magnetic resonance operating room for your hospitality, professionalism, and skill.

When blocks seemed insurmountable and another rewrite too daunting, Luke, Daniel, Matt, and Bekica have helped to keep everything in perspective, along with many friends of Bill W.

And finally, thanks beyond measure to my friends Linda Grey, who brought her genius as an editor to the final rewrites of this book, and Eben Alexander III, M.D., whose remarkable gifts as a physician, surgeon, and scientist made the whole project possible. Whenever I needed neurosurgical facts or techniques, Eben was always there. Any errors or oversights are mine, and are doubtless due to my neglecting to review them with him.

MSP

SYLVAN MAYS, M.D., STOOD BY THE VAST WINDOW OF his fifth-floor office and gazed out at the countryside, where late afternoon shadows were lengthening across the Iowa River. At fifty, he had just gone over ten million in net worth and was one of the few physicians who had actually seen his income increase since the advent of managed care. The decision to remain in Iowa had certainly been the right one. For sure, he had his detractors. Success always brought those. He was too entrepreneurial, some said—a big fish in a small pond, too intent on building himself into a neurosurgical version of DeBakey or Menninger.

What's so wrong with that? he wondered. DeBakey and Menninger were world renowned and respected, doing good on a global scale. What was so wrong with wanting to emulate them?

The gleaming seven-story Mays Institute for Neurological Surgery had put Iowa City on the map and brought millions of dollars in research and industrial development grants to the university. Now, his robotics team was closing in on a real prize—the first microrobot to be approved by the FDA for use in neurosurgery. A preliminary application had already been submitted. Six months, maybe less, and the few remaining bugs in the system would be worked out. As it was, he was revered for cranking through more brain tumor cases than anyone else in the country. Now, with several researchers on the robotics project, and Sylvan Mays' name on every scientific article the group generated, he was gaining recognition as a top researcher as well.

He checked his watch. Five minutes or so before Frederick Wilson was due. As with his previous appointment, Wilson had insisted on being the very last patient of the day. At first, Mays had been put off by his prospective patient's demands. But what a find he'd turned out to be! Wilson was eccentric as could be, yet ready to reward handsomely anyone who did him good service. A quarter of a million in cash just for evaluating his case. Four times that when the surgery was completed, plus a healthy donation to the Institute. Wilson was the patient of a surgeon's dreams, except that his tumor was bad—as bad as any so-called benign tumor could be. A slow-growing subfrontal meningioma with some extension, steadily compressing normal brain tissue. Progressive neurologic difficulty had begun. Now, the only choices Wilson had were surgery or a stuttering, inexorable death.

Mays was sure he would be able to get to the tumor, but not without doing some damage—maybe a lot of damage. Then there was the actual dissection. He had probably excised more tumors like this one than almost any other surgeon in the world; if he couldn't do it, it was doubtful anyone could. But even for him, the dissection would be chancy. Wilson had come to him impressively well informed, and had asked specifically about the robotics system. Rather than risk losing him to some other surgeon, Mays had chosen to tell him that employing the robot in the OR was possible, but not definite. *By no means definite.* Hadn't those been his exact words? The exaggeration had been necessary initially. Now, it was time to back off.

The trick, as with all cases like this, was to hang crepe—to stress the dangers inherent in the surgery and lower the patient's expectations to the point where even a marginally successful operation would be welcomed as the work of a genius. The man had seemed reasonably easygoing and understanding enough at their first meeting, yet he was sharp, too. That much was certain.

But so was Sylvan Mays. Until Mays had the chance to study the MRIs, he had refused to talk in anything but generalities. Today, though, they would have to get down to business—to go over the specific anatomical challenges and potential surgical stumbling blocks inherent in Wilson's case. First, it would be necessary to dispel Wilson's belief that the only way to reach his tumor was by means of a robot.

Mays wandered over to what he thought of as his wall of fame—dozens of photos and testimonials from world leaders and other celebrities. "Neurosurgeon to the Stars," one publication had dubbed him. "Brain Tumor? Head for the Cornfields," another had headlined. "Is This Heaven? . . . No, It's Iowa—Unless You Need a Neurosurgeon."

"It damn well *is* heaven," Mays said out loud.

He paced to his desk and hit the intercom.

"Yes, Syl?"

Sandy had used his first name. The waiting room had to be empty.

"Mr. Wilson arrive yet?" he asked, just in case.

"Not yet. There's no one here at all at the moment. No one at all. . . . Hint, hint."

As always, Sandy Alter's flirting over the intercom immediately turned Mays on. At thirty-one, she was a hell of a gal Friday, with an aerobics instructor's body and a wicked imagination in bed. And even more exciting, after almost a year, she didn't want anything from him other than a night or two a week, enough cocaine to elevate their lovemaking from great to sublime, and no talk about his wife or kids. Could life get any better?

"I wish we could do it right now," he said. "Tonight can't come soon enough for me."

"Me either."

The stiffness inside Mays' slacks intensified. At that moment, through the intercom, he heard the outside office door open and close.

"Mr. Wilson," Sandy said. "Nice to see you again."

The intercom was switched off, then on again, and she announced Wilson's arrival.

Mays positioned himself behind his desk, on which lay Wilson's file, took a deep, calming breath, and asked Sandy to send him in.

Okay, Sylvan, he thought. *It's showtime.*

Frederick Wilson limped into the office, a cane in his right hand and an elegant black leather briefcase in his left. He set the briefcase down, shook Mays' hand enthusiastically, and lowered himself into one of the two mahogany chairs on the patient's side of the desk. He was dressed as he had been on his first visit to the office—dark suit, conservative tie, white shirt. His thick gray hair was brushed straight back, and his beard and mustache—equally gray—were neatly trimmed. His intelligent dark eyes were partially veiled by heavy-rimmed spectacles with lightly tinted glass.

As so often happened, Mays found himself seeing his patient with Superman-like X-ray vision, staring beyond Wilson's face, eyes, and skull at the fleshy tumor that was infiltrating and displacing his brain. *Poor bastard*.

"You've verified the deposit?" Wilson asked in a modest accent that Mays had decided was probably German or Russian.

"Barclays Bank, Grand Cayman. In my name. Yes. Yes, I have."

"There will be no tax problems that way . . . for either of us."

Eccentric. Mysterious. Clearly a man of wealth and breeding, yet with no health insurance. Electronic cash transfers only. When the time came, Wilson would speak to Bob Black, the hospital administrator, and transfer funds for his inpatient treatment. But first, Mays had had to pass muster in an interview that lasted most of an hour. His background . . . his training . . . his family . . . his interests outside of medicine . . . his specific experience with the kind of tumor Wilson had . . . and finally, the status of his robotics research. Mays knew he had acquitted himself well, and was not in the least surprised when Wilson had called the next day to inform him about the money deposited in Grand Cayman and to formally accept him as his surgeon.

"So," Wilson said now, "I have offered money for a service and you have agreed to provide it. I have given you a down payment for that service and you have accepted. We have set a fee to you and to this institute when the service is rendered that will total well in excess of a million dollars, tax free. It seems, then, we have entered into a business arrangement."

"I . . . I guess I never thought about what I do that way before, but yes, I suppose we have."

"Excellent. Let's talk about expectations, then."

"Yes. I think at this point that's quite appropriate."

Mays straightened himself in his chair, cleared his throat, and met Wilson's gaze with an expression that he hoped was sufficiently grim. Now was the time to begin to paint the picture of guarded pessimism. But before the surgeon could say another word, Wilson began speaking.

"Given the benign nature of my tumor, and the magnificent qualifications, experience, and skill you have described, I expect nothing less than a complete cure. I expect to be speaking as well as I am now, to be walking without a limp, and to have full use of my senses and my intellect."

"But—"

"I also expect to have no evidence of residual tumor on a postoperative MRI study."

"But—"

"Is that clear?"

Mays felt a sudden chill.

"I . . . I expect an excellent result, of course, but I can't make those sorts of promises. No surgeon can."

"You've told me you are the best in the world at this sort of surgery. You told me your robotics system was capable of bypassing the usual route from my skull to the tumor."

"I said it was *potentially* capable of that, yes. But I also said our robotics project was still in the experimental stage."

"And you accepted my money without hesitation."

"Yes, but—"

"Then I expect full satisfaction."

"I understand. However—"

"Dr. Mays. Close your mouth, please, and listen carefully. I have not paid you a quarter of a million dollars to debate this point. I expect you to perform the way you have promised me you can. To guarantee that I get your best work, my people are currently observing your wife and daughter. When the day of my surgery arrives, they will be entertaining your family at a place of my choosing until I am safely out of danger, and your radiologist as well as one of my choosing has reviewed my MRI films. When I know that I am safe, unharmed, and free of tumor, your wife and daughter will be returned to you. They will be treated well, I promise you that."

Mays felt as if he were being strangled. There was nothing in Wilson's manner or expression that suggested flexibility. The man must be insane.

"I . . . I can't agree to this," he finally managed. "No surgeon can."

"Our arrangement has been established. I have the right to expect complete satisfaction. I have the right to recourse if you fail."

"You're not buying a used car from me, Mr. Wilson. This is neurosurgery."

"Precisely why I have sought out the very best, which you assure me you are. The terms are nonnegotiable, Dr. Mays."

The shirt beneath Mays' armpits was soaked. He felt as if his bowels might let loose at any moment.

"I refuse," he managed, with forced bluster. "I refuse to be bullied and threatened, and I refuse to operate on you under these circumstances. Go find yourself another surgeon. There are plenty of them as qualified as I am."

"That is not what you told me at our first meeting."

"All right, all right, there are only a few. But that makes no difference. I will not operate."

"Dr. Mays, I am very disappointed in you."

"I don't give a damn that you're disappointed, Wilson. I won't be pushed like this. Be reasonable, man. This is brain surgery we're talking about. Nothing is certain in brain surgery. Christ, man, nothing is certain anyplace."

Wilson sighed.

"That is where you are wrong, Doctor. One thing is very certain."

He calmly opened his briefcase and extracted a heavy pistol with a long silencer on it. Without waiting for another word, he aimed from his chest and fired.

Mays saw the muzzle flash, and actually heard the spit of the shot. But he would never appreciate the perfect placement of the bullet hole, exactly equidistant between the bridge of his nose and his hairline. An expression of amazement froze on his face, and his head jerked backward, then slowly drifted forward until it slammed onto the desk.

Frederick Wilson took his file and every piece of paper with any reference to him, and placed them all in his briefcase. Then he carefully wiped the arms of his chair. He stopped by the door to ensure that he had overlooked nothing, then stepped out into the reception area. The receptionist smiled up at him.

"Well, that didn't take long," she said. "Did Dr. Mays want to see you in the office again?"

"No," Wilson replied, without the hint of an accent. "He didn't say a word about that."

He removed the silenced pistol from behind his brief-case and, from ten feet away, firing almost nonchalantly from his hip, put a shot in precisely the same spot on Sandy's forehead as he had on Mays'. Then he placed all potentially incriminating files and papers in his case, hooked his cane over a chair, and, without any sign of a limp, strolled back into Mays' office. He was upset by the disappointing session with the surgeon, although not with his decision to terminate the relationship. The man was a pompous ass. A few thousand to the bank manager in Cayman would transfer the quarter million back into his account. And that would be that for his dealings with Sylvan Mays.

After a final check to ensure he had removed all trace of his ever having been at the Institute, he retrieved his cane, reacquired his limp, locked the outer office door behind him, and hobbled off down the hall.

CHAPTER 1

THEY WERE NEARLY THREE HOURS INTO THE OP-
eration and not one cell of the cancer had yet been removed. But by neurosurgical standards, three hours was
still well within the feeling-out period—especially for a
procedure involving experimental equipment. And despite huge progress recently, ARTIE most certainly
remained experimental.

"Let's try another set of images with enhancement of
the tumor, please."

To a physician, all growths, benign and malignant,
were tumors, although the term "cancer" was generally
reserved for malignancies—those tumors capable of
spreading to distant organs. This particular cancer, a
glioblastoma, was among the most virulent of all brain
tumors.

Staring straight ahead at the eight-inch monitor

screen that was suspended from the ceiling to her eye level, Jessie Copeland set her gloved hands down on the patient's draped scalp, which was fixed by heavy screws to an immobile titanium frame. The physical contact wasn't technically necessary. From here on, ARTIE would be doing the actual surgery. But there was still something reassuring about it.

"You playing gypsy fortune-teller?" Emily DelGreco asked from across the table.

"I just want to make certain the guy hasn't slipped out from under the sheets, gotten up, and run away while I'm trying to decide whether or not our little robot pal is in position to begin removing this tumor. For some reason ARTIE's movements forward and left feel sluggish to me—not as responsive to the controls as I think he should be."

"Easy does it, Jess," Emily said. "We always expect more from our kids than they can ever deliver—just ask mine. The sensors I'm watching, plus my monitor screen, say you and ARTIE are doing fine. If you start feeling rushed, just say 'Berenberg.'"

Emily, a nurse practitioner, had been on the neurosurgical service at the Eastern Massachusetts Medical Center for several years before Jessie started her residency. The two of them, close in age if not in temperament, had hit it off immediately, and over the intervening eight years had become fast friends. Now that Jessie was on the junior faculty, Emily had moved into the tiny office next to hers and worked almost exclusively with her and her patients. Neither of them would ever forget Stanley Berenberg, one of the first brain tumor cases the two of them had done together. His operation had taken twenty-two hours. They did the delicate resection together without relief. But every minute they spent on the case proved worth it. Berenberg was now enjoying an active retirement, playing golf and carving birds, one of which—a beautifully rendered red-tailed hawk—held sway on the mantel in Jessie's apartment.

"Berenberg . . . Berenberg . . . Berenberg," Jessie repeated mantralike. "Thanks for the pep talk, Em. I think ARTIE's just about ready to start melting this tumor."

Jessie had decided to apply to medical school five years after her graduation from MIT with a combined degree in biology and mechanical engineering. She had spent those five years working in research and development for Globotech, one of the hottest R and D companies around.

"I didn't mind making those toys," she had told neurosurgical chief Carl Gilbride at her residency interview, "but I really wanted to play with them afterwards."

Under Gilbride's leadership, the Eastern Mass Medical Center's neurosurgical program, once the subject of scorn in academic circles, was a residency on the rise, drawing high-ranking applicants from the best medical schools in the country. Jessie, who was comfortably in the middle of the pack at Boston University's med school, had applied to EMMC strictly as a long shot. She was astonished when, following the interview, Gilbride had accepted her on the spot. There was, however, one proviso. She had to agree to spend a significant amount of time in his lab, resurrecting work on an intraoperative robot that a now-departed researcher there had abandoned.

Working in Gilbride's lab throughout her residency while carrying a full clinical load, Jessie had learned that her boss's true forte was self-promotion, but she had been elated to spearhead the development of ARTIE—

Assisted Robotic Tissue Incision and Extraction. The apparatus was an exciting fusion of biomechanics and radiology.

Now, after some preliminary animal work, she and ARTIE were finally in the OR.

Over the past few years, Jessie had viewed countless video images produced by the intraoperative MRI system. What she was studying now was the continuous, three-dimensional reconstruction of the brain beneath the intact skull of the patient—images that could be rotated in any direction using a track-ball system bolted to the floor beside her foot. The on-screen presentations of the MRI data were undergoing constant improvement by the extraordinary genius geeks in Hans Pfeffer's computer lab. And Jessie could not help but marvel at the pictures they were producing. The malignant tumor and other significant structures in the brain could be demarcated electronically and colorized to any extent the surgeon wished.

Jessie had always been a game player—a fierce competitor in sports, as well as in Nintendo, poker, billiards, and especially bridge. She was something of a legend around the hospital for the Game Boy that she carried in her lab coat pocket. She used it whenever the hours and tension of her job threatened to overwhelm her—usually to play the dynamic geometric puzzle Tetris. It was easy to understand why the MRI-OR setup excited her so. Operating in this milieu, especially at the controls of ARTIE, was like playing the ultimate video game.

MRI—magnetic resonance imaging—had progressed significantly since its introduction in the early 1980s. But the technique had taken a quantum leap when White Memorial Hospital, the most prestigious of the Boston teaching hospitals, had designed and built an operating room around the massive MRI magnet. The key to developing the unique OR was the division of the seven-foot-high superconducting magnet into two opposing heads—"tori," the manufacturer had chosen to call them, a torus being the geometric term for any structure shaped like a doughnut. The tori were joined electronically by under-floor cables, and separated by a gap of just over two feet. It was in this narrow space that the surgeon and one assistant worked. The patient was guided into position on a padded sled that ran along a track through a circular opening in one of the magnets. Jessie understood nearly every aspect of the apparatus, but that knowledge never kept her from marveling at it.

"Let's do it," she said, crouching a bit to peer under the video screen and make brief eye contact with her friend. "Everyone ready?"

The scrub and circulating nurses acknowledged that they were, as did the radiology imaging fellow and the team working the console outside the OR. Through the glass viewing window, Jessie could see radiologist Hans Pfeffer—Ichabod Crane with a stethoscope in one pocket, a calculator in the other, and an IQ that had to be off the charts. The imaging system was as much his baby as ARTIE was hers. He had been watching, motionless, for every minute of the three hours. Now, as their eyes met, he simply nodded.

"Come on, ARTIE," Emily said. "Do that thing that you do."

The flexible robotic surgeon, three-quarters of an inch long and a third of that in width, was packed with microelectronics and gears. The guidance console by Jessie's right hand was connected by microcable to six pods—tiny sets of pincers—three to a side. The pods enabled ARTIE to move along—and, where necessary, even through—the brain with minimal damage to the structures it passed. In addition to the guidance cable, ARTIE carried two other fine tubes, one capable of delivering ultrasonic waves powerful enough to liquefy tumor cells, and the other, a hollow suction catheter, designed to remove debris or to implant slivers of radioactive isotopes. Not counting the tubes and cable, the remarkable little robot weighed less than two ounces.

Jessie stretched some of the tension from her neck and began the meticulous process of liquefying and removing the large glioblastoma. She had inserted ARTIE up through the patient's nose and into the cranial cavity, and then guided it to the diseased tissue. The tumor would have been virtually inoperable by conventional methods because of the normal brain tissue that would have been destroyed in the process of simply reaching the spot. ARTIE had made it with only minimal damage to healthy brain. Test one, passed with honors.

"He's working perfectly, Jess," Emily said. "Just don't let him forget for a moment that's *brain* he's sucking on."

"To do that I'll have to change his program. I have him thinking he's operating on kidney. I thought he'd be less nervous that way."

The two women communicated with each other directly, while overhead cameras recorded the operation. They spoke over their shoulders to the nurses and technician, and by microphone to the team managing the console. Although neither of them was large, gowned as they were, surgeon and assistant virtually filled the spaces between the huge MRI tori. As long as neither of them keyed the microphone, by keeping their voices low they could conduct a conversation in virtual privacy. But at the moment, there was no need to speak. It was time to begin the actual operation. For a silent, motionless minute, they shared the appreciation that for the next three to ten hours, a narrow, twenty-six-inch space would be their world.

Bit by bit, Jessie began the dissection of the cancer, dissolving the cells with ultrasound and removing the resulting debris. As the procedure progressed, Emily monitored the various parameters within ARTIE and occasionally broke the viselike tension with small talk about the latest examples of Carl Gilbride's florid egomania, about her two teenage sons, or about Jessie's life—especially her mother, Paulette, whose shameless determination to do something about her forty-one-year-old daughter's single status was a cartoon that never failed to amuse them. From here on, Emily was the supporting player, but she handled her role well. The two of them had spent so many hours together in the operating room that they functioned essentially as one. But today a third player had been added—a tiny robot that might, with time, revolutionize neurosurgery.

An hour passed with little conversation. To Jessie, it seemed like a minute. Every microscopic movement of the robot had to be visualized in three dimensions: anterior, posterior, right, left, up, down, and every diagonal in between. She asked the console tech for *Scheherazade,* one of a dozen or so CDs she had on file to be played while she operated. The slow, hypnotic music instantly softened the hollow, tiled silence. The electronically enhanced tumor as displayed on the monitor was crimson—a deadly hydra, its many tentacles probing deep into the dark blue of normal brain. ARTIE, the defender of the realm, was bright yellow. Delicately, deftly, Jessie directed its snout and the ultrasonic sword it wielded. Bit by bit the crimson receded. Bit by bit the blue expanded—swollen but intact brain, filling the void where the tumor had been liquefied, then aspirated. Another hour passed. Dave Brubeck replaced Rimsky-Korsakov on the sound system. Two of the eight tentacles and a portion of the cancer's body were now gone.

Still, to Jessie, ARTIE's responsiveness in one particular maneuver seemed slightly sluggish.

"Em, is there anything the matter?" she asked. "I still feel out of sync some of the time. There's a choppiness when I try to back ARTIE up. Have you checked each of the pods?"

"I will. . . . I don't see anything striking, although numbers five and six are spinning a bit more rapidly than the others. I'm not sure, but I would think that's just because they're moving through liquefied tumor and aren't actually connecting with solid tissue."

"Maybe. I'm telling you, Em, we've still got a lot to learn about this little fella."

Jessie suddenly stopped humming along to Brubeck's "Take Five." Something was definitely wrong with ARTIE.

"Em, check the pods again, please," she said with unmistakable concern.

When she called for ARTIE to move right, forward and posterior, the robot gave a sharp jab to the left.

"The problem's in five and six," Emily replied. "RPMs are staying up. They're not shutting off."

"Jessie, you're drifting posterior and left," Hans called in over the intercom, his English perfect although his Dutch accent remained pronounced. "A millimeter . . . more now. . . . You are closing in on brain stem."

Disaster. Jessie battled the controls, but she could see that ARTIE wasn't responding the way it had been. From beneath her hair guard, sweat beaded across her forehead. Several drops fell onto her glasses.

"Wipe, please, John," she said, turning her head briefly so the circulating nurse could dry her with a cloth sponge. "My glasses, too."

The image on the screen was devastating. A rim of blue had begun to appear between one of the crimson tentacles and the robot. ARTIE was veering away from the cancer and through normal brain tissue toward the densely packed neurons of the brain stem, where even a millimeter of tissue destruction, properly placed, could be lethal.

"Jess, you were right," Emily said. "Things just went haywire on the panel here. Five and six are continuing to spin. And now four is acting strange. It's like ARTIE's had a stroke or something."

"Damn," Jessie muttered, tapping rapidly at the key that should have reversed the malfunction.

Communication between the panel and ARTIE had somehow been disrupted. An overheat someplace? A computer glitch? Jessie cursed herself for not delaying the procedure until Skip Porter returned from having his painfully abscessed molar taken care of. A wizard with electronics, Skip was her lab technician and knew ARTIE at least as intimately as she did. But the truth was, with the robot buried deep in the brain, all the knowledge in the world wasn't going to salvage the operation.

The blue rim expanded.

"You're well into brain stem now, Jessie," Hans reported.

Unspoken was the estimate of the neurologic damage that had already been done. Jessie could feel the deflation of her team's energy and enthusiasm. There had been such high hopes for this day, ARTIE's first under actual OR conditions. Somebody switched off the stereo.

Now there was only dense silence.

Jessie stepped back, clear of the tori, and looked over to Hans Pfeffer, shaking her head sadly. Then she moved back to her spot by the table. It would take an hour or more to back ARTIE out, if they could do it at all.

Across from her, the expression in Emily's eyes, framed by her hair cover and mask, was grim.

"Thank you, everyone," Jessie said suddenly. "You all did a great job. ARTIE's close. Really close. But I guess he's not quite there yet."

She shut off the power to the robot, then took a scalpel and sliced through the control cord.

"Hans, thank you," she said. "I'll retrieve ARTIE at autopsy, and then we'll give him an autopsy of his own."

"Sorry, Jess," Emily murmured.

Jessie pushed the monitor screen up toward the ceiling and pulled down her mask.

"Me, too," she said.

She hated losing. God, how she hated losing. But at least this defeat hadn't affected a living patient.

She pulled the drapes free and loosened the screws from the cadaver. Pete Roslanski had had a miserable six months before his glioblastoma took him. The tumor had already done irreversible damage when it was diagnosed. Surgery was out of the question. ARTIE, which even now had yet to be approved by the hospital's human experimentation panel, could not have been used in any event. It had been a wonderful gesture on Pete's and his family's part to allow his body to be operated on this way.

"It's a step at a time," Emily said. "And today was a big one for ARTIE. He's almost there, Jess. Just keep doing what you've been doing, and you're both going to succeed. Just be grateful no one's pushing you."

"Yeah," Jessie said flatly. "I am grateful for that."

CHAPTER 2

ALEX BISHOP PICKED UP THE STACCATO TAPPING OF Craft's cane half a minute before he actually spotted the man approaching from his left. Still, he remained motionless, as he had been for most of an hour, pressed against the base of a tree, with a clear view of all the accesses to the F.D.R. Memorial. Mel Craft, now the deputy assistant head of the directorate of CIA operations, had promised he would come alone, and given their history, he had every reason to keep his word. But Craft was the ultimate Company man, and Bishop was nothing if not cautious. Surviving seventeen years as an operative in some of the diciest spots on earth was a testament to that.

It was six in the morning. Pale sunlight filtered through a broken sky and sparked off the wind-whipped chop on the Potomac. It had been nine months since Bishop had last been in D.C. By and large he couldn't stand the place, but he considered the area around the river to be as beautiful as anything any other city had to offer. Two runners and a bicyclist passed the blind man, each unable to keep from glancing back curiously at him. No threat there. Bishop made a final visual sweep of the area and left his concealment, moving stealthily across the thick grass toward Craft. He was still five yards away when the deputy turned toward him.

"It's okay, Alex," he said in his heavy Mississippi drawl. "I'm alone."

"There's a bench twenty yards to your left. I'll meet you there."

"Jesus, Alex, if you can't trust me, you are in a pretty damn sorry state."

"You're right about that," Bishop murmured.

He watched until Craft was seated, then turned his back to the river and made a wide, wary arc before settling down at the far end of the bench, three feet away from his onetime partner. At forty-five, Craft was two years older than Bishop. But the torture that had ended his fieldwork, plus the twenty-five inactivity pounds he had put on since then, had added a decade to his looks.

"I can smell your gun," Craft said. "What is it, under a newspaper?"

"The *Post*."

"I'd like to tell you to put it away, that you don't have anything to be so paranoid about."

"But I do, right?"

"Alex, you were supposed to report in a month ago to begin your new assignment training the incoming class at the farm."

"I can't. Things are finally starting to break."

"The powers that be already consider you a liability.

And you know as well as I do that's a very unhealthy thing to be considered, even if you're not."

"Mel, one of the powers that be is *you*. You've got to stall things for me."

Craft removed his mirrored sunglasses and rubbed at the scarred craters where his eyes once had been.

"I can't control some of the people you've upset by going AWOL," he said.

"You've got to, Mel. Malloche is in trouble. He's got a brain tumor of some sort."

"How do you know?"

"I found out about the tumor from a source in France. The entire staff of an MRI lab in Strasbourg was wiped out, each with a single center shot to the forehead. That shot is the only thing Malloche has ever done with any consistency."

"So?"

"So, a week ago the bastard surfaced here in the U.S.—in *Iowa* of all places."

"How do you know? You've never even seen the guy. Almost five years chasing after him, and you've never even seen his goddamn face."

Bishop ignored the jab.

"A neurosurgeon named Sylvan Mays and his secretary were killed in his office. Center forehead shot. One apiece."

"I still don't see—"

"Mays was one of the top neurosurgeons in the world. He's developing a kind of robot that can reach tumors that were considered inoperable."

"So why did Malloche kill him?"

"I figure Mays didn't know who he was dealing with, and made some promises to Malloche that he couldn't keep."

Craft shook his head.

"Alex, there's a pretty large contingent on Capitol Hill and even some people at Langley who don't even believe Claude Malloche exists."

"You know better."

"What I know is that it's over, my friend. The agency gave you three years, then four, then five. Now they want you home. I'm sorry you didn't get him, Alex. But now you've got to accept that it's over."

Bishop slid a foot closer, tightly gripping the .45. Even blind and ten years out of the field, Mel Craft had more killing skills than most operatives.

"You thought it was over for you in El Salvador, too," Bishop said.

Craft took a deep breath, then exhaled slowly. After fifteen hours of unspeakable torture at the hands of a right-wing death squad, he had been sightless, hopeless, and praying for death. Then the commotion had begun. A minute or so later, Alex Bishop was untying him, having killed all seven of Craft's captors—three with his bare hands. El Salvador was Bishop's trump card, and he had just played it.

"Okay," Craft said finally. "What do you want?"

"Malloche is headed for a hospital in Boston."

"How do you know?"

"There are only three other places in the country that are doing the same sort of research as Mays. This surgeon in Boston is the one people tell me is farthest along. If I can find that information out, Malloche knows it, too. I'm willing to bet he's headed there right now."

"I'll do what I can, but I can't promise anything. They want you real bad, Alex. In the fold or in a box."

"I need some time, Mel. I need a cover to get me inside, and I need a contact at the local FBI. And all of it's got to be done real quick and real quiet. Malloche always seems to know who to pay off."

"And who to *knock* off. You really think this is it?"

"If it isn't, I promise you, I'm done."

"If I can't convince Stebbins and his internal affairs thugs to back off, you may be done anyhow."

"That's my problem. Will you at least try?"

"If I do, I don't want to hear any of that 'remember El Salvador' shit again. Agreed?"

"Agreed."

"If it had been you tied to that chair, I would have tried the same harebrained one-man attack you did."

"I believe you would have."

"But this is no time to be harebrained, Alex. You've been part of this organization long enough to know how berserk internal affairs can get about someone they feel is a loose cannon. And operating inside this country definitely makes you one of those."

"By the time they find me, it'll be over."

"Don't underestimate them."

"I won't, Mel. I've stayed alive this long by not underestimating anyone. But if they come after me, they'd better send someone who wants to get me as much as I want Malloche. And I don't think that person exists."

"I'll do what I can. Just watch your back."

CHAPTER 3

". . . 'YOU MAY LOSE THE VISION IN ONE OR BOTH of your eyes.'"

"As long as it's only one or both."

"Okay, then. Initial here. . . . 'You may lose the use of one or both of your arms.'"

"Arms? I mean, really. What do I need arms for, anyhow? Show me *one* unhappy amoeba. I can scratch my back on a tree like the bears and eat pie like those guys in the county fair. Mmmmmm."

"Initial. . . . 'You may lose the use of one or both of your legs.'"

"Jessie, please."

"Sara, hospital policy says I have to read this neurosurgery op permit to you out loud, and you know what a policy nerd I am. So stop giving me a hard time and let me finish."

"Giving *you* a hard time? It's *my* damn brain tumor."

"Touché."

Jessie set her clipboard aside and sat down on the edge of Sara Devereau's bed. Sara, an elementary school teacher with three kids, was only thirty-nine. She was facing a third operation on an astrocytoma that had been maddeningly tenacious. Her first procedure, done five years ago by Carl Gilbride, might or might not have been adequate. Jessie had her opinion, but with only the op note and X rays to go by, she knew it wasn't fair to judge . . . even him.

She had assisted him on Sara's second operation, nearly two years ago. When he announced he had finished the case, Jessie felt certain he had not been aggressive enough. But what could she do? At the time, she was chief resident. He was chief of the department.

Following the second procedure, she had gone out of her way to get to know Sara. Their contacts outside the hospital weren't frequent, but they did manage a lunch or a late-afternoon drink from time to time, and twice Jessie had been invited to Sara's home. The woman had taught her more about courage, more about taking life as it came, about adjusting to calamity, than any other patient she had ever had.

As she and Sara grew closer, Jessie had tried to understand—to place herself in Gilbride's shoes that day; to forgive. But she could never free her memory of the overwhelming apprehension and helplessness she had felt the moment he suddenly stepped back from the table and announced that he had completed the reoperation on Sara, and had gotten as much tumor out of her brain as was necessary to effect a long-term favorable outcome. He had then stripped off his gloves and gown in the theatrical way that was his trademark and hurried from the

OR to catch a plane to speak at an international conference, leaving Jessie to replace the skull flap and close the scalp incision over a cancer that she strongly feared had been inadequately excised.

Sara's "long-term favorable outcome" had lasted just twenty-two months.

A few weeks before, with the sudden development of headaches and thickened speech, Damocles' sword had finally fallen. The news from the MRI was grim. The surgery Sara was facing this time had a chance of being curative, but only a slim one. Her response to the devastating report was typical—whatever had to be done, should be done. She and her family would deal with it and make the best of it. If the cancer could possibly be overcome, she was determined to be the one to do it. As long as she was aware and moving about, she had precisely the same gift as did everyone else in the world—this day.

But she had insisted that this time Jessie perform the operation. And Gilbride, clumsily masking his relief, had turned over the reins.

Jessie and Sara were in room 748, one of ten private rooms on the neurosurgical floor, which occupied the seventh of eight stories of the Surgical Tower. Over the five years since its grand opening, the forty-five rooms and offices on Surgical Seven had been more of a home to Jessie than her Back Bay apartment.

It was nearing four in the afternoon. Jessie had just arrived on Surgical Seven for patient rounds, following an hour in pathology during which she had helped extract ARTIE from the late Pete Roslanski's head. Tech Skip Porter, his jaw swollen like a plum from his dental encounter, had taken the tiny robot to their lab for a painstaking, under-microscope dissection. Jessie suspected that it wouldn't be long before they had some answers. Upset though she was over ARTIE's failure to complete the operation, she was pleased with the way it had performed in the early going, and totally relieved that she had gone with a trial run on a cadaver. From the early work guiding the robot through watermelons, to testing on pigs, then finally primates, she and Carl Gilbride had improved their technique just as she and Skip had improved ARTIE's. Now, as soon as Skip had made a diagnosis, they would consider gearing up ARTIE-2 for another cadaver trial. Then, who knew? Maybe Gilbride would be ready to make a presentation to the human experimentation committee.

For the moment, though, ARTIE had to be Skip's problem. Sara Devereau was just the first of twenty-two patients on the two file cards Emily had prepared for afternoon rounds. Jessie, locking in a commitment that would force her to leave the hospital before eleven for the first time this week, had agreed to meet her friend Eileen at a duplicate bridge game at seven forty-five. But Sara was also a friend, and the only one of the twenty-two who was pre-op for tomorrow. If there was any rushing to be done, it would not be in room 748. If Jessie couldn't make it to the Cavendish Club, Eileen could always drag her husband, Kenny, away from his computer for the evening to play with her.

Emily's extensive training, years of experience, and superb clinical judgment made it easy for Jessie to delegate responsibility to her. After sending her off to see the first few patients, she closed the door and returned to her spot on the edge of Sara's bed. In a little more than twelve hours, their lives would be joined in a mortal struggle against a virulent, resilient cancer, that was eating away at Sara's ability to move and think. There were things that needed to be said between them.

"Tomorrow's going to be tough," Jessie began.

Sara's eyes held none of their usual playfulness.

"I'm running out of steam, Jess."

"I know you are. I would have cracked long ago. You've been a titan. Everyone around here has gotten stronger from watching the way you've handled things—especially me. Sara, you and I both know I'm not God. But I promise you I'm going to do everything in my power to make this third one the charm."

"I never questioned that, but it's good to hear anyhow. You know, it's funny. I'm ready—at least as ready as I'm ever going to be—for the surgery. But I keep having this weird, unanswerable question running through my head. How am I ever going to know that I didn't wake up from the anesthesia? Isn't that silly?"

"No. It's hardly silly. It's the ultimate question in every surgical patient's mind. They just don't always express it as eloquently as you did. But in your case, at least, the question's not unanswerable."

"It's not?"

Jessie shook her head.

"No. Because you're not going to be under. Sar, I went over the MRIs again. This damn thing is very close to a lot of important centers. Speech, motor, facial movements. I need you awake if I'm going to push this dissection to the limit. You'll get a local and some sedation, but no general except in the very beginning. In exchange, I give you my word that I won't sing during the operation."

Sara mulled over the offer.

"No singing, huh? . . . Okay, it's a deal."

"We'll use continuous MRI monitoring of the procedure."

"But not that little robot you told me about?"

Again Jessie shook her head.

"I don't think he'd improve matters. This will be your third operation. There's a sort of scar-tissue superhighway right down to the tumor. I can get there through the scar without causing any problems. Getting enough of the tumor so that your body's natural defenses can take care of the rest—that's the test. But I was always pretty good at taking tests."

Sara reached out and took Jessie's hand.

"My chances this time?"

Jessie pondered the question with solemnity.

"That depends," she said finally. "Have you been giving generously when the plate's been passed around?"

"Of course."

"In that case, I think we're in good shape. I'm a pretty experienced surgeon, and God only knows you're a damned experienced patient. Together with the power of your offerings to the church, I don't see how we can miss."

"What if I said I never give anything when that plate comes around?"

Jessie squeezed her hand and smiled.

"I'd still tell you we were okay . . . because *I* give— every chance I get. You can't be too careful in this neurosurgical business, you know."

SURGICAL SEVEN, LIKE the floors below it, was a broad circle, serviced by a bank of four elevators and one stairway. The nurses' station and supply rooms occupied most of a central core, along with the kitchen, conference room, and two examining rooms. Near the elevators was the six-bed neurosurgical ICU. Around the core, with views ranging from neighborhood rooftops to urban vistas, were thirty patients' rooms, with a total capacity of fifty. The circular hallway between the core and the rooms was known—especially by the nurses—as the Track.

In addition to the elevators and main stairway, a narrow auxiliary staircase joined Surgical Seven with Surgical Eight, which housed the neurosurgical operating rooms and recovery room. Because of shielding requirements and the massive weight of the superconducting magnet, the MRI operating room was in the subbasement, hewn into the surrounding rock.

The offices of the neurosurgical faculty, including Jessie's, were spaced along a broad corridor that extended west from the elevators and connected Surgical Seven with the main hospital. The corridor, lined with black, spoke-back Harvard chairs, also doubled as the waiting area for outpatients.

Suddenly bleary, Jessie promised Emily she'd be back to finish rounds in twenty minutes or so and headed to her office. What the tension-filled hours with ARTIE in the OR had started, the session with Sara Devereau seemed to have finished off. She badly needed time alone.

"Contrary to what you might have been led to believe, gender does matter in our business. The two most powerful influences—one positive, one negative—that will define you as a physician will both be that you're a woman."

The words were Narda Woolard's, a med school professor of surgery, and a role model for Jessie from the day they met. Rather than trying to convince female med students to ignore issues of gender when competing with men for university appointments and other positions, Woolard ran a seminar on how to capitalize on them.

"The deep sensitivity and empathy intrinsic to most women will make you that much better a physician regardless of the specialty you choose. But those same qualities will make medicine harder on you than on most men . . . especially if you choose a specialty like oncology, or critical care, or certain branches of surgery, where a fair percentage of your patients are going to suffer and die in spite of everything you can do for them."

Jessie's office was a lilliputian, one-window cubicle, made to feel even smaller by dark cherry paneling. A desk, two chairs, a locked filing cabinet for patient records and journal articles, and a set of shoulder-to-ceiling bookshelves on one wall all but filled the room, although she had managed to personalize the space with a couple of small watercolors, some framed photos from her rafting trip down the Colorado, and a planter.

Narda Woolard's words were echoing in Jessie's head as she sank into her chair. She did five uninspired minutes of Tetris and set a timer for fifteen minutes. Then she put her feet up on the desk, leaned back, and closed her eyes. Usually even fifteen minutes was long enough for her to drift off, enter some sort of REM sleep, and awaken rejuvenated. This time, her thoughts refused to slow. Early on in her internship, a cynical resident, already in advanced burnout, first exposed her to what he called Fox's Immutable Laws of Medicine: *Good guys get cancer. Trash survives.* Who Fox was, the resident never explained. But Jessie had seen the laws hold too many times ever to ignore them. And Sara Devereau was an exceedingly good guy.

Could Sara have been cured by a properly aggressive initial operation? Jessie had wondered this many times. Had Carl Gilbride even given the case much thought? How would he have felt if he had been to Sara's house?

Met her husband? Her kids? Would he have spent an extra hour or two at the operating table? Gone after those few extra tumor cells? Fat chance. Throughout her experience with the man, Jessie had never heard him admit to so much as a shortcoming, let alone an actual mistake—and there had been many over the years. . . .

What difference does it make now, anyway? Tomorrow morning Sara would have her last shot at a surgical miracle. The envelope was going to have to be pushed and pushed some more. Walking, sight, arm use, speech . . . there was no telling what would have to be risked—even sacrificed—in the interest of getting all the tumor. And there was no predicting what was going to be left of Sara after the operation was done.

Go to hell, Fox, whoever you are!

"Jess?"

Emily had opened the office door and was peering in. Jessie realized that she'd been out cold, tilted back in her chair, orbiting Neptune. Her timer, which she had apparently shut off, was clutched tightly in her lap. Forty-five minutes had passed.

"Whoa," she said, shaking the cobwebs loose, brushing some wisps of hair away from her eyes, and fumbling for her glasses on the desk. "I don't think we're in Kansas anymore, Toto."

"You okay?"

"Let's just say I needed the rest."

"I'm glad you got some. Ready to finish rounds?"

"I am."

"It shouldn't take too long. Oh, before I forget, there was a call for you at the nurses' station just a little while ago from Dr. Mark Naehring."

"The shrink?"

"Exactly. Remember that show he put on at grand rounds?"

"Who could forget it? That poor woman."

Naehring was a psychopharmacologist. In front of an amphitheater filled with two hundred or so physicians and other practitioners, he had used a combination of drugs to rapidly and very effectively hypnotize a middle-aged woman with profound emotional illness. He then extracted, for the first time, a terrifyingly vivid description of childhood sexual abuse at the hands of her father and his brother, at times both at once. Naehring then used more medication and posthypnotic suggestion to remove all memory of his patient having shared anything. He would introduce her revelations gradually in their therapy sessions, making use of a video where needed.

"Hopefully, the breakthrough helped her in the long run," Emily said.

"Do you have any idea what he wanted?"

"I do. He's heard about the functional MRIs we're doing to map patients' brains while they're awake during surgery, and he wondered if he could come into the OR sometime and watch you do it. He believes some of the drug combinations he's been using might be useful in keeping patients sedated but completely responsive."

"Interesting. Did you invite him to observe Sara's operation?"

"I did. He'll be at a conference all day tomorrow. He said to please call him next time."

"Terrific. Hey, maybe he can use some of those meds on me," Jessie said. "He can probe me to find out how I could have turned out the way I have with a mother who spent years grooming me to be the perfect happy homemaker for some lucky guy."

"What a failure she's been. Imagine having to live with your daughter growing up to be one of the finest neurosurgeons around."

"Okay, okay, you can have that raise. Now, how's our service doing?"

"Not bad, actually. I've seen everyone but Dave Scolari."

"Any problems with the others?"

"Let's see. Mrs. Kinchley wants to change rooms because Mrs. Weiss snores. Mr. Emspak wants to pull the shunt out of his head and go home because he has tickets to the ball game this weekend. Mrs. Davidoff is in her sixth day without a bowel movement. She won't let us discharge her until she has one. I told the nurses that whoever gets her emptied out wins dinner for two at the Top of the Hub."

"Courtesy of her HMO. Anything else?"

"Dr. Gilbride's patient, Larry Kelleher, has a fever. I couldn't find much, so I ordered blood cultures and the usual tests."

"Carl's patient with a post-op fever? Not possible!"

"I know. I know. I couldn't believe it myself."

They were still trading digs at their department chief when they entered room 717. New England Patriots linebacker Dave Scolari looked up at them impassively. He was a beautiful man—twenty-six years old, six foot three, with a 250-pound body that could have been chiseled from granite. He was also paralyzed from the neck down as the result of a fluke helmet-to-helmet hit. Surgery had stabilized his cervical fracture, and he had gotten back some movement in his hands, but the outlook for major recovery was guarded. Scolari, a fearless warrior on the field, had all but given up.

"Something funny?" he asked.

Jessie apologized, silently cursing herself and Emily for not regaining their composure before going in to see a patient—especially Dave. One of her coverage partners had done the surgery on Dave's neck, then had gone on safari, so over the intervening weeks, she had spent a fair amount of time with him. Initially, he had responded to her, teasing her about looking too young to be a neurosurgeon, even calling her Doogie Howser. But as the reality of his situation and his prognosis hit home, his enthusiasm began to wane. Now, though he tried being civil and went through the motions with his therapists, it was obvious to everyone that the spark was gone.

"More cards," she said, gesturing to the walls, which were virtually covered. "I'll bet most of them are from beautiful women."

"I haven't looked. The nurses hang them up."

Jessie took one down and studied the photo of a woman who had to be a professional model.

"Maybe you should read them. This one gives her phone number."

She showed Dave the photo, but got little reaction.

"Nice looking," was all he said.

Jessie conducted a quick but thorough exam. His grip seemed marginally less feeble than it had been.

"Dave, I think there's improvement here. I really do."

"Come on, Dr. Copeland. There's been no change. You know that as well as I do."

"No, Dave, you *don't* know that as well as I do. I love playing games, but not this kind. If I say you're improving, you're improving. You've got to stop this. The more negative you are, the less you'll benefit from the therapy you're getting, and the less your body will respond to any of those X-factors that go into the medical miracles we're always hearing about. I'm sorry to sound so sharp. I hope you know that I'll do anything I possibly can to help you. But you've got to help yourself."

Scolari looked away.

"Sure," he said. "Anything you say."

Jessie wondered how she would respond to having life as she knew it end with the ghastly suddenness his had. No more neurosurgery, no more walks, no more volleyball at the Y, maybe no more dressing herself, or even feeding herself. Did she have what it would take to retool? She knew there was no way she, or anyone else, could really answer that question until they were where Dave Scolari was now. She set her hand on his shoulder. The muscle tone was gone, and she knew that atrophy had already begun. But some bulk was still there.

"You just do your best," she said, clearing a rasp from her voice. "Whatever hand you're dealt, fair or not, is going to be your hand. Just try to do your best, Dave, and chances are some good things will happen. Say, listen. I've got an idea. Do you think you could handle having a quadriplegic friend of mine come and visit you? His name's Luis Velasco, and he's quite an incredible person. . . . Dave?"

"Whatever."

"I'll take that as a yes. I'll call Luis tonight. Hang in there, pal."

Jessie followed Emily out of the room.

"Let's intensify his therapy," she said. "Make sure they're doing enough electrostimulation."

"You really think he's getting stuff back?"

"I'm sure of it. Not a breakthrough, but definitely something. Dave's just too depressed right now to accept the change and work with it. That's understandable, too. When your idea of activity is knocking someone's block off on a football field, a little flicker of a couple of fingers just doesn't cut it. We can't let up on him, though. Any guy who thinks I look too young to be a neurosurgeon is definitely worth saving."

Emily took Scolari's chart off a rolling rack and wrote orders for the intensified therapy. Then she and Jessie headed for room 710, a double that, for the past few days, had been occupied by only one patient—thirteen-year-old Tamika Bing. Before they reached the room, Jessie stopped and flipped through the girl's chart.

Seven days had passed since Jessie performed the excision of a glioblastoma infiltrating deep on the left side of Tamika's brain. The operation had gone as well as she could have hoped, given the nature of the problem. Tamika's motor function, a major concern, had been completely preserved. But the teen's ability to connect with words appeared to have been lost. With that realization had come a devastating depression and an inertia even more disabling than Dave Scolari's. Only the threat of tubes down her nose had gotten her to eat anything. And getting her to leave her room and take a walk was out of the question.

Friends, family, nurses, social workers, psychiatrists, Jessie—no one had made a dent.

"What am I going to see in there?" Jessie asked now.

"Guess," Emily replied.

"Any ideas?"

"The shrink wants to start her on an antidepressant."

"Ugh. As if having her brain messed with surgically isn't enough. Well, I guess we don't have another option. Has she used the laptop her mother brought in?"

"Nope. Her mom says she was on it all the time at home, and even took it to school. Apparently it was her prized possession. She won't touch it."

"Poor baby."

Tamika's half of the room was as cheerful as the nurses and her mother could possibly make it, filled with cards, letters, pictures, stuffed animals, candy, magazines, and a portable CD player with headphones. In the middle of the comfortable clutter, propped in bed at almost ninety degrees, the girl sat, her wide, dark eyes staring straight ahead at nothing in particular.

Fox's laws.

"Hi, Tamik," Jessie said. "How're you doing?"

The two of them had gotten along well—very well—right up until the surgery. Since then, the teen hadn't acknowledged her at all. This moment was no different.

"I see you haven't opened the CD I brought you," she said, holding up the rap album she had picked out for the girl. "Want me to put it on?"

Nothing.

"Come on, Tamika. At least write me something—anything. Type it if you want."

Jessie centered the portable computer on the Formica tray table across Tamika's lap.

Nothing.

She looked to Emily for guidance, but the nurse only shrugged. A quick exam, a final try to get some sort of response from their patient, and they turned to go. Carl Gilbride was standing in the doorway, watching them.

The neurosurgical chief was, as always, impeccably dressed and groomed—tan suit, silk tie, wing tips, gold Rolex, starched and pressed lab coat, perfectly straight name tag—*Carl W. Gilbride, Jr., M.D.; Chief of Neurosurgery*. His wavy brown salon-cut hair and his round, rimless glasses helped produce an image that reminded Jessie of an SS interrogator in a grade B war movie.

"Carl, hi," she said lightly. "I thought you were going to be off lecturing for the day."

He stood motionless in the doorway, glaring at her.

"What in the hell did I just hear about you doing a case with ARTIE in the operating room?" he said, giving no indication he cared about the girl in the bed behind her. "Just who the fuck do you think you are?"

CHAPTER 4

"CARL, PLEASE. TAKE A DEEP BREATH AND TRY TO stop snarling at me like I just shot a white rhino. I didn't hurt anyone or do anything wrong. At least I don't think I did. Pete Roslanski was dead. *A cadaver!* He and his family wanted his body to serve some purpose beyond fertilizing the north forty of some cemetery. You were away. I couldn't have asked your permission even if I wanted to."

Jessie and Gilbride confronted each other across the table in one of the examining rooms on Surgical Seven. She had managed to curtail his tirade in Tamika Bing's room before it got any more abusive, and to lead him down the hall. The teenager, who had surely overheard what was said, had reacted not at all. She merely lay there as she always did, propped up in whatever position the nurses had chosen for her, staring straight ahead at nothing.

Gilbride's fury had only marginally receded. He still looked like a bullfrog being squeezed tightly from below. Over the years Jessie had served in his residency and worked in his lab, he had lost his temper with her any number of times. Enduring his explosions went with the territory. And in truth, she really wasn't treated much differently from any of the others who were on his B list. His A list consisted of those who never expressed a viewpoint or treatment approach different from his. And that sort of obsequiousness she was simply incapable of displaying—or even faking, as most of those who *were* on the A list did.

She suspected that merely having two X chromosomes would have also been enough to disqualify her from the A's. She had been the first—and to this point the last—female resident Gilbride had taken into his program, and the only woman on the neurosurgical faculty. It took just a few months of her residency—and of his snide, offensive, at times near-illegal asides—for her to understand how desperately the man must have needed her technical expertise in his robotics lab to have accepted her. There was even a rumor that he had once let slip his belief that she would wash out of the program before a year was out, and end up working full-time on his research.

But on the plus side, she wasn't playing the résumé-and-wait game every year in a field dominated by XYs, and she had a damn good job in a hospital that had risen to near the top of neurosurgery programs. She had friends like Emily and Hans Pfeffer, almost universal respect from her colleagues at EMMC, and at last count was the busiest surgeon in the department, next to the bullfrog himself. And finally, she had ARTIE, which, although technically Gilbride's, was a child she was determined to see into adulthood.

In the interest of continuing her work, she could handle whatever Gilbride dished out, as long as he didn't demand she compromise her beliefs too much. But the scene in Tamika's room had represented a clear-cut escalation in the tension between them. Gilbride had never chastised her in front of a patient before, let alone so harshly.

She took pains to maintain eye contact with the man and focused on two objectives: first, to defuse his anger before he said something irreparable, and then, to try to find out exactly why he was so steamed over what she had done. The clock over Gilbride's left shoulder read almost six-thirty. Her chances of making it to the Cavendish Club in time for the bridge game were almost as remote as the chances of her playing well now even if she did.

"Carl, I'm sorry," she began, not completely certain for what she was apologizing.

"You should be. What right did you have to tie up an entire operating room team, plus the radiologists, without clearing it with me?"

"Bill Wellman had canceled his OR case. The team was just waiting around for their next case, and Pete Roslan—"

"Dammit, Copeland, I'm not done talking. Why is it you always have the bullshit ready before anyone even has a shovel?"

"Sorry."

"You know, I carry a beeper just like you do. You could have paged me."

Jessie could have enumerated the many times Gilbride had gone ballistic because she or one of the other B-listers *had* paged him for something less than a nuclear spill on Surgical Seven. Instead, she muttered another apology. This fire was simply going to have to burn itself out.

"You've done good work in the lab," he went on. "I have no complaints about that. But I think you tend to forget that *I* had started developing ARTIE before *you* ever came on board here. Those grants that pay for you, Skip, and all that equipment are *my* grants. The patents on ARTIE have *my* name on them. You aren't his adopted mother, you're his nursemaid and his tutor. If you forget that fact, you'll be history around here. I promise you that."

Jessie sighed.

"Exactly what did I do that upset you so?" she asked.

"You brought our research out into the open, that's what you did. How many people were there today?"

"I still don't—"

"How many?"

"I don't know. Ten or eleven."

"Jesus. I'm surprised you didn't insist on having someone from anesthesia there, too."

Jessie came perilously close to admitting that, in fact, a friend from that department had stopped by, and would have returned had the procedure not been terminated so abruptly. But why was Gilbride so upset about the number of observers? The chief didn't wait for her to ask.

"Copeland, operating with ARTIE prematurely may have jeopardized the whole project—on more than one level. There's a race going on here—a race that ultimately could be worth hundreds of millions of dollars, to say nothing of a place in medical history. It's damn serious business—serious enough that the police came to see me last week to question me about where I was when that fatuous womanizing Sylvan Mays got himself killed; serious enough that Terwilliger and his group at Baylor are bad-mouthing us and our work every chance they get, and may have cost us grants I've applied for from the NIH and the MacIntosh Foundation. I was expecting to hear from both of them weeks ago, and there hasn't been a word. Then there's that son of a bitch at Stanford. His robotics work may or may not be as far along as ARTIE. The way that he holds his cards so close to the vest, it's hard to tell. They may actually be ready to go with patients. I don't know. But I do know that they are in direct competition with us for every cent in grant money we get for this project. If word gets out that you had a major failure in the operating room, there's no telling what the fallout will be."

"But—"

"There's more, dammit. Just shut up and let me finish. I've already submitted our application to the human experimentation panel here at the hospital. When word gets out that ARTIE ate away half of this poor stiff's brain stem, what do you think they're going to do?"

"It was a minor technical problem. I'm almost sure of it."

"Really? And suppose it was operator error? You've had more screwups in the animal lab than I have—many more."

Yes, because I was trying to do much more complicated maneuvers than you've ever risked, Jessie wanted to shout.

"I suppose operator error is always possible," she said instead, her fists balled at her sides. "But I think I was on top of things. Whatever it turns out to be—even if it's that I have more practicing to do—it's got to be better to know about it now than when we're operating on a live patient."

"That is beside the point. I didn't bring you into my lab to end up second to that bozo from Houston or any of the others. If Terwilliger scoops us on this because we had to go back to the drawing board, there's going to be hell to pay."

"I'm almost certain the problem is mechanical and will be easily correctable. Skip is working on it now."

"I know. I just came from there. He works for me, remember?"

How could I possibly forget? How could anyone forget that we all do?

"Look, Carl, I'm sorry. From now on I won't even change a lightbulb in ARTIE without clearing it with you."

"See to it that you don't. Now, I want a detailed op note and Skip's report on my desk by morning."

"But—"

"I don't care if you have to type it yourself. I want it."

Without waiting for a response, Gilbride stalked off.

Jessie checked the time and pictured Eileen excitedly pulling out the convention card the two of them used, then heading off to the bridge club, which was a good half hour from her house. It was too late now for her to talk her husband into playing. With any luck, there wouldn't be some inept loner hanging around the club waiting for a partner, and Eileen could play with the director. Jessie used Information to get the number of the Cavendish.

"Ray, Jessie Copeland here. . . . Yeah, I know, I know. I miss seeing everyone there, too. Actually, I was planning on playing with Eileen tonight, but I'm not going to be able to make it. Do you think you could play with her? . . . Ralph Pomm? The guy with the horrible toupee? Ray, he's kind of tough to play with. Can't you match him up with someone else? . . . I see. Okay. Tell Eileen I'm sorry, and that I'll call her tomorrow."

Ralph Pomm—self-centered, loudly opinionated, and pedantic. Everything she and Eileen hated in a partner.

Well, Eileen, Jessie thought as she headed back toward her office, *at least he's not Carl Gilbride.*

CHAPTER **5**

CHAPTER **5**

JESSIE'S DAY OF RECKONING WITH SARA DEVEREAU
began at five in the morning with fifteen minutes of
stretching and two dozen push-ups, followed by a cup of
decaf and half a melon, a quick shower, and finally two
games of Pin Bot—the full-sized pinball machine that
occupied a significant portion of her living room. It was
clear from the pile of covers on the floor by her bed that
her sleep had been fitful, although as usual, she had no
clear recollection of any dream. If a nightmare was responsible for the bedding pileup, she was reasonably certain that a bug-eyed bullfrog had played a leading role.

As always on a day when she was scheduled to operate, Jessie felt keyed up—excited and on edge. She was
the starting pitcher in a World Series game, but with no
hope of being taken out for a reliever no matter how
hard she was being hit. Facing a day as the principal in

the neurosurgical operating room was a rush few would ever experience. And Jessie loved the feeling.

One of the fringe benefits of being a surgeon was not having to build up a wardrobe of business clothes. Scrubs and a lab coat were always as fashionable in the hospital as they were functional. Jessie dressed in sneakers, khakis, a button-down shirt, and a blue cardigan, and spent a minute in front of the bathroom mirror, applying a bit of lip gloss and some mascara. Her shoulder-length hair was still mostly chestnut brown, but each day, it seemed, there were a few more gray strands. Monique, the Newbury Street stylist she saw every couple of months, had started pushing for a cosmetic response.

Maybe someday, she thought, fixing her hair back with a turquoise clip. *Right now you've got a little neuro-surgery to do.*

She trotted down three flights and exited her building by the basement door. A year or so ago she had won a lottery among the tenants in all of the apartments that allowed her to pay through the nose for one of the parking spaces behind their building. On days like this one—rainy and raw—the absurd tariff seemed almost worth it. Swede, her five-year-old Saab, had begun to nickel-and-dime her, and was especially cranky in rainy-and-raw. Still, out of loyalty, she was totally devoted to the machine. Today Swede turned over on the first try—a good omen.

Traffic to the hospital was so light that Jessie made the drive to parking lot E in fifteen minutes. Her assignment to E—an eight-minute walk to the hospital—easily counterbalanced her success in the apartment building lottery. Monthly petitions to the parking office to move to one of the garages had yet to be dignified with a response. As she hurried, jacket over head, to the hospital, she reminded herself for the hundredth time to get an umbrella.

By the time Jessie arrived on Surgical Seven, Sara was floating through a drug-induced haze. Her husband, Barry, and their three children were at her bedside.

"Hey, I was beginning to think you weren't going to show up," Sara said thickly.

"Wouldn't miss it for the world," Jessie replied. "At last the chance to look into that goofy brain of yours and find out what really makes Sara Devereau tick."

"Tell me something. How come I got all that pre-op medication and I'm still scared to death?"

Jessie grinned and took her friend's hand.

"Beats me," she said. "I guess you're just chicken. Listen, Sara, we're going to do it this time. If it's humanly possible to beat this thing, we're going to be fearless, and we're going to do it."

Jessie knew that the pep talk was as much for her own benefit as her patient's, and she suspected Sara knew it as well.

"Fearless," Sara said. "I trust you, coach."

"What can we expect?" Barry asked.

Jessie knew better than to measure her response too much. Sara's kids were not naive. They had been through this twice before.

"The tumor is right alongside some vital neurologic structures," she began, "including the nerve packages that control Sara's right visual field, right arm, and right leg. But we've got to be especially careful operating around what's called Wernicke's area. That's the center that controls speech and language."

"Mom could lose her ability to speak?" the oldest child, Diana, asked.

"Yes. I certainly hope not, but that's a possibility. And maybe even to *understand* speech."

Jessie could see nine-year-old Jared's eyes begin to

well up. She moved aside so that the boy could take her place beside his mother. *Enough,* she decided. The rest would be between her and Sara.

"There is one thing you all need to know," Jessie added. "Even if this operation is the total success I hope it will be, we might not know the results for a while—days, even weeks, afterward. Brain tissue has been pushed aside by the tumor. Once the tumor is gone, normal tissue will fall back to where it used to be. But there is always swelling of the brain cells when there is any manipulation or injury, and there might be a period after the operation when things don't work right. Please don't get discouraged if that happens. After the first twenty-four to forty-eight hours, things should improve tremendously. Now, if you don't have any other questions, I'm going to go and get ready."

She hugged Barry and shook the children's hands, whispering to each to be brave. Telling them not to worry would have been foolish.

JESSIE MADE QUICK rounds on her patients, then spent twenty minutes studying Sara's MRIs and reviewing her operative plan. The tumor was in a temporo-parietal location, just above the ear on the left side, just adjacent to the nerves of Wernicke's area. Speaking . . . understanding spoken and written words . . . reading . . . writing. The biggest danger of the operation would be failing to get out enough tumor to effect a cure. But the risk of having Sara Devereau living out her life in a hell devoid of expressive and receptive language was not far behind. Loss of a limb or a visual field was one thing. Permanent loss of the ability to communicate or to be communicated with was something else again.

Knowing too much and fearing that she didn't know

enough, Jessie followed her pre-op ritual, walking slowly and deliberately down the eight flights to the subbasement. Then she paused briefly before a pair of glass doors before stepping into the world of MRI-assisted surgery.

By the time Jessie emerged from the dressing room after changing into fresh scrubs and her OR Keds, Emily was in the prep area, shaving Sara bald with a disposable, double-edged safety razor. Thousands of hours and hundreds of thousands of dollars had gone into making anesthesia and surgical equipment insensitive to the MRI's massive magnets, which, themselves, were never turned off except in the event of some mechanical disaster. Once into the OR, even the most insignificant metal object would be snatched across to the housing—a missile with deadly potential. Ultimately, it had been less expensive to build a small prep area than it would have been to develop and manufacture non-ferromagnetic razors.

On the wall of the prep area was a blown-up photo of a janitor, smiling broadly as he pushed an industrial-sized floor buffer along. A red circle and slash had been painted over the picture, which was actually posed for and taken by the residents after an EMMC maintenance worker had missed the multitude of warning signs and cheerfully buffed his way into the MRI operating room. The huge buffer, ripped from his hands and sucked chest-high across ten feet of air, slammed against one of the tori with destructive force. Shutting down the semiconductors to remove the buffer had cost tens of thousands of dollars and closed the operating room for weeks.

"How're things going?" Jessie asked.

"Excellent pre-op meds," Emily said. "She's just passing the second star to the right. Sara, I think you'll love this new hairdo."

"Hey, what works for Michael Jordan works for me," Sara replied dreamily. "Your scalpel sharp, Doc?"

"We're all set," Jessie said. "The plan is to put you to sleep until we finish the noisy parts."

"I never did like listening to my skull being drilled."

"When you wake up, you'll be on your side with your head fixed in a frame."

"I remember."

"You'll have an airway in your throat, but we'll take it out when we need you to talk. You'll also have on the pair of special goggles I showed you. The goggles will project words or pictures. I may ask you to describe some things you see with one or two words, or else just to think about them. While you're doing that, we're going to be making a map of the parts of your brain that are working at that moment. It's called a functional MRI."

"Functional MRI," Sara echoed.

"Jessie," Emily cut in, "I hate to spoil this highly informative session, but I think she's probably too squashy to get much out of it. You have already gone over all this, yes?"

"Yes. I'm just . . . I don't know . . . trying to be thorough."

"That's fine. Listen, we're going to do great."

"Yeah," Jessie replied, with less enthusiasm than she had intended.

"I mean it."

"Thanks. I know. Anesthesia here?"

"Yup. Byron Wong."

"Radiology?"

"Everyone's here. And I'm ready. You can do this, Jess."

"Yeah," Sara muttered, as if from down a long tunnel. "You can do this."

"I only wish I didn't have to," Jessie said. "See you inside."

As she turned and headed for the sinks to begin a lengthy scrub, Jessie was thinking about the cocktail party catch phrase she had heard so many times . . . *I mean, it isn't exactly brain surgery.*

BULKY IN HER surgical gown, Jessie stepped into the narrow world between the MRI tori just as anesthesiologist Byron Wong and the circulating nurse slid Sara through the opening in the magnet to her left.

"We'll keep her out with propofol and midazolam," Wong said, "but not too deep. It'll take just a minute or two to wake her up when you're ready. She'll be uncomfortable being on her side for I don't know how many hours, but thanks to the midazolam, when we're all done, she won't remember how miserable she was."

"If a tree falls in the forest, and there's no one around to hear it . . ." Jessie said, bolting Sara's head into the frame that would hold it motionless throughout the surgery.

"Pardon?"

"Nothing, nothing," Jessie said, setting the crosshairs of three lasers so that they would intersect at the center of where she visualized the tumor to be, targeting things for the MRI. "I was just wondering how much someone is suffering if they have complete amnesia for the time when the suffering happened."

"You're very deep," Emily said.

"I know that. I know I am."

The mindless banter between the two friends would continue on and off throughout the operation. Emily had developed a sixth sense as to when Jessie needed the connection, and when she simply had to be left alone with her thoughts and the awesome responsibility of her job. Because of the teaching hospital's demand that the residents assist on as many cases as possible, there was constant pressure on Jessie to use them. And, remembering her own residency, generally she did. But for the most difficult cases, she still always stood her ground and insisted on Emily. If she was the World Series pitcher, Emily DelGreco, wise and experienced, was her favorite catcher and lucky rabbit's foot rolled into one.

After a thorough antiseptic prep, they spread out sterile drapes especially designed for the narrow work space between the tori. Then she and Emily adjusted their MRI screens. It was time. Jessie closed her eyes for several seconds and cleared her mind with a few deep breaths, until one word dominated her thoughts: *steady*.

"Ready, Byron?" she asked, her eyes still closed.

"All set."

"Holly?"

"Ready to go," the tech at the outside console said through the speakers.

"Ted?"

"Viva Las Vegas," the radiologist replied.

Jessie opened her eyes slowly.

"Suction up," she said. "Scalpel, please."

WORKING WITH PRACTICED quickness, Jessie made a question-mark incision just over Sara's left ear, then worked the scalp away and began freeing up the temporalis muscle—the broad muscle that closes the jaw. All the while, she was concentrating on locating the upper branch of the facial nerve and the vessels arising off the temporal artery. Cutting through any of those structures would have permanent consequences.

"Nice job," Emily whispered as she helped move the temporalis aside. "Real nice."

Jessie called for the bone drill and made a series of large holes that she then connected with a smaller bit.

"Carpentry's done," she said as Emily wrapped the bony segment in wet gauze and passed it back to the scrub nurse. Jessie then ran her fingers over the thick membrane covering Sara's brain. "The dura's pretty badly scarred down," she reported.

"You mean Gilbrided down," Emily whispered.

"Shhhh," Jessie said, her eyes smiling above her mask. "Let me be sure my microphone's off before you say anything about our esteemed leader."

With each progressive layer, the surgery became more demanding. Damaging the veins in the dura, some of which were bound in scar tissue from the two prior operations, could easily cause a stroke.

"When you're hot, you're hot," Emily said, suturing back the membrane after a perfect dissection. "What do you think Paulette would say if she saw how her little girl spends her days?"

Jessie ran her fingertips over the folds of Sara's cerebral cortex.

"We're going to do a rapid imaging sequence with contrast," she said. "Have the IV gadolinium ready." She shut off her microphone. "My mother's more interested in how I spend my *nights*. Or should I say how I *don't* spend my nights. She thinks I never date."

"I guess that means she's not wrong *all* the time."

"Hey, watch it. I date, and you know it."

"Example?"

"That lawyer from Toronto. The one I met when I went to Cancun. I even flew up to Canada for a couple of weekends with him. Remember?"

"Jess, I hate to tell you this, but that was almost two years ago."

"I've been busy. Gadolinium in, please. Besides, all he talked about was how much opportunity there would be for me in Canada. When I suggested *he* might like Boston, I thought he was going to have a seizure. Look, look, there it is, Em. Great pictures, Ted. Perfect. Just think of all those chemists who called gadolinium a useless rare earth element. Surely someone should have known that a hundred years later we were going to invent magnetic resonance imaging and it would be the perfect contrast material. That just goes to show you—never discount anything. Byron, ten minutes and I'm going to want her to start waking up. Em, you get her goggles on while I expose this beast. Holly, how about something mellow—maybe that Irish harp CD. We're going to get this sucker. We're going to get every bit of it."

Mapping by MRI was the key. Mapping tumor. Mapping functioning brain. Superimposing the two. Melting one with ultrasound. Leaving the other intact.

Speed was also important. Although brain swelling was generally well controlled during surgery, it was always a concern. The more the swelling, the more the blurring between thinking tissue and tumor. Jessie hummed along with the harp as she worked, melting obvious tumor with the ultrasonic selector as Emily helped suction out the resultant debris. Soon, the obvious tumor was markedly depleted. The general anesthesia had been turned off. Sara Devereau, her brain widely exposed, was awake.

Now we see who's a warrior, Jessie said to herself.

"Sara, it's me. Everything's going great. Can you hear me?"

"I can," Sara replied hoarsely.

"Remember, you're in that frame. You can't move."

"Can't . . . move."

"Open your eyes, please, and think about what you're seeing. Don't say anything unless I ask you to. Just think it."

Functional magnetic resonance—another miracle—was based on detecting the chemical change in hemoglobin where thinking brain was using extra energy and drawing extra oxygen from the blood. Jessie had been around for much of the development of the technique, but it still astonished her. *Amazing,* she thought as she worked. . . . *Amazing . . . amazing . . . amazing. . . . And the geek shall inherit the earth. . . . That's it, sweet baby . . . just keep thinking . . . just keep thinking.*

Jessie watched the map of Sara's functional gray matter develop on the monitor screen. Moments later, the radiologist superimposed the tumor on it. Then, as quickly as possible, Jessie began melting cancer cells once more, all the while getting closer and closer to thinking brain.

"What do you see, Sar? Tell me what the guy's doing?"

"Ski-ing."

"And now?"

"Run-ning."

"She's starting to swell," Jessie whispered. "Jesus, is she swelling. Byron, please give her fifty of mannitol."

"Fifty going in."

"What do you see, Sar? Talk to me. Talk to me."

"M . . . ma . . ."

Jessie felt her aggressive approach to the resection begin to blunt.

"Em, there's too much swelling. Everything's shifting, getting distorted. Byron, give her some steroids. Make it ten of Decadron."

"Ten in."

"Easy, Jess. You can only do what you can do," Emily said.

"Sara, what do you see? Sara? Em, suck here. Right here."

God, I'm too deep. I know I am.

Jessie was far less emotional in the operating room than she was in the rest of her world. But even at her coolest, she was not the ice cube some surgeons were. With the reality of a partial or complete loss of communication for her patient on the line, Jessie knew she was tightening up like a heated bowstring. The sudden swelling and the intertwining of normal and abnormal cells had made further surgery impractical, if not impossible. Maybe she had gotten enough already, she reasoned. Maybe Sara's own immune system could take care of whatever was left behind.

I don't think I can go any further.

"Sara, it's Jess. Tell me what you see. . . . Say something. . . . Anything. . . . Come on, baby, say something."

The best Sara could muster was a guttural groan.

"Em, I don't know," Jessie said. "I'm right there. I'm right at speech pathways. Maybe in them already. It's like the tumor's just melted into brain."

"You want to stop?"

"I . . . I don't know."

This was it—the moment she had prayed would never come. She had allowed herself to hope for an operation that was perfectly clean—everything crystal clear and well defined. No overwhelming scarring, no dangerous swelling, no wrenching decisions. She surveyed the edema distorting Sara's brain. If anything, it had gotten a little worse. *Too soon,* she told herself. It was still too soon to tell if the mannitol and Decadron would reduce the

swelling. But as things stood, there was still some definition of structure—not much, but some. If she waited for
the treatment to work and instead the swelling wors-
ened, the chances of avoiding critical speech areas, and
probably other structures as well, would be even slimmer
than they already were. The bowstring tightened.

The only safe thing to do, she decided, was to stop.

Before she could voice that decision to Emily, the
door to the OR pushed open and a man strode in wearing scrubs and a mask, but no covering over his rip-
pling brown hair nor his spit-polished wing tips. . . .
Gilbride.

"Jessie, where's Skip Porter?" he asked with not so
much as an acknowledgment that there was brain
surgery going on, let alone on a former patient of his.

Jerk.

"Skip? He had some emergency oral surgery yesterday. I think he went to have it checked before coming in
today. He usually only works afternoons on Mondays
anyway."

"Well, I need him. The president of Cybermed was at
the meeting this morning. He's in my office right now
and he wants a look at ARTIE."

Jessie looked down into Sara's incision. The swelling
was no better, but thank God, no worse.

"The prototype from yesterday has been taken
apart," she said through clenched teeth. "ARTIE-Two
should be around."

"Well, it isn't. I looked all over the lab and I can't find
it. Cybermed has the clout to make ARTIE number one
in the area of intraoperative robotics. And here I can't
even produce the damn thing."

Beneath her mask, Jessie calmed herself with a
lengthy exhale.

"Did you look in the cabinet over the central sink? That's where we always keep both ARTIEs locked up."

"No, I . . . The cabinet with the combination lock?"

"Exactly. You had us set the combination for your birthday, remember?"

"Oh . . . yes. It's been a while since I . . . since I needed to do any work in that lab. I'll go check. Carry on."

Gilbride turned and was gone. Just like that. Not a word about Sara Devereau. Jessie wondered how much of the conversation Sara had heard, and whether it registered that the surgeon who had done her first two operations had breezed in and out without even acknowledging that she was on the table.

Jessie felt the bowstring relax. Her shoulders sagged comfortably. The tightness in her jaw vanished. Gilbride had just saved her from making a decision she would have regretted for the rest of her life. There was still tumor in Sara's brain—too much tumor for Jessie to believe her body could fight for long.

Fearless.

In the heat of the moment, with her friend on the table, swelling distorting the anatomy, and faced with a tumor among the most difficult she had encountered, Jessie had lost her objectivity. She had forgotten her promise to her friend and to herself.

Fearless.

"Ted, I want a new set of images of this sucker," she heard herself say. "Everybody, this is the captain speaking. I want you all to just hunker down and let your honeys know you might be late for dinner. We're going to be at this for a few more hours."

CHAPTER 6

BOSTON'S FLEET CENTER WAS A NEAR SELLOUT.
Pacing about the carpeted VIP room, Marci Sheprow
could hear the crowd, like the white noise of the ocean.
Both were sounds familiar to her. She had spent the first
nine of her eighteen years living at home with her parents on Cape Cod. The next eight she had lived, essentially, in a Houston gymnasium, training with several
dozen other gymnastics hopefuls. But unlike the others,
Marci had made it to the pinnacle of her sport. Two
Olympic golds and a bronze. She was back living on the
Cape now, more often than before, anyway. And when
the time came, maybe after college, she planned to take a
piece of the millions she had already banked and buy a
place near her parents.

She had no intention of competing in the Olympics
again, but every time she said that, her coach and parents

just smiled. They knew as well as she did that there was little about competitive gymnastics she didn't love. And now she was riding a wave of incredible popularity, especially in New England.

"Hey, babe, what gives?"

Shasheen Standon, Marci's closest friend on the U.S. team, was eating a pear, and offered a bite.

"No, thanks. My stomach's a little queasy, and I've got a little bit of a headache."

"It must be a virus. It sure can't be nerves. You ain't got none of those."

"Come on. You of all people know that's just b.s."

Marci was famous on the team and in the press for her calm, almost blissful demeanor when she performed. She was approachable, though—not like those Russian and Romanian ice maidens. Still, her routines were described in the *New York Times* as "breathtakingly daring." "The whole package," another writer gushed.

"You know," Shasheen said, "now that you mention it, you don't look that great. Remember, this is only an exhibition. Maybe you should pack it in tonight. Let us second stringers have center stage."

Marci punched her friend lightly on the arm.

"A team gold and an individual silver on the uneven bars. Some second stringer you are. I may cut back on my routine, but I can't back out. I'm local. Do you have any idea how many family and friends I have out there? You stayed at my house last night. You know."

"That was a pretty wild scene, that's for sure, especially that Uncle Jerry of yours. Well, just go easy. Leave out some of the crazy Sheprow moves."

"Maybe. Maybe I will."

Marci bent over and effortlessly touched the carpet with her palms. At five foot five she was on the tall side for a gymnast, but she was remarkably lithe and the strongest girl on the team. She was also 100 percent athlete, totally in tune with her body. And tonight, she simply didn't feel right. She went up on her toes and snapped her hands across her body, then up toward the ceiling. To the casual observer, she would have looked lightning quick. But she knew that she was unnaturally aware of her right leg when she flexed at the ankle, and that her right arm felt slightly sluggish as well. They had been on tour for more than a month, with shows sometimes three nights in a row. Maybe she was just wearing down.

Across the room, Shasheen was entertaining several of the girls and coaches with one of her stories. Marci smiled. *Talk about loose.*

"Five minutes," the promoter called into the room. "Five minutes, everyone. Marci, that deal with the governor's going to happen at intermission. I told his people you felt uncomfortable being singled out, but they reminded me that you're the only one on the team from Massachusetts, and that the small print in our contract says we have to cooperate with this sort of thing. It's just a plaque of some kind. Your folks'll love it."

"Viva Sheprow," Shasheen cheered with her typical sly edge.

The others laughed and applauded. At one time or another, everyone on the team had had differences with the others, but by and large they had stuck together pretty well. Marci bowed to the group and nodded to the promoter that she was okay about the plaque. She pulled on her warm-up jacket and tried, unsuccessfully, to shake the strange leaden feeling from her right arm. Finally she zipped up and followed the others out to the arena.

As Marci had anticipated, there were few empty seats in the house—probably the biggest crowd they had drawn on the entire tour. Through the playing of the national anthem and the introduction of the team, Marci tested her muscles—fingers, hands, arms, shoulders, neck, legs. *Better,* she thought. Everything felt better. She went up on her toes again. No real problem. Well, maybe a little weirdness.

What in the hell is going on?

She was scheduled to perform on the balance beam and uneven bars, as well as the vault. Then she and two others were to do a series of synchronized tumbling passes. Maybe she could beg off that.

"You okay, Marse?" Shasheen asked.

"Huh? Oh, yeah. I'm okay, I guess."

"What did you say?"

"I said I'm okay."

"Marci, you're not speaking right."

"I'm okay."

Her words sounded fine now. This was like the flu, she thought, or some kind of sugar thing. She typically wouldn't eat for hours before a competition, and even though this was only an exhibition, she should never have had a frappe and sandwich. The loudspeaker announcer called the eight of them to their places. Shasheen was starting on the uneven bars. Marci would be vaulting.

"Knock 'em dead," Shasheen said, giving her a thumbs-up as she headed across the arena.

"Yeah," Marci whispered to no one. "You, too."

She followed a teammate toward the head of the runway leading to the vault horse. Her individual gold medal was on the balance beam, but of all the events, vault was the most natural and automatic for her. Again, her right arm and leg seemed heavy. She felt confused and, for the first time, frightened.

Knock 'em dead.

Marci watched her teammate do an adequate vault, then heard her own name reverberate through the vast arena.

Mom, something's wrong with me. What should I do?

Marci looked to her left, where her parents, sister, relatives, and friends took up most of three rows. Barbara Sheprow, with her flaming red hair and the white suit she had bought for the occasion, beamed at her and pumped both fists in the air.

Mama?

Marci suddenly became aware that the entire Fleet Center had become eerily silent. Everyone was watching her . . . waiting. She hadn't even begun going through the mental prep to vault.

She turned toward the runway, shaking her hand and contracting the muscles in her arm. If she waited any longer, there was no telling what she would feel like.

You can do it. There are no judges. Just do a decent vault. Nothing special. Go for it.

The silence in the arena was replaced by a nervous buzz.

It had to be now.

Marci rose on her toes and began her sprint toward the horse, arms pumping. She knew her speed was down, but it was too late now. She could pull it off. Even feeling lousy, she could pull it off.

A step before the take-off ramp, her right leg seemed to disappear. When she planted it, there was almost nothing there. She was airborne, but not nearly high enough to complete a vault. Panicked, she reached out reflexively for the horse, but her right arm failed her completely. She did an awkward, clumsy turn in the air and fell heavily on the horse. Air exploded from her lungs. She toppled forward helplessly. Her consciousness began to fade. The last sound Marci heard before blacking out was the cracking of bone in her wrist.

CHAPTER 7

"JESSIE, DEL MURPHY HERE. ARE YOU FREE TO MEET ME
in the ER?"

It was just after nine when Jessie answered the page
from Murphy, the neurologist on call. She was taking a
short break in her office, but for much of the past five
hours she had been in the neurosurgical ICU. Sara
Devereau had shown no signs of regaining consciousness
following what had turned into a ten-hour battle to remove enough tumor from her brain to give her a chance
at a cure. Jessie had a dreadful sensation that her friend
was not going to awaken with intact neurologic function
if, in fact, she woke up at all.

"I can be down in just a few minutes," she said. "What
do you have?"

"I have Marci Sheprow."

"The gymnast?"

"She blacked out during an exhibition at the Fleet Center tonight, fell, and broke her wrist. The fracture's been set and casted by Bill Shea. But he didn't like her story of passing out, and called me. I've gone over her. She's stable, but she's got some neurologic findings, and I just got a look at her MRI."

"I don't like the sound of that."

"Probably not as bad as it could have been. Come on down."

Jessie splashed some cold water on her face and made another quick stop in the unit. Sara, her eyes taped shut, was hooked to a ventilator by a clear polystyrene tube that ran up her nose, down the back of her throat, and between her vocal cords. In addition, the usual array of catheters, monitor cables, and other tubes were connected to her.

"She looks so peaceful," Barry Devereau said.

"She is, in a way. Certainly, she's in no pain."

"But there's a battle going on."

"There's a battle going on, all right," Jessie echoed flatly. "I don't expect there to be any change tonight, Barry."

"I'm going to stay just the same. I have someone with the kids."

"The nurses'll take good care of you. I'm backing up the residents and covering for all private cases tonight. I take calls from home, but at night I can get back here in no time at all."

"I don't know how you do it."

Jessie rubbed at the fatigue stinging her eyes.

"It's not all that hard," she said, "as long as you don't look in the mirror."

·   ·   ·

"NO, I WILL not have a resident touching my daughter, and that's final. I want this . . . this Dr. Copeland down here now."

Jessie stood outside the doorway to room 6 in the ER, vainly searching for a way to avoid having to deal with Marci Sheprow's mother. Del Murphy had warned her about the woman as they were reviewing the MRIs. Aggressive, entitled, smart, protective, and very suspicious.

"Not frightened?" Jessie had asked.

"Not that I can tell. At least not that she lets on."

Del had correctly read the MRIs as showing a very localized, well-defined tumor—almost certainly a low-grade meningioma—pressing between the inner skull and Marci's brain on the left side, directly over the areas controlling movement of the right arm and leg. If there was such a thing as good news for someone with a brain tumor, this diagnosis and location was it.

Jessie made a futile attempt to smooth some of the wrinkles from her lab coat and scrubs, and cursed herself for not thinking to replace them before coming down. Then she noticed that she still had on the pink canvas Keds she had worn in the operating room. *Lord.* One look at those and Barbara Sheprow would probably be on the phone, calling an ambulance to spirit her daughter across town to White Memorial.

"Oh, well," she breathed, and stepped into the room.

She introduced herself first to Marci, then to her mother. The Olympic gold medalist, an icon well known in virtually every country in the world, looked frail and very young. But the spark in her green eyes belied that impression. Barbara Sheprow glanced over at Del Murphy uncomfortably.

"I . . . I expected a . . . what I mean is, Dr. Murphy didn't say you were . . ."

"A woman?"

"That, yes, and so young."

"I'm afraid I can't do much about the woman part," Jessie said, "but, I can be very reassuring about not being too young."

"I didn't even know there *were* women neurosurgeons," Marci's mother said, pushing.

A dozen flip remarks crossed Jessie's mind, but stopped short of her tongue.

"There aren't too many of us, Mrs. Sheprow, but there are some. And as you might suspect, we've all had to be twice as good to make it to where we are. As I hope Dr. Murphy will affirm, I'm a very well trained and experienced neurosurgeon."

"I appreciate the reassurance," Barbara said, sounding not at all reassured. "I had Marci brought here because Bob McGillvary, our doctor down on the Cape, knew Dr. Shea, the orthopedist who fixed her wrist, and Bob referred us to him. I . . . I never dreamed we'd be needing a neurosurgeon."

"Well, at this point, I'm not certain what you need. But I do know that to do my job right, *I* need to hear in Marci's own words what happened tonight."

Barbara Sheprow looked over at her daughter. Jessie could almost hear the woman weighing her options. This was the mother of an Olympic champion, Jessie reminded herself—a woman used to dictating to others, not to being dictated to herself. Finally, Barbara stepped aside and motioned for Jessie to go ahead.

Del Murphy mumbled something about seeing a consult and returning in a little while, and left the room, perhaps sensing that as long as he was there, Barbara

Sheprow would be directing her clinical concerns to him. Under Barbara's watchful eye, Jessie's history-taking and neurologic exam lasted half an hour. During that time, she could sense a pleasant rapport developing between herself and Marci, who was brighter and more philosophical than she had anticipated. The MRIs and current neurologic findings suggested that surgery did not have to be done on an emergency basis. But the nature of Marci's sudden weakness and loss of consciousness shouted a clear warning. There was no question an operation was in her near future.

Finally, Jessie had all the information she needed. Marci's father and younger sister were brought in from the waiting room.

"This is Dr. Jessie Copeland, Paul," Barbara said to her husband. "She's on call for the neurosurgical department. It's her job to evaluate Marci and give us her opinion as to what's happened."

Not exactly a vote of confidence, Jessie thought.

She slid the MRI films into the two view boxes and described to Marci's father what she had found.

"When would you be doing this procedure?" Paul Sheprow ventured when Jessie had finished her explanation.

Jessie could see the man's wife stiffen.

"Now, Paul," Barbara admonished, "no one has said anything about *who* would be doing Marci's surgery, let alone *when,* or even *whether.*"

"But I thought—"

"Please, dear. Dr. Copeland, is this the best hospital for Marci to be having this surgery?"

"It is certainly *one* of the best. We have a great deal of significant research going on, and we do a lot of brain tumor surgery."

"We?"

"The department, I mean."

"And where do you rate in that department?"

"Mother!" Marci exclaimed. "Give her a break."

"I will not. This isn't exactly deciding who is going to do your nails."

"If I've got to have an operation, I think she'll do fine."

"I'll tell you what, Marci. When it's your child's head someone wants to operate on, I'll let you decide whether they should or not, and who should do it."

"Look," Jessie said, "there are forty or fifty neurosurgeons in Boston. Any one of them would be happy to give you a second opinion, and also a second choice. I want you to be totally confident in me or whoever does this surgery. Having this kind of operation is frightening enough without your having doubts about the surgeon."

"If you did the procedure, when would you do it?" Barbara asked, not acknowledging Jessie's words of reassurance.

"This is a benign tumor in that it doesn't spread to other sites in the body," Jessie replied. "And as I pointed out, it appears to be the kind of meningioma that is the easiest for us to remove. But the skull is a closed container, and there is pressure building up. The episode tonight was a pretty strident warning."

"So you're saying soon."

"Two days, three. I wouldn't wait much longer than a week."

"And are there other treatment possibilities? Radiation? Chemo?"

Jessie shook her head.

"Barb, Dr. Copeland sounds pretty confident in herself," Paul ventured.

Barbara Sheprow never had the opportunity to tell her husband to keep his thoughts to himself. For at that moment, lacking only a flourish of trumpets, Carl Gilbride swept into the room followed by two residents. He was as impeccably dressed as Jessie was rumpled, and he exuded stature and confidence.

"Mrs. Sheprow, Mr. Sheprow, Marci, I'm Dr. Gilbride, the chief of neurosurgery here at EMMC," he said, shaking hands with the parents, while cutting Barbara off from Jessie like a champion wrangler. "I had just stopped by the hospital to check on a post-op patient, and heard you were here."

What post-op patient? Jessie wanted to scream. A news flash on TV, a call from the orthopedist or from someone else—those were possibilities. But not a nine o'clock drop-in to check on a post-op. *Give me a break!*

The passing of the surgical baton took just five minutes. If only Gilbride were as masterful in the OR as he was in situations such as this one, Jessie thought, Sara Devereau might never have needed two re-operations.

"Dr. Copeland is one of our finest young surgeons," Gilbride said after his cursory exam and glance at the MRI. "I assume it was her opinion that an operation is necessary on this meningioma, and fairly soon."

Finest young surgeons. Jessie swallowed back a jet of bile. Gilbride was only six or seven years older than she was, if that.

"We'd be pleased to have the chief of neurosurgery handle this," Barbara said, carefully avoiding eye contact with her.

Jessie could see Gilbride's chest puff like a pigeon's.

"Well," he said, "I'm certain that for someone who has brought such glory to us all, we can free up an OR whenever we need one. There is some danger in waiting, and it's been my experience that people are much happier just getting this sort of thing over with."

"I agree with you there," Barbara said.

"Good. My recommendation is the day after tomorrow. I'm scheduled to present a lecture at the Midwest neurosurgical meeting in Chicago that day, but the topic is research that Dr. Copeland has been assisting me on. I'm sure you won't mind standing in for me there, Jessie, yes?"

"Well, actually, I have Sara Devereau in the ICU right now and—"

"You can fly out tomorrow, give the talk at eleven the next morning, and be back by evening. The department will fly you there and you can take my room at the Hilton. The staff here'll be happy to cover your patients for the short time you'll be gone. After all, we are a team."

Jessie was already inching back toward the door. For sheer gall, stealing a patient this way fell short of some of Gilbride's past showstoppers, but it was right up there. She wondered if the uncomfortable heat in her cheeks was translating into anything people could see.

"That will be fine," she said. "Marci, good luck with all this. Dr. Gilbride is a very good surgeon. You'll be back on the balance beam before you know it."

The girl clearly looked embarrassed, but said nothing. It was as if she had seen her mother in action too many times to bother.

"Thank you, Jessie," Gilbride said, oblivious to the silent exchange. "Alice, in my office, will have the carousel of slides and your tickets ready for you first thing in the morning."

The best Jessie could manage was a tight-lipped nod. "Thanks," she said. "Good luck."

Feeling perilously close to tears, she hurried out of the ER and back up to Surgical Seven. She rarely tried to contain herself if she felt like crying, even in public. But dammit, she vowed, there was no way Carl Gilbride was going to be the cause.

AT TEN THERE was, as always, still more to do, but Jessie decided that a fifteen-hour nonstop workday was enough. Gilbride's obnoxious performance in the ER hadn't broken her spirit, but it had surely left a dent. She felt totally stressed. Her back and neck ached, and she was frantic for a protracted soak in the tub.

The hospital was located not far from some of the toughest neighborhoods in the city. There was a shuttle that ferried employees to the various parking lots, but at night it only ran at the time of shift change, between ten forty-five and midnight. Jessie was in no mood to wait forty-five minutes. She had made the walk by herself any number of nights without incident, trusting her instincts, her New Balance cross-trainers, and the cylinder of Mace in her purse.

She made a quick, final sweep through Surgical Seven, wrote some orders, and changed back into her civvies by the OR. Then she headed to the main lobby.

Carefully avoiding eye contact with any of the gaggle of reporters waiting for news of Marci Sheprow, she signed out with the operator and left the hospital. The night was moonless—dark and cool, with fine, wind-whipped mist. On evenings like this one, Swede was not at its most reliable. For Christmas, Jessie planned to get it a complete physical with a new battery and whatever else was recommended by the specialist. If it let her down tonight and didn't start, she decided, that checkup was going to come much sooner, and would include a colonoscopy.

For whatever reason—maybe the heavy darkness, she thought—Jessie kept checking over her shoulder as she walked briskly to parking lot E. At one point, she actually thought she heard footsteps. The mist was building toward a steady rain. By the time she crossed the gravel to her car, she was running. She fumbled with her keys, then unlocked the door and slid behind the wheel. Relieved, she quickly locked the doors, then sat there, panting. Finally, she slipped the key into the ignition and turned it. Nothing. Just an impotent click.

"Oh, Swede," she groaned, staring out at the dimly lit parking lot.

The rain was increasing. Around her, the windows began to fog. She opened hers a crack, then tried the wipers, which worked, and the headlights, which did also. *Not a dead battery*. She turned off both and tried the ignition again. Nothing. Suddenly, a sharp rapping on the passenger window startled her and seemed to stop her heart for several beats.

"Y—Yes?" she managed.

"Open the window, please," a man's voice said. "Security."

Jessie leaned over and smeared a circle in the condensation with the side of her hand. All she could make out was a blurred face. She opened the window an inch.

"Identification," she said.

The man, rainwater dripping off the hood of his poncho, quickly held up a hospital ID. Grateful, Jessie didn't bother reading the name. She opened the window another few inches.

"My car's dead," she said. "The battery seems okay, but nothing happens when I turn the key."

"Can you pop the hood, please?"

Jessie did as he asked and felt the car dip from his weight as he bent over the engine. The beam from his flashlight intermittently swung up from under the hood and dispersed across the fogged windshield. Jessie opened her window as far as she could without getting soaked.

"Do you need any help?" she called out.

"I don't think so. A wire's come off the ignition. I've just about got it back on. There. Try it now."

Jessie turned the key and Swede rumbled to life.

"Bless you," she murmured.

The guard appeared at the driver's-side window. His face was largely hidden by his poncho, but what Jessie could see looked pleasant enough.

"You're all set, ma'am," he said. "I was just heading back to the hospital when you came running by. I'm glad I decided to wait."

"Well, I sure am, too, I can tell you that. Do you have a car here?"

"No, I was walking."

"Well, get in. I'll drive you back."

"I'm soaked. I don't want to get your—"

"Come on, get in. This car doesn't care, and neither do I."

Jessie leaned over and opened the passenger-side door.

"Thanks," the guard said, sliding in.

"That's my line," Jessie said.

The man, about her age, was tall and broad shouldered. He had deep-set, dark eyes and the sort of rugged looks that women into Hollywood hunks might not have found attractive, but that she had always liked.

"It got nasty in a hurry out there," he said, pushing his hood back from his closely cut, light brown hair.

"I'm very grateful to you for sticking around. Did I look that helpless?"

"Hardly. I'm new on the job, and to tell you the truth, after a career in the Marines, it's a bit boring. A woman running through the rain at this hour definitely caught my attention. I appreciate the ride back."

"It's my pleasure. I'm Jessie Copeland, one of the doctors at the old place."

She extended her hand. The guard's thick fingers enfolded it.

"Well, I'm pleased to meet you, Dr. Copeland," he said, noting that Jessie was better looking than her photo in the hospital directory. "My name's Bishop. Alex Bishop."

CHAPTER 8

NOT SURPRISINGLY, CARL GILBRIDE'S "ROOM" AT THE
Chicago Hilton was a suite. It had been hard for Jessie to
leave Sara in the care of one of the other neurosurgeons,
but there had been absolutely no improvement in her
level of consciousness or neurologic function. And Jessie
strongly believed there wouldn't be any over the day she
would be away. The symptoms and clinical course of
cerebral edema—brain swelling—were impossible to
predict with any confidence. Some post-op patients were
alert within a few hours despite significantly increased
intracranial pressure and documented swelling on their
MRIs, while others, with much less edema, awoke only
after being out for days, weeks, or even months.

It was midafternoon when Jessie had called Barry
Devereau with the lack-of-progress report. Then she
had changed for the trip in the on-call room. Marci

Sheprow's impending surgery, scheduled for first thing in the morning, was, of course, the talk of the hospital. Coming down the Track earlier in the day, Jessie had seen Barbara Sheprow approaching and had actually ducked into a patient's room rather than open the curtain on what was certain to be a strained, even embarrassing, interaction with the woman. She also felt some relief each time she walked past the gymnast's room and the door was closed. She knew she was allowing herself to become a player in Gilbride's theater of the absurd, but she was also able to acknowledge that she was only human. By the time she had picked up Gilbride's slides from his secretary and taken a cab to the airport, she was ready to get away from Eastern Mass Medical Center— even if it was only for a day.

On the flight to Chicago, she had resolved to try harder to accept the fact that nothing she could ever do would change her department chief one iota. That grand decision did little to boost her spirits.

One thing that did give her a lift was her brief contact with Alex Bishop, the hospital guard who had reconnected the wire in Swede's ignition and kept a miserable evening from becoming even worse. Bishop was a former medic in the Marines, and was in the process of applying to Northeastern's physician's assistant program. He seemed incredibly intense, but he also had a droll, self-deprecating humor that appealed to her as much as his looks.

After stepping out of her car, he had said, "Well, see you around."

She had nearly replied, "When?"

Jessie set aside the notes she had made for her presentation, opened the closet, and took out the two suits she had brought to Chicago—one a conservative charcoal gray befitting the stand-in for Carl Gilbride, and the other a butter yellow number with a short straight skirt and cropped jacket. It was no contest. The yellow outfit made her feel feminine and yes, maybe even powerful. And who knew, perhaps some guy who was neither married nor lethally self-absorbed would be in the audience. Emily was right. It had been too long. It was time to get her nose out of people's cranial cavities and look around.

She wandered out to the sitting room of her suite and called the neurosurgical ICU at Eastern Mass Medical. As she had anticipated, Sara's condition was unchanged. Jessie had known better than to expect any improvement, and yet she had held her breath, waiting for the terse report.

Gilbride's presentation, as it turned out, was scheduled for one in the afternoon, not eleven in the morning as he had told her. She could have gone down to the lecture hall to listen to some of the other talks. Instead, she decided on a nap. First, though, she took a twelve-dollar mason jar of cashews from the in-room minibar and washed some of them down with a few swallows from a three-dollar can of diet Coke. God only knew, she had earned the indulgence. With any luck, sometime in the future the expenses for her trip would float across Gilbride's desk, and there they'd be—fifteen bucks' worth of cashews and Coke. She opened a five-dollar Toblerone bar for good measure, and set it aside after one small bite.

I'm a vindictive enemy, Gilbride, she thought as she checked off the three items on the minibar tally sheet. *Take that! And that!*

The phone rang with the wake-up call she had requested, anticipating that the strain of the past two days and whatever Freudian factors were at work might have her napping through her presentation. She arranged for a delayed checkout and gathered her things for the talk, which Gilbride had modestly titled "Robotics and Intraoperative MRI: A Marriage for the Ages." Finally, after one last survey in the mirror, she headed down ten flights to the Northeast Salon.

Gilbride and Copeland, she was thinking. *A Marriage for the Ages.*

JESSIE WAS INFINITELY more comfortable teaching a small group of residents or students than she ever would be standing up before a crowd. She was grateful that most of this talk was commentary on slides, with the house lights down. Except for the clearing of throats and an occasional cough from among the 150 or so attendees, she felt alone much of the time, lecturing in a cocoon of darkness. Carl Gilbride, a master at such presentations, had interspersed his charts and photographs with a number of cartoons, some of which were unabashedly sexist. Jessie had weeded out the most offensive ones, and then appalled herself by leaving in two of the borderlines, just to show the almost-all-XY audience that she could be one of the boys.

She had been allotted forty-five minutes and was pleased and relieved to realize that, with seven minutes left, she was done. She turned on the house lights from the lectern and asked for questions. Three microphones had been placed along the center aisle. Immediately one surgeon was up at each one—a good sign that the entire crowd hadn't drifted into dreamland. The first two questions were softballs—simple clarifications she could easily handle. Both men—neither of whom looked like potential spice for her personal life—complimented her on an excellent presentation and fascinating research. *So far, so good,* she thought as the two physicians were quickly replaced at their microphones.

The third questioner was a tall black neurosurgeon from California named Litton, a researcher in one of the programs developing a competitor for ARTIE. In their brief encounters with each other, Jessie had found him to be impressively intelligent and absolutely humorless. He had arrived fifteen minutes late, during one of the brief lights-on periods of her talk. She sensed trouble even before Litton began speaking.

"Dr. Copeland, Ron Litton, Stanford University, here. I want to congratulate you on an excellent presentation of fascinating research into the field of intraoperative robotics. But there is one thing troubling me."

"Yes?"

"You said that to this point you've done some work with your ARTIE on animals and cadavers."

"That's right."

"And that you and your department head, Dr. Gilbride, had begun making preparations to submit a proposal for approval by your hospital's committee on human experimentation."

"That's exactly what I said, yes."

"Then I would suggest that perhaps you and your chief of neurosurgery should get on the same page. I was several minutes late arriving for your presentation because I was glued to the television in my room. CNN, to be precise."

"Dr. Litton, I don't understand what that has to do with our submitting a human experimentation proto-col."

"Dr. Copeland, I certainly hope you have approval from that committee already. Because according to the

news and the interview with Dr. Gilbride that I just
watched, earlier today he used your friend ARTIE to ex-
cise and successfully remove a tumor from the brain of
the Olympic gold medal gymnast Marci Sheprow."

CHAPTER 9

"DR. GILBRIDE, WOULD YOU SAY THAT FROM WHAT YOU'VE seen of Marci Sheprow so far, your surgical robot has scored a perfect ten?"

Gilbride, looking earnest and professorial, met the cameras covering his press conference warmly.

"Nothing in neurosurgery can be taken for granted, Charlie," he said, tenting his fingers, "but at the moment, Miss Sheprow is looking very good, and we're expecting a rapid recovery. The trauma associated with traditional surgery was certainly diminished through the use of our intraoperative robotics."

Come on, Carl, have you no shame?

Jessie sat slumped in stunned silence on the couch in her suite, watching her boss perform for the cameras and at least two dozen microphones bunched on the table before him. To his left, propped on an easel, was an artist's graphic rendering of Marci Sheprow's head, the location of her meningioma, and the path followed by ARTIE. It was as if Gilbride were General Schwarzkopf and Marci's brain Iraq. It appalled Jessie, but did not at all surprise her, that he had commissioned the artwork *before* he did the surgery.

"Dr. Gilbride, Pat Jackson, Associated Press. Could you give us some idea of the future of robotics in neurosurgery?"

"In *all* of surgery, Pat. Advances in medicine are coming so fast. People forget that CT scans weren't in general use until twenty years ago, and MRIs just over half that. Ultrasound's been around since World War Two, but with nothing like the sophistication we have today. Now there's fiber optics, which has made all of the various scopes possible, and looming on the horizon is robotics. The potential is limitless, and I've told the researchers in my department that it's full speed ahead in this area."

Jerk.

Jessie wondered about her future at EMMC. Had Gilbride left her any option but resignation? He had lied to her about getting ready to apply for authorization from the human experimentation panel. The five-member panel was largely made up of his cronies. Clearly he had already gotten approval from them for a clinical trial with ARTIE, and was just waiting for the perfect case.

And then there was the matter of Marci Sheprow's tumor. It wasn't much of an exaggeration to suggest that a reasonably competent neurosurgeon could have successfully removed her meningioma with a Black & Decker drill, a teaspoon, and a Swiss Army knife. This was hardly the sort of case for which ARTIE was being developed. But only the few who were present when

Jessie was working on Pete Roslanski's tumor knew how much damage ARTIE-2 could have done to Marci's brain had it malfunctioned the way ARTIE-1 had. No wonder Gilbride had gone haywire about her cadaver trial. He was already primed and waiting for the right moment to make history. The technical problem she had encountered, however remediable, would create a major glitch in his plans should word filter back to the human experimentation panel. Enter Marci Sheprow—a morsel just too tasty to pass up.

The news conference was continuing, but Jessie had seen and heard all she cared to. She left her suit and underwear where they fell on the bedroom floor and stood in a steaming shower for twenty minutes, washing herself over and over, as if she could somehow scrub away the contamination from her association with the man.

She dried her hair, then pulled on jeans and a crew-neck sweater and packed up her things for the flight home. It would be fairly late by the time she returned to the hospital and it was doubtful she'd have to be dressed up to face the press. Even if someone did manage to connect her to ARTIE, so what. She was just the robot's nursemaid. Gilbride was its press agent.

She started out of the room, then returned to the minibar and added a three-dollar bag of M&M's to her purse.

Take that!

THE PHALANX OF satellite broadcasting vans parked in front of the hospital was the first giveaway that Jessie had seriously underestimated the media's devotion to Marci Sheprow, and their fascination with the technology that had saved her life. There were security guards everyplace she looked, and clusters of news and camera people in the main lobby and hallway. As she showed her ID to a guard, several reporters began calling out questions to her on the off chance that she had something—anything—to do with Marci. Others began shuffling toward her like extras in a zombie picture.

Jessie hurried up to the OR dressing room on Surgical Eight and changed into scrubs and a lab coat. Then, full of nervous tension, she raced down to Surgical Seven.

Marci was still in the NICU. Jessie had planned to stop in and see her after she had checked on Sara, but Barbara Sheprow caught her eye as she passed and motioned her in.

"How was your talk?" Barbara whispered, conscious of her sleeping daughter.

"It went fine. I'm so pleased with what I've heard about Marci's operation."

The gymnast was off all life support, and looked to be breathing comfortably.

"She's opened her eyes several times, and has even spoken. But mostly she's been sleeping."

"That's certainly normal."

"Dr. Copeland, I hope there're no hard feelings about my decision to go with Dr. Gilbride on this."

"This isn't a contest, Mrs. Sheprow. It's your child's life. You've got to be as comfortable as possible with her surgeon. I wouldn't want to be that surgeon if you weren't."

Without waiting for further conversation, she brushed some hair from Marci's forehead, studied her perfect, unlined face, and said a silent prayer of thanks that nothing had gone wrong during Gilbride's grandstand play. Then she left. Barbara was obviously ecstatic with the decision she had made in choosing Gilbride. Jessie hoped she would never know how shamelessly her daughter had been used.

Sara remained on assisted ventilation, but the covering neurosurgeon's notes stated that she had begun gagging a bit on the breathing tube—a slightly hopeful sign. He had also reported a flicker of movement on Sara's left side. *Flicker of movement.* A brilliant, vibrant teacher and mother of three, and that was what her world had been reduced to. *At the moment,* Jessie reminded herself. *At the moment.* But she also knew that every passing hour with minimal or no progress, each passing day, made a recovery without major deficits less likely.

Jessie did a brief neurologic exam, which revealed no reflexes, poor muscle tone, and nothing approaching even the flicker her covering doctor had described. This was not just a battle, this was Sara's Armageddon.

Looking down at her friend, she wondered how Barry and the kids would react to the news that she had decided to resign from the staff. What about Tamika Bing and Dave Scolari and Mrs. Kinchley and her other patients? What about Skip Porter, and Hans, and all those who had helped breathe life into ARTIE? If only Gilbride had stayed on his side of the line. Minimal, unavoidable contact she could have handled. Now, she was being forced to make a choice that would only hurt people—most prominently, she reflected sadly, herself. She wrote a few perfunctory orders on Sara and headed, downcast, toward the ward, intending to make quick rounds on her patients before heading home. The unit charge nurse called to her before she reached the doors.

"Jessie, hi," the nurse said, handing over an envelope with Jessie's name printed on it. "Dr. Gilbride said you would probably be in here tonight. He left this for you."

More than curious, Jessie thanked the nurse and hurried to her office with the envelope before opening it.

MEMO
From: Carl W. Gilbride, M.D.; Chief, Department of
     Neurosurgery
To: Roland Tuten, M.D.; Chairman, Professional
     Standing, Credentials, and Promotions Committee
Re: Jessie D. Copeland, M.D.; Instructor in
     Neurosurgery

Dear Dr. Tuten:
    I am writing to inform you of my intention to recommend Dr. Jessie D. Copeland for a promotion from clinical instructor to Assistant Professor of Neurosurgery, effective as soon as I receive approval from your committee. Dr. Copeland has served this department and Eastern Massachusetts Medical Center with distinction, and has been especially instrumental in the development of our program in intraoperative robotics. It is my intention to reward her for these efforts with this upgrade in her academic rank.

Assistant professor—a serious step toward tenure; a significant raise in pay. Jessie stared down at the memo. She had believed herself to be two years away from a promotion, maybe three—if she got one at all. She also knew that she would be leapfrogging several members—*XY members*—of the department. She wasn't a militant feminist, but she couldn't deny her satisfaction at the idea.

"I wanted to wait to speak with you until you had read that."

Carl Gilbride, looking no less fresh than he had during his press conference hours ago, stood in her doorway. Jessie held up the memo.

"In the outside world they throw people in jail for accepting a payoff like this," she said.

Gilbride slipped inside the office and closed the door behind him.

"Call it what you wish," he said. "Either way, you've earned it. I knew you'd be upset by what happened today."

"I'm worse than upset, Carl. I'm horrified and furious, and . . . and mortified. ARTIE wasn't ready for something like this, and you know it."

"That's not what Skip Porter told me. He said that . . . that little problem you had the other day was purely mechanical—a broken wire, not any design or computer flaw. Besides, when is a new technique or drug ever *really* ready? At some point, clinical scientists have just got to take the bull by the horns and do it."

Jessie shook her head slowly.

"Spare me, please," she said.

"Jessie, I appreciate all you've done with ARTIE. But I also don't think *you* appreciate some of the realities of financing a research-oriented neurosurgical department."

"Carl, you placed that girl in danger for no reason."

"If there was any trouble with ARTIE, I was set to open her up and go after her tumor that way. And don't say the device was used for no reason. Look at these."

Gilbride withdrew a large, stuffed manila envelope from his briefcase and passed it over. It contained dozens of congratulatory e-mails, phone messages, faxes, and even several telegrams. Patients from countries around the world were already contacting Gilbride, asking him to take a crack with ARTIE at their "inoperable" tumors.

"Please, I was hopeless until now," one fax read. "I have nothing to lose. Please help me."

"Congratulations," Jessie said, hoping her tone reflected her lack of sincerity.

"Two of those faxes and one of those telegrams are from agencies that could or do help fund our research," Gilbride said, reaching across the desk to separate them from the others. "Here."

The telegram was from the medical director of Durbin Surgicals. Jessie knew that a good portion of the work on ARTIE had been done with their help through a grant that was in Gilbride's name, but for which she had written the application.

Dear Carl. We at Durbin are proud that research done in part under one of our career development awards has made such an impressive impact. Congratulations to you, Dr. Copeland, and the rest of your staff. I suspect when you apply for a renewal you will find smooth sailing.

"And look. Look at this one. It's from the executive director of the MacIntosh Foundation in Los Angeles. You've heard of them?"

"Of course."

Dear Dr. Gilbride,
Congratulations on your successful use of intraoperative robotics in the case of Marci Sheprow. As you know, the MacIntosh Foundation is committed in part to the furtherance of medical science as it directly impacts the public. I know you have

been anxiously awaiting our response to your recent grant application to our agency. We are impressed with what you have accomplished, and will be evaluating your research for one of our Class 1 awards, which, as you may know, has a minimum value of three million dollars. I will be contacting you directly should we require any further information, or should our grant awards committee reach a decision on your application.

Sincerely,
Eastman Tolliver
Executive Director

"Three million," Jessie said, genuinely impressed.

"Just the beginning. Because of this case, we're going to be right up there with the elite programs in the country. My guess is that by the time this week is over, we'll be getting more referrals and doing more tumor cases than any other program around. We're also going to have tremendous clout when it comes to competing with places like Stanford and Baylor for money—especially with Iowa no longer in the picture."

"Carl, I appreciate all you're saying. But I just can't forgive you for lying to me about not having the human experimentation approval."

"I didn't. The day after Marci presented to you in the ER I pushed through the approval. Not before."

Jessie eyed him suspiciously.

"You can provide me proof of that?"

"If you want it. Jessie, I understand you're angry. People get angry with me all the time. It's part of running a department and pushing it toward the top of the heap. But I don't want the department to lose you. That's what this promotion is all about. Now, what do you say?"

By claiming that he had not lied regarding the HE panel's approval, Gilbride had opened the door just a sliver for Jessie to remain at the hospital. It was really all she wanted.

"My guess is it's going to be pretty crazy here tomorrow," she said, her voice neutral.

"I think you could say that."

His smug expression said he knew he had won. Jessie thought about demanding written proof of the date the HE committee had approved ARTIE. But she knew Gilbride well enough to suspect he could produce such a document even if it belied the truth. And why should she hurt herself, Sara, and her other patients over this, anyhow? she thought. Better to try to do things on her terms—to take the promotion and begin making some discreet inquiries to other neurosurgery departments in the city and around the country.

"I'll do what I can to help you out," she said.

"Spoken like a true team player," Gilbride replied.

CHAPTER 10

ALEX BISHOP HAD TAKEN A FURNISHED STUDIO IN
a clapboard tenement a mile from the hospital. It was
midnight, and his shift at the hospital had just ended. On
the way back to his room, he stopped at a convenience
store for some Diet Pepsi, a dozen Almond Joy candy
bars, and several packs of nicotine gum. His last cigarette
had closely followed his decision to hunt down Malloche.
Until the man was behind bars or dead, no more smokes.
That was the deal he had made with himself, and it had
been a bear of a promise to keep. Periodic nicotine gum
or patches helped keep the craving under reasonable
control, but nothing had touched his substitute addiction
to Almond Joys, which was now up to five or six bars a
day. Each morning he did a hundred push-ups and four
times that many sit-ups as penance.

The tenement was in a fairly tough neighborhood.

Bishop headed there half hoping some punks might try to shake him down. He was going through one of those periods when he simply craved action. But he knew this just wasn't the time. He needed to show whatever restraint was necessary to keep from calling attention to himself.

Everything was coming together.

The robot-assisted operation on Marci Sheprow had eliminated what lingering doubt he had regarding Claude Malloche's choice of a surgeon. The Mist, as some called the elusive, genius killer, was either on his way to Eastern Mass Medical Center, or he was already there. And Carl Gilbride was to be his surgeon. It hadn't been easy to gather information discreetly on Gilbride, but gradually a picture of the man was beginning to emerge. And thanks to the ignition wire he had loosened on Jessie Copeland's car, before too much longer, the pieces of the Gilbride puzzle that were missing would be filled in by her.

What Bishop knew so far was that Carl Gilbride was an empire builder, much like Sylvan Mays had been. He had a humble background, and had begun living above his means as soon as he could. Now, he was an autocrat, forging a department that was already considered among the best in the country. Socially, he and his wife were tight with Boston's upper crust. Mrs. Gilbride was on the board of the symphony.

Did Gilbride seem like someone Claude Malloche could buy? Based on the information Bishop had gleaned so far, the answer was unequivocally yes. If the price was right, would he do the surgery even if he knew who Malloche was? That question remained to be answered.

Getting close to Jessie Copeland was going to help fill in the gaps and also make it easy for him to get a fix on the neurosurgical patients on Surgical Seven and in the outpatient department. Through his offhand inquiries, he had heard nothing but good things about her, and he felt fairly certain from some of what had been said that she was not that tight with Gilbride. In that respect, she was just what the doctor ordered. His initial impression was that she seemed too nice and too feminine to be earning a living cutting into people's brains. But he had known a number of nice, exceedingly feminine women in the agency who were quite capable of blowing a person's brains to bits if the job required it.

It would all have been so much easier if only he had gotten one dependable look at Malloche, just one. But the Mist never did business personally, and when he did come into the open to any extent, he used disguises and very often, substitutes. This time, though, he was nearing the end of the line.

Bishop's studio was on the third floor of the rickety four-floor walk-up. He hadn't slept much since coming to Boston, but still, he was pleased to note, his legs had some spring. He reached his apartment door and had his key in hand when he stopped. The two hairs he had set in place between the door and the jamb were gone. They might have fallen or been blown free, but there was no breeze at this level. His .45 was inside the room, wrapped in a towel beneath a corner of the mattress. There was no way he could have brought it in to work. Running away now would ruin any chance he had to get Malloche. If someone had been in his apartment, or was there now, dealing with the situation immediately was his only option. And the fire escape was his only chance.

Bishop crept softly up to the fourth floor, then up the narrow flight to the roof. Totally under control, with the arm strength of a gymnast, he swung himself over the roof's edge, lowered himself onto the wrought-iron fire escape by the fourth floor, and inched down a flight. The curtains to the west window of his apartment were drawn, but he could just make out furniture shapes through a narrow opening between them. The lights were off, but there was some illumination from the south-facing window just over the pullout that was his bed. From what he could see, the place looked empty.

For five minutes, ten, he remained crouched on the landing, motionless, peering in. Then suddenly he saw movement just to the left of the door. A man, solidly built, arose and went into the john for a minute or so, then returned to his spot. Bishop couldn't be positive, but it appeared the intruder was carrying a gun loosely in his right hand. He continued observing between the curtains until he felt certain the man was alone. A gun in trained hands versus surprise. Under most circumstances, Bishop knew, he would take his chances with his reflexes and the gun. This time, he had no choice. He might well end up cut to shreds before he reached his target, but the windowpanes were small and the wood framing them was old. Besides, this wouldn't be the first time he had gone through a window—in either direction.

He took an Almond Joy from the plastic bag, opened the wrapper, and took a bite, careful as he always was to get the right mix of coconut, chocolate, and almond. What remained of the bar he held on to as he stepped up on the railing of the fire escape. He flipped it against the window lightly enough to produce a sound but preserve some ambiguity. Then he reached up and grasped one of the stairs leading to the fourth floor.

The intruder warily approached the window. Bishop didn't wait for him to open the curtains. A feet-first entry would have been safer, but infinitely less effective.

Instead, Bishop pulled his uniform jacket over his head and dove straight in. Wood and glass exploded into the room. His head hit the man in the midchest like a medicine ball, while his hand latched onto his wrist. He hyperflexed the joint and the gun clattered free even before the two of them had hit the floor. A sharp elbow to the jaw, followed by a powerful backhand to the opposite cheek, and it was over. Five seconds—maybe six.

Bishop rolled over the pieces of wood and shards of glass and had the muzzle of the man's Smith & Wesson .38 jammed up under his chin before his cobwebs had cleared. The intruder was beefy enough—taller than Bishop by a couple of inches, and a good twenty to twenty-five pounds heavier. But he was just a kid.

"Scoot toward the door!" Bishop snapped. "I don't want to kill you, but I will if you give me any trouble."

When he could reach the switch, he flipped on the overhead light. *Kid, indeed!* The man looked like a collegiate football player. Twenty-six, tops. He was bleeding from the corner of his mouth and from a fairly decent gash on his forehead that was going to require some stitches. To his credit, or perhaps his discredit, he didn't seem that frightened. Bishop straightened up and moved several feet away.

"Stay flat on your back, legs together, arms out," he said. "Just like a snow angel. Okay, who sent you?"

"Internal affairs. I wasn't supposed to hurt you, just talk to you."

"Thank goodness for that. And what were you supposed to say?"

"That this is your last chance to come back to the farm."

"How did you know where to find me?"

"They told me you were here at the hospital. I spotted you yesterday and followed you here. Can I get up now?"

"No. If all you were supposed to do was talk to me, you could have done it there."

He took his cell phone and dialed a number in Alexandria, Virginia. Clearly, Mel Craft had been sleeping.

"Mel, it's me, Alex. Internal affairs sent someone after me."

"Damn. Where is he now? How badly is he hurt?"

"He's on the floor of my apartment. Nothing that a few stitches won't take care of. Christ, Mel, he looks like he's seventeen."

"I'm twenty-eight."

"Shut up! Mel, how did they find me?"

"How do you think? I.A. knows we were partners and what you did for me. Hell, everyone knows. The bastards must have had my phone tapped when I made those calls to Boston for you. I never told them a thing. I didn't have to. Alex, I told you in D.C. If they want you, sooner or later they'll get you."

"Not with this kind of punk, they won't. Mel, talk to them. Tell them I let Dennis the Menace here off with nothing more than a scolding. Tell them I need to be left alone for two weeks."

"I'll tell them, Alex, but I can't make any guarantees. And Karen and I are leaving first thing in the morning for ten days in Brazil. I'll do what I can before I go."

"Right now."

"Okay, right now. Alex, the last five years have changed you—hardened you in ways that no one who knows you thinks are good. You'd be much better off if you'd just let the whole thing drop."

"Five hundred people, Mel. That's how many that

bastard or his men have killed. Five hundred. Probably more."

"Says you, Alex. Let it go."

"Tell them to give me my two weeks, or promise them for me that the next twenty-something they send after me will be shipped back to them in a bag."

"I'll do what I can. I'm glad you took it easy on the kid."

"I think he is, too. Have a good vacation, Mel."

CHAPTER 11

CHAOS.

Two days had passed since the successful surgery on Marci Sheprow—two days of reporters and faxes, telegrams and news briefings and CNN broadcasts. For Jessie, all Carl Gilbride's triumph had meant was more work. Since her return from Chicago, she had, to all intents, been covering her practice and his.

The bright spot for her was the embryonic connection that had developed with Alex Bishop. Yesterday, a chance meeting in the cafeteria had led to a half-hour "date" for coffee later that evening. As she had sensed during their ride back through the rain from lot E, there was much more to the man than one might have expected. He was two years older than she was and well past a marriage that had produced no children. While in the Marines, he had finished college with a degree in philosophy and had seen action in the Gulf. He liked the same sort of movies she did and seemed to be better read, although since she left for medical school thirteen years ago, most people were. And to top matters off, his looks were even more appealing to her than they had been that first night. As things were left, they would try to meet in the cafeteria again tonight, same time, same seats.

Although she hadn't gotten home from the hospital until almost 1 A.M., Jessie had set her alarm for five o'clock and headed back in. With the exception of two new cases—an elective aneurysm resection for tomorrow, and a pre-op to be done on a tenacious glioblastoma—her service was pretty much as it had been. Tamika Bing was still in her near-catatonic state despite the best efforts of psychiatrists and physical, occupational, and speech therapists. Mrs. Kinchley and Mrs. Weiss were complaining in private about each other to the staff, then each denying she had ever said any such thing when the matter was brought up to the pair of them.

Of all Jessie's patients, only Dave Scolari seemed changed. His eyes were noticeably brighter, and he smiled warmly as she came into his room.

"Hey, Doc, how goes it?"

"It goes. I stopped by last night, but you were asleep. I see you've been getting more mail."

She motioned at the cards and letters that were open on his tray table—an interest she hadn't seen from him before.

"My mom handles them for me. We've started answering some, too. I just tell her what to say and she writes it down."

Jessie felt her heart leap. She had seen enough medical miracles to know that faith and attitude were prime ingredients.

"That's great, Dave. I'm glad you're doing that," she said. "So will a lot of people be when they get your reply."

"There's something else I have to show you," he said, looking like a kid who had just brought home an unexpected A.

His jaws tightened into the grimace of extreme effort, and his eyes narrowed with strain. Then suddenly, shakily, his right arm came off the bed. At the same time, his fingers moved. It was subtle—reeds in a gentle breeze. But in neurology, movement of any kind meant intact nerve conduction pathways.

"I can do the other side a little, too," Dave said.

Jessie took his hand in hers, then hugged him.

"Oh, Dave. This is the best," she said, wondering if he fully appreciated the mammoth implications of his minute movements. "This is just the best."

"That friend of yours, Luis, keeps coming by to see me. He's quite a guy."

"Oh, he is that," Jessie said. Luis was an artist and Boys Club coach who had taken his life in many wonderful directions since the tragic auto accident that had paralyzed him.

"After he left, I just decided I was going to do this. I tried for hours. Then, last night, all of a sudden, I could. I haven't told anyone yet. I wanted you to be the first."

"It's a tremendous step forward, Dave. Just wonderful. Now you've got a heck of a lot of work to do."

"I'm ready," Scolari said.

Jessie sailed through the rest of her rounds. When she arrived back at her office, just after eight, a plump, dowdy-looking woman in her fifties was seated outside in one of the waiting area chairs. It took several seconds before Jessie realized it was Alice Twitchell, one of

Gilbride's office staff. "Quiet," "competent," "colorless," "proper" were the words she had always brought to Jessie's mind.

"Hi," Alice said somewhat sheepishly. "I guess I'm on loan to you from Dr. Gilbride."

Now what?

Jessie unlocked her door and motioned the woman inside.

"You're on *loan* to me?"

"Dr. Gilbride said that for a while, you were going to help him out screening referrals and handling some of the calls."

"He told you that?"

"He did. In fact, here are some messages and memos to get you started."

Alice handed over a stack of papers.

"I don't believe this," Jessie couldn't keep herself from saying. "I just don't believe this. Exactly where are you supposed to work?"

Alice shifted uncomfortably, but held her place.

"Dr. Lacy's on vacation for two weeks," she said. "For now, I'm to be across the hall in his office. The phone people will be here in just a few minutes to add a line to your phone and hook me up with you. Dr. Copeland, I can see you're upset. I'm sorry. This wasn't my idea."

"I know, Alice. I know. It's just that I was already working twenty-six-hour days. I don't know what more he expects me to do."

But Jessie did know precisely what Gilbride expected her to do—everything that got in the way of his next press conference or television appearance. She could go to him, ask why she was getting the secretary and the extra work, and why not one of the other surgeons, but there was no reason to bother. Gilbride would have some disparaging remark about each of the others' ability to get organized and get things done, sandwiched around some smarmy praise for her. No, he would say, Jessie was the logical choice—the *only* choice to keep the place moving while he was doing what had to be done. He would be sure to mention teamwork a dozen or so times, and dress it up with reminders of her intimate knowledge of ARTIE, as well as of her impending accelerated promotion. Gilbride was a total jerk, but he was also a damn sly one. Jessie glanced at the first memo.

"Here, Alice," she said, resigned, "write a letter to these people thanking them for the donation to the department that they dropped off in Marci's name, and also for their note. Assure them that the money will go directly to neurosurgical research."

"Thank you, Doctor," Alice said.

CHAOS.

The referral calls started at nine and continued unabated for the rest of the day. Pennsylvania, Utah, Canada, London. Private doctors, individuals, even other neurosurgeons. Several frantic patients simply showed up at the hospital, begging for Gilbride's evaluation. Almost all of them had significant disease. Apparently, Gilbride had also given Jessie's name to the hospital public relations people. Reporters for a number of lesser-light publications and broadcasting stations were being patched up to her for comment.

Midway through the day, Gilbride called. By that time, Jessie's clinic appointment book was filled for weeks, and she had actually begun to book some of those patients in to her surgical schedule before seeing them in order to hold the OR time, anticipating that she would agree with their referring physician that surgery was necessary.

"So, Jessie," Gilbride said cheerfully, "I'm down here at Channel Four, getting set for their call-in show. How goes it?"

"How do you *think* it goes, Carl?"

"I spoke to Alice. She says you're doing fine, and that the cases are rolling in."

"Oh, they're rolling in, all right. We're very busy. But then again, we were busy before all this started. Carl, these people want you, not me."

"But Alice says you've been scheduling them for yourself."

"Some of them. Some just hang up when I tell them you're not available."

"I hope none of those hang-ups were HCs."

"HCs?"

"Highly connected. You know, senators, big businessmen, celebrities, foreign diplomats—the kind of people who can pump prestige into a program like ours just by walking through the doors."

Jessie felt nauseated and had to remind herself for the thousandth time that nothing she could ever say or do was going to change Carl Gilbride.

"You mean like Marci," she said.

"Precisely. Those are the ones who need to be referred directly to me. Teamwork."

"Yeah, sure, teamwork."

Gilbride simply steamrolled over her sarcasm.

"What about that guy from the MacIntosh Foundation?" he asked. "Any word from him?"

"Not yet."

"Well, let me know as soon as you hear anything about that."

"Three million. I remember. Carl, I can do this for a little while, but not indefinitely."

"I assure you, once Marci's out of the hospital, all this will begin to die down."

"I certainly hope so."

"Remember, HCs should be referred to my office right away. Alice is doing her best to work them into my schedule as quickly as possible."

"HCs to CG," Jessie said acidly. "I just noted it down."

FOLLOWING THE AGENCY attempt to ambush him in his apartment, Alex stopped going anywhere unarmed— opting for his .38 revolver holstered beneath his left pant leg. It was ten o'clock, and as he had done the evening before, he had left his assigned area to wander through Surgical Seven, taking note of any new patients and targeting any male between thirty and fifty-five for further investigation and observation. This time, though, he had a guide. Jessie Copeland had met him in the cafeteria for the second evening in a row, but they had been together for less than ten minutes when she was called back to the floor to check on a patient. Unaware that he had already been there several times, she had invited him to come along to get a firsthand look at where she worked and what she did.

While she was in with her patient, Bishop wandered down the hall a few doors, glancing into the rooms. The hospital computer had already told him that there were currently forty-four patients on the neurosurgical service—only seven of them possibles. After a brief check, he was fairly certain that none of them was Malloche. Still, he managed to obtain fingerprints from the rooms of five of the men to send to Paris. Interpol had two sets of prints on file they felt might be Malloche's. With Malloche it was always *might be*.

Jessie came out of room 713 and hurried down to him. She wasn't exactly a knockout, he was thinking, but she was certainly good looking in a bookish sort of way, even when she was harried and overtired, which seemed to be most of the time. It bothered Bishop to have lied to her about himself, but in truth, not that much. In his job, the ability to lie seamlessly was a survival skill—one he had perfected over years of practice. When he had his man, he would set things straight with her. Meanwhile, he had no intention of trusting her or anyone else any more than he had to.

It made things easier that she seemed attracted to him. The more they talked, the more he learned about Gilbride and the rest of the service. Perhaps under other circumstances, he would have been open to exploring the possibilities between the two of them. But this wasn't other circumstances. He had bet the ranch on nothing more than a hunch, and he had less than two weeks to amend five years of failure. If he was wrong about Malloche coming to EMMC, or if the Mist eluded him in some way, not even a surgeon like Jessie Copeland would be able to put Humpty together again.

"Hi," she said. "Sorry to take so long."

"No problem."

"Actually, there is. The guy I just went over needs a spinal tap, and he's got so much arthritis in his spine that the resident just can't get the needle into the right space."

"So you're going to do it?"

"I'm going to try. From the time I was a medical student, no matter what happened in the hospital, I could always look over my shoulder and know there was someone with more experience watching out for me. Now that I'm the attending surgeon, when I look over my shoulder, no one's there."

"I think I'd faint."

"I doubt it. You don't look like a fainter. Besides, I don't think you made it through the Marines by passing out."

"Actually, you're right. I hold it all in and then get sick later when no one's around. Listen, you just go ahead and tap that guy's spine. I'd better get back on my loop or I'll get sacked before I even get my first paycheck."

"It was great talking with you again, even if it was just for a little while. You're kind of funny. I like that in a security guard."

Bishop sensed she wanted plans to be made for them to see each other again, but she had already gone more than halfway in that regard.

"So what do you think?" he asked. "Would you like to try and get together outside the hospital sometime?"

"Wait. You mean there's an 'outside the hospital'?"

"I can prove it."

"Then let's. The night after tomorrow is a definite possibility for me."

"Oops, I'm on the schedule. How about the night after that?"

"Um, I'm on call."

"Lunch. Lunch tomorrow," he said.

"Maybe. Just call first. Gilbride's celebrity has come at a price, only I'm the one who's paying it. This dating stuff is easy, huh?"

"Don't worry. Not much that's worthwhile is."

Bishop left the neurosurgical floor and headed down the long corridor past Jessie's office and the others. There was something about her that unsettled him. Maybe it was her unassuming confidence, maybe her eyes and the way she smiled at him. In spite of himself, he knew he was wondering what it would feel like to hold her. His love life over the five years he had been after Malloche had consisted of nothing more intense than scattered one-night stands, some with professionals. That was the way he wanted it. Not once over that time had he become emotionally entangled with a woman. Jessie Copeland was one to beware of.

Distracted, he hurried around the corner, and nearly collided with an elderly, stoop-shouldered janitor who was mopping the floor outside Carl Gilbride's office.

"Oh, excuse me," he muttered, barely looking at the man as he passed.

"Have a good night, Officer," the old man said.

Claude Malloche, his hair and fake mustache snow white, continued his mopping until he was certain the security guard was gone. Then he pulled a device from his pocket, opened the door to Gilbride's suite in less than fifteen seconds, and dragged his mop and bucket inside. Quickly, he crossed the receptionist's office, entered Gilbride's, and closed the door behind him. The high-powered light and camera he took from his pocket were espionage quality. He spread out all the papers on Gilbride's desk and rapidly photographed each one. Next he turned to the file cabinet.

Twenty minutes and three rolls of film later, Malloche was back in the hallway, humming the melody of a French folk tune as he nonchalantly worked his way toward the exit.

~~~~~~~~~~~~~~~~~~~~~~~~~~~~~~~~~~~ CHAPTER **12**

IT SEEMED HARDLY POSSIBLE TO JESSIE, BUT OVER
the next few days, life for her at the hospital became even
more hectic and exhausting. In addition to her thirteen
inpatients, she was covering Gilbride's large service as
well, while the chief continued to stump for publicity,
new patients, and grant money like a manic politician.
More than once, Jessie had to rein in her anger by remembering that harboring resentment was like drink-
ing poison and then waiting for the other guy to die.

In the office, the calls, referrals, inquiries, letters, do-
nations, and requests for interviews, personal appear-
ances, and patient appointments made life a whirlwind,
second-to-second affair. Even Gilbride's unflappable secretary Alice Twitchell seemed to be fraying at the edges.

Then there were Jessie's inpatients. She visited Sara
in the NICU three or four times a day. Although Sara re-

mained comatose, she *was* breathing on her own and showing other very soft signs that the coma was getting lighter. Not exactly startling improvement, but certainly no setback either. Jessie had resigned herself to being encouraged by anything even slightly positive. But she also knew her objectivity in Sara's case had flown south. It was wrenching to see the expressions on Barry's and the kids' faces as they tried to come to grips with the reality that this might be all they got back of their wife and mother.

Dave Scolari was a different story. He was moving both arms fairly easily now, and even showing some action in his legs. Jessie's quadriplegic patient, Luis Velasco, had become something of a fixture in Dave's room—a cheerleader who saw in the linebacker the chance for a level of recovery that he, himself, would never be able to achieve.

After more than a week, Elsa Davidoff had finally managed a bowel movement and had been shipped off to a rehab center. Jessie wondered what the insurance utilization review people would say when they got a look at the reason for six additional hospital days. Actually, she didn't care whether the UR people approved or not. If nothing else, she was striking a blow for pre-managed-care kindness and patients' rights by honoring the elderly woman's demand that she not be sent out to rehab until her colon had proven it could function.

Marci Sheprow was out of the NICU and, in fact, only a day or two from being out of the hospital altogether. Her family and Gilbride held twice-daily press conferences in the hospital auditorium, and late this afternoon, Marci herself would be wheeled down to participate for the first time.

Jessie had tried to take advantage of the gymnast's

celebrity by wheeling her into Tamika Bing's room. Marci was charming and patient, but her visit evoked nothing from the mute teenager. Tamika, her laptop still open but untouched on her tray table, looked as if she knew who her visitor was, but she reacted no more than that. Soon, the utilization folks would be nipping at the department's heels about her hospitalization, and plans would have to be made for her discharge. Jessie was pulling out all the stops to keep her as an inpatient because the therapists and psychiatrist were still hopeful and still pushing. She knew there was no way she would get approval to cover an in-hospital stay at a rehab center, and it was certain Tamika's mother, who was holding down a factory job, wouldn't be able to take her for daily outpatient therapy.

Alex Bishop continued to be a pleasurable island in the madness. Although they had yet to manage any extended time together outside the hospital, they had walked around the neighborhood for half an hour last night, and he had visited her on Surgical Seven a number of times. He continued to be a source of little surprises, including a better than passing knowledge of opera and, once she had given him instructions and turned over her Game Boy, a deft hand at Tetris. With her demanding on-call schedule, and his assignment to the evening shift, she feared they might be doomed to an unending in-hospital courtship. The drastic initial measure she opted for was to meet him tomorrow at noon in the North End—Little Italy—for lunch and two hours of strolling the shops and uninterrupted conversation. If the neurosurgical service managed to survive when she was tied up in emergency surgery, it could manage while she was tied up in veal scallopini.

Jessie's aneurysm case, which she had done in the regular neurosurgical OR, had gone beautifully, but in the MRI-OR, the post-Marci deluge of patients had intensified an already existing problem—no available time. Marci's three-and-a-half-hour case notwithstanding, the usual MRI-guided operation took anywhere from five to seven hours. Adding prep and clean-up time, that meant each of the two specially trained teams could do one case a day. A third team could be assembled from parts of the other two when absolutely necessary, but to try to do more than two cases a day was to ask for burnout and shaky judgment from the staff.

Already, the MRI-OR schedule was booked solid for more than three weeks. A number of those cases were appropriate for ARTIE, although Jessie was still uncertain whether she or the robot were ready. Patients with brain tumors were being reassured, as much as Jessie and Emily could justify, that waiting around at home for a few weeks would not lessen their chances of a successful operation . . . unless, of course, there was a sudden complication like bleeding into the tumor or rapid pressure buildup from the unanticipated obstruction of spinal fluid flow.

Although Jessie did most of the preliminary patient evaluations, a number of the MRI cases were going to be Gilbride's—all of them high visibility. Some of the new patients Gilbride dashed by and met on the fly, while the more important ones he would see in an evening office session. The lowest-level HCs he would not meet in person until they had been checked into the hospital the morning of their operation. Jessie knew that at this pace, with all Gilbride's distractions and his marginal surgical skills, disaster was just a cut away.

It was six in the evening when the intensity of the day finally began to ebb. There were enough patients for

Jessie still to see, and enough paperwork to catch up on, to keep her in the hospital until ten, but the way things had been going since *the* operation, home by ten-thirty was tantamount to a vacation day. Her first stop would be the NICU to check on her post-op aneurysm patient, and also on Sara. Not surprisingly, though, before she could leave her office, the phone was ringing again. Also, not surprisingly, the caller was her department chief with more work for her.

"Jessie, hi," he began. "Sorry to be calling you so late about this, but I'm in the middle of taping *Talk of the City* for Channel Five, and I didn't check in for messages until a few minutes ago."

"That's okay," Jessie replied dully. "What do you need?"

"Do you remember me reading you a cable from a guy named Tolliver at the MacIntosh Foundation?"

"Yes, I remember. It's hard to forget three million dollars."

"Well, I just got word that he's coming to check out our setup personally."

"That's terrific," Jessie responded with little enthusiasm.

She sensed what was coming next.

"There's just one problem. I've been invited to do a phone interview on the *Imus in the Morning* radio show at nine tomorrow, then I'm meeting with the hospital administration to discuss some extra lab space for the department. So I've arranged to have Tolliver contact you when he arrives at the hospital. Just show him around and be your usual charming self. Whatever he wants to see or do is fine."

"But—"

"Take him out somewhere for lunch if I'm not back.

Maybe that Sandpiper place. Just turn in your expenses to Alice and the department'll take care of reimbursing you. She's a real peach, isn't she? Listen, the producer's waving at me for something. I've got to go. Keep up the good work, Jess. Three million will buy a helluva lot of research."

Before Jessie could insert a word, she was listening to a dial tone.

"All bleeding eventually stops," she muttered, picturing Alex Bishop marching off into the sunset with a plate of veal scallopini. "All bleeding eventually stops."

Jessie's post-op aneurysm patient, a thirty-eight-year-old, high-powered businessman named Gary Garrison, was awake and lucid.

"Any stock tips?" she asked.

"McNeil. They make Tylenol. If this headache of mine doesn't let up soon, I'm going to push their stock up all by myself."

Jessie had him describe the pain and location. Then she checked his neurologic status and used an ophthalmoscope to examine the arteries, veins, and optic nerves on the back surface of his retinas, searching for the changes that warned of brain swelling.

"Not serious," she proclaimed, finally. "Between your initial hemorrhage and what I did in getting that artery clipped, the structures in your skull have had quite a bit of trauma. They're allowed to hurt. One more day, I suspect, and you'll start to feel much better. Feel like leaving the unit?"

"Not really."

"Good enough. That's all I have to hear. I'll explain things to your HMO in a way they'll understand."

"You're the best, Doc."

Jessie wrote out some orders and passed them to one of

the nurses. Then she headed into Sara's room. A candy striper stood at the bedside, massaging cream into Sara's hands. The volunteer, whom Jessie had never seen on Surgical Seven before, was a waiflike brunette, maybe in her late teens, with wide, dark eyes and close-cropped hair.

"Hi," said Jessie, startling the girl, who was engrossed in her work. "I'm Dr. Copeland."

"Oh . . . hi. I'm Lisa. I just started here."

"Welcome to Oz. It looks like you've caught on quickly. I'm sure Sara appreciates the hand massage."

"Thank you. I did a lot of volunteer work in hospitals when I was in high school. Now, I'm taking a semester off from college, but I wanted to do something that mattered while I was figuring out what comes next."

"I thought you looked a little old to be a candy striper."

"My mother says I'm a little old to be taking time off from college," the girl said, grinning.

"Hey, I'm a neurosurgeon, and I *still* don't know what I want to do when I grow up. Have you thought about medicine?"

Lisa blushed.

"I . . . I don't do very well in the sciences," she said. "I'm considering working with kids—probably because I think I'm destined to always look like one. Do you want me to leave?"

"No. Of course not. I want you to keep at it. Sara Devereau is very important to me. And I believe that things like hand massages play a significant role in a patient's recovery. I'll be back a little later. Thanks for what you're doing here."

"Thanks for talking with me," Lisa said. "Most of the doctors I've dealt with seem too stressed to stop and talk to anyone."

CHAPTER 13

LATE THE NEXT MORNING, EASTMAN TOLLIVER, THE three-million-dollar man, arrived at Eastern Mass Medical on schedule. Jessie had returned to the hospital at six feeling irritable and frustrated. Instead of spending a few relaxing hours away from the hospital with the first man in whom she had been interested in a couple of years, she would be baby-sitting a foundation bureaucrat.

Gradually, though, as it usually did, her practice lifted her spirits. Her patients were all improving, or at least were no worse. Sara, though still unconscious, continued to show signs that her coma was becoming lighter. Shortly after rounds, Jessie successfully revised a spinal fluid drainage shunt in a long-term tumor patient—a nice procedure when it went well, simple and life-saving. And finally, Marci Sheprow had gone home, and with her went the stress of avoiding eye contact with her mother. The fallout from her surgery would go on indefinitely, but at least that chapter was closed.

Jessie had expected the worst from her job as escort to Tolliver. In fact, their time together proved a most pleasant surprise. He was distinguished looking, with dark, intelligent eyes, hair graying at the temples, sharply cut features, and perhaps ten pounds of excess weight. In addition, he was charming, urbane, and intelligent, and best of all, a seasoned bridge player.

Over crab Louis at the Sandpiper, they talked about the game, about his six years as executive director of the MacIntosh Foundation, and of course about ARTIE and Carl Gilbride. In what seemed like only minutes, an hour and a half had flashed by. During that time, Jessie had used her cell phone to answer a half dozen pages, the last few dealing with the burgeoning group in her waiting area.

"It's really enjoyable talking with you," she said, "but I'm afraid that if I don't show up at my office soon, the patients waiting for me are going to unionize. What time this afternoon will you be meeting Carl?"

Tolliver absently twisted his thin gold wedding band and looked at her strangely.

"I assumed you knew," he said.

"Knew what?"

"I spoke with Dr. Gilbride by phone this morning shortly after I arrived at the hospital. Apparently last night he was invited to be on the *Today* show tomorrow morning. He's leaving directly from his commitment at the medical center and flying down to New York to meet with the producers. He'll be back at noon, right after the show. Meanwhile, you were right there to wine and dine me as he promised, and as you have done most charmingly."

"I . . . I'm really sorry I didn't know," she said. "And did he say I would be your hostess until he gets back?"

Tolliver's expression suggested he was used to the conflicts and spur-of-the-moment schedule changes that accompanied dealings with highly successful people.

"He did say something like that," he replied, "yes."

"Eastman, I'm a little embarrassed. I would have loved to have spent the afternoon and evening with you, showed you some of the city, or even played some bridge. But I'm on in-house call tonight."

"Actually, as I told Dr. Gilbride, I have no problem starting the formal part of my visit tomorrow, because I really could use a bit of rest and relaxation. Maybe I'll stop back this evening and follow you around. But most likely I'll see you in the morning after I watch Dr. Gilbride on television."

"Either way would be fine."

Jessie said the words sensing that she wasn't being perfectly honest. She really did prefer he stay at his hotel tonight rather than come back to the hospital to follow her around. Alex's shift would be starting at three.

"Are you sure you'll be all right?" she asked. "For obvious reasons, I can't have you in to see patients. But you can wait in the lab with our robotics technician until I'm done. After that I'll be happy to show you around the hospital."

"I promise you I am very resourceful. Besides, I came to the hospital straight from the airport. I'd like to check in at the bed-and-breakfast where I'll be staying."

"Not a hotel?"

"Wherever possible, I prefer to have the foundation's funds go toward medical research. Besides, this place comes highly recommended by our travel people. I have been promised that it is warm and charmingly decorated."

"Where is it?"

Tolliver referred to a sheet in his jacket pocket.

"Hereford Street. They said it was walking distance from the hospital."

"Only if you really love to walk. It's in the Back Bay, not far from where I live. With luggage, I'd suggest a cab; without luggage, good shoes."

"A cab it will be. I have been told that this B-and-B has a small but well-equipped exercise room. I think I shall avail myself of it this afternoon. Looking fifty in the eye is powerful motivation."

"Exercise . . . exercise. I vaguely remember once knowing what that was. I'm jealous."

They walked the three blocks back to the hospital.

"Well, thank you," Tolliver said after retrieving his bag from Jessie's office. "I believe I'm going to enjoy my days here. And I hope Carl Gilbride knows what a jewel he has in you."

"Oh, he tells me all the time," Jessie replied.

WHEN JESSIE HAD finally finished seeing the last of her patients, Alice Twitchell brought in yet another stack of messages, hospital charts, and other Carl Gilbride–generated flotsam.

Jessie flipped through the pile.

"Lord," she said. "There's a couple of hours' worth of work right here. Well, at least I'm through with the out-patients."

Alice grinned at her sheepishly.

"I'm afraid I have to tell you that there is one more patient for you to see. He and his wife have been here for almost two hours. His name is Rolf Hermann. He's a count or something from Germany, and he has a brain tumor. Apparently his wife spoke with Dr. Gilbride by phone. Now they're camped outside his office, and she's insisting that they're not moving until they see him. Dr. Copeland, he's staying over in New York tonight."

"I know. Goodness, a German count. Talk about your HCs."

"Pardon?"

"Nothing. Nothing. Listen, you go ahead and get a TV moved up to your office so we can watch the boss tomorrow morning. I'll go talk to the Count."

"He's an impressive man. And his wife is very beautiful."

"Thanks for the info. Dr. Gilbride didn't say anything at all about this fellow to you?"

"No. As you know, he's been forgetting to mention a lot of things lately."

Kill!

"Well, take the rest of the day off as soon as you can, Alice," Jessie said sweetly. "I'll see you in the morning."

While Jessie and the other surgeons in the department used the Harvard chairs lining the corridor as their waiting area, Gilbride had an anteroom of his own—a walnut-paneled, leather-furnished space across from his equally elegant office. The Count and his wife looked born to be in rooms as richly appointed. Seated across from them were two men and a woman in their late twenties, each of them trim, athletic, and dressed expensively. They were presented by Hermann's wife as the Count's sons and daughter—not her children, Jessie noted, but his. None of them stood to greet her.

Rolf Hermann, powerfully built, could have been forty but, judging by his children's ages, was at least ten years older than that. He was square-jawed and craggy, with thick, jet black hair, pomaded straight back. He shook hands with Jessie and greeted her in heavily accented English. His wife, who introduced herself as Countess Orlis Hermann, was stunning. In her early forties, perhaps even younger, she had a high fashion model's bearing and figure. Her fine porcelain face was perfectly offset by straight sun-blond hair, artistically cut just above her shoulders. Her beige suit almost certainly owed its existence to some exclusive designer. From the first moment of their meeting, the Countess's pale blue eyes remained fixed on Jessie's like a magnet, leaving no doubt in Jessie that this was a woman accustomed to having life go her way.

"Well," Jessie began, clearing her throat, "it's very nice to meet you both. I'm . . . an assistant professor of neurosurgery here at Eastern Mass Medical."

"That's very nice," Orlis said in fluent English, much less accented than her husband's, "but we came to see Dr. Gilbride. I'm afraid an assistant *anything* just won't do."

Rolf stopped her with a raised hand and spoke to her forcefully in German. Orlis calmed visibly.

"I'm sorry," Jessie said, "but Dr. Gilbride is in New York until tomorrow afternoon."

"But that's impossible," Orlis said. "He said we should come today." She held up an envelope of X rays. "My husband has a tumor in his head. Dr. Gilbride said he would remove it."

Jessie could tell from the Count's expression that he was taking in every word.

"In that case," she said, "I'm certain he will. But until tomorrow, he's two hundred miles away."

"This is just not acceptable."

Clearly the calming effect of the Count's words had already worn off.

"Countess Hermann," Jessie said, "for the past week

Dr. Gilbride has been extremely busy. For the same reason you heard of him all the way across the Atlantic, so have others from all over the world, many of them very seriously ill. I have been helping with the initial evaluation and scheduling of most of these new patients. I will be happy to do the same for your husband. But not here in the waiting room."

This time, Rolf Hermann leaned over and spoke softly into his wife's ear. He squeezed her hand, completely enveloping it in his massive paw.

Orlis's lips tightened. Finally, she nodded and passed the X rays over.

"Where do you want us to go?" she asked.

"My office can hold the three of us," Jessie replied. "Your family would best wait here, or else in the chairs in the hallway just outside my office."

Orlis gave the orders in German, and the Count's children nodded.

"They will come to your office," she said. "They and their father are very close. They are very concerned about him."

Jessie led the entourage down the hall. Rolf Hermann walked rigidly upright with determined strides, although there was, Jessie noted, the slightest hitch in his right leg. She left the younger Hermanns in the corridor and motioned the couple to the two chairs by her desk. Orlis evaluated the space disdainfully, but finally took her seat.

"My husband understands English perfectly," she said, "and he can speak it, although not as well as I. For that reason he has asked me to tell you his story."

"That's fine, as long as you know, Count, to speak up at any time. This is no school exam or contest here. It is your health. I promise you will not be graded on your English."

For the first time, the Count's smile held genuine warmth.

"Thank you very much," he said carefully. "Orlis, please."

"Two and a half months ago," she began, "my husband had a fit—a shaking all over during which he soiled himself and became unconscious. What do you call that?"

"A seizure."

"He had a seizure. We took him to our doctor, and he ordered those X rays."

Jessie placed two of the MRI films onto the fluorescent view boxes on the wall to her right. The dense tumor, almost certainly a rather large subfrontal meningioma, glowed obscenely amid the much darker normal brain tissue. The location was dangerous, and the shape of the tumor suggested that it was the type of meningioma that was poorly contained, with extensions infiltrating the brain tissue surrounding it. An ARTIE tumor if ever there was one.

"The tumor is right here," Jessie said, pointing it out.

"Yes, we know. Our doctor referred us to a brain surgeon, but he gave us no confidence that he could remove my husband's tumor without causing a good deal of damage. Our doctor then suggested we search for a surgeon in London or in the United States. We were in the process of doing that, and already had Dr. Gilbride's name on a very short list of candidates, when he performed his miraculous operation on that young gymnast."

"I see. Well, I'm sure Dr. Gilbride can help you. But you must know that surgery such as this is risky. Parts of the tumor are situated right alongside normal brain tissue. The dissection is extremely difficult. There may well be residual neurologic deficits."

"We would prefer to speak with Dr. Gilbride about that."

Jessie felt overwhelming gratitude that the Count would not be her patient.

"Very well," she said. "He should be back sometime tomorrow afternoon. You can come back then."

"Excuse me, Dr. Copeland, but we have traveled a long way, and we have no intention of leaving this hospital."

"But—"

"My husband has had two seizures. If he has another, I want him here. We intend to pay in cash, so we will have no problem with your insurance or your health care system. I will be happy to leave enough money with your hospital administrator in advance to cover all the expenses of our stay, including my husband's surgery."

"Mrs. Hermann, I don't know if we can do this."

"Then I suggest you speak to the director of your hospital. I will be happy to speak to him as well."

"I guess I'd better do that."

Jessie went down the hall to Alice Twitchell's temporary office, and was rather easily able to reach Richard Marcus, the hospital president. A few minutes later, she was back in her office. Marcus had confirmed what she already knew—running a hospital was all about money.

"The president of the hospital will be happy to meet with you in his office. We have a private room available on Surgical Seven, the neurosurgical floor."

"Actually, we will need two. The Count's children plan to stay near him as long as he is in the hospital. I assure you they will make it their business to be in nobody's way. We will pay whatever rate you charge."

Jessie knew better than to argue, and it was clear from the way the Count held his arms tightly folded across his chest that he had no intention of intervening again.

"Countess," Jessie said, "if Dr. Marcus says it's okay, and we have the room, you get the room."

"And private nurses."

"We have agencies that can provide you with that. The head nurse on Surgical Seven will know how it's done. Anything else?"

"Yes. I wish to know when my husband's surgery will be performed."

"Now *that* I absolutely cannot tell you. For one thing, that's Dr. Gilbride's decision. For another, our MRI-assisted neurosurgical suite is booked solid. It may be some time before your husband can be fitted into the schedule."

Countess Orlis Hermann's smile was patronizing in the extreme.

"We shall see about that," she said.

IT WAS AFTER seven when Jessie caught up with Alex in the cafeteria. He and another security guard were sitting together. She was about to head back to the floor when he spotted her and waved her to join them. Wanting not to seem too eager, she grabbed a salad, some chips, and a decaf, and stopped to say a few words to a resident she barely knew. By the time she ambled over to Alex's table, the other guard had left.

"I was going to call you to meet for dinner," he said, "but some guy went berserk in the ER, and Eldon and I had to deal with him. Then Eldon insisted we take our dinner break together."

"Why did he leave?"

Alex's grin reminded her of Clint Eastwood's.

"I guess he left because I asked him to," he said.

"Oh," Jessie managed, hoping she looked more composed at that moment than she was feeling. "Well . . . how's your day?"

"Actually, they've scheduled two too many guards on this shift, so it's been pretty light. They offered me the chance to go home."

"And you didn't take it?"

"The choice was an empty apartment and a Mel Gibson video versus the chance to get together with you, *and* get paid for it."

"Oh," she said again. "I like that you say what's on your mind."

"That may be why I've never won any popularity contests. How's your day been?"

Jessie's beeper went off before she could answer. She glanced at the display.

"It's the ER," she said. "Hold that last question."

In less than a minute she was back.

"Trouble?" Alex asked.

"Big-time. An eight-year-old boy's being brought into the ER by ambulance right now with a gunshot wound to the head."

CHAPTER 14

FROM THE MOMENT THE CALL CAME FROM THE RESCUE squad that they were on the way in with eight-year-old Jackie Terrell, the clock began ticking. Jessie and Alex left the cafeteria and raced to the ER.

"Mind if I come and watch you work if my supervisor okays it?" Alex asked.

"If it's okay with him, it's okay with me, so long as you don't expect any attention."

"I'll go call him."

Jessie had already instructed the ER nurse to mobilize the OR, CT scan people, and blood bank, and to locate the neurosurgical resident on call.

The twin dragons they would be battling for the child's life were tissue damage and blood loss. Either could be lethal. The rescue squad had reported heavy bleeding, typical of a gunshot wound to the organ in the body with the richest blood supply. As usual, the paramedics and emergency medical technicians had done their jobs well. Two IV lines were in, plasma volume expanders were running, and pressure was being applied to the obvious bleeding points. But to Jessie, the most important piece of information they had radioed in was that although the boy was unconscious, there had been some definite purposeful movement on his left side. In neurosurgery, movement meant hope. And hope demanded speed.

Throughout Jessie's training, there was an unofficial competition among the residents to see who could get a head trauma patient with an open skull fracture or gunshot wound through labs and CT and into the OR the fastest. Anything over ten minutes from ER door to OR table was automatically disqualified from consideration.

The ER was bedlam on two fronts, neither of which had anything to do with Jackie Terrell. A full cardiac arrest was being worked on in the major medical room, and in one of the trauma rooms, the surgical residents were dealing with a stabbing victim. Jessie knew that what she needed most right now was an experienced nurse who knew her way around head trauma and around EMMC. What she got instead was a new grad named Larry Miller, eager to please but very green.

"Please page Emily DelGreco and get her down here right away" was Jessie's first order.

The neurosurgical resident on duty, Steven Santee, was in the ER when she arrived, preparing a stretcher for their case in one of the available trauma rooms. He wasn't the sharpest of his group of residents, and certainly was not the one she would have chosen to assist her on this case, but he was a damn hard worker.

"Don't bother, Steve," she said. "We're going right

from the door to CT. Just keep bugging the lab. I want
ten units of O-negative blood in the OR when we arrive.
We'll use them until we get the kid cross-matched. It'll
be your job to draw blood on him unless the rescue people did it when they started his lines."

"They're two minutes out," Larry Miller called down
the hall. "Emily said she'll meet you in the OR and will
have everything ready when you get there. Anesthesia's
on the way there, too. So are the nursing supervisor, a
scrub nurse, and a circulating nurse. Do you want me to
come with you?"

"With Emily meeting us, we may be okay. But then
again, I may need another pair of hands."

"Will I do?"

Jessie hadn't noticed that Alex had come into the ER.
Now, she sized up the situation.

"You don't mind being a gofer for blood and instruments?"

"Hardly. You sure it's okay for me to help in the
OR?"

"Hey, I'm the surgeon. It's okay if I say so. And you
won't faint on me?"

"We already discussed that, remember?"

"Well, then, stick around. As soon as the kid gets
here, we're going to CT. You be the motor for his
stretcher. Steve and I will do the evaluation. Emily will
make sure the OR's got everything we need, and do what
she can with the lab."

Santee, Larry Miller, Emily, and now Alex. A ragtag
medical army if ever there was one—especially poised to
battle such potent foes. But at least, as far as Jessie knew,
there were no expanding egos on the team. Each of them
would do whatever she needed—no questions asked, no
improvising.

Jessie felt energized, but she had dealt with enough gunshots to be frightened as well.

"They're on the drive," Larry Miller called out.

"Steve," Jessie said, "take a minute and get what history you can from the rescue squad, especially the caliber of that bullet. Alex, Larry, we get the stretcher and go. I want this kid in the OR within eight minutes."

At that instant, the doors to the ER glided open and the battle began in earnest.

"Drive-by shooting," an EMT said breathlessly, handing over their paperwork. "We assume it was a handgun. The poor kid was just in the wrong place at the wrong time."

"Thanks," Jessie called out, as Alex took over at the rear of the litter. "You can pick up your stretcher at CT. Just have someone follow us."

There was a CT scanner that served the ER alone. In fifteen seconds, Jackie Robinson Terrell was on the table. Jessie's heart ached as she looked down at the naked child, spattered all over with his own blood. His body was as perfect as most eight-year-olds'—not an ounce of excess fat, muscles just beginning to become defined. His smooth, chocolate skin was unscarred. But the pressure dressing on his head was soaked through with crimson.

The entry wound, just behind the child's left ear, was in a bad spot, but it could have been even worse. An inch to the right, and it would have shattered the torcular—the bony ridge at the base of the skull that protected the confluence of the straight and sagittal sinuses, the largest blood-filled cavities in the brain. Had the torcular been hit that way, Jackie Terrell would still be on the sidewalk, covered from head to toe with a sheet, lying in a pool of his own blood. Now, at least, he had a chance.

"Poor little guy," Jessie murmured as she checked his

pupils for size and responsiveness to light. "Poor baby. Larry, could you please go back to the ER and see where this child's parents are. If you find them in the next minute, bring them here. Otherwise, explain what's happening and bring them to the Surgical Eight waiting room. Then go save us an elevator in the Surgical Tower." She turned to Lydia Stewart, the radiologist. "Stew, give me just five cuts through the hemispheres and two through the posterior fossa, please. As soon as you're done, we're out of here, so please hurry."

"What do you think?" Alex asked.

Jessie shook her head.

"I don't know. His pupils are still mid-sized. That's a good sign. But he's got no corneal reflex, and he's losing blood fast. He was probably just playing out there—maybe thinking about what he wanted for his birthday. . . ."

She shook her head as if clearing it, then reached over and took two lead aprons from the wall, handing one to Alex.

"Is this necessary?" he asked.

"That depends on whether or not you think your gene pool is worth protecting. Listen, when we get to the OR, I want you to put on scrubs and stay on hand. We really are short-staffed and I may need you to run errands."

Jessie held Jackie Terrell's little hand as the CT scanner whirred. Moments later, the radiologist called out that the views were on the screen. The pictures were grim. Fracture lines everywhere, a massive collection of clotting blood, and definite brain destruction. It was as if an egg had been dropped onto concrete from ten feet, but had somehow stayed together.

"We're out of here," she said, motioning Alex to help her lift the boy onto a gurney.

They hurried through the hospital to the bank of elevators in the Surgical Tower. Larry Miller was there, holding the doors of one car open. Standing back a ways were a dozen or so curious onlookers, anxious to check out the emergency before going about their business. The three of them squeezed into the elevator with the gurney. For eight floors, Jessie's arm was pressed tightly against Alex's. As the doors parted, he briefly squeezed her hand.

"Good luck," he said.

"This way, quickly," she replied, racing to the front of the stretcher. "The men's dressing room is right over there. Cap, mask, shoe covers, and scrubs."

Jessie checked the time as she and Larry Miller exploded into OR-2 with Jackie Terrell. Almost nine minutes. Not a prizewinner, but good enough. Emily was there, scrubbed, gowned, and ready to begin prepping the child's scalp. The anesthesiologist, Byron Wong, stood by his instruments, set to slip in a breathing tube and connect his other highly sophisticated monitoring equipment. Ten units of uncrossmatched O-negative blood were arranged on a tray by his station. With almost no antibodies to the proteins in type A or type B blood, nor to the Rh factor protein, O-negative blood could be treated to absorb most of what antibodies *were* there, and then used for emergency transfusions until properly cross-matched blood could be obtained. Not optimum, but then nothing about this case was close to that.

As Jessie and Wong were transferring the child from the stretcher to the OR table, he suddenly cried out and flailed with his left hand, actually hitting Wong on the shoulder.

"Jesus," Jessie said, "he's moving. We've got a chance."

Steve Santee poked his head in.

"Dr. Copeland, Jackie's mother is in the family room. His father is a bus driver. They're trying to locate him now."

Excuse me, Mr. Terrell, but we wonder if you could drive on over to Eastern Mass Medical. Your eight-year-old son has been shot in the head. . . .

The notion made Jessie cringe.

"Get scrubbed, Steve," she said. "Emily, after he's intubated, get two units running. I want him left ear up. Do a quick prep, then stay next to me. Steve'll work across from us. I'm going to say a word to the boy's mom and then scrub. I want to make the incision in two minutes. Three tops."

"You've got it," Emily said.

Charlene Terrell, an expansive woman with a gentle face, was wringing her hands. An older woman, who introduced herself as a family friend, sat with an arm around her.

"We're going to operate in just a minute," Jessie said after brief introductions. "Jackie's been hurt very badly."

"He's a wonderful boy," Charlene sobbed. "Please save him. He's our only child."

"I'll do my best."

"Thank you, Doctor. Oh, thank you so much."

"One thing. Is he left- or right-handed?"

"Jackie? Oh, he's right-handed. You should see him throw a ball. He's only in third grade, but he already can play with the middle-school kids."

"Thank you, Mrs. Terrell."

Grim.

Jessie hurried to the prep room. At this point she had neither the time nor the inclination to go into any of the gunshot-wound details with her patient's mother. Until the operation was completed, there was nothing she could say that wouldn't make a very bad situation worse. Right-handed meant that most of the vital speech and movement centers were on the left side, precisely around the bullet's path. Tamika Bing's situation, only with right-sided motor deficits as well.

As she scrubbed, her concentration was almost exclusively on the child and on the surgical approach she was going to take. *Almost.* One corner of her mind was dominated by a spinning tangle of images—Alex Bishop, Carl Gilbride, Marci Sheprow, Sara Devereau, Tamika Bing, Eastman Tolliver, Orlis Hermann, and the Count, tossing about along with multiple reminders to herself that she wasn't the one who had pulled the trigger and shot the eight-year-old. Nor was she God. She was simply the one who was on call, and who was doing her best to save the child.

"You ready?"

Alex had come up from behind and was standing a few feet away.

"Ready as I'll ever be," she replied. "You can stand behind me to either side. There's a riser you can step up on to give you a better angle."

"I'm praying for the kid," Alex said.

Jessie's eyes locked on his.

"You keep on doing that," she said. "I never refuse help."

THE APPROACH JESSIE had settled on was pretty standard—a wide scalp flap around the entry wound, drill away as much bone as necessary, and then go for the large collection of congealing blood that the CT scan had located just above and behind Jackie's ear. Retrieving the bullet and working around the other fracture fragments would come later in the case. The child was anesthetized now, so there would be no more movement, no cries. But the team was driven by what they had seen.

Quick but careful, Jessie said over and over to herself. *Quick but careful.*

"He's losing a lot of blood," Emily said. "The rescue squad brought tubes in, so the lab has had a head start with the cross-match."

"When do you think we'll have the blood?"

"Five minutes, no more."

"Hang a couple more units of O-negative, Byron. Alex, could you please call the blood bank and find out how much longer?"

"Right away."

Emily elbowed her friend.

"Nice helper," she whispered.

Jessie glanced up at Steve Santee, who was engrossed in suctioning the persistent bleeding.

"Behave," she shot back, her voice shielded by the sound of the aspirator. "That's it, Steve. Suck right here. We're doing fine."

"They'll be ready in the blood bank in a minute," Alex said, returning to his riser.

"Maddy," Jessie said to the circulating nurse, "this is Alex Bishop from security. He's also soon to be a physician's assistant student at Northeastern. Would you please take him with you to the blood bank and bring us back eight units."

Quick but careful.

Around the bullet hole, the child's skull was like broken pottery. Jessie removed most of the shards and much of the clot, while Emily and Steve continued aspirating blood, keeping her field clean. The bullet had stopped short of crossing the midline, but had damaged a good deal of brain before it did.

Jackie? Oh, he's right-handed. You should see him throw a ball.

Alex and the circulator returned with the blood, and he again took his place on the riser.

Jessie forced herself to remember some of the miracles she had seen since entering neurosurgery—the patients who should have died, but instead ended up living quite functional and rewarding lives. Meticulously, she picked off the bleeders, cauterizing them by running electric current through her bipolar forceps. Bit by painstaking bit, the ooze lessened. And as it did, the extent of the damage became clearer.

"Just keep up with blood loss, Byron," Jessie said. "It's still hard to predict, but I will say that I've seen worse."

"You're doing an incredible job," Emily said. "Alex, I hope you have a good view of this, because you're never going to see a gunshot case handled better."

This time Jessie threw the elbow. She knew Emily was saying things just to keep her from getting too tense, but she was beginning to regret having confessed her newly evolving connection with the man.

"Quit it!" she whispered.

"A little advertising never hurt," Emily whispered back.

The bullet had entered at a slightly upward angle, shattered the inner table of the skull, and ricocheted to a halt just to the left of the midline. Jessie recovered it with ease, then began cleaning away tissue that was clearly damaged beyond healing.

Maybe Jackie Robinson Terrell will throw again, she was thinking at the moment the anesthesiologist said, "Everything all right? I'm getting a drop in pressure."

"I don't see—"

Jessie never finished the sentence. A sudden, continuous gush of dark, venous blood welled into the surgical field from beneath the posterior skull. Jessie's heart rate rocketed.

"The occiput *was* fractured!" she cried out. "The torcular's torn." The bone fragments over the network of vital blood vessels had been held together so tightly by the bleeding and swelling around them that the CT scan hadn't shown the fracture lines. "Byron, pump in every ounce of blood you have and send for more! Steve, let's get the boy facedown immediately!"

"But the sterile field—"

"To hell with the sterile field! This child's going out!"

"I need him supine if I'm going to be of any help in keeping his pressure up," the anesthesiologist said.

"Byron, he's got to be prone! If I can't get at this bleeding, nothing you do matters. Scalpel, please. Scalpel, dammit!"

Frantically, with no attempt at continued sterility, Jessie cut away the posterior portion of Jackie Terrell's scalp. The bone over the torcular was split down the middle, and blood was pouring out from the sinuses beneath it.

"Suck here, Steve! Em, you, too! Byron, we need more blood! Oh, Jesus!"

"The Doppler monitor on his chest is recording something," Wong said. "I think it's air in his heart."

Jessie continued packing the bleeding area, but it was like trying to sandbag a waterfall.

"Pressure?" she asked.

"Forty. Jessie, there's definitely air being sucked into his circulatory system. His heart's filling with it."

"Blood! We need volume!" Jessie ordered, unwilling yet to believe what she was hearing. "Put the table in Trendelenburg position. Adjust it until he's not bleeding out or sucking in air!"

"Pressure zero," Wong reported. "The air embolism is huge now. Heart rate is dropping. . . . Flat line. We've got flat line."

Jessie fought a few minutes more. Then she stared down at the blood, which continued to well up over her gloves but was now slightly frothy from the air that had been sucked through the damaged sinuses into the child's circulatory system.

"That's it," she heard her voice say from a million miles away. "There's no sense in continuing anymore."

For a full minute, no one in the operating room moved. Then Jessie shook her head.

"I'm sorry, everyone," she said hoarsely. "I'm really sorry. Each of you did a great job."

ALONE IN HER office, Jessie stared out her single window at a pair of swallows that had settled on her ledge. It had been hell telling Charlene Terrell that her son had died on the operating table—hell trying to explain to her that what ultimately killed her child couldn't have been anticipated and couldn't have been fixed.

One of the things Jessie had come to accept as a neurosurgeon was that many of her patients would never be perfectly, or even reasonably, intact after their surgery. All that was available to those cases and their families was to move the goal markers of their lives—the expectations—and to start over from wherever they could. But this—the inhuman senselessness of Jackie Terrell's injury, the sudden, unforseeable catastrophe in the OR— this was more pain than she ever wanted from her specialty. Gilbride, Tamika Bing, then Sara, and now this. Maybe it was time to consider moving to the lab for a while. Or maybe it was time simply to realize that she didn't have the steel plating necessary to make it as a neurosurgeon. Lost in her thoughts, Jessie barely heard the gentle knock on her door.

"Yes, come in," she said after clearing her throat.

Alex Bishop slipped in and closed the door behind him.

"Hi."

"Hi, yourself."

"I thought maybe you could use a little cheering up."

"A little cheering up might elevate me to miserable."

Except for Emily, there was no one in Jessie's world that she would want visiting her at this moment. Yet Alex Bishop, with his wonderful, troubled eyes, and his gentle voice, was a welcome sight.

"Your nurse told me there was no way anyone could have predicted that cracked bone when it didn't show on the CT scan," he said. "She told me you had saved that kid's life, but when you removed the clot you also re-leased the pressure that was holding the pieces together, and the crack opened up."

"I guess."

"It was awful for all of us to go through. It must be ten times as hard for you."

"Thanks for understanding that. I'll never get used to this sort of thing."

"I hope you don't."

She put her hands on his, then stood and let him hold her for a time.

"I'm glad you came up here," she said.

CHAPTER **15**

JESSIE SPENT A RESTLESS NIGHT IN ONE OF THE
tiny on-call rooms, rebreathing lungfuls of stale air and
answering just enough phone calls to keep from reaching
any deep, renewing sleep. She awoke for the last time at
six, vaguely aware that she had been dreaming of Jackie
Terrell racing through a brilliant, sunlit day over a carpet
of emerald grass, chasing an endless succession of fly
balls.

Throughout the evening, reporters had paged her to
ask about the boy. They all were referred to the hospital's
public relations people, who read or faxed them a state-
ment she had helped to prepare. Undoubtedly, Eastern
Mass Medical Center would be on the front pages for the
second time in a week. This time, it was doubtful the
item would stimulate any three-million-dollar grants.

Jessie showered, pulled on a fresh set of scrubs, and

tried a brief meditation. Still, as she headed over to the cafeteria for her usual in-house fare—sesame bagel with sliced tomato and cream cheese, coffee, and a banana—she felt unprepared for another frenetic round of post-Sheprow neurosurgical clinic. The four physicians she joined in the doctors' dining room were engaged in what had become the standard, almost exclusive, mealtime conversation at the hospital—a can-you-top-this of managed care horror stories and jokes.

Generally, Jessie's zeal to make rounds on her patients and get her day going kept her from spending more than fifteen or twenty minutes with the breakfast crew. Today, although the stories and humor were as stale as the air in the on-call room, she couldn't pull herself away. She even tried out a joke she had recently heard about the managed care executive who died and went to heaven, only to find out God had limited him to a three-day stay. The polite reaction from the others told her they had already heard it.

Finally, at seven-fifteen, she paged Emily and met her on Surgical Seven for rounds. Their patients were reasonably stable. As Jessie anticipated, Gary Garrison's headaches had begun to abate. He was still frightened of a rebleed from his aneurysm, though, and jumped at her offer of one last day in the ICU. Dave Scolari's hands and arms were making remarkable progress, and his legs were showing encouraging strength as well. A miracle. They were heading out of Dave's room when Emily mentioned Jackie Terrell for the first time.

"Did you see the *Globe* this morning?" she asked.

"Nope."

"They wrote about the heroic efforts of the doctors at Eastern Mass Medical."

Jessie knew her friend well enough to leap ahead some steps.

"I'm okay about it, Em," she said. "Honest, I am. I'm not blaming myself for something even the radiologist couldn't see. It's just so damn sad, that's all."

Emily put her arm around Jessie's shoulder.

"I know, pal. I know it is. I went home last night and demanded that my kids turn off the tube and snuggle up with me on the couch for half an hour."

"Good move. They're great guys."

"Speaking of guys . . ."

Jessie smiled coyly and shrugged.

"Dunno," she said.

"You do, too. I can see it all over your face. Did he come to see you after the case?"

"Maybe."

"Ohmagosh, you really are bit, and it sounds like he might be, too. I think that's great."

"We'll see. Look, I'm sorry for being in such a testy mood this morning. Gilbride's off being famous again, so I'm facing another crazy day in outpatient. It's like he opened this dam of referrals and then just swam away."

They turned in to the next patient's room, a tumor case of Gilbride's. Jessie was surprised to see Lisa Brandon, the candy striper who had been with Sara, seated at the bedside.

"Evening shift one day, day shift another," Jessie said. "Are you going for some sort of volunteer-of-the-year award?"

Lisa shifted uncomfortably.

"I hope it's all right that I'm here again. Actually, there isn't much for me to do at home, and I really like helping the patients."

"In that case we're lucky to have you. Work all three shifts if you want. Why not? I do."

Jessie introduced Lisa to Emily as a leader in the don't-know-what-to-do-when-I-grow-up club, and Emily proclaimed herself a founding mother of the organization.

"Cute kid," Emily said after they had left the room.

"She's no kid. She's in her early twenties."

"Have you looked at the birth date on your driver's license lately, honey? She's a kid."

IT WAS MIDAFTERNOON. Jessie was in Carl Gilbride's office waiting for Eastman Tolliver to join the two of them for what would essentially be catch-up rounds for Gilbride on his patients. He had returned from New York City a short while ago in triumph—a full ten minutes on the *Today* show, followed by an interview with the *Times,* a hastily called grand rounds presentation at Columbia Presbyterian, and a lunch meeting with a robotics manufacturer interested in cutting some sort of deal for ARTIE. Now, after finally telling his secretary to hold all calls, he was shamelessly pumping Jessie for any information that would give him an edge in his quest for a three-million-dollar grant.

"So what do you make of this guy?" he asked.

"Carl, I only spent an hour or so with him yesterday. He's pleasant, and very interested in our program. That's all I can say. I expected he might come in for rounds this morning—I invited him—but he called and said he'd wait until you got back."

"Did he seem angry I wasn't here?"

"Not really—at least not as far as I could tell. He seems very, I don't know, Californian. Sort of laid-back."

"Surely he must understand that I would never have

left him hanging except that this was all very important stuff."

"Critical. How many times does a body ever get invited to be on the *Today* show?"

"Exactly. So, what's his background? What are his interests?"

"He hasn't been at the MacIntosh Foundation all that long—six years, I think he said. Before that he was a college professor of some sort."

"He's bright, then?"

Bright enough to see through you, I fear.

"Yes, that was my impression."

"Mine, too," Gilbride said. "I think we should—"

Gilbride was interrupted by his secretary buzzing in with the announcement that Tolliver had arrived. The foundation director strode into the office and greeted them both with vigor.

"Dr. Copeland, I'm terribly sorry to hear of that child's death," he said.

"Thank you," Jessie replied, noting that her department chief hadn't mentioned a word about the case.

"I was in your cafeteria and heard some people talking about what a heroic job you did by even getting the boy to the operating room."

Jessie sighed.

"The whole thing is very tragic."

Tragic. The word seemed to galvanize Gilbride into action. It was as if he couldn't stand to let any negative connotation hang in the air.

"So, Eastman," he said, clearing his throat for a transition, "what do you think of what you've seen so far?"

Tolliver's expression flickered annoyance at Gilbride's inappropriate lack of subtlety. Jessie was as certain she saw the reaction as she was that her chief hadn't.

"So far, so good," he said. "But I'm still anxious to learn more about ARTIE, and to watch him in action."

"Well, I can't say that I blame you," Gilbride said. "I believe we are seeing the future of neurosurgery—perhaps even of all surgery—in our little robot."

"Have you experienced any problems with the device?"

"Some mechanical glitches, but nothing major."—Unseen by either man, Jessie rolled her eyes.—"Even though we're doing cases now with ARTIE," Gilbride went on, "we're still working with him in the lab. The search for perfection isn't just the motto of our research unit, it's the rule. We see the next generation of the device being even smaller, more maneuverable, and more powerful than the one we're using. I believe it's no exaggeration to say that at some point, not that far down the road, the surgeon interface between the robot and the MRI may be eliminated altogether. The device could simply be inserted beneath the patient's skull and turned loose, as it were."

"Sounds like something straight out of science fiction," Tolliver said.

"So were Jules Verne's submarine and rocket to the moon," Gilbride responded, now clearly on a roll. "MRI-assisted surgery is merely in its infancy. The future is limitless."

Jessie felt her gut knot. Just a short while ago, a mechanical malfunction had caused ARTIE to rip into the normal brain tissue of her cadaver-subject. Still, she knew better than to so much as mist on Gilbride's three-million-dollar parade—at least not until she was ready to start searching for a new position. If Gilbride wanted to compare himself as visionary with Jules Verne, so be it.

"Well," Tolliver said, "you certainly make a good case for your invention. However, before I return to California, I would hope to see this ARTIE perform an actual operation. Is that possible?"

Gilbride's bluff had been called. Not surprisingly to Jessie, Eastman Tolliver had no intention of buying a pig in a poke. If the MacIntosh Foundation was going to lay heavy money on a device, he wanted to see it in action. Jessie knew what was coming next.

"So, Jessie," Gilbride said, turning to her, "you have my OR schedule. Are there any cases appropriate for ARTIE?"

No, Carl. As a matter of fact, at this stage of the game, there are no cases anywhere that are appropriate for ARTIE.

"Actually, Emily has the OR schedule. We'll be meeting her in the ICU. You can decide for yourself once you've gone over it and met your new patients."

"And I shall." Once again Carl cleared his throat, signaling he was about to transition. "So, then, shall we make our way to the ICU?"

ROUNDS BEGAN SMOOTHLY enough, with Gilbride at his bombastic best, leading an entourage that included Jessie, Emily, two other nurses, two medical students, two residents, and the foundation director on a leisurely patient-by-patient tour—first of the unit, then of the rest of the floor.

By and large, Gilbride's patients were docile and seemed happy to have their surgeon back and grateful he had stopped in to see them. There were, however, three of the sharper ones who made snide or angry remarks about his lack of involvement in their cases. Jessie wasn't certain whether the cynicism was ignored by Gilbride or simply went over his head. But the jab of one elderly patient, Clara Gittleson, clearly hit home.

"Dr. Gilbride," she said crisply, "I have to tell you that I never knew how little attention you were paying to me until Dr. Copeland and Emily started coming around."

Gilbride mumbled something that might have been an apology. A nerve twitched at the corner of his mouth. He asked Jessie a number of questions about the woman's post-op mental status. Finally, he suggested that a psych consult might be in order to deal with what was obviously a combination of depression and reaction to post-op medications. Jessie glanced over at Tolliver, who seemed unaffected by the exchange but remained steadily focused on Gilbride.

As they headed for the next room—Rolf Hermann's—Jessie lagged back and subtly motioned for Emily to join her.

"Have you been in to see Orlis yet?" she whispered.

"Dragon Lady? Oh, yes. I stopped by a few hours ago while I was checking to make sure everything was in place for the emperor's return. She wanted to see me about as much as she wants to see a zit on that perfect face of hers." Emily adopted a passable German accent and added, "I vish only to speak viz Ducktor Geelbride."

"Well, Orlis, be careful what you wish for. You just might get it."

"I can hardly wait."

"Dr. Copeland," Gilbride called out from outside the door, "would you mind terribly continuing on rounds with us?"

Jessie hurried up to the group, presenting the next patient as she arrived.

"Count Rolf Hermann is a fifty-three-year-old married German man, the father of three, who was perfectly healthy until he experienced the first of two seizures about six weeks ago. Evaluation in Europe led to these MRIs."

Jessie knew better than to upstage Gilbride by identifying the tumor or giving any clinical opinions. Instead, she merely nodded to Emily, who took Hermann's MRIs off a stainless steel rolling cart and slid them onto two of the view boxes inset in the wall across from his room. Gilbride's thoughtful pacing back and forth in front of the films was clearly for the benefit of Tolliver and perhaps the medical students, because all of the others could have made the correct diagnosis from a passing train.

"Well," he said finally, "it appears what we have here is a large subfrontal meningioma, wouldn't you say, Dr. Copeland?"

"I would, yes, sir."

"Well, what do you think of this tumor as appropriate for our intraoperative MRI with robotic assist?"

Jessie knew that if any case was ideal for ARTIE, this one was. But she still had serious reservations.

"I think ARTIE would be one way of getting at it," she said, choosing her words carefully.

"Excellent. We're in agreement, then. Mr. Tolliver, here's your case. Dr. Copeland, is there anything else you think I should know about this fellow?"

"Not really."

"Well, then, let's go meet the man."

"He speaks some English," Jessie said, "and understands it completely, but his wife does most of the talking."

The room, which was large for a single, was packed even before the arrival of the medical entourage, with Orlis, her husband, and his three grown children sharing space with a considerably overweight private-duty nurse. Jessie introduced Gilbride, feeling as if she were passing off the baton in a barefoot relay race across hot coals.

"Well, it's a pleasure indeed to meet you," Gilbride said. "However, before we conduct our business, I must ask your children and nurse to wait in the hall. We are a teaching hospital, and after I bring everyone in who is making rounds with me today, I'm afraid this room will get a bit crowded."

"You will not be bringing everyone in," Orlis responded. "Count Hermann will not take part in any medical circus."

"Ka-boom!" Jessie whispered to Emily.

The initial test of wills between Gilbride and the Countess lasted through several exchanges before the Count intervened and brokered a compromise. Jessie and Emily would stay, along with Hermann's older son, Derrick, a man with watchful eyes, strongly built like his father, but with little resemblance beyond that. Tolliver, who observed the conflict and resolution from the doorway, smiled understandingly and motioned that he would be waiting in the hallway.

"Now, then," Orlis said, immediately seizing the initiative, "exactly what is the procedure you intend to do on my husband, and when will it be done?"

"I will answer each of your questions in due time, dear lady. But not until I have had the chance to examine my patient." He turned from her and continued speaking with a deliberateness that bordered on patronizing. "Count Hermann, I am pleased to make your acquaintance. I look forward to the successful treatment of your problem."

"I wish that will be so," the Count said.

Orlis, her expression stony, stood aside as Gilbride

did a more painstaking and meticulous neurologic examination than Jessie had ever seen him perform.

Spare me, was all she could think. It was comforting and amusing to know that a few feet away, Emily was thinking the same thing.

"An excellent exam," Gilbride said finally, putting his reflex hammer and the tuning fork used to test vibratory sense back into his lab coat pocket. "Excellent. Count Hermann, your neurologic exam is surprisingly good. Your tumor is rather slow-growing and non-malignant, which means it does not spread to distant parts of the brain, or to other organs. However, it is taking up increasing amounts of space, and has begun compressing normal brain tissue. You will need surgery to remove it."

The Countess inserted herself between the two men, making no attempt to hide her impatience to hear something she did not already know.

"Do you intend to use the same device you used successfully on that young gymnast?"

Almost in spite of himself, Gilbride glanced at Jessie. She looked away.

"Well, yes," he said. "I suspect we will do this operation in the MRI operating room, and we probably *will* use our robotic assistant."

"We don't want probably," Orlis said sharply. "My husband came here because you said you had something to offer that other neurosurgeons did not. I want everything necessary to be done for him. He is a very special man and helps a great number of people."

Gilbride rose to meet the challenge.

"I appreciate your anxiety, Madame," he replied, "but I feel I must remind you that I am the surgeon. If I think robotic assist will help us remove your husband's tumor, that is what we will use. And if not, well then, we shall not. I hope that is clear?"

Orlis looked to the Count, who nodded his agreement. Then she thrust back.

"When will the operation be done?" she asked.

Gilbride turned to Emily.

"You have the OR schedule?"

Emily, clearly unwilling to be anyplace but on the sidelines of this battle, handed the notebook over to Jessie.

"We're limiting ourselves to the MRI operating room?" Jessie asked.

"Precisely," Gilbride replied.

"Okay. The room is maxed out for three weeks. We have two cases a day booked every day, including Saturdays."

"But I have promised Mr. Tolliver I would be doing an ARTIE case that he could observe. We need to fit Count Hermann into the schedule by the end of the week."

Jessie sighed.

"Tomorrow Dr. Wilbourne from Infants and Children's has his case scheduled first thing in the morning. In the afternoon is the re-op on Terence Gilligan. He's in the unit right now and not doing well. He really needs to have his surgery done as quickly as possible. The day after tomorrow, your patient, Lindsay Pearlman, is first. She's quite symptomatic, and I think there would be a serious risk in delaying her. After her is that man you're going to do with the surgical team from China. They're all flying in tomorrow. Thursday I'm doing Ben Rasheed in the morning. He's been postponed twice, and he really has to be done soon or something disastrous is going to happen. It might be possible to push the Thursday afternoon case into next week. That's your re-op on the Hopkins boy."

"What are you trying to say?" Orlis demanded.

"In my opinion," Jessie went on, "the best we could do—the very best without endangering patients who are much more unstable than Count Hermann—would be three days from now in the afternoon slot."

"That is ridiculous and unacceptable," Orlis snapped.

"Orlis," the Count said, holding up a calming hand.

The Countess took a deep breath and exhaled slowly.

"Dr. Gilbride," she said, nearly shaking, "my husband has had two seizures already. I want this surgery done tomorrow or Wednesday at the very latest."

"Jessie," Gilbride said, "I would rather not keep Eastman here any longer than necessary."

Jessie shrugged.

"These cases are really in critical shape," she said. "I would hate to delay any of them any more than they already have been, and I don't think you want to tell the Chinese they're being bumped."

Gilbride studied his fingers, clearly weighing the political and malpractice implications of putting off a case and having some sort of catastrophe befall the patient.

"Thursday afternoon it is," he pronounced finally.

Orlis's porcelain face reddened.

"This is unacceptable," she said again.

Gilbride seemed to enjoy having the upper hand. Clearly this was one HC who had pushed him too hard.

"Furthermore," he said, "I would suggest that you and your family check into a hotel until Thursday morning."

"We are paying in cash, Dr. Gilbride. We have Dr. Marcus's permission to occupy our rooms, and we will not be leaving."

"Suit yourself, Countess."

"Dr. Gilbride, I want you to know that we are not accustomed to this sort of treatment."

"Mrs. Hermann, I assure you there are a number of other neurosurgeons in the city."

Without waiting for a response, Gilbride swung around and led Emily and Jessie from the room. Eastman Tolliver was waiting just outside the door, where he couldn't have helped but hear everything that had transpired. Jessie tried unsuccessfully to read anything into his expression. Removing Rolf Hermann's tumor by any method was hardly going to be a stroll in the park. And although confidence was as essential a quality in a surgeon as a steady hand, the line between self-assuredness and hubris was a fine one. Jessie wondered now if Gilbride's determination to impress Eastman Tolliver had just pushed him across it.

CHAPTER 16

JESSIE HAD JUST FINISHED DINNER WITH ALEX IN the cafeteria when she was paged to an in-house number.

"This is Dr. Copeland, returning a page."

"Ah, yes, Jessie. Eastman Tolliver here. I hope I'm not interrupting you."

Jessie looked over at Alex, who had cleaned their table and was now pointing at his watch and motioning that he was leaving. "See you later," he mouthed.

"No," she said to Tolliver. "You're not interrupting anything."

"I wonder if at some point this evening we might talk for a bit," Tolliver said.

"Is there a problem?"

"No, nothing like that. I just had some questions that I felt you might better be able to answer than Dr. Gilbride."

I'd really rather not get involved in this grant business any more than I already have been. . . . Nothing personal, but I think you should direct any questions you have to Carl. . . . I am absolutely beat, and I had hoped to make it an early night tonight. . . .

In the few seconds it took her to answer, Jessie rejected half a dozen responses that were each more accurate than the one she ended up giving.

"Of course. Where are you now?"

"In the library going over your—I mean Dr. Gilbride's—grant application, and boning up on my neurosurgery."

"I can be done by nine. Will that be too late?"

"Nine will be fine."

"Tell you what. Meet me in the lobby. You can escort me to my car, and I'll drive you to your place. We can talk on the way."

Over the next hour Jessie returned eleven phone calls—seven of them for Gilbride. There appeared to be no letup in the frenzy he had created with his gold medal operation. It was actually five after nine by the time she had changed out of her scrubs and made it to the lobby. Eastman Tolliver was there, dressed conservatively in a lightweight tan suit, button-down white shirt, and muted tie. Perhaps sensing that she had had a long day, he wasted no time on small talk.

"So," he said as they descended the stairs from the main entrance, "Dr. Gilbride has told me that he has a case scheduled Thursday afternoon in which he will probably be using your robotic assistant. I am planning on returning to California shortly after I observe that operation. I was hoping that before I leave, we two might talk a little business."

"Business?"

"Yes. I would appreciate it very much if you could tell me about your recent misadventure with ARTIE."

Jessie looked over at him, stunned.

"Misadventure?"

Tolliver's dark, intelligent eyes sparked.

"I didn't come all the way to Boston just to be charmed by your department chief," he said, "although I have been positively disposed toward him thus far. I came to learn about your work and to gather the information necessary to make what will amount to a four-million-dollar decision."

"Not three?"

"Probably not. And please, don't feel you are breaking any confidences. Dr. Gilbride has encouraged me to speak with whomever I wish."

Jessie couldn't help but be impressed with the man's thoroughness. Pleading ignorance at this point hardly seemed appropriate.

"Well, I don't know for certain what you mean by misadventure," she said, "but I assume you're talking about the procedure I did on a cadaver not too long ago."

"Precisely."

"ARTIE was functioning perfectly, but a microcable snapped, and I lost control of him. It was that simple."

"Could that happen again?"

"I would hope not, but speaking as a former engineer, I can tell you that with something mechanical anything can happen."

"But the design of these cables is as good as it can be?"

"If a thing is man-made it can be improved upon," Jessie replied, "but for the moment, I would say yes, the guidance system on ARTIE is as good as we can make it."

"Did you participate in the decision to use the device on Marci Sheprow?"

Again, Jessie stared over at him.

"Eastman, I seldom get too nervous performing brain surgery," she said, "but the possibility that I might say something that will cost my department a four-million-dollar research grant is another matter altogether. Perhaps we should discuss all this with Carl."

"I'm sorry. Jessie, yours is not the only program in intraoperative robotics that has applied to us for financial assistance. To make the fairest decision, these are the sorts of things I need to know—the reason I came all the way across the country to evaluate your program firsthand."

Jessie thought for a time, then shrugged.

"No," she said simply. "Carl made the decision to use ARTIE on Marci Sheprow without consulting with me. Nor did he have to. It's his department, his lab, and his invention."

"But you're the principal researcher, yes?"

"I think you know the answer to that."

"I believe I do. And I want you to trust that your response will be kept strictly confidential."

"I have a degree in mechanical engineering."

"I am aware of that."

"Well, I was hired as a resident with the understanding that I would spend some time in the lab working on ARTIE. So I guess you could say I was the principal researcher on the project. But believe me, Dr. Gilbride has been on top of things every step of the way."

"I have no doubt that he has. The operation Dr. Gilbride was referring to, it will be Count Hermann, yes?"

"Yes, it will. I suppose you heard that when you were in the hall."

"It was difficult *not* to. In fact, after I overheard the exchange between Dr. Gilbride and the Countess, I made a point of stopping by later to speak with the Hermanns."

"The Countess actually talked to you?"

"I found both of them quite easy to converse with."

"She's pretty angry at us."

"Perhaps. But I believe she is simply frightened for her husband. It seems to me that she loves him very much. Tell me, Jessie, in your opinion, is the decision to use ARTIE on Count Hermann the correct one, or is this just being done on my account?"

Jessie looked over at him, but said nothing.

"Please," he implored. "It's very important that I know how you feel about this."

Jessie felt her mouth go dry. Tolliver was extremely intuitive, and clearly had been asking questions around the hospital. She wondered if he sensed that she didn't believe ARTIE was ready to be used on anyone—or, more to the point, that anyone, including her, was competent enough with the device at this juncture to use it on a difficult patient. Even assuming that ARTIE had no further mechanical problems, the ability to see a tumor in three dimensions and to guide the robotic unerringly through normal brain tissue would come only with time. For sure, she felt her skills improving with practice, but she still wasn't confident enough to lay one of her patient's lives on the line.

She knew she was going to have to lie to Tolliver, risk costing her department a four-million-dollar grant, or pick her words with the care of a soldier on land-mine detail.

"I believe the technical problems I encountered have been dealt with," she said. "I also believe that ARTIE has a great deal to offer to patients whose tumors are difficult to reach."

"In the right hands."

Jessie unlocked Swede's door for Tolliver and waited to reply until she had pulled out of the lot.

"Dr. Gilbride is a skilled surgeon with a great deal of confidence in himself," she said finally. "That confidence is job one in our specialty. Without it, a neurosurgeon might just as well pack it in."

Jessie could feel Tolliver studying her, deciding whether to push the matter any further.

"Thank you, Jessie," he said at last. "I am most grateful for your candor. You have my word that any other questions I have I'll ask Dr. Gilbride."

IN HIS MIND, forty-eight-year-old Terence Gilligan had never lost a fight. He had been beaten in the ring a number of times and, on occasion, pummeled. But he had never really lost because he had never broken. Even when his knees refused to straighten, he had never given up. The British had beaten on him, too. He was one of the Rowdies—an arm of the IRA in east Belfast that was noted for its toughness. They had rousted him, hauled him in to the station house, and slapped him around for hours. But they always came away empty. And gradually, they came to know not to bother with Gilligan.

This brain tumor thing was no different, he thought now. Those rotten cells would come to know the same as the Brits—don't bother with Gilligan.

He had been through so much in his life, it was hard to believe he was lying in a bed in the intensive care unit of a hospital in Massachusetts, with tubes stuck in almost every bloody opening in his body. But that was the way things were. First the girl from South Boston, visiting her ancestral home, then the flight from Ireland to be with her, and finally the merging of his life with hers, her family, and the rest of the Americans.

Gilligan coughed against the huge tube that passed down his throat, connecting his lungs to a breathing machine. Forty years of fags had done his breathing in. Now it seemed like forty years since he had last smoked one. With the friggin' tube down, he hadn't been able to speak to anyone for days, neither. Did they even know he could hear them? Understand them—at least some of the time? Did they even know how uncomfortable he was? Or that he was aware of tomorrow's trip back into the operating room to try and clean out the brain tumor that had regrown, it seemed, in just a few months?

Shit, what lousy luck. If the bullets don't get you, the cancer will.

Gilligan shifted his weight, trying to find a comfortable position. He could barely move with all the bloody tubes, to say nothing of the straps around his wrists and ankles that kept him from getting at them.

"Mr. Gilligan, hold still now. It won't do you any good to pull out your breathing tube."

Gilligan blinked, trying to focus through the dim light on the woman, who was backlit from the outside hallway. She spoke with a heavy accent, though not one he immediately recognized. He waved at her with one hand as best he could.

Pain medicine. If you can't run some bloody fag smoke down this tube, at least give me some more pain medicine so I don't have to think about it.

"I'm from anesthesia, Mr. Gilligan," the woman said

gently. "I'm here to give you some medicine to help you sleep before your surgery tomorrow."

Well, it's about friggin' time.

The woman came closer. She was wearing a long white coat, a mask, and something covering her hair. From what he could see, her eyes looked nice enough, and her voice, not much more than a whisper, was soothing. She had a syringe full of the sleeping medicine in her hand.

"Just hold still, now, Mr. Gilligan," she said. "You'll be feeling better in just a short while."

She slipped the needle into the IV tubing and emptied the syringe.

Bless you, Sister. Bless you.

"Sweet dreams."

Almost before he realized it, the woman was gone. Still there, though, was her perfume. Odd, Gilligan thought. Of all the many nurses and woman doctors who had cared for him, none had worn any perfume that he could remember. He forced himself down into his pillow and waited.

How long did she say it was going to take to work? How long has it been?

Suddenly, a strange, unsettling emptiness filled his chest and throat—the sensation of his heart flip-flopping.

"Somebody go in and check on Gilly," he heard one of the nurses say. "He's starting to have runs of extra beats. They look ventricular."

Extra beats. Now what in the hell does that—?

"Quick, Becky, Gilly's fibrillating!"

The extra beats in Gilligan's chest exploded into a terrifying vacuum, and he knew, well before he lost consciousness, that his heart had stopped beating.

"Code ninety-nine, room seven! Call it in!"

Hurry, girls, hurry!

"Get the cart. Molly, call Dr. Dakar!"

"Code ninety-nine, Surgical Seven ICU! . . . Code ninety-nine, Surgical Seven ICU! . . ."

Hurry! . . . Fix me! . . . I'm dying!

"He's still in fib."

"Give me three hundred joules. Get ready to defibrillate!"

Oh, God, please . . .

"Three hundred!"

Oh, God . . .

"Okay. Ready, everyone . . . Clear! . . ."

CHAPTER 17

THERE WAS A PALL OVER SURGICAL SEVEN WHEN
Jessie arrived at work. Terry Gilligan, something of a
mascot on the neurosurgical service because of his dense
brogue and infectious wit, was dead. His cardiac arrest
had occurred during the early-morning hours and was in-
tractable to the heroic efforts first of the nurses, then of the
entire code team. He had been on assisted ventilation because of a seizure and borderline pulmonary reserve, and
his tumor was a bad one. But no one had come close to
giving up on him.

On a morning that had begun so badly, Jessie was relieved that at last Carl had opted to stay around and see
patients. With only her own work to attend to, her day
gradually smoothed out. But nothing prepared her for
what she found waiting when her afternoon clinic was
over—waiting in room 6 of the neurosurgical ICU.

When she arrived, the ubiquitous candy striper, Lisa Brandon, was rubbing lotion into Sara Devereau's feet.

"Well, hi," Jessie said. "Here you are again."

"Here I am," Lisa said cheerily.

"You know, everyone on the service is pulling for you not to figure out what you want to do with your life, Lisa. You're far too valuable as a volunteer here."

Lisa brushed aside some slips of dark hair.

"That's very kind of you to say, even if it isn't true."

"Ah, but it is. You're doing a great job with the patients—this one in particular."

"Thank you. Well, I think we have a surprise for you here."

We? Jessie looked quickly at Sara. Reasonably peaceful, but deeply comatose. Still, something about Lisa's proud expression made her pulse jump a notch.

"Luckily, I'm one of the few neurosurgeons in the world who likes surprises," she said.

"Okay, then," Lisa replied, "here goes." She raised her voice. "Sara, it's Lisa. Dr. Copeland's here. Can you open your eyes?"

For two fearfully empty seconds there was nothing. Then, suddenly, Sara's eyelids fluttered and opened.

"Oh, God!" Jessie exclaimed, grasping her friend's hand. "Oh, God. Sara, it's me, Jessie. Can you hear me?"

Sara's nod, though slight, was unequivocal.

"She started responding to me about an hour ago," Lisa said. "I almost called you, but then I asked the nurses when you were expected, and they said you'd be up soon."

Jessie barely heard the woman. Tears welling, she was stroking Sara's forehead and looking into eyes that were clearly looking back at her.

Conjugate gaze intact . . . pupils midposition, reactive, her surgeon's mind automatically recorded. She reached over and grasped Sara's other hand as she had at least once every day since the surgery.

"Sara, can you squeeze my hands?" she asked.

The pressure, faint but definite, and equal on both sides, broke the dam. Jessie made no effort to wipe aside her tears.

"Oh, Devereau," she said, "where in the hell have you been?"

Sara's lips struggled to form a word. Over and over again they opened and closed. Finally, there was the faintest wisp of a sound.

"J . . . Jessie," she said.

Jessie turned to Lisa.

"Did you tell the nurses?" she asked.

"No. I thought you might want to."

"Well, you're right. I do want to." She crossed to the door. "Hey, everyone, room six. On the double. Our patient has something she wants to say!"

BECAUSE OF TERRY Gilligan's death, the entire MRI-OR schedule was moved up. Tomorrow's morning case would now be Gilbride's operation with the team of Chinese neurosurgeons. In the afternoon, Jessie would operate on Ben Rasheed, a fifty-year-old black laborer and father of four, who presented with severe weakness in his left arm and leg, and was found by Jessie to have a rather large tumor on the right side of his brain—almost certainly an astrocytoma. The sooner the tumor could be removed and graded for malignancy, the sooner appropriate post-op therapy could be instituted—most likely radiation.

With a potentially difficult case tomorrow, followed in the evening by her first real date with Alex, Jessie decided to head home at eight—for her a quite reasonable hour. After reviewing Rasheed's films again, and making some notes regarding the surgical approach she would use, she took the shuttle to lot E and drove to the Back Bay.

She straightened up her apartment, defrosted some lasagna she had made a month or so ago, and ate it between shots in one of her higher-scoring games of Pin Bot. It had been two years since she scraped together every bit of cash she had and bought the one-bedroom condo. Generally, she felt the apartment served her needs quite well, although her feelings about it often mirrored what was transpiring in the rest of her life. Tonight, with Sara awake, Alex looking like he might be the start of something good, and an exciting OR case in the afternoon, the place felt perfect.

At ten o'clock, when her beeper went off, she had just brewed a cup of Earl Grey, run a steaming tub, lit several scented candles, and set out her favorite huge bath sheet. The callback message on the LED was from the evening shift nursing supervisor on Surgical Seven. Being paged by the extremely capable nurse when she wasn't on call was unusual, Jessie thought—unusual enough not to ignore.

"Dr. Copeland, I'm really sorry to call you like this," the woman said, "but Dr. Sanjay is up here from anesthesia. Apparently there's some problem with Ben Rasheed."

"What kind of problem? I just went over him this morning."

"Oh, it's nothing medical. Dr. Sanjay says Ben told him he wasn't having surgery tomorrow. Wait a minute—here he is."

Jessie steeled herself for what she knew was going to be a struggle—understanding Sanjay, who spoke perfectly good English, but so rapidly and with such a dense Indian accent that he was always hard to follow.

"Your patient, Mr. Rasheed, tells me he is not going to have his operation tomorrow afternoon. Instead, he is going to have it in two days' time. According to your patient, someone named Hermann will be taking his place."

Jessie covered her eyes with her hand. What in the hell had the Countess done now? Borne by her years of making decisions as a surgeon, she ticked off her possible courses of action in seconds, discarding each as impractical, given the circumstances, the hour, and the personalities involved. Finally, only one option remained.

"I'll be there in twenty minutes," she said. "Go ahead about your business. I'll page you after I've had the chance to speak with Mr. Rasheed."

AT TEN-THIRTY in the evening, the ride to EMMC took just fifteen minutes. The best part about coming to the hospital at such an hour was that there would be parking spaces in the central underground lot. Throughout the ride, Jessie tried to find some explanation for Ben Rasheed's sudden refusal to be operated on tomorrow other than that he had sold his OR time to Count Hermann. But no other rationale made sense.

As she turned in to Longwell Street, which ran along the back of the hospital, she peered up at the Surgical Tower. From this side, her office was visible seven stories up. Suddenly, she pulled the Saab over and stopped. There was a light on in her office. Moments later, the silhouette of a figure passed behind the sheer white curtain. *Housekeeping?* Hard to believe at this hour, she decided.

She hurried into a parking spot and raced through the basement to the Surgical Tower elevator. She stepped from the car on seven, hesitated, and then used a nearby house phone to call security, hoping that Alex was around. Instead, her call was answered in two minutes by the guard whom she had seen in the cafeteria with him, a bear of a man named Eldon Ellroy.

The corridor outside the offices was on evening-light status, with every other fixture dark. There was no light coming from beneath any of the doors, including hers. Gently, silently, Ellroy tried the knob. Locked. Then Jessie inserted the key, turned it, pushed the door open, and stepped back into the corridor. Nothing. Ellroy reached around the jamb and switched on the light. The tiny office was empty. He motioned her inside, and she confirmed that there was nothing out of place. Ellroy reassured her kindly that ever since the hospital started cutting back on electricity, security had been getting many more calls such as hers. Then he left.

Jessie stood in the silence, still tensed. The papers on her desk and in her drawers seemed in order, but she couldn't shake the feeling that someone had been there. Finally, she marginally convinced herself that the light and silhouette she had seen were in one of the orthopedists' offices on Surgical Six. Turning off the light and carefully locking the door behind her, she headed to the ward and Ben Rasheed's room.

Rasheed's ebony face, set off by a clean-shaven scalp, was thick-featured, deeply lined, and, to Jessie, handsome. His outsized, heavily callused hands could easily have palmed a basketball. He had a spirit that made him one of Jessie's favorites, and loved to tell stories about his life as a bodyguard, chauffeur, and construction worker, and to drop the names of the famous people with whom he had, at one time or another, crossed paths.

Rasheed's half of the double room was adorned with

photos of his wife and children. As soon as he saw Jessie at the doorway, he playfully ducked beneath the sheets. She pulled up a chair and waited. Rasheed stayed where he was.

"I ain't comin' out until you say you're not mad at me," he announced.

"Ben, I *am* mad at you. You can't do this."

Slowly, tortoiselike, Rasheed emerged. His expression was deadly serious.

"Doc, I *got* to," he said.

Jessie took a calming breath.

"Okay, okay. Start from the beginning."

"A few hours ago, this woman come to see me. She spoke like, I don't know, like a Nazi in a war movie."

"I know who she is."

"Okay. Well, she says that her husband's very sick and needs an operation bad, but that he can't get no time in the operatin' room for two days. She says that if I change places with him, an' let him have my time, I could have his."

"How much money did she offer you?"

"I . . . I promised I wouldn't say."

Jessie was about to demand to know, but then realized there was no need. Ben Rasheed was anything but dumb. He knew what was at stake for himself. If he was making this decision, the money had to be enough for him.

"Ben, this is potentially a very dangerous thing for you to do," she said. "You've already had some major symptoms. With this type of tumor, things can come apart very quickly. That's one of the reasons we've put you in the hospital to wait for your operation."

"I know that. But I also know you won't let nothin' bad happen to me."

"Ben, that's a little naive. The longer we wait, the

more chance something bad *will* happen. And if it does, I can't make any guarantees."

"But you said that about the operation, too, Doc. No guarantees. I know this tumor in my head might kill me whether I wait an extra day or I don't. I got four kids, a wife, an' a mortgage, an' I got nothin' in the bank an' no life insurance. For what this lady's gonna pay me, I'm willin' to roll the dice. Christ, for that kind of money, if she wanted my kidney, I'd hand it over. I know you're angry with me, Doc. I'm sorry 'bout that. But a man's gotta do what a man's gotta do."

Jessie knew that were their roles reversed, she would have made the same choice.

"Okay, I'm not angry with you, Ben," she said. "One thing, though. You don't have to tell me the amount, just tell me the terms."

"Some now, more after the guy's operation."

"I want you to get it all up front. Mrs. Hermann has cash. I'm certain of it."

"You gonna talk to her about that?"

"You bet I am," Jessie said.

THE EXCHANGE WITH Orlis Hermann was brief and to the point.

"I don't know how much you offered Ben Rasheed, Mrs. Hermann," Jessie said, "but I want it paid in full before the Count's operation tomorrow."

"Or what?" Orlis asked.

The two women faced off across the dimly lit hospital room, with Rolf Hermann and one of his sons looking on. Jessie refused to blink.

"Or I'll do whatever is necessary to get your husband taken off the MRI-OR schedule and pushed back to his original slot."

"I have already spoken with Dr. Gilbride about the change in schedule. He wants to do this operation as quickly as possible."

"I don't care," Jessie replied. "I believe he also wants to keep me on his staff."

Orlis studied her resolve, then said simply, "Mr. Rasheed will have his money tomorrow morning."

"One more thing. If I hear of you interacting with any of my patients again without my permission, I'll move heaven and earth to have you and your family shipped to another hospital. Is that clear?"

"Get out," Orlis Hermann said. "Get out of here this instant."

Jessie stormed from the room, left word with Sanjay, the anesthesiologist, that his afternoon case had changed, and hurried down to her car. She was determined that Orlis Hermann wasn't going to ruin what had been a wonderful day. With any luck, the water in the tub would just take a little heating up. She was at the parking attendant's booth when she realized that her purse was still on the chair in her office.

"Sorry, but you can't leave your car there," the sleepy attendant told her when she tried to park it off to one side.

Weary of conflicts, Jessie turned around and eventually pulled into the slot she had just left. She took the elevator back to Surgical Seven, inserted the key in her office lock, and opened the door. As she was reaching for the light switch, a strong hand snatched her wrist and jerked her inside. At the same instant, the man's other hand clamped tightly across her mouth.

CHAPTER 18

EVEN BEFORE SHE HEARD HIS VOICE, JESSIE KNEW it was Alex.

"Jessie, it's me," he whispered. "I'm going to let go. Just promise me you won't scream. . . . Do you promise?"

She nodded. His grip lessened and finally released altogether. Jessie turned, rubbing her mouth, and glared at him through what light the filmy curtains permitted. She felt as if she had been gored.

"I knew you were too good," she said.

"I'm sorry."

"Can I turn the light on?"

"How about the one on your desk?"

Jessie switched it on and moved quickly to her own chair before he could stop her or object.

"That was you in here a while ago, too, wasn't it?" she said.

"By sheer chance I looked out the window just as you pulled over to the side of the street. I wasn't sure, but I thought it was you."

Jessie forced her lips tightly together until she was certain she could speak without crying or screaming. Absurdly, she flashed on the tub in her apartment, and the tea, and the candles. Alex just sat there, arms folded, waiting. At least there was nothing smug in his expression, she thought. At least there was no half-assed, knee-jerk attempt at fabricating some lame explanation for why he had twice broken in to her office.

"Well," she managed finally, "you haven't killed me, so I assume I'm going to get some sort of tale to convince me you're not just a low-life snoop or thief or pervert— something like that you're an undercover cop working on a case?"

His smile was uncomfortable.

"Actually, I'm CIA."

"Uh-huh."

"Well, sort of CIA."

"Sort of."

"We get paid by the CIA, but we function pretty independently. I should say functioned. We've been broken up and those of us who are still alive have been sort of decommissioned."

"We?"

"An antiterrorist group, I guess you'd call us."

"Does your 'group' have a name like SPECTRE or SMERSH?"

"No. No name."

"ID?"

"No."

"A phone number?"

"Not really. There's a guy in Langley who'd probably vouch for me, but he's on vacation."

"On vacation. . . . Alex, what were you doing in my office?"

"I'll tell you, but I need you to promise you'll give me the benefit of the doubt."

"Benefit of the doubt? Until I hear a reasonable explanation for what you just did, I'm not promising to give you the benefit of anything."

He studied her for a time, then sighed.

"I was getting ready to go through your patient records," he said.

"Of course. You broke into my office to go through my patient records. What else? I should have guessed that right away. How foolish of me." Jessie felt herself coming unraveled.

"I wish you wouldn't do this," he said.

"What I'm going to *do* in about ten seconds is call the police."

"If that's what you think you have to do, I won't stop you."

"Is this some sort of bluff? You think if you tell me it's okay to call the police, I won't?"

"No. No bluff. Listen, if I go out to get something from my locker, will you wait here for me?"

"Are you going to bolt?"

"No."

"Look at me! Are you going to take off?"

"Jessie, that's the last thing I'm going to do. Will you wait here? There are lives at stake."

"My, my, such high drama. Go ahead. I'll wait. But before you go, I want to tell you that I'm feeling a little used by you, for whatever silly reason. And I hate that feeling.

So whatever it is you're going to go and get from your locker had better be good, or else don't bother."

Bishop stood slowly and, never taking his eyes from her, backed out of the office. Jessie sat there, staring unseeingly at the elegant paperweight Emily had given her last Christmas, feeling too stunned and disappointed to move. She knew there was nothing Alex could tell her that would erase the hurt. She thought about just leaving—going home to bed. If she stayed and Alex didn't come back, she'd be relieved. If he did return, she'd probably not believe anything he told her anyway. So why not just go?

Shit!

Employee lockers were in the subbasement. Jessie timed out five minutes, and was about to head home when Bishop returned carrying a large manila envelope. He looked relieved to see her still there.

He sat down, cradling the envelope in his lap. "What I told you before is the truth. For years I've worked undercover for a branch of the CIA. Mostly I've been in Europe."

"Go on," she said, interested in his story, but disinclined to believe it.

"Have you ever heard of Claude Malloche?"

"No."

"That's not surprising. Not many people have. In fact, in some places he's called the Mist or some equivalent, suggesting that he really doesn't exist. But he does. He kills for a living. A prime minister or a plane full of tourists, Malloche really doesn't care as long as the price is right. He's French by birth, but he comes and goes— Germany, the Balkans, Russia. He has places all over. I have reason to believe that he or those who work for him have killed more than five hundred people, if you count the jetliner explosion over Athens five years ago, and the one over the Canary Islands two years ago."

"I thought Arab terrorists were blamed for that Athens one," Jessie said, upset with herself for participating in his tall tale.

"The money was Arab, and one of their splinter groups claimed responsibility, just like the Algerian separatists took credit for the Canary Islands disaster. But Malloche blew up both planes for those groups. I'm certain of it. "

"And why are you so certain?"

"Because, for five years now, tracking down Claude Malloche is all I've done."

"Pardon me for stating the obvious," Jessie said, "but it would appear you're not very good at your job."

Bishop sighed.

"Unfortunately, there are a few important people in Washington who agree with that assessment," he said. "In fact, they're the same ones who aren't even convinced there is a Claude Malloche. They think he's a figment of the CIA's imagination, used to explain every assassination or bombing we're unable to solve."

"Like Santa Claus gets credit for Christmas presents."

"Jessie, you have every right to be furious with me. But please, just hear me out."

"Go ahead."

"Malloche is like the bull's-eye at the center of a target. Surrounding him is a small organization I have heard called the Dark—maybe ten or twelve men and women who are suicidally loyal to him. They are the only ones who ever have contact with him—and live. And around that group is another ring of supporters, much more diffuse and less informed, and then another ring. So far the network has proven impossible to penetrate very deeply. We've lost several people trying. Those at the center have no political agenda other than money. Malloche himself is ruthless, brilliant, incredibly careful, and absolutely without regard for human life—*other* humans' lives, that is."

"And you've been chasing him."

"At the moment, I'm all that's left of a unit that once was six. Four of the others have disappeared, and are presumed dead. One is teaching recruits. I can't get more men or more money to keep after Malloche."

"Because people in Washington don't think he exists."

Bishop looked as if he were about to speak, then nodded instead.

"Do they know *you* exist?" Jessie asked.

"They've demanded that I stop what I've been doing and return to Virginia to join my former partner and become an instructor for new recruits to the agency. I'm overdue to report by almost a month now. They've already sent a man here to bring me back or kill me."

"And did you kill him?"

"I could have, but I didn't. Next time they send someone, I will probably have to."

"That's great to hear. There really isn't a phone number I could call to verify all this?"

"Not really."

"How do you get paid?"

"I don't think I do anymore. But when I did, it was a rather complicated, convoluted process."

"Of course. Forget I asked. You have a photo of this Malloche?"

"Maybe. Maybe dozens. He doesn't look the same in any two of them."

"Fingerprints?"

Bishop shook his head. "Maybe," he said again.

"Okay, no definite photos, no definite fingerprints, no definite proof he exists. No pay stubs to prove *you* exist. What has all this got to do with me and my patients?"

Bishop extracted some eight-by-ten-inch photographs from the envelope, hesitated, then handed several of them over.

"These are pretty gruesome," he said, "but after watching you in the OR with that child, I know you can handle it."

The photos were of corpses—one man and two women in white coats, another woman, quite young, in street clothes—taken in a medical clinic of some sort. Each of them had been shot in the center of the forehead, right above the bridge of the nose.

"Explain."

"These photos were taken about three months ago by the police in an MRI clinic in Strasbourg, France, right on the border with Germany. The shot placement is a trademark of Malloche's. It's the only thing I've ever found him to do with any consistency. Look."

He passed over several more photos of various victims. Each had been shot in virtually the same place.

"Two months ago," Bishop went on, "I was able to question a man in one of those outer rings I spoke about, but one not that far from the center. It's a break I've worked years for. The guy had been picked up by the police in Madrid in connection with a political killing there. They had him on video from a surveillance camera. He offered to cut a deal in exchange for being allowed to disappear. One of the arresting officers had known me for years, and when he found out what the killer was bringing to the table, he contacted me imme-

diately. Basically, what the guy said was that Malloche
has a brain tumor and that he's looking for a doctor to
operate.

"I began sending out alerts to the FBI in this country,
and the equivalent agencies throughout Europe, although I always knew he'd surface in the U.S. or, a remote possibility, in Italy or the U.K."

"Why those places?"

"You tell me."

"The finest neurosurgeons, the best equipment."

"With the U.S. head and shoulders above the others."
He extracted another set of photographs from the envelope and continued. "Three and a half weeks ago, a
prominent neurosurgeon in Iowa was shot to death in
his office, along with his secretary."

"Sylvan Mays. He was involved in the same sort of
robotics research we are."

"Exactly. Did you know him?"

"I've heard him speak at some conferences, but we'd
never really met. I think Carl Gilbride knew him pretty
well."

"From what you do know of this Dr. Mays, do you
think he's the sort who might have come to Claude
Malloche's attention?"

"Perhaps. If Malloche really exists."

"Do these help convince you? I got them from the
Iowa City police. The one sprawled out on the floor is
Sylvan Mays. The one at her desk is his receptionist."

"Same bullet holes."

"Malloche has a thing about witnesses. Mays' wife
says he had been talking about coming into a lot of
money, but he wouldn't say how, and there's no extra
money in any of his bank accounts. I have a feeling Mays
had already agreed to do Malloche's surgery, and then

something went wrong. Malloche decided he didn't trust him, or Mays tried to back out for some reason."

"Bad idea, it would seem. Okay, Alex, I've seen enough."

"You believe me?"

"Hell no. And if this Claude Malloche really does exist, I have no reason to believe you're not him."

"Jesus. Jessie, I'm telling you the truth. I'm certain Malloche has learned all he can about robotic surgery and Marci Sheprow's operation, and has decided to have Carl Gilbride perform his surgery."

"Then why not go to Carl?"

"I've checked around. I get the sense that Gilbride would be willing to cut almost any corner—or any deal—depending on what was in it for him. I don't know if I can trust him. I don't have time to check on whether or not he has made any major deposits over the last couple of weeks either, so I've just got to go with my gut. And my gut says Malloche is here or he's gonna be here real soon. Five years, Jessie. Five years and this is the best shot I've had at the bastard—maybe the last shot."

"Well, good luck, and good night."

Jessie stood to go.

"Please, wait, Jessie. I told you that our unit had lost four men."

"Yes."

"Well, two of them were killed when an informant we trusted sold us out and we were ambushed by Malloche's people. One of those men who was killed was my older brother, Andy. I was wounded. He was dragging me to cover when he was shot by a long-range sniper right here." Bishop pointed to the spot just above the bridge of his nose. "His killer fired from nearly half a mile away. Malloche is one of the very few people on earth who could have made that shot."

"If that's really true," Jessie said, "I'm sorry. I honestly am. Now, I'm going home."

"Wait! Dammit, Jessie, please. I need your help. This is my last chance. I'm not going to give up and go teach at their secret agent school, and the agency is going to keep after me. If I kill one of their men, they'll just send someone better."

"I think you should give up."

"With Mays dead, this seems like the obvious place for Malloche to go—especially after Gilbride got all that publicity for operating on that gymnast. So far, though, I haven't been able to figure out whether or not Malloche is here. Since I arrived, I've been lifting prints off glasses and other things from every new male patient who's come onto the neurosurgical service. I've sent them to Interpol, and today I brought them to D.C. in hopes of matching them to any of the two or three dozen maybes I've gotten on Malloche over the years."

"And?"

"Nothing. I've got to know more about each of the patients. And when we determine which one Malloche is, I may need help capturing him. There are just too many doubters. I need him alive. But even dead, I have a chance to identify him."

"What do you mean?"

"The witness in Spain, the one who told me about Malloche's brain tumor?"

"Yes?"

"His name is Cardoza. He claims he's seen Malloche—several times. He looked at all the photos I showed him, but refused to say whether any of them was or wasn't Malloche. He wanted to cut a deal for passage for him and his family out of Spain, and enough money to set them up wherever they went."

"Why didn't you make the deal?"

"How could I trust him? He was still in prison. He could have pointed out anyone."

"But now you trust him?"

"I do. Apparently Malloche found out Cardoza had been speaking with us. A few weeks ago, his apartment was blown up. As I said, he was locked up, but his wife and kid weren't so lucky. The police in Madrid have him someplace safe for now, and they're moving him around. But Malloche has money to burn, so it's only a matter of time before someone on the force takes a bite and sells Cardoza out. They offered to take him out of the country for the time being, but he refused. He wants Malloche dead."

"What about the photos, then?"

"A dozen or so nos, one maybe. That's the best he could do. The maybe is so blurred that it could be anyone. As soon as I have a suspect, Cardoza'll be flown over."

"This is just crazy. You're working this case all by yourself?"

"I have a little help from the local FBI. Not much, but a little."

"So who killed Cardoza's wife and child?"

"What?"

"If this Malloche is as good as you say at killing, it's a little hard to believe he hasn't killed Cardoza as well. And if this whole phantasmagorical story of yours is true, it would seem you had quite a bit to gain from blowing up that family in Madrid yourself."

Bishop's look held genuine admiration.

"You know," he said, "the truth is, if I had thought of doing it, I very possibly might have. But I didn't."

"Killing an innocent woman and a child?" Jessie said. "How noble."

"I told you I didn't do it," Bishop replied, "but I also told you how much getting Malloche means—how many lives his capture or death will save."

"Well, either way, I don't see how I could possibly be of any—" Jessie felt a sudden chill. She took several deep breaths through her nose, trying to maintain some composure. "Alex, or whatever your name is, tell me something. That car trouble you saved me from, was that rigged?"

There was the briefest hesitation, during which Jessie was certain Bishop was mulling over whether or not to lie.

"I . . . Jessie, I was desperate to learn about Gilbride," he said. "I needed to get inside the neurosurgical service quickly. From what I could tell, he wasn't someone I could trust. You were. I had to get close to you."

"Jesus."

"I'm sorry. I really am. Jessie, I admit the way I met you and some of what I told you about myself was contrived, but none of what I've told you tonight has been. I'm sorry I had to lie, but I need your help. I'm *begging* you to help."

"Get out!"

Bishop stood.

"Jessie—"

Jessie leaped around the edge of the desk and punched him viciously on the side of his face. Then she pushed the photos at him. He clutched them clumsily against his chest and backed into the hall.

"Alex?" she said less stridently.

He took a step back into the doorway.

"Yes?"

She moved forward and slapped him, raising a crimson, palm-shaped welt on his cheek.

"I'll think about it," she said.

She slammed the door in his face.

CHAPTER **19**

MIDNIGHT . . . TWELVE-THIRTY . . . ONE. LYING
in her darkened bedroom, Jessie watched the time pass on
the lighted dial of her clock radio. One-thirty . . . two. She
remembered a vial of sleeping pills in her medicine cabinet from some bygone era in her life. Although she hadn't
taken any in years, and they were probably expired, she
seriously considered trying one or two. Finally, she picked
up the novel she had been inching through at a page or
two a night, and padded out to the living room couch. She
was wearing her usual sleeping garb—an extra-large
T-shirt, this one from Earth Day. Nothing more.

She was furious at Alex's deception, but even more,
she was angry at herself for buying into it. Fairy tales
were tales—it was as simple as that. And expectations, as
often as not, led to pain.

Keep your expectations in check, tend to business, and good things will come, she told herself. Alex Bishop was nothing more than a pothole in the road of her life.

She set the book aside and tried some warm milk. Nothing was going to calm her thoughts. Gratefully, Ben Rasheed's selling his OR time had left her with a relatively light day ahead. If she had to endure a night without sleep, so be it. She had the proven constitution to work thirty-six hours with little or no rest, although her body inevitably paid the price when she did.

Was Alex telling the truth? she asked herself.

The photos were impressive, but they could just as easily belong to the killer as to the CIA. The sicker the man, the slicker the lies. Who said that? Maybe no one. Maybe the line was all hers. The slicker the man, the sicker the lies.

Two-thirty.

Jessie queued up a ball in Pin Bot and lost it between the flippers after just five seconds or so—a catastrophe that could have been avoided by a right-hand nudge that was usually routine for her. This simply wasn't going to be her night for anything. She opened the novel again, read a few sentences, and then set it aside. The questions kept rumbling through her mind like tanks.

How could Alex be so certain Malloche was headed to Carl for his surgery? Was he really the dogged CIA pursuer making an expert guess based on five years of tracking down his prey, or was he one of Malloche's people, or even Malloche himself, in the process of making up his mind about who would cut on him? If Malloche was Mr. Thorough, as Alex claimed, it only made sense that he would check up on Gilbride and the whole neurosurgical service at EMMC before letting Carl drill open his head. And what more reliable, efficient way to do that than to start up a romance with one of the surgeons in his department?

Why in the hell couldn't it all have been real?

She rubbed at the exhaustion stinging her eyes as she again confronted the most troubling question of all: What if Alex was telling the truth? What if he *was* so set on capturing this Malloche that he would use her as he had? And even if she ever did come to trust what he was saying, could she possibly agree to help him? What about the patient/physician confidentiality she so treasured? Did it not extend to Gilbride's patients—even to one who might be a killer?

The telephone startled her so that she sloshed some of the warm milk onto her thigh.

"Hello?"

"Jessie, it's Alex. Please don't hang up."

About to do just that, Jessie kept the receiver to her ear.

"What do you want?" she asked.

"I need to talk to you."

"No!"

"Jessie, please. Everything I told you in your office was true. Deceiving you the way I have was stupid and cruel. I'm sorry I did it. I'm under tremendous pressure, and in the world I come from almost nothing matters more than getting the job done. But it was still a dumb mistake."

"Okay, you've apologized. Good night."

"Wait!"

"Dammit, Alex, you've hurt me. I don't want anything more to do with you. Now—"

"Listen, Jessie. Malloche is in your hospital right now. I'm almost certain of it. If I'm right, there's a good chance people are going to be killed—maybe me, maybe you, maybe even some of your patients."

Jessie sensed herself freeze at the last possibility. She felt certain Alex knew that she would. *Damn him!*

"Where are you?" she asked finally.

"I . . . I'm right outside. I've been here for a couple of hours, thinking. I had decided to leave and not try to speak with you until the morning, but then your light went on."

"So you knew where I lived and which one was my apartment. Why am I not surprised?"

"Jessie, I'm going to get Malloche no matter what. But it would be a hell of a lot easier and maybe a lot safer for everyone with your help."

Jessie chewed anxiously on her lip, wishing she was anyplace else.

"Ring the bell. I'll buzz you in," she heard herself say.

Her condo was on the third floor. There was a security camera mounted downstairs in the outer foyer. Channel Two. She switched on the TV and flipped to the channel. Alex, wearing a light windbreaker, entered the outside door and looked up at the camera as if he knew she would be watching.

The doorbell sounded. She went to her bedroom and pulled on a pair of sweatpants and a hooded sweatshirt. She then stood by the intercom box, reminding herself that, Malloche or CIA, the man she was about to allow into her apartment at two-thirty in the morning was a professional killer. The bell sounded again, and she buzzed him in. Then she opened her door and watched him trudge up to the top of the wide, carpeted stairway that had once graced a sea captain's mansion.

"Thanks for seeing me," he said.

Fatigue etched his face.

She motioned him to an easy chair and took a place on the end of the sofa farthest from him.

The sicker the man, the slicker the lie, she reminded herself.

"What do you want from me?" she asked.

Bishop leaned forward.

"I'm almost certain Rolf Hermann is Claude Malloche," he said. "In fact, I've contacted the people in Madrid. They're in the process of sending Jorge Cardoza over here right now. There are many factors in favor of Hermann being Malloche, and not many against it. That wife of his is what made me suspicious of him in the first place. Although I've never seen her, I've been told that Malloche has a remarkably beautiful wife—a former recruit of his from Austria. Her name's Arlette. Not Orlis."

"The Countess seems pretty cold, all right," Jessie said, "but Rolf actually seems like quite a nice man, and he barely speaks English."

Alex laughed disdainfully.

"My bet is he can speak it and half a dozen other languages without an accent. I've got people in Europe trying to see if there even is a Count Rolf Hermann, but that could take time."

"You don't have a lot of that, I'm afraid. Hermann's being operated on tomorrow afternoon—hell, it's *this* afternoon now."

Bishop looked startled.

"I thought he was on the schedule for Thursday."

"His wife paid off one of my patients to switch. Dr. Gilbride is operating on him as the second case later today."

"If I tip my hand and make a move on Hermann before Cardoza gets here to identify him, and I'm wrong, I'll most likely have ruined everything. Malloche will hear about it. I don't know how, but he will. He'll go someplace else, and I'll lose what is probably my last chance."

"But you think it's Hermann."

"Right age, right build, right wife, right timing, European. Yes, I think it's him. And those so-called children of his. They're bogus. I'd bet on it. If he's operated on today, when will he be ready to leave the hospital?"

"Assuming there are no unusual problems from the surgery, it could be anywhere from five to seven days. But this is a tough tumor. Given its location"—*and the flaws in Carl's surgical technique,* she wanted to add, but didn't—"there is the significant possibility, even with our robot helping with the operation, that there will be damage to some intervening structures. If that happens, he could be in the hospital much longer."

Jessie suddenly realized that she had just crossed the line and disclosed information on a patient. If she allowed Alex to hang around her, it wouldn't be the last time. She was either in, or she was out.

"In that case," Alex was saying, "I'm not going to do anything that will interfere with the surgery. If I'm right about Hermann being Malloche, and if there is a God, the man will end up permanently paralyzed from his eyebrows to his toes—totally aware, but immobile forever. The perfect justice."

"Your justice, maybe," Jessie said. "I'd like you to go now."

"But—"

"You've apologized to me, you've said your piece, you've asked me to help you. Now I'd like you to leave me alone. I told you in my office I would think about getting involved. At the moment, I'm disinclined even to speak to you anymore. If that feeling changes, you'll hear from me."

Their eyes met, and Jessie quickly looked away. She couldn't stop remembering the hour after Jackie Terrell's death—Alex's touch, how much his caring and insight into how she was feeling had meant to her. Well, he wasn't going to get to her again. Intellectually, she was becoming inclined to believe what he was telling her. But she was not ready to forgive the lies.

Alex stood and seemed for a moment as if he had something else to say. Then he simply shook his head in frustration.

"Thanks for listening," he said as he left.

CHAPTER 20

THERE WAS AN ELECTRIC TENSION SURROUNDING the MRI operating room as one by one the players began to assemble for the robot-assisted tumor extraction on Count Rolf Hermann. Jessie stood outside the room, watching the silent, slow-motion ballet through the heavy glass observation window, and wondering if the broad-shouldered man being ministered to by the anesthesiologist was, as Alex had claimed, the ruthless, remorseless killer of hundreds.

To her right, Hans Pfeffer and the console tech were checking and rechecking their instruments. Jessie pictured the action a floor above them where, in the cluttered, space-age computer center, half a dozen geek geniuses were preparing their remarkable machines to process the imaging data sent to them by the massive MRI. Their focus throughout this operation would be not on the patient, but on the tumor and the normal structures surrounding it. In addition to Pfeffer, a Dutchman, there were scientists from Germany and Sweden, Russia and Israel and the U.S. And for the next four or five hours, the life of a man they had never laid eyes on would be in their hands.

It was well within her rights for her to watch the surgery, but Jessie still felt obligated to get Carl's permission. Although she had spent significantly more hours than he had working ARTIE through any number of test matrices and animal models, as well as the ill-fated effort on Pete Roslanski, she felt like the understudy, asking the star if she could watch from the wings. For a few seconds, it seemed that Gilbride might actually refuse her request—surprising, given that he relished an audience for his performances.

"Well, Jessie, I certainly don't mind you hanging around during the procedure," he said, finally, "but with Eastman Tolliver on a riser behind me, and Skip Porter in the OR as well to keep an eye on ARTIE, I think it might be a bit crowded in the room. How about you watch the proceedings outside on the screen in the console area."

"Actually, that's what I was planning on doing," she replied.

"Fine, then. I've gone over ARTIE most thoroughly with Skip, and both of them appear to be in perfect working order."

He chuckled at what was, for him, a raucous joke.

"That's great."

"The tumor is sitting pretty for a transsphenoid approach—up the nose and in."

"Up the nose and in," Jessie parroted, trying to sound more enthusiastic than sarcastic.

Hermann's meningioma was, indeed, the ideal tumor in the ideal location for ARTIE. But Jessie remained unconvinced that Gilbride—or even she herself, for that matter—was fluid enough, and comfortable enough with guiding the apparatus, to risk using it on a patient—even one who might be a remorseless killer.

It was nearly two in the afternoon of a day that had started clear and sunny, but had clouded over by noon. Jessie estimated she had slept at most for an hour and a half, just before dawn. For once, she was glad she was not the one operating.

Skip Porter entered the console area from the scrub room, waved a dripping hand at Jessie, and backed into the operating room to be toweled off, gowned, and gloved by the scrub nurse. He was tall, gangly, and refreshingly free of ambition, with bleached blond hair and a ragged goatee that reminded Jessie of Shaggy in *Scooby Doo*. He also had a commitment to perfection in his work, and a practical understanding of electromechanics that rivaled any Jessie had encountered at MIT. If Skip was nervous about his second case with ARTIE and Gilbride, he hid it well. His report to Jessie on the Marci Sheprow surgery was that both robot and surgeon had performed admirably, and that the tumor dissection, however straightforward, had been flawless. But he knew, as did Jessie, that Rolf Hermann's complex meningioma presented an infinitely greater challenge.

ARTIE-2 was sterilized and covered on a steel tray. Porter would check it out one final time as he attached it to the port next to the guidance panel where Gilbride would be working.

There were seven in the OR now: the scrub and circulating nurses, anesthesiologist Pramod Sanjay, a med student rotating through Sanjay's service, a neurosurgical resident from Ghana named Danl Toomei, who would be Gilbride's assistant, Skip, and of course, the patient. Next to arrive was Eastman Tolliver, looking fit and trim in his sky blue scrubs. His eyes smiled at Jessie from above his mask as he came over to shake her hand before entering the OR.

"I must say, this is all very exciting," he said.

"Yes, it is," she replied, "although I'm not sure Count Hermann would share our enthusiasm."

She nodded at the scene through the window, where the anesthesiologist was sliding Rolf Hermann through the central opening of the MRI and into position between the huge tori, where his head could be bolted to the circular immobilization frame.

"Quite a remarkable scene," Tolliver said. "Most impressive."

Carl would be pleased to hear you say that, Jessie thought.

"I've been down here dozens and dozens of times as observer *and* surgeon, and it still amazes me," she said. "To someone who hasn't seen it before, it must be like landing on another planet."

"Perfectly put. I'm very excited. Well, I guess I'd better get in there."

"You'll have the best view looking over Carl's right shoulder. That way you can watch the patient, the control panel for ARTIE, Dr. Gilbride's hands, and the MRI screen."

"Excellent. That's where I'll set up, then." He looked through the observation window and added, "I'm going to say a prayer for that poor man."

And I'll say one for Carl.

"In the OR, prayer is always a good idea."

Tolliver lingered for a few more seconds and then entered the operating room.

Eight in. Moments later, with the arrival of a translator, there were nine. One to go. The crowd around the console outside the OR had swelled as well. Danl Toomei's back was about all anyone could see through the observation window, so most were clustered near the twin screens—one projecting the surgical field from an overhead camera, and the other displaying a duplicate of the images being transmitted to Gilbride and his assistant from the computer center.

Surgical theater at its best, Jessie thought. *Hog heaven for Carl Gilbride.*

Moments before Gilbride made his appearance, Jessie's attention was drawn through the crowd to the safe area—the area thirty feet or so from the OR door, beyond which scrubs did not have to be worn. Alex Bishop was there in his hospital security uniform, leaning casually against a thick, concrete-covered support pillar. There was nothing casual, though, in his eyes or in the set of the muscles of his face. He was alternating between scanning the observers and peering as best as he could manage through the window into the OR.

His gaze connected with hers, and he nodded briefly. She returned the gesture and then shrugged her bewilderment at the whole deal.

Where's the truth, Alex? she wondered. *Where's the truth?*

For a time the images of bodies arranged in a grotesque tableau, with bullet holes in their foreheads, occupied her thoughts. Her unpleasant reverie ended abruptly when, hands up, palms in, dramatically banging the scrub room door into the wall as he backed through it, Carl Gilbride crossed before the multitude and entered the OR.

Let the games begin, Jessie thought as Gilbride was quickly gowned and gloved. Having seen his often rushed and awkward technique in the OR, Jessie realized that ARTIE, with its meticulous, microscopic abilities, might well represent an improvement.

She scanned the two monitor screens. The operative field was prepped and ready. The color-enhanced image of Hermann's brain tumor, displayed by the crew upstairs, had excellent resolution. At the moment, normal brain tissue was navy blue, and the meningioma canary yellow. Blood vessels, appropriately, were crimson. On the other side of the observation window, all the principals were in position. Although Gilbride was largely screened from her by the resident, Jessie could see Eastman Tolliver on an eight-inch riser, watching intently from over Carl's right shoulder.

A four-million-dollar grant . . . Claude Malloche . . . Count Rolf Hermann . . . Alex Bishop . . . so much was riding on the next few hours.

"Ready, Dr. Sanjay?" Gilbride asked.

"No problems," the anesthesiologist said.

"Dr. Toomei?"

"Ready, sir."

"Mrs. Duncan?"

"All set," the scrub nurse replied.

"Dr. Pfeffer?"

"At your command, sir," the radiologist called out.

"Well, then, scalpel and periosteal elevator, please."

The approach to getting ARTIE into place was straightforward. With the Count fully asleep, a probe would be inserted through a small incision up one nostril, and a half-inch hole would be drilled through the skull where the bone was thinnest. A fine guide wire would be fed in through the opening, and ARTIE would then be sent in along the wire, and directed to the anterior edge of the meningioma. If all went well, most of the two hours or more that would have been spent simply reaching the tumor by traditional methods would have been saved, to say nothing of the elimination of much of the damage to intervening structures.

Go, ARTIE! Jessie cheered. *Go!*

The insertion went perfectly, and was accompanied by murmurs of amazement from those in the crowd, when Gilbride announced he was in position and ready to begin the dissection. Jessie had to admit grudgingly that the neurosurgical chief was handling the controls of their invention quite expertly.

The ultrasound liquefaction and removal of Hermann's tumor began uneventfully. Gilbride, working with appropriate care, seemed firmly in control. In spite of herself, every few minutes, Jessie's attention drifted away from the screens and over to where Alex was watching. From time to time, he was gone, no doubt going through the motions of his security job. But mostly he was there, up against his pillar, watching.

"Okay, Dr. Sanjay," Gilbride said. "I think it is appropriate now to awaken our patient for some functional MRI mapping."

Jessie studied the tumor image on the screen. About a third of the meningioma had been removed—the most accessible part. There was still a good deal that could have been melted away before Hermann's cooperation was needed. It was almost as if Gilbride was stalling—doing whatever he could to delay an attack on the portion of the tumor that was most intimately adjacent to normal brain.

It took a while for the anesthesia to lessen. During that time, Gilbride continued to pick away at what remained of the bulkiest portion of the tumor. Jessie was watching the monitor nonstop now. She was certain no one else appreciated it yet, but several times, Gilbride had started

ARTIE off in the wrong direction, then quickly reversed. He seemed to be having trouble with the spatial relationships between the views of the tumor and the movement of the robot. To Jessie, ARTIE was essentially a video-game race car, able to move in any direction, but with controls that were in a fixed position. So when ARTIE was moving in one direction, a right-hand move on the control panel meant a right turn. But in the opposite direction, a right turn meant going left on the controls, and in between, there were literally an infinite number of permutations. To a video-game junkie like Jessie, the moves were second nature. But she could see that as the field of surgery grew smaller and smaller, Gilbride was having more and more trouble maneuvering.

Twice he turned off the audio and called Skip Porter over for a whispered exchange. Both times, apparently assured by Skip that the robot was functioning properly, Gilbride returned to the surgery.

"Count Hermann," he said now, "lift your right hand a bit if you can hear me."

The translator, a nurse who had translated on occasion for some of Jessie's patients, spoke from behind Gilbride, just to Eastman Tolliver's left. Despite his adequate comprehension of spoken English, it had been the Count's decision to have commands relayed to him in German. If Alex was right about the man's facility with languages, Jessie was thinking, the request was part of the charade. Through the overhead camera, Hermann's chest, where his hands rested beneath the drapes, was visible. Immediately after Carl's order was translated, the Count responded with the requested movement.

The operation proceeded for another twenty minutes. Jessie wished the overhead camera was focused on ARTIE's control panel rather than the essentially static operative field. That view, along with the MRI, would have told her a great deal. Again and again now, as the dissection became more difficult, she saw Gilbride miss once, even twice, before directing the robot along the proper course. The errors were minuscule hitches—like the feints of a prizefighter before striking in the other direction. But they were errors nonetheless. She was certain of it.

As ARTIE ate more and more into the tumor, closer to normal brain, Gilbride was clearly having more and more difficulty controlling its movement. At one point, where fibers of normal brain had to have been damaged by an errant thrust, Hans Pfeffer looked over, caught Jessie's eye, and shook his head grimly.

Alex, perhaps reading her expression and intensified concentration, managed to connect with her long enough to mouth the words, *What's happening?* Her response was a shrug.

Gilbride placed the LED goggles on his patient and requested a functional magnetic resonance sequence, the brain mapping alternating with more dissection. Twice, Hermann seemed unable to follow commands. Both times, ARTIE was slightly off course. This was no mechanical failure. The technique, at this level, was simply beyond Gilbride's ability. At one point Jessie thought he might back the robot out—admit he could go no further and simply opt for a full, open craniotomy. But Gilbride persisted. She wondered if it was getting to the point where he was pitting Rolf Hermann's brain against a four-million-dollar grant.

Another muted conversation with Skip. Another helpless gesture by the research technician.

ARTIE is functioning fine, Jessie could almost hear him whispering.

Hans Pfeffer made his way over to her and pulled her aside.

"Do something!" he whispered.

It was the most animated she had ever seen the laconic Dutchman.

"You have a suggestion?"

"There's the microphone. Tell him to stop. The robot's just not ready for this."

Oh, ARTIE's ready, all right, she wanted to reply. *Ready and able.*

"Hans," she whispered back, "Carl is chief of this department, and one of the most powerful men in this hospital. He controls my job, and I would bet a good portion of your research funds as well. Nobody would survive busting in on him in the middle of a case with an audience like this. Nobody."

There were concerned murmurs in the crowd now as first the other radiologist then the two neurosurgeons observing the case picked up on what was happening.

"Get in there!" Hans whispered. "Jessie, get in there before—"

Pfeffer stopped in midsentence. He and Jessie stared at the screen where a faint gray puff had just appeared, right at the snout and just to the left of ARTIE, clearly outside the boundary of the tumor. The smudge was tiny but unmistakable, and it was definitely expanding. A deep arterial hemorrhage—the neurosurgical equivalent of a nuclear explosion. Guided off course by Carl, one of ARTIE's pincers had torn an artery. Seconds later, Gilbride's strained voice came over the intercom.

"Dr. Copeland, are you still out there?"

Jessie ran to the microphone over the console.

"I'm here."

"You see what's going on. ARTIE's malfunctioning. Could you come in here, please?"

On the screen, the hemorrhage was continuing to grow. Count Rolf Hermann had begun writhing as the pain caused by rapidly building pressure deep within his brain overcame the twilight anesthesia that had been used for his functional MRI.

"Pramod," Jessie ordered to the anesthesiologist, "put him to sleep and drop his pressure. Give him forty of Lasix and a hundred of mannitol *stat*. Carl, I'll be right in."

The crowd parted as Jessie made a quick check to be certain she was wearing no metal, pulled on a hair covering and mask, and hurried into the OR. The scrub nurse was waiting with gloves and a gown. Danl Toomei stepped back from his spot between the tori across from Gilbride to allow her in. As she moved into his place, she looked over at Gilbride. What she could see of his face was blanched, but there was no way to read his eyes. Above and behind Gilbride's right shoulder, looming like a surgical specter, seemingly transfixed by the scene, was Eastman Tolliver.

"Enhance the hemorrhage, please," Jessie said.

"Roger that," one of Pfeffer's people in the lab upstairs replied.

In seconds, on her screen and Gilbride's, the blood leaking into Hermann's brain was transformed into a crimson grid. Almost certainly, the torn vessel was a branch of the left anterior cerebral artery.

Gilbride cut off the sound. He leaned forward so that no one but Jessie—not the scrub nurse, not even Tolliver—could hear what he was saying.

"It . . . the robot just broke down," he whispered. "I couldn't control it."

"I know," Jessie responded.

"That hemorrhage is huge already. Pressure's building. What should we do?"

"Fry it," Jessie said simply. "Do you mind if we switch sides so I can get at ARTIE's guidance console?"

Gilbride hesitated. It required no telepathy to know why. His patient's life versus the humiliation of giving up the principal surgeon's spot in front of a large audience—for most not a difficult call, but for Carl, gut-wrenching. Jessie was about to remind him that he could always blame the disaster on a mechanical defect, when he apparently reminded himself.

"Come on over," he said.

Jessie took her position at the control panel and switched on the microphone.

"Hey, guys," she called to the crew upstairs, "see if you can get me some sort of enhancement of the left anterior circulation and a leaking artery just branching off it. I'm going to try and swing ARTIE around and cauterize the tear."

"We copy," came the heavily accented voice of Israeli programming wizard Manny Geller.

The neodymium-YAG laser—YAG for yttrium aluminum garnet—was a relatively recent addition to ARTIE, giving it the power to cauterize along with its existing abilities to melt tissue with ultrasound and to suction debris and fluid through a fairly large tube. This would be the first time Jessie had used the laser on human tissue. But there was no time to open up Rolf Hermann's skull and go after the bleeder directly.

The image beamed down from the computer lab was exactly what Jessie wanted.

"There it is," she said. "See?"

The leaking vessel was microns from ARTIE. The

trick would be to back the robot up and turn it slightly. Slowly, but with unerring control, Jessie completed the maneuver.

"Okay, cross your fingers. Ready, aim . . . fire."

She depressed the button controlling the laser beam. The blood surrounding the leak instantly boiled. Immediately, the expanding hemorrhage stopped. For one minute, two, they stood there in silence, watching the screens.

"Jessie," Hans Pfeffer called in, "the bleeding's stopped and the repair seems to be holding. Well done. Well done."

Someone standing near Pfeffer began clapping, then several more joined in, the sound reverberating through the speakers in the OR. Moments later, the OR staff in the room was applauding as well—all except the man standing across from her.

"Nicely done, Doctor," Gilbride said, loud enough for all to hear. "I'm afraid it's back to the drawing board for our friend ARTIE."

"Before we bring ARTIE out, I want to try and aspirate as much of the hemorrhage as we can."

"Please do. After Count Hermann wakes up, we'll have to discuss removing the rest of the meningioma sometime in the future."

Jessie stared at her boss, but said nothing. She had seen enough miracles, including the one in NICU 6 right now, to know that anything was possible. But the truth was, Rolf Hermann, or Claude Malloche, or whoever the man lying there was, had about as much chance of waking up from this tragedy as she did of winning the lottery.

CHAPTER 21

KNOWING THE SPACE-AGE EFFICIENCY OF THE
hospital grapevine, Jessie was certain that word of the fiasco in the MRI-OR had spread throughout the hospital by the time Rolf Hermann was transferred to the NICU on Surgical Seven. His condition was listed with the switchboard operator as critical, but that really did not tell the whole story. The Count's pupils were dilated and unreactive to light or any other stimulus. The Babinski sign—an upward movement of the great toe when the sole of the foot is stimulated—was present bilaterally, signifying that there was essentially a functional disconnection of the brain from the rest of the body.

Carl Gilbride was distracted and irritable, and several times snapped at the nurses as his patient was being transferred to the unit bed. For brief moments, Jessie actually felt some sympathy for the man. But in the main, she was disgusted with him and not a little embarrassed for the department. The combination of his hubris, greed, and inflated opinion of his surgical skills had led him to a series of decisions that would ultimately cost a life and, in all likelihood, a four-million-dollar grant as well. Now he had insisted that Jessie accompany him into the family room to speak with Orlis Hermann and the Count's sons and daughter. Orlis was waiting for them in the family room along with her stepdaughter and one of her stepsons. Jessie mused on where Hermann's other son might be at so critical a time, then took a seat behind Gilbride. As she surveyed the family, she wondered if Rolf Hermann's beautiful wife could really be, as Alex claimed, an assassin and hardened mercenary, and if the grown offspring, sitting there statue-like, could be nothing more than bodyguards, chosen from Claude Malloche's elite inner circle. If these people were capable of murdering Sylvan Mays, who hadn't even performed an operation on Malloche, how would they treat the ones who had botched it?

Tone it down, Carl, she was thinking. *Tell them it's bad, but for God's sake, don't tell them it's hopeless.*

"Well," Gilbride said, tenting his fingers in a blatantly pensive pose. "I'm afraid the news isn't good. Things started off well enough, and we had a good deal of the tumor removed, but then we ran into some . . . problems."

"Problems?" Orlis said stonily.

"Mrs. Hermann"—Gilbride paused as if searching for words—"during the operation, your husband had a fairly large hemorrhage into his brain."

"A hemorrhage? From what?"

"I can't say for certain. Sometimes, during major surgery, arteries just . . . rupture. In this case, with the

Count's tumor situated so deep in his brain, it's possible that an artery might have been nicked and bled."

Orlis quickly translated in German for the Count's offspring. The son asked a question, which she answered. Jessie tried to get a read on the group, but failed completely. If they were all killers, then they were damn fine actors as well. If they weren't killers, then Alex was either dead wrong, or a deadly sham himself.

"What can we expect now?" Orlis asked.

Please, Jessie pleaded silently. *Please tell them there's hope.*

If Gilbride handled things right, at least there might be time for Alex to make a move before anyone got hurt.

The neurosurgical chief shook his head grimly. His expression was tight and severe. Jessie had seen the look before. The man was preparing to paint the bleakest picture possible in hopes that any improvement would make him look good. It was exactly what she had been praying he would not do.

"Well," he said, tenting his fingers again and looking down at them, "the hemorrhage was quite extensive. Dr. Copeland and I were able to use our intraoperative robot to cauterize the vessel and stop the bleeding, but I'm afraid by that time a good deal of damage had been done. I—"

"Dr. Gilbride," Orlis said, her blue-white eyes impaling him, "would you please stop mumbling and stalling and tell us if my husband is going to survive this."

No! Jessie's thoughts screamed. *Don't react!*

"Mrs. Hermann," Gilbride replied, clearly frayed, "I know you're upset, but I do not appreciate being spoken to like that."

"I brought you a man who was completely intact, and

you hand me back a . . . a vegetable. What do you expect, praise?"

Jessie couldn't remember the last time she had seen Gilbride so uncomfortable. He stood and faced Orlis, his arms folded across his chest, his cheeks flushed.

"Mrs. Hermann, you and Count Hermann read all the possible outcomes of his operation and attested in writing to your acceptance of them. Now, we'll continue doing everything we can for him. When there is any news to report, we'll find you. In the meantime, beginning tomorrow afternoon, for the forty-eight hours I'm in New York, Dr. Copeland will be covering my service."

"New York!" Orlis exclaimed, almost in unison with Jessie.

"I'm due to sit on a panel at a very important conference tomorrow afternoon at NYU," Gilbride said with far too much pride in his voice.

For God's sake, Carl, can't you hide that outrageous ego for once? Our lives could depend on it.

"Dr. Gilbride," Orlis said with chilling calm, "I promise you that if you leave Boston with my husband in this condition, you will regret it."

Jessie expected a combative response from her chief. Instead, Gilbride just stood there, transfixed by the woman.

"We'll talk about it in the morning," he said finally, in a strained, unnatural voice.

Without so much as a glance at Jessie, he turned and hurried from the room.

Jessie forced herself to remain still—not simply to leap up and follow him.

"He's very upset," she managed to say.

"You'd best speak with him, Doctor Copeland," Orlis replied with her same frightening calm. "Tell him I meant what I said. I don't want him leaving this hospital for any reason other than to go home and rest. If he deserts my husband, he will regret it."

Regret as in Sylvan Mays? Jessie wondered.

"I'll tell him," she said.

"RAISE YOUR RIGHT hand. No, Devereau, your *other* right hand. Are you ragging on me?"

"Just . . . want see . . . if you were pay . . . attention," Sara said thickly.

With great effort, she raised her right arm off the bed and issued a clumsy but unmistakable thumbs up. Jessie answered her in kind.

Progress, progress, progress, she chanted to herself. All that ever mattered in neurosurgical post-ops was progress. And progress Sara most certainly was making.

Shaken by the exchange with Orlis, Jessie forced herself to focus through the neuro check on her patient. Orlis . . . Alex . . . Gilbride . . . Malloche. In the kind of acute-care medicine she practiced, distraction was often the touchstone to disaster. She was beginning to feel smothered. She badly needed to talk to *someone* about what was happening. Emily DelGreco was the only candidate.

Jessie wrote down the order to keep Sara in the NICU, although clinically she no longer needed it. The nurses on the floor were quite good, but the ones in the unit were special, with a bulldog determination to do whatever was necessary for their patients' recovery. Until utilization review began making a fuss, or the bed became needed for someone else, or Sara jumped up and demanded a transfer herself, she would remain right where she was.

By the time Jessie had finished writing, Sara was asleep, exhausted. Jessie brushed her cheek gently, then headed to the phone at the nurses' station.

Emily had begged off work for the day. There was a show at her younger son's school. Jessie hoped she could reach her at home. It would be a huge relief to share the burden Alex had placed on her.

Emily's oldest, Ted, answered.

"Mom's not here, Jessie. She went out an hour or so ago. I thought she was with you."

"Why would you think that?"

"She got a phone call, then she said she had to go to the hospital for a while."

"Did she say who called her?"

"Nope. I just assumed it was you."

Jessie shifted nervously. The DelGrecos lived in Brookline, just a short way from Eastern Mass Medical. If she had left an hour ago, she would be here by now.

"Your dad home?"

"Nope. He almost never gets home before seven."

"When he does, would you ask him to page me at the hospital?"

"Sure."

"And if you hear from Mom, tell her the same thing."

"Okay. Is something the matter?"

"No, no. Just some stuff going on with one of the patients that I want to check with her about. This place is so huge that your mom's probably in another part of the hospital right now. I'll have her paged."

"You still have that pinball machine in your apartment?"

"Of course. You'll have to come over sometime soon and play. As I recall, you came close to my record last time."

"Hardly close. But I'd like another try. That was fun."

"Take care, Ted."

Jessie set the receiver down and immediately paged Emily. Fifteen minutes went by without a return call. Jessie was hunched over Sara's chart, writing a progress note, when Alex Bishop startled her from behind.

"Hey, Doc," he said softly.

"Jesus, don't sneak up on me like that! Clear your throat or something."

"Sorry." He looked about to ensure no one was listening. "Can I talk to you?"

"Alex, I still don't know if I feel comfortable saying anything to you about our patients."

"You don't believe what I've told you?"

"I . . . don't know what to believe."

He passed over a piece of paper.

"Here's a phone number in Virginia. Ask for a man named Benson, Harold Benson. He's head of internal affairs at the agency. They're the ones who are after me. He knows me and what I've been doing these past five years. If you tell him the situation and ask him nicely, he might say who I am."

"It won't prove anything. These phone things can be set up."

"Okay, then, Doctor," he said, his eyes narrowed and hard, "play it any way you want. I said I was sorry for not starting with the truth. I can't do any more than that. With or without your help, I'm going to bring Claude Malloche down. If people get hurt in the process, it'll be on your head as much as mine."

He turned and started down the hall.

"Wait," Jessie called out, stopping him. "What do you want to know?"

Alex walked slowly back. The intensity in his eyes was still there, but not the unsettling hardness.

"Thank you," he whispered. "What's the situation?"

"Your friend Hermann, or Malloche, is in room two on a vent," she said, feeling relief at having made a decision.

"So I saw. Is he going to wake up?"

Jessie shook her head.

"Stranger things have happened," she said. "But in my opinion, if he wakes up, look for a star in the east."

"How long can he go on like this?"

"I couldn't say. Hours? Weeks? I've been surprised both ways."

"But he's not going to wake up."

"He had a hell of a hemorrhage. There's been pretty massive brain damage. That's all I can say."

"Okay. As far as I know, Jorge Cardoza will be on his way here from Madrid tomorrow. If Hermann is still on the respirator, we'll have to find a way to get Cardoza into the hospital without having him run into the wife."

"If it comes to that, I'll see what I can do to help. Right now, Orlis is in a pretty foul mood."

"Her name's Arlette, remember?"

"Orlis, Arlette—whoever she is, she just threatened Dr. Gilbride."

"She did what?"

"He said he was flying to New York tomorrow to be on some sort of panel, and that I'd be in charge of the Count while he was gone. She told him he'd regret it if he did. Carl was pretty shaken up."

"Good. That could save his life. Maybe it's time to tell him what's going on—who he's dealing with."

"And you're certain who that is?"

"Virtually. Interpol hasn't been able to come up with any match for the fingerprints I sent them. But that's not surprising. They have a few dozen sets on file from assassinations that are believed to be Malloche's work, including those murders at that MRI clinic in France. But it's possible not a single one belongs to him."

"Or they could all be Malloche if he's more than one person."

"Nice theory. But he's only one person all right. That guy right in there. How did Gilbride screw up so badly in the operation?"

"He shouldn't have read his press clippings after the Marci Sheprow surgery. That's how."

"If Malloche dies, I want his body."

"If Malloche dies, I want protection for Carl and me."

"I'll find a way. Meanwhile, we're going to stay on the job."

"We?"

"I told you I had a little help."

"But—"

"That's all I can say." He scribbled a phone number on a piece of progress note paper. "This is an answering service here in Boston. They have instructions on how to contact me if necessary. If anything happens to Hermann, just call and tell them. We'll wait it out until Cardoza arrives. Meanwhile, if Malloche dies, I'll be going after his body, his wife, and those three junior killers. Once we get a positive ID from Cardoza and then get Arlette Malloche and her so-called stepchildren into custody, we'll learn what we need to know."

"You scare me, Alex."

"Sometimes, even after all these years, I scare myself.

Jessie, I know how difficult it was to decide to help me. Thank you for trusting me."

"I don't," she said.

JESSIE WATCHED AS he made his way down the corridor, pausing just long enough to glimpse into room 2 as he passed. *Five years.* Almost as long as it had taken her to complete her neurosurgical residency. It was a hell of a long time to chase an obsession—especially with so little success. Now, with no firm proof that the patient in 2 was Malloche, and with the man so near death, it was possible Alex's quest would end not with a bang, but with the whimper of lingering uncertainty.

Jessie checked the time—nearly twenty minutes since her page to Emily had been sent. She wondered if Emily's beeper could possibly be malfunctioning or might simply have been turned off. At that instant her own pager sounded. The display gave Alice Twitchell's name and extension.

"Oh, Dr. Copeland, I'm so glad you answered so quickly," Carl's meticulous assistant said. "I'm in Dr. Gilbride's office with Mr. Tolliver. He's having a severe headache—a migraine. He told me to page you and not to bother trying to find Dr. Gilbride. Could you possibly come down and have a look at him?"

"I'll be right over," Jessie said. "Alice, do you by any chance know where Emily DelGreco might be?"

"Gee, no, Dr. Copeland," the woman said apologetically. "I have no idea."

CHAPTER 22

WHEN JESSIE ARRIVED, EASTMAN TOLLIVER, WEAR-
ing gray slacks and a navy blue blazer, was supine on the
Moroccan leather sofa in Carl's waiting room, a pillow
under his knees, his feet hanging several inches over the
armrest. He held the crook of his elbow pressed tightly
across his eyes, and was actually trembling with discomfort. There was a wastebasket strategically placed on the
rug beside him. Alice Twitchell was trying to move his
arm enough to get a damp washcloth onto his forehead.

"Eastman, it's me," Jessie said, kneeling at his side.
"Can you hear me all right?"

Tolliver nodded.

"It's beginning to let up," he said hoarsely. "I've had
these before."

His speech sounded just a little bit thick.

"How long has it been this time?"

"Fifteen or twenty minutes," Alice said. "Dr. Gilbride was supposed to meet Mr. Tolliver forty-five minutes ago, but he called to say he'd be late."

"We had some business to attend to in the unit," Jessie said.

She gently removed Eastman's arm from across his face.

"You look a little peaked, my friend," she said, beginning her neurological evaluation with the observation that the skin fold on the right side of his mouth was marginally less pronounced than that on the left. "Could you open your eyes? . . . Good. Now, follow my finger if you can."

Pupils midposition, reactive . . . Slight weakness in lateral gaze, right eye . . . Possible slight droop, right lid . . .

"Eastman, could you show me your teeth, as if you were smiling?" *Possible facial weakness, right . . .* "Please stick out your tongue. Good. Now, squeeze my hands." *No obvious upper extremity weakness.*

"It's letting up," Tolliver said.

"Good. Eastman, when's the last time you saw a doctor for these headaches?"

"I don't know. A couple of years, maybe. He said they were migraine headaches."

"Do you take medicine?"

"Over-the-counter sometimes. That's all."

Jessie walked over to where Alice Twitchell stood watching.

"Alice, please call the ER and have them send a surgical resident, a gurney, and a nurse up here, *stat*," she said. "Then call radiology and tell them I'm going to need an MRI tonight."

"Yes, Doctor."

Alice scurried away.

The color had begun to return to Tolliver's face, and his eyes no longer seemed glazed over. The abnormal neurological findings were persisting, but while they were potentially a harbinger of serious pathology, like an aneurysm or a tumor, they were also consistent with certain variations of migraine. Fortunately, Jessie knew that with the technology at her disposal, it wasn't necessary to guess—or to wait very long.

"Eastman, how is it now?"

"Quite a bit better."

"Good. I've noticed some things in the rather incomplete exam I just did that concern me. I think you should have a few blood tests and an MRI."

"Are you sure I need all that?"

"I'm very sure. Your symptoms and my findings are quite possibly all due to migraine headaches, but I can't be positive. It may be fine for you to travel back to California, but not before we see your MRI. Have you had one before?"

"No, I haven't," Tolliver said, still lying motionless enough so that Jessie knew his pain was persisting.

"Okay," she said, "just take it easy. The stretcher will be here before long. Don't try to sit up."

"You're the boss."

Carl Gilbride cleared his throat to announce his presence in the doorway.

"What's going on here?"

"Oh, hi, Carl. Mr. Tolliver's having a headache. Twenty or twenty-five minutes now, pretty severe. He has a history of migraines."

Gilbride approached the sofa.

"Eastman, how are you feeling?"

"Not perfect, but improved, thank you."

"Well, that's excellent news. Excellent. I've made dinner reservations for us at the Four Seasons. But you can feel free to rest a bit more for now. We have plenty of time. The chef there is the best in the city."

"Um, Carl, could I speak with you for a moment?" Jessie asked.

"Certainly, what is it?"

"In your office."

"Oh, nonsense," Tolliver cut in. "Carl, Dr. Copeland has had a chance to examine me. She is concerned enough to want me to have an MRI and some blood tests."

"For a migraine?"

"Carl," Jessie said, "Eastman had a slight right facial droop, a little bit of thickness of his speech, and maybe some eye signs as well."

Without excusing himself, Gilbride inserted himself between her and Tolliver, and peered down at the man's face.

"Follow my finger, Eastman," he ordered, repeating some of the maneuvers Jessie had already done. "I don't see anything," he pronounced.

Not, I don't see anything *now*, Jessie noted. The implication in his words and tone was that there was nothing the matter—that the observations that had so concerned her were inconsequential. Jessie steeled herself for a confrontation. Whether or not the signs were still present was immaterial. They *had* been there, and many serious neurological conditions had waxing and waning findings at some stage. Her patience with her department chief had just about run out. Tolliver saved her from a potentially destructive blowup.

"Look, Carl," he said. "I like a good meal as much as the next fellow, but I also want to be certain this headache is a plain old migraine. It hurt like the devil."

"Very well, then," Gilbride replied in a voice that already had some pout in it, "I'll call down and see if we can get a CT scan."

"Carl," Jessie said, "I've got a team from the ER on their way up here right now to bring Eastman down for some bloodwork and an MRI."

Unseen by their patient, Gilbride glowered at her.

"That's fine," he said icily. "More than I would have done for what seems like a garden-variety migraine, but if Eastman doesn't mind missing dinner, we'll do it. I'll take over from here and walk him down."

"Actually, Carl," Tolliver said, "I'd prefer it if Dr. Copeland continued as my doctor."

"But—"

"I know it upsets you, but I am the patient. And at the moment, if it is all right with Dr. Copeland, she is my choice."

Was Tolliver's unequivocal insistence on her some sort of comment on the bungled surgery? Jessie suspected so. Whatever the reason, she felt nothing but delight.

"I'll be more than happy to honor your request, Eastman," she said, carefully avoiding eye contact with her chief.

At that moment, both Jessie's and Gilbride's beepers went off almost simultaneously. Then the phone across the hall in Gilbride's office began ringing.

"It's the unit," Jessie said.

"Mine, too."

Alice Twitchell came racing over breathlessly.

"Dr. Gilbride," she said, "Count Hermann has had a cardiac arrest. They're working on him now, but they want you over there. Dr. Copeland, the people from the ER are on the way up."

"Thank you," Jessie replied.

"Oh, that's just awful news about Count Hermann," said Tolliver. "Simply awful."

Gilbride looked almost apoplectic. Jessie imagined that there was no place on earth he would less like to be than supervising the resuscitation on his recent surgical calamity.

"Jessie, I'd appreciate it if you would honor Eastman's request and function as his primary physician," he said, through nearly clenched teeth. "Meanwhile, I'd best hurry on over to the NICU."

"I'll be up to help as soon as I can. Carl, have you seen Emily around?"

"DelGreco?"

"Yes."

"Not today I haven't."

"Thanks," she said, but he had already hurried off.

Moments later the elevator arrived, and the team from the ER emerged.

Jessie introduced Tolliver to the resident and nurse.

"Eastman, you're in good hands for now," she said. "While they're getting your tests done, I'm going to run over to the unit and see if I can help Dr. Gilbride. I'll see you downstairs in just a little while."

"I have the utmost confidence in you," Tolliver said. "Let's hope this is nothing serious."

"Let's hope that, indeed," Jessie replied.

But as she aided Eastman onto the stretcher and helped wheel him over to the elevator, every bit of instinct and intuition she possessed was telling her otherwise.

CHAPTER 23

PHILANTHROPIC DIRECTOR COMES TO EVALUATE
neurosurgical program and ends up needing an emergency MRI. . . . Patient he watched be operated on has
catastrophic result, then has cardiac arrest.

What else could possibly go wrong? Jessie wondered as
she hurried down the corridor of the office wing and
through the doorway to the Surgical Tower. As a medical
student, and even as a resident, she had always been excited by the frenetic action and drama of a full code 99.
Now, while she accepted them as an essential part of the
hospital, codes no longer held any allure. Their outcomes
were, more often than not, preordained. Patients could
frequently be hauled through the initial crisis, but unless
the underlying problem was dealt with, and quickly, it
was just a matter of time before their next code 99.

Catherine Purcell, the evening nursing supervisor and a long-term veteran of the hospital wars, was standing just outside the doorway to room 2.

"Hey, Catherine," Jessie said, "how goes it in there?"

"I think the Grim Reaper is well ahead. The patient was sort of stable, then suddenly he lost his pressure and went into V. fib. Now even that rhythm is degenerating. Thank God Joe Milano from cardiology is running the code."

"Is Dr. Gilbride in there?"

"Oh yes, he certainly is. What's with him, Jess?"

"What do you mean?"

"He stopped by the unit an hour or so ago to check on Count Hermann. Two of my nurses were talking and one of them laughed. Gilbride thought they were laughing at him, even though both of them claim he wasn't even the topic of conversation. He called me and is threatening to have the nurse who laughed disciplined or even kicked out of the ICU."

"Which nurse?"

"Laura Pearson."

"Jeez. These nurses can be harsh at times, but of all of them, she'd be the least likely to say anything unpleasant about anyone. Carl's just a wreck over this calamity, I think—hypersensitive for a while. He'll get over it."

"He'd better. I have a black belt in defending my nurses. Does the Count have any chance brainwise?"

"Not much. I'd better get in there and see if I can lend a hand."

"If you have a chance, speak to Gilbride about Laura."

"Will do. Catherine, have you by any chance seen Emily?"

"DelGreco? No. But I've only been wandering around the wards for a couple of hours. If I do see her, I'll tell her to give you a page."

"Thanks."

There was the usual code 99 crush of bodies in room 2 of the neurosurgical ICU—nurses, med techs, a respiratory tech, an anesthesiologist, and several house officers, with a couple of medical students thrown in just to increase the critical mass. And of course, there was Carl, still in his spotless, starched lab coat, standing just close enough to the action to act as if he were in charge, while deferring—at least Jessie *hoped* he was—to the medical resident and to cardiology fellow Joe Milano, each of whom was far better equipped to handle a code than any staff person.

Rolf Hermann had been detached from the respirator. A respiratory tech was squeezing a breathing bag to ventilate him through his endotracheal tube. The bedsheets had been thrown aside. Hermann's naked body looked vulnerable, although the man was over six feet tall and quite sturdily built. In addition to the breathing tube, he had a monitoring/blood-drawing line in the radial artery at one wrist, an infusion line in a vein higher up in his arm, a tube through his nose and down into his stomach, connected to suction, and a catheter draining his bladder into a plastic bag that hung below the bed. There were cables connecting the EKG leads on his chest to the monitor, and others snaking up from an oximeter on one of his fingers and a port on the arterial line. Viewed this way, he looked like anything but the deadly, merciless killer of hundreds who had been the object of Alex Bishop's obsession for five years. But illness and injury were great equalizers, and count or killer, there he was.

Jessie worked her way through the crowd to Carl's side.

"How's it going?" she asked.

Gilbride kept his eyes fixed on the action. He looked frazzled and irritated.

"What in the hell did you say to Tolliver that turned him against me?" he said out of the side of his mouth. "Joe, have you given him any IV bicarb?" he called over to the cardiology fellow.

"We don't use it anymore," the fellow called back.

"I knew that. I just thought this might be an exception. I think we should shock him again, yes?"

"After we give him some more epi, Dr. Gilbride."

"Right. Give him the epi, then shock."

"Carl," Jessie said, "I didn't say anything at all to him except what you know—that he needs an MRI."

"Four million dollars," Gilbride said, pausing theatrically between each word. "That's what that man holds in his hand. Get ready to shock, everyone. Go ahead, Joe."

"We're shocking. Everyone clear! Now!"

There was a muffled pop from the paddles that the cardiologist held pressed against Hermann's left chest, and four hundred joules of electricity were sent streaking through the Count's body. His arms flapped off the bed, then fell back down heavily. His legs flared out, then relaxed. Five seconds passed with no response. Then the cardiograph pattern on the monitor showed one beat . . . then nothing . . . then suddenly another . . . and another.

"I'll be damned," Jessie said, marveling at the quickness and skill of her younger colleagues, and trying to remember that once, not that long ago, she was as good at all this as they were now.

Helped by a heavy dose of cardiac medications, Rolf Hermann's heartbeat rapidly stabilized, and his blood pressure rose from zero to sixty to ninety. His blood oxygen content rose as well. The patient was a save . . . at least for the moment.

"Do you think he arrested because of increased intracranial pressure?" Jessie asked.

"Maybe," Gilbride replied, still looking straight ahead. "I'll give him some more diuretic and up his steroids. If Porter hadn't mistuned that damn robot of his, none of this would be happening."

Jessie was about to leap to Skip's defense, but decided against it. Gilbride was on a knife's edge as it was. This was not the moment.

Hermann's pressure and pulse were holding steady. One by one, the room began emptying out. This round, at least, had gone to the caregivers. But Jessie knew that the Reaper was, if nothing else, patient. Barring a miracle inside the Count's skull, another round wasn't far off.

"Do you think we could talk for a couple of minutes?" she asked.

"I've got to go speak to the Dragon Lady about her husband's latest crisis. You know, if you hadn't admitted these people to my service without waiting for my approval, none of this would be happening."

Jessie refused to be provoked.

"What I have to say won't take but a few minutes," she said. "It has to do with the Count and his wife."

"I've got to go speak with Hermann's family. Then I'm going to go down and check on Tolliver. After we confirm that his MRI is negative, there's still time for me to get him to the Four Seasons and maybe smooth things over. I can't believe he was in the OR for this fiasco."

Neither can I, Jessie thought.

"Carl," she said firmly, "I want a few minutes with you. Right now. It's very important."

Startled by her tone, Gilbride looked directly at her for the first time. Still, he appeared distracted and unfocused.

"I'll . . . um . . . meet you in the conference room in just a minute," he said. "I need to see what the cardiologist wants to do here."

Jessie went directly to the nurses' station and had most of Emily's home number dialed when she set the receiver down. If Em had checked in or returned home, her son Ted would have told her to call Jessie. He was that kind of kid. One more hour, she decided. If there was no word from her by then, it would be time to panic.

The small conference room was located just to one end of the unit. Jessie waited there only a minute or two before Gilbride arrived. He had the look of a treed animal. To the outside world, he was still the king of robotic surgery, in demand at hospital conferences and on talk shows. But his immediate universe was coming unraveled. He perceived himself, not without justification, to be the brunt of cruel jokes throughout the hospital. He was in the process of having a very highly connected post-op patient die of surgical complications. And perhaps worst of all, the man holding the purse strings of a four-million-dollar grant had all but issued a vote of no confidence in him by choosing to be cared for by one of his junior faculty.

"So," he said brusquely, "what do you want?"

"I . . . I want to talk to you about Orlis and Rolf Hermann," Jessie said, wondering how she was going to pull this one off.

"Go on."

"This may be hard for me to explain, and hard for you to accept, Carl, but I have reason to believe that Hermann may not be a count at all, and that both he and his wife may in fact be quite dangerous."

Gilbride's anger gave way to absolute incredulity. Jessie could read his thoughts.

Now what kind of goddamn trouble are you trying to cause me? Haven't you done enough?

"I don't understand," he said.

Jessie tried as best she could to explain about Alex Bishop and his theories. She could tell by Gilbride's expression and body language that he was simply not equipped for another assault on his academic fiefdom—especially one with no objective proof whatsoever.

"This is insane," he said when she had finished. "You think these are the people responsible for Sylvan Mays' murder?"

"It's quite possible."

"And this man—this Bishop—he's masquerading as a hospital guard but he's actually CIA?"

"That's what he says, yes."

"But he hasn't given you any concrete proof of that?"

"He gave me a phone number of someone in Virginia that he said might vouch for him."

"But you haven't called?"

Jessie felt as if she were being cross-examined by a hostile attorney. She felt herself pulling in.

"No," she said. "I couldn't see the point."

"So what do you want me to do about all this?"

"I want you to be careful, Carl. Especially with things going so poorly for Hermann. I don't want to cross Orlis in any way until Bishop has the chance to sort out what's going on. And that includes your not going to New York tomorrow. I'll help you talk to her right now about what's going on with her husband. But let's not do anything to rile her."

"She doesn't frighten me one bit," Gilbride said, clearly at the end of his tether. "And I don't know who this Bishop is. But before I disrupt my service and go accusing anyone of anything, I want to see some proof. Until then, I'm still the chief of this department, and I'll make any decisions that need making regarding our patients. Now, I would like you to accompany me into the family room to update Countess Hermann on this latest development."

Jessie followed Gilbride into the room, where Orlis Hermann was waiting, this time with all three of the Count's offspring. The session lasted less than ten minutes, and was even more unpleasant than the last one, with Gilbride stumbling through yet another blame-anyone-but-himself explanation of another tragic Rolf Hermann outcome. The woman almost certain to be Hermann's widow before too much longer received the news of her husband's cardiac arrest stoically, but her chilling gaze, locked every moment on Gilbride, made Jessie shudder.

"You will do everything you possibly can to save my husband's life," was all Orlis said when he had finished.

Then she nodded toward her stepsons and stepdaughter, and the four of them stood in unison and marched out the door. The last of them had just left when Jessie's beeper went off, directing her to an extension she didn't recognize.

"Em," she said out loud, hurrying over to the phone.

Her call was answered instead by the radiologist on duty. Jessie listened intently, then turned slowly to Gilbride.

"That was Don Harkness in radiology," she said. "He wants to review the findings on Eastman Tolliver's films with us."

I guess it's not a migraine, she wanted to add, but didn't.

In strained silence, the two of them took the elevator down to the basement and crossed through the tunnel to the MRI unit in the emergency ward. Don Harkness, a veteran radiologist, greeted them and then motioned toward the view box and Tolliver's films.

"Well, I'll be . . . ," Jessie murmured.

Gilbride and Jessie looked at each other in amazement. The tumor in Eastman Tolliver's head was slightly smaller than Rolf Hermann's, and a bit more to the left of center—not an identical twin, but certainly fraternal.

"The man's got problems," Harkness said. "A subfrontal meningioma, I should think. Big 'un, too. Now, that's one you don't see every day."

CHAPTER 24

ALTHOUGH SHE WASN'T ON CALL, JESSIE HAD chosen to spend the night in the hospital. Her closest friend had vanished. No note, no call, no signs of personal trouble, no hints of emotional instability, no evidence of an abduction—just a phone call to Emily at home . . . then she was gone. Jessie had been too worried to go home.

It was not yet six-thirty in the morning when she awoke in one of the windowless on-call cubicles, momentarily disoriented in the pitch darkness, her mouth desert dry, her lungs burning from four hours of inhaling stale air. She switched on the bedside lamp and was grateful to see the cup of water she had left on the scarred table beside it. Wetting her fingertips, she rubbed some water on her eyelids, then drank the rest and sank back onto the pillow. Dreamlike, the highly charged events of the previous night drifted into focus.

Eastman Tolliver had taken the unfortunate news of his MRI results about as Jessie had expected—a dismayed, softly uttered curse, followed by an attempt at a brave smile, and finally a resigned declaration that he would do whatever it took to beat the tumor. These were, Jessie knew, only baby steps in the process of coming to grips with the nearly unfathomable diagnosis of a brain tumor. The heavy work would take place over the few days remaining before surgery. And while the depth of the success of that work was unpredictable from patient to patient, it often had a major bearing on the outcome of the treatment.

"Maybe it's all the time I've been spending around the patients here," Tolliver said, "but while they were wheeling me down here, I had this feeling it was going to be . . ."

His voice drifted away, and for a brief while, he stared up at the ceiling. He then stated his decision to stay in Boston and have his surgery performed at EMMC. Gilbride made several hardly subtle efforts to insert himself as the physician of record, but Tolliver would have none of it.

"I've made up my mind, Carl," he said. "I know what happened to poor Count Hermann could have happened with any surgeon, but I've watched Dr. Copeland in the operating room, and I've spoken with her patients, and I have chosen Dr. Copeland to do it. It's as simple as that. It says a good deal about you that you have a surgeon of her caliber on your staff."

"Whatever you say," Gilbride managed, barely unclenching his jaws.

"However, when I do go into the operating room," Tolliver went on, "I'd like to know that you'll be there as a consultant."

"Of course."

Jessie suggested an immediate admission to the neurosurgical service, and promised to schedule Tolliver's operation as soon as possible. Tolliver convinced her instead to allow him to return to his room to gather some things and to call his wife, Kathleen. She would then fly in from California as soon as she could arrange for someone to take her place in caring for her mother, who was incapacitated by Alzheimer's disease. However, Tolliver was quick to add, setting a time for surgery should not be predicated on his wife's arrival. He wanted it done as quickly as possible.

"Just get this thing out of my head," he said.

Two hours after his release from the emergency room, Eastman Tolliver had returned to EMMC and was admitted as a patient to Surgical Seven.

Meanwhile, Jessie had left the hospital and driven over to the modest two-story house Emily shared with her husband, Ed, and their two sons. Jessie felt that Ed, a software engineer at a firm in Cambridge, responded to the crisis less emotionally and more analytically than Emily would have done had he been the one to have disappeared. But there was no misinterpreting his anxiousness. At Jessie's urging, he called the Brookline police and an hour later an officer did stop by more out of courtesy than concern. The man had clearly encountered too many of these situations to get worked up about this one at this point.

"It's almost always some sort of misunderstanding," he said, in a clumsy and totally ineffective attempt to calm everyone. "A meeting or an appointment that Mrs. DelGreco's certain she told you about, but didn't—something like that."

Jessie rolled her eyes. Emily was as meticulously organized as anyone she knew, and considerate to a fault.

The policeman then pulled Ed and Jessie away from the boys and asked them about the possibility that Emily was seeing someone else.

"I suppose anything's possible," Ed replied clinically.

"Nonsense!" Jessie exclaimed. "Emily tells me when a *movie star* is attractive to her. If she was involved with someone else I guarantee you I'd know about it. I suspect it's police procedure to wait a certain amount of time before considering a person actually missing, but in this case you shouldn't waste time waiting, Officer. Emily is an incredibly responsible woman. She would never disappear like this without telling anyone—unless she didn't have the chance."

The policeman had responded with patronizing reassurance that they would do whatever was necessary as soon as it was clear Emily had been missing at least twenty-four hours.

Jessie finished the last of the water from the bedside table, and forced herself to use the narrow, molded-plastic shower.

What in the hell happened to Emily?

The question overrode all her other thoughts. She searched with little success for an explanation that worked with all she knew of the woman. Finally, she began ticking through a list of scenarios that didn't jibe with what she knew. Maybe there *was* another man. Ed DelGreco was a decent-looking guy, and certainly bright, but he was dry as toast. It wasn't an impossible stretch to believe that Em could have left Ed and run off with someone. But it was inconceivable that she could have done it to her boys. No, something bad had happened to her. Jessie felt almost certain of it.

Was it possible that Emily's disappearance had something to do with the Count and Orlis Hermann? Had

she seen or heard something she shouldn't have? Jessie
pondered those questions for a time, then toweled off,
pulled on a fresh set of scrubs, and fished out the number Alex had given her.

"Four-two-six-nine-four-four-four," a woman's sterile voice said.

"Alex Bishop, please."

"You may leave a message."

"Can you get it to him?"

"You may leave a message."

"Okay, okay. Ask Mr. Bishop to page Dr. Copeland,
please." Jessie hesitated, then added, "Tell him it's important."

Em, where in the hell are you?

Jessie joined the breakfast bunch in the cafeteria, but
found it impossible this day to tolerate their humor.
Making rounds on Surgical Seven was the only thing she
felt she could handle. With the exception of Ben
Rasheed, who would remain a ticking bomb until his
surgery later that day, her service—nine patients right
now—was in excellent shape. Making rounds on the
group would have to be a boost to her spirits, and starting early would give her some extra time to talk with
each of them.

As always since Sara's surgery, Jessie started her
rounds in NICU room 6. Although it was only seven-
thirty, she was not that surprised to find Lisa Brandon at
work, using lotion to massage Sara's back.

"So, how's my patient?"

"Just . . . good," Sara said.

Lisa helped her onto her back and cranked up the
bed.

"I'm going to see if the nurses have anything for me
to do," she said. "See you later, Dr. Copeland."

"Thank you, Lisa."

Sara's neurologic exam showed signs, albeit not striking ones, of continuing improvement in many areas. Voluntary movement present in all extremities with some decent leg strength. . . . Cognition good. . . . Speech somewhat disjointed but largely discernible. . . . All twelve pairs of cranial nerves intact. Clearly, Sara was nearing the edge of the woods. She was certainly ready to be moved out of the unit and, barring a major complication, could be in a rehab facility within a week.

One friend a virtual miracle, one friend missing. . . . *Patrons with heart conditions should refrain from taking this ride.*

The two women talked for a time, although Jessie carried most of the conversation. They spoke about the weather and movies, Sara's kids and Jessie's personal life, and even what it was like to be operated on while awake. And finally, Sara drifted into an exhausted sleep. Jessie pushed herself up from the edge of the bed and was heading out of the room when she noticed a thin volume on the bedside table, folded open, with a passage circled in pencil. It was Shakespeare's *Richard III*. The marked passage was probably one Barry Devereau had read to his wife—perhaps many times.

> *True hope is swift, and flies with swallow's wings;*
> *Kings it makes gods, and meaner creatures kings.*

"Hang in there, Sara," Jessie whispered. She headed into the hallway, then added, "Em, you hang in there, too."

"Dr. Copeland, there's trouble in two," a nurse called out.

Jessie hurried to Rolf Hermann's bedside. His daughter was asleep in the guest chair, a pillow bunched be-

neath her head. A cardiac pacemaker wire, inserted after
the code 99, had been added to Hermann's array of tubes
and monitor cables. It was a temporary wire, inserted
through a blind stick into the subclavian vein beneath
the Count's right collarbone and threaded down until it
made contact with the inner lining of his heart. The
pacer control box to which the wire was connected was
taped to his upper arm.

Pacemaker, IV, breathing tube, mechanical ventilation, catheter, feeding tube, eyes taped shut. Rolf
Hermann or Claude Malloche—whoever he was—was
more dead than alive. The code 99 had been a success,
but the underlying cause of his cardiac degeneration,
which was most likely a disruption of the nerve pathways from the brain regulating his heart rhythm, remained unchanged. And now, another grave situation
was developing. His blood pressure, as displayed on the
monitor screen from the cannula in his radial artery, was
75/30 . . . and dropping.

A normal heartbeat pattern on the monitor with a
falling blood pressure. Cardiac pump failure—the sort
of circulatory collapse that not even a pacemaker could
help. Rolf Hermann was on the barge, as the residents
often put it—on the barge and about to cross the river of
no return.

"Hang a dopamine infusion, please," Jessie said to the
nurse. "Then call the cardiology fellow, the neurosurgical resident, and Dr. Gilbride."

Hermann's daughter woke up with a start, and appeared lost and alarmed. She was in her early to mid-
twenties, lithe, with short, straight brown hair and an
aquiline nose that dominated her face. Jessie patted her
shoulder to calm her, then led her out into the hall and
turned her over to one of the nurses, with instructions to

go find Orlis and to bring the whole group to the family room. Rolf Hermann's heartbeat hadn't stopped yet, but it was going to.

Jessie sighed and turned to the unit secretary. There was no sense in just sitting around waiting for the inevitable.

"Code ninety-nine, NICU two," she said. "Please call it in."

CHAPTER 25

AFTER THE MEDICAL NIGHTMARE COUNT ROLF Hermann had been through, his death would be almost anticlimactic. With his ventilator-driven respirations, the cardiac meds, and the pacemaker, he was essentially being continuously resuscitated. He could go on indefinitely this way so long as his heart continued to circulate blood with enough force to perfuse his organs. But the drop in blood pressure was a signal that his pump was failing. Speeding up his heart rate with the pacemaker might help for a while, Jessie thought—long enough at least for the room to fill up once again with the usual crush of combatants and onlookers. But the ultimate negative outcome was approaching rapidly.

The cardiology fellow, Joe Milano, was still on call, and in fact had been on his way up to check on Hermann and his pacemaker when the code 99 was broadcast. He rushed into the room, checked the monitor screen, then slid into place beside Jessie.

"I had the pacer set to take over if he dropped below seventy," he said. "Now he's pacing at one-twenty."

"His pressure had dropped to seventy-five," Jessie replied. "We've hung some dopamine, and since there's no fluid in his chest that I can hear, we're pushing fluid to increase his circulating volume. But I thought that increasing his rate with the pacemaker might drive up his pressure some."

"And look, it has," Milano said, gesturing to the pressure readout of 79. "That was a heck of a good move—especially for a neurosurgeon."

"I was a doctor once, remember? Any other ideas?"

Milano checked the clear plastic urine collector hanging from the bed frame.

"There's not much pee. Has this been emptied recently?"

"Three hours ago," a nurse responded. "There wasn't much output then either."

"We can push the pressors and start pumping on his chest," Milano said. "If we do that, we're sort of committed to a balloon pump assist as well. As usual, it's hard to know where to draw the line."

"The family wants everything possible done," Jessie said.

"Is it worth trying to put a shunt into his head? It's almost certain the fallout from his cerebral hemorrhage is causing this, along with some underlying cardiac disease."

"There's no evidence for an acute obstruction of the outflow of spinal fluid from his brain. That would be the only neurosurgical condition we might be able to remediate in the OR. His problem is massive brain swelling, not acute hydrocephalus. A shunt wouldn't help."

"And his brain swelling's not going away?"

Jessie shook her head. "No," she said, glancing over at the doorway and wondering when Gilbride might appear. "It doesn't look like it."

"In that case it seems like we're swimming against the tide regardless of what we do."

"Pressure's down to seventy again," the nurse said.

Her tone was a none-too-subtle request that one of the physicians in charge make a decision whether to plow ahead with meds and chest compressions or stand back and let Hermann's pressure keep on dropping.

"It's too bad," Milano said softly. "The guy comes all the way over here from Germany to have his operation, and ends up like this."

"Sixty-five," the nurse said.

"I don't know," Jessie said. "My head is telling me we'd better pull out all the stops. My heart says that doing that is a cruel and expensive exercise in futility."

She looked past the crowd to the hallway again. Carl Gilbride wasn't there, but Alex Bishop was, dressed in his brown security force uniform. He caught her eye and asked the obvious question with a gesture. She replied with a barely perceptible shake of her head. At that moment, Gilbride strode past Alex and into the room. Despite having left the hospital at ten last night for what Jessie assumed was a decent night's sleep, and despite his spotless lab coat and designer shirt, he looked haggard and edgy.

"What's going on here?" he demanded.

"Pump's failing," Milano said.

"So, get it going."

Gilbride looked reproachfully at Jessie.

"How long have you been here?" he demanded.

"Ten minutes or so."

"And you're not doing anything?"

"We were just discussing whether it was appropriate and fair to send for a balloon assist pump."

"Milano, get him through this," Gilbride ordered. "I don't care what you have to do." He turned to Jessie. "Because of you, I've canceled appearing on a panel in New York City that was very important to me. And now I get here and find you just standing around."

"Begin compressions," Milano said to the medical resident, the resignation in his voice making it clear the order was against his better judgment. "Someone please call down to the CCU and have the intra-aortic balloon pump brought up here. Might as well call the cardiac surg people as well to help with the insertion."

"I'll call them," Jessie said quickly, anxious to get out of the room.

She was furious at Gilbride's public rebuke, but she was also a bit sheepish that she hadn't been as aggressive as he was being. Still, dead was dead. And the most exhaustive, expensive interventions in the world weren't going to bring back Rolf Hermann's brain or, for that matter, his heart.

She hurried past Alex with just a brief nod that he should follow. Then she stopped at the ward secretary's desk, called the coronary care unit, and asked to have a nurse wheel up the balloon pump. The apparatus, a long balloon that was inserted into the abdominal aorta through an artery in the groin and inflated with each heartbeat, could raise the blood pressure in some cases of pump failure. Next Jessie put in a page for the cardiac surgery team. Finally, she walked down the hall to a small alcove opposite the only empty room in the NICU, and motioned to Alex that the coast was clear.

"Is he going to make it?" he asked at once.

"Define *make it*," Jessie replied. "Joe Milano, the cardiologist, is damn good, but I don't think anyone's *that* good. Do you know that I called you early this morning?"

"I do, yes. I'm sorry. They just reached me with the message."

"What were you doing?"

"I was off getting a hearse."

"A hearse?"

"A hearse, the black dress suit, the subdued tie, the works—all courtesy of the greedy folks at Bowker and Hammersmith Funeral Parlor. They have even offered their cooler to stash Hermann's body in until Jorge Cardoza gets here."

"Very clever. When will he be arriving?"

"This afternoon. His plane lands at three. Is Hermann still going to be among the living by then?"

"Define *living*. I was ready to call it quits on the resuscitation before Carl got here. But he canceled an appearance in New York because of the Count, and now he's determined the guy's going to survive this."

"It'll be dangerous bringing Cardoza into the hospital. There's a chance one or another of Hermann's so-called family knows him."

"Well, speaking as a betting woman, my money's on your not having to."

"Will you help me get Hermann out of the hospital? I know where the morgue is, but I don't know much about the protocol."

"Jesus, Alex. I'm still not even certain who you *are,*

and you want me to risk my career by stealing a body from my own hospital?"

"Forget I asked."

"I'll do it. I'll do it. But listen. You've got to help me, too. I'm very frightened about my nurse practitioner, Emily."

"What do you mean?"

"She's disappeared. According to her son, yesterday evening she got a phone call, then said she was going to the hospital. He assumed it was me calling, but it wasn't. She hasn't been heard from since, and I'm very worried."

"Has her family called the police?"

"Yes, but they won't do anything until she's been missing at least twenty-four hours."

"Missing, huh. That is a little worrisome. She's never done anything like this before?"

"Never. That's why I called you. I want to make a deal. If I help you with Hermann, I want you to get your FBI friends involved right away in finding Emily."

"I don't know if—"

"No deal, no body. And I mean it. I want them on the case today no matter what the Brookline police say."

"I'll do my best."

"Look at me, Alex. Right here in my eyes. . . . Dammit, I wish I could tell when you're lying."

The nurse from the coronary care unit raced by, pushing the orange-crate-sized intra-aortic balloon pump ahead of her.

"Go ahead back in there," Alex said. "I won't be far away."

"Why don't you use the time right now to keep your end of the bargain and call your FBI friends? Emily DelGreco. Her number's listed in the Brookline directory under Edward DelGreco."

"Okay. Okay. You're like a frigging pit bull."

"There's a side of me that pit bulls run away from. You came dangerously close to bringing it out once. For both our sakes, don't do it again."

She hurried away without waiting for a response, and rejoined the throng in room 2.

The blood pressure readout on the monitor showed 50 now. Rolf Hermann's skin was gray, mottled with deep violet. His eyelids were taped closed. A respiratory tech was using a breathing bag to supply him with 100 percent oxygen. By any definition, the Count was far more dead than alive. Still, the team, driven by a frantic Carl Gilbride, pushed on. The resident continued pumping on Hermann's chest while Joe Milano gave med orders to the nurses. And now a cardiac surgical resident was on the scene as well, preparing Hermann's groin for the insertion of the intra-aortic balloon, and calling out his supply needs without checking to see if anyone was listening. It was a medical circus maximus, and at the center stood Carl Gilbride, no more effective than Nero might have been while watching Rome burn around him.

Jessie was torn between diving in to relieve the exhausted resident who was doing the chest compressions, and simply skulking off to a quiet corner of the hospital until the madness was over. Finally, she decided on a compromise, and moved to a spot next to Gilbride. There was a particular favor she wanted to offer him when it was appropriate to do so.

"Any change?" she asked.

"You might have started all this sooner," Gilbride said, never turning away from the action.

"I'm sorry," she replied, unwilling to take the bait and start up an argument about the definition of futility.

"It doesn't look good."

The pressure was down to 45—poor even for artificial external cardiac compressions.

"That chest pumper's running down," Jessie said. "I think I'll take over."

"Nonsense. You're an assistant professor. Pumping is a resident's job."

He called out and caught the attention of the neurosurgical resident. Then he pointed at Hermann's chest and pantomimed the order that the man take over the cardiac compressions. To Jessie, it was as if Nero was now demanding that a bucket of water be tossed on the conflagration. The personnel transfer took place on the bed without missing a beat, but the pressure readout remained essentially unchanged. Five more minutes passed. Fifteen people—residents, students, nurses, technicians, faculty—had been tied up for the better part of an hour now. Thousands of dollars in equipment, medications, and lab tests had been expended.

"Balloon's in and functioning well," the cardiac surgery resident announced.

"Stop pumping, please," Joe Milano requested.

The room was suddenly silent save for the beeping of the monitor, the puffs of the Ambu breathing bag, and the soft thump of the intra-aortic balloon assist. Every eye was fixed on the monitor. For a time, maybe a minute, maybe two, the blood pressure reading stayed at 50. Then slowly, like the orbit of a dying satellite, it began to deteriorate. Down to 47 . . . 42 . . . 40. Seconds after the pressure hit 40, Rolf Hermann flat-lined. No one moved. The silence in the room continued as everyone on the resuscitation team waited for Carl Gilbride to decide whether or not it was over.

There was nothing from him. Not a word.

Finally, Joe Milano spoke up.

"Dr. Gilbride, I appreciate how much you want this guy to make it. But I'm not sure what else we can do."

"This all should have been started sooner," Gilbride said.

He turned and stalked from the room.

Jerk.

"That's it. Thank you, everyone," Jessie blurted, hurrying after Gilbride, and catching up with him at the nurses' station.

"Sorry," she said, wanting to throttle the man.

"Where're his wife and the others?"

"Waiting in the family room."

"Well, I suppose I'd best get this over with."

"Be careful. Remember what I told you about her."

"What you told me is nonsense. Killers! Fake security guards! I just want to get this whole business over with. I never should have canceled my appearance in New York. Never. And now Mrs. Levin has developed a headache and a fever on the day she was supposed to be discharged. As soon as I finish with the Countess, I'm going to have to perform a spinal tap on her."

"Would you like me to do it?"

"I think you've done enough for one day."

"How about Orlis? Do you want me in there with you when you speak to her?"

"I think I can handle that myself as well."

"Okay," Jessie said. She crossed her fingers for luck and went for the brass ring. "How about the death certificate? Can I fill that out for you?"

Gilbride mulled the request over, then finally said, "I suppose so. As long as you make sure the cause of death is listed as cardiac, because that's what it was."

"Cardiac arrest, due to arteriosclerotic heart disease,

with meningioma as a coincidentally existing condition. How does that sound?"

"It sounds like the way it should be. Now, if you'll excuse me, I have a great deal to do."

"So do I," Jessie murmured as he walked away.

CHAPTER **26**

IT TOOK NEARLY TWENTY MINUTES FOR THE nurses to clean up room 2. They removed all the tubes and lines from Rolf Hermann's body and untaped his eyelids. Jessie offered to help, but was shooed away. Instead, she sat behind the counter of the nurses' station filling out the death certificate—the one piece of paperwork that would be necessary to remove the Count's body from the hospital.

> **Please print in black pen only.**
> > **Cause of Death: Cardiac Arrest**
> > **DUE TO: Cardiogenic Shock**
> > **DUE TO: Arteriosclerotic Cardiovascular Disease**
> > **Co-existing Condition: Subfrontal Meningioma**

A few properly placed words and *poof*, Gilbride's wish had been granted. A surgical calamity would go into the books as a coronary. And unless the family demanded the certificate, no one would be the wiser. Difficult though Orlis was, Jessie did not think that idea would occur to her. Deservedly or not, Gilbride was off the hook.

The pen is mightier than the scalpel.

Jessie smiled at the thought as she block printed in the final pieces of demographic data. She looked up just as Orlis Hermann and Rolf's daughter came down the hall and entered his room. A minute or so later, they emerged and approached her.

"So," Orlis said with chilling matter-of-factness, "my husband is dead."

"We're all very sorry," Jessie replied, standing.

"Your Dr. Gilbride didn't seem all that remorseful when he spoke to us just now."

"I assure you, he was. He kept everyone in there doing the resuscitation long after most doctors would have stopped."

"What do we do now?"

"If you were local, I would say all you needed to do was call a funeral home. Coming from another country, I'm not sure. If you don't mind waiting in your room out there on the floor, I'll speak to the nursing supervisor. She knows all the rules. I assume you're planning to take the Count back to Germany."

"We are."

"I'm sure that complicates things somewhat, but I think the first step is still calling a funeral home. There's paperwork that needs to be done here as well. Dr. Gilbride has quite a caseload, so I've offered to do it for him. But there may be some delay—a few hours, per-haps."

Jessie was rambling deliberately, hoping that Orlis

would agree to stay around the hospital, as Alex needed her to.

"I don't mind," Orlis said. "I need to get my husband's things together anyway."

"Will the Count's sons be in to see him?"

"No. They are off on business right now. They should be back shortly, but there is no need to keep Count Hermann's body up here until they arrive. Although they were very close to their father, they are not sentimental in that way."

"Fine. I'll take care of everything, and I'll be in to see you as soon as I have information."

"Do that. . . . Dr. Copeland?"

"Yes."

"Your chief killed my husband. You do know that."

A knot of tension materialized in Jessie's chest. Whether or not Alex was right about Orlis Hermann being Arlette Malloche, the woman *was* absolutely chilling. Jessie chose her words carefully. She had no desire to defend Carl Gilbride, but this was hardly the situation in which to allow principle and emotion to get in the way of common sense. Even if Orlis Hermann was nothing more than the Count's distraught wife, she was still a potential litigant against Gilbride, EMMC, and probably Jessie as well. If she was, as Alex believed, a murderer capable of extreme vengeance, then there was no reason to provide her with any more justification for violence than she already had.

"What I know, Mrs. Hermann," she said, "is that your husband had a large brain tumor that was unfortunately situated in a spot that was technically very difficult to reach. The more difficult the location of such a tumor, the more likely there will be complications. We really are sorry."

"Tell me something honestly, Dr. Copeland. Would this have happened if you had done the surgery?"

The question caught Jessie by surprise. In all her dealings with Orlis Hermann, she never once felt the woman had the least interest in what she could or could not do in the operating room. A myriad of responses to the question flashed through her head—none of them truthful.

"I hope you will understand that I cannot possibly answer that question," she said finally. "I've had my share of surgical triumphs just as Dr. Gilbride has, but I've had some surgical tragedies as well."

For a few moments, Orlis Hermann stood there silently, her eyes locked on Jessie's. Then, almost imperceptibly, she nodded.

"We will be waiting in our room for word from you," she said.

She took her stepdaughter by the arm and led her away. Moments later, Alex appeared at Jessie's side.

"What'd she say?"

"She'll be waiting to hear from me about what to do with the body."

"Time frame?"

"I told her it could be a few hours before I have any information."

"Great. Nice going. If worse comes to worst, the body will just be missing, and she'll have to wait around until it's found."

"Unless that makes her suspicious and she takes off."

"I have that possibility covered, I think. She's being watched."

Jessie looked at him queerly.

"Watched by whom?" she asked.

"I'll tell you soon."

"Oh, I just love secrets," she said with unbridled sarcasm.

"I gave my word."

"As long as *I* can count on your word, too. You know, Alex, as hard a woman as Orlis is, and as many awful things as you think she and her husband have done, I believe she's feeling a deep and genuine hurt over what's happened to him. And you know what? So am I."

"In that case, maybe I should bring out those photographs again," Alex replied. "I have no sympathy for that woman or her husband. I only hope he somehow knew he was dying when that artery started bleeding into his brain. I can't tell you what a joy it will be, to be the one shoving Claude Malloche's body into a hearse."

"Vengeance is mine, sayeth the Bishop."

"Amen."

"Pardon me for saying it, but would your brother have endorsed this five-year vendetta of yours?"

"My brother's dead. The choices I've made are mine. But the answer to your question is yes. We were both recruited by the agency right after college. We both knew what we were getting into. We both felt like patriots serving our country, and we both hated our country's enemies. If Malloche had any credo at all, it was an absolute loathing for America and Americans. If he had killed me, Andy would have hunted him to the ends of the earth."

Jessie sighed.

"In that case, we should get moving."

"Do you have a plan?" he asked.

"Yes, but it's complicated, so pay attention."

"Ready."

"Okay. First, I give you this paper. Second, you change into your undertaker suit. You got this so far?"

"Go on."

"Next, you come and haul off the body."

"That's it?"

"I checked. It's essentially self-serve. You stop at the pathology department desk, show them the death certificate, and sign a log. After that, no one cares. It's yet another example of the cardinal rule of moving about a hospital: If you look like you know what you're doing, as far as anyone is concerned, you know what you're doing."

"I've noticed that, playing hospital guard."

"People's first option is always the one that isn't going to cause them any extra work. I'm going to put that principle to the test right now."

"How?"

"Just to make sure everything's in place when you make your appearance as Digger O'Dell, the friendly undertaker, I'm going to tell the nurses I need a break from this floor and from Carl, and offer to spare someone the job of accompanying the security guard when he wheels the body down to the morgue. I don't think it would be wise for you to play the guard *and* Digger, but if you hurry, I'll still be down there waiting when you drive up in your hearse."

Alex looked about to ensure no one was watching, then took her hand in his and held it for several seconds.

"I'll meet you in the morgue," he said.

He had disappeared around the corner before Jessie realized that she hadn't even thought about pulling away from him.

JESSIE ASSISTED TWO nurses in transferring Rolf Hermann's body to a gurney. Then she and the guard, a paunchy man named Seth, who seemed to pale at the sight of the Count's corpse, headed off for the morgue.

Five hundred murders. It was hard enough for her to accept that any man could be responsible for such horror, let alone that it was the one lying beneath the sheet. Cunning, thorough, brilliant, paranoid, meticulous. Those were just some of the adjectives Alex had used to describe Claude Malloche. Now, it seemed, the monster's headstone might read:

"Here lies a man who made only one mistake in life. He chose the wrong surgeon."

The morgue was in the basement of the main hospital. It consisted of an unlocked room, adjacent to the autopsy suite, with twelve stainless steel refrigerated boxes built into the wall for body storage. Formaldehyde fumes hung heavy in the air. There was no one around, so Jessie left Seth waiting with the gurney and walked through the autopsy room and across a corridor to the pathology office, where an indifferent secretary slid a black loose-leaf notebook across her desk to log the body in.

"I think the funeral home is on its way over," Jessie said, paving the way for Alex's imminent arrival.

The woman mumbled, "Yeah, okay."

No problem here, Jessie was thinking.

She returned to the morgue, where Seth had posted himself in the hallway outside the door.

No problem here either.

"Listen," Jessie said, "I just spoke to the funeral parlor, and they're sending someone over right away. Why don't you go on back to work. I'll stay here until they arrive."

"You sure?"

"It's fine. I'm sure."

Jessie watched until the grateful guard had headed down the passageway to the elevators. Then she reentered the morgue and lifted the sheet from Rolf Hermann's gray, mottled face. Gradually, the stagnant blood in his capillaries would be drawn by gravity into the dependent tissues, and his complexion would assume the pallor of death. From her first encounter with a dead body in anatomy, corpses had not particularly affected her—even the ones whose demise was grisly. Hermann was no exception. Perhaps it was the ability to detach that had made her so successful as a surgical student, then later as a resident. Whatever the reason, looking down at the body now only made her wonder about Claude Malloche—and about the man who had hunted him for so long.

Five years, she was thinking. Alex Bishop had given up five years of his life for this. Hermann's eyes were open a slit. Jessie peered at them, wondering about all they had seen during their life, and what had driven the man behind them.

"Jessie?"

The woman's voice, from behind her, brought her heart rocketing to her throat. She whirled, pulling the sheet back into place over Hermann's face in the same motion. Nursing supervisor Catherine Purcell stood, arms folded, just inside the door.

"Oh, hi," Jessie managed. "You startled me."

"I can see that. Sorry. Is there a problem?"

"No, not really. I was just wondering about the guy. I did his admission workup for Carl, but I never really got to talk with him. Because of the language barrier and his wife's bossiness, almost everything went through her."

Jessie's mind was racing. Alex would be here any-time. Catherine Purcell was one of the sharpest people in the hospital, and his looks were striking. It was reasonable to think she might recognize him.

"The nurses in the unit told me you had walked the Count down here," Catherine said.

"They were busy, and I just wanted to get off the floor for a while. Weren't you on last evening?"

"Betty Hollister's got the flu. I told her I'd cover. You need help loading him into the cooler?"

"No . . . ah . . . the funeral home called the floor before we left and said they'd be right over. I didn't see any sense in moving him around any more than necessary. Have you heard something about Emily? Is that why you're here?"

She worked her way toward the door.

"No. I heard she's still missing. I have no idea what could have happened."

"I'm really worried."

"In that case, I'm worried, too. But I came down to find you because I'm worried about someone else—Carl. I think he's losing it."

"You mean like going crazy?"

"I mean exactly that."

"Catherine, could we maybe leave here to talk about it? The fumes are starting to make me queasy. The funeral guy knows to stop at the path office. I left the death certificate there."

"Certainly."

Nicely done, Jessie was thinking to herself as they reached the bank of elevators. The doors parted and Catherine stepped into the car at the moment the doors to the next car opened and Alex emerged, dressed in an ill-fitting black suit and pushing a narrow stretcher. There was only a moment for their eyes to meet, but in that moment, Alex saw inside the elevator, assessed the situation, and looked down.

"He's in the morgue," Jessie said. "The pathology office has the certificate."

"Thank you," Alex said.

"I could swear I've seen that man someplace before," Catherine commented as the elevator doors glided shut.

Jessie's pulse leveled off at two hundred or so and began to slow.

"I imagine this isn't his first trip here," she said hopefully.

"No, I suppose not."

"About Carl?"

"Oh, yes. You remember I told you last night how he was absolutely certain Laura Pearson and another nurse were laughing at him, and threatened to have her fired?"

"Yes."

"Well, now he's up on Surgical Seven, shrieking at the nurses because there are none of the special spinal tap sets on the floor that he insists on using."

"Oh, yes. The famous Gilbride kit."

Jessie tried to stay focused on Catherine and their conversation, but she kept picturing Alex, alone in the morgue, loading the body of his nemesis onto a borrowed stretcher for the trip to a hearse. *Five years.*

"Special spinal needle, special pressure monitor, special clamps, special drapes, special disinfectant," Catherine was saying. "Everyone else uses the standard, disposable kits, but Carl insists on his wacky setup."

"I know. He insists that the residents use it, too, but unless he's watching they never do. It's become sort of a joke passed on from class to class. It's just one of those power things, Catherine. Carl demands the kits simply because he can."

"Well, now he's up there berating anyone and everyone because there aren't any."

"He's stressed. This Count Hermann thing has turned his world upside down. Surely central supply must have some of his sets made up and sterilized."

"One, thank God. They're sending it up now. But Jessie, you've got to do something to calm the man down before we have a mass walkout on our hands. Or before I slip twenty of Valium into his butt. He's always been hard on people, but never this abusive. It's really appalling."

"I'll do what I can."

They heard Gilbride ranting the moment the doors opened on Surgical Seven.

"You know how much time I've wasted up here, waiting for this? I could have seen half a dozen patients in my office! From now on, I want at least two Gilbride kits on this floor at all times, is that clear?"

Clutching the sterile, towel-covered tray that held his precious spinal tap set, Gilbride was still railing at one of the nurses as Jessie approached.

"Carl?"

He whirled to face her.

"I don't want to hear anything from you either, Doctor," he snarled. "This is my service, and I'll run it my way. Now, if you'll excuse me."

He was muttering unintelligibly as he turned away. Just behind him, Jessie could see the candy striper, Lisa Brandon, emerging from Sara's new room. She was looking back over her shoulder into the room, saying something about getting more lotion. To Jessie, watching the catastrophe develop, the collision seemed to take place in slow motion. Gilbride took two rapid steps backward and was turning when he slammed into Lisa, driving her back a few feet and almost knocking her down. The Gilbride kit—the only one in the hospital— went clattering to the floor.

For two or three stunned, silent seconds, Gilbride could only stare down at the broken tubes and contaminated instruments. Then he transferred his gaze to Lisa.

"God damn it!" he bellowed. "Who the hell are you?"

Without waiting for a response, he reached down and snatched Lisa's laminated ID from where it was clipped to her jacket pocket. He studied the picture, then looked at the woman, then looked back at the ID.

"I . . . I'm sorry," Lisa stammered. "I really am. It was an ac—"

"What in the hell kind of an ID is this?"

"What do you mean?" Lisa asked.

Jessie took a step closer. To her left, Orlis Hermann and one of her sons were standing by the door to their room, taking in the scene.

"I mean this thing is fake. The ID number doesn't start with a V like all volunteers' numbers do, and you can't possibly have gotten this just three weeks ago, because if you did, you'd still be in orientation, and not up here putting your hands on my patients and smashing into me. Now, who in the hell are you?"

He nearly shrieked the words.

"Dr. Gilbride, if we could just speak in private," Lisa said, urgently, but quite calmly and with surprising authority.

"Nonsense! I want security called. I want you out of here right now."

"Dr. Gilbride, please, I—"

Gilbride turned to the unit secretary.

"Get security up here right now," he bellowed. "In fact, tell them to call the police."

Jessie kept her eyes on Lisa Brandon, who appeared furious and somewhat uncertain as to what to do, but not at all intimidated.

"Dr. Gilbride, quiet down," she said firmly. "I *am* the police. FBI."

She handed him a leather case with a badge. Then, just as quickly, she took a step forward, produced a pistol that had been concealed above her boot, and leveled it expertly at Orlis.

"Don't move, Mrs. Hermann," she said. "Or should I say, Madame Malloche."

Orlis just looked at her, her lips pursed in a strange half-smile.

"Madame Malloche will do just fine, dear," she said. "Arlette Malloche."

There was a momentary silence, which was broken by the soft, distinctive spit of a silenced revolver. A dark hole materialized in the center of Lisa Brandon's forehead, just above the bridge of her nose.

"Oh, God!" Jessie cried, rushing toward her as the FBI agent lurched backward and fell heavily to the floor.

"Don't move and don't bother checking her," a man said. "I couldn't possibly miss at this range."

Jessie's head swung toward the voice. Standing in the doorway of his room, the silenced pistol in his hand still smoking, was Eastman Tolliver.

CHAPTER 27

THE MOMENT LISA BRANDON'S BODY HIT THE TILED floor, Arlette Malloche and her team of three "stepchildren" were in action. Armed with semiautomatic weapons, moving with speed and skill, they fanned through Surgical Seven as if perfectly prepared for the situation.

The woman who had posed as Hermann's daughter dashed from room to room, disconnecting the phones and throwing them into the hallway. The younger of her "brothers" hauled a suitcase from their room and raced out toward the doors connecting the tower portion of Surgical Seven with the main hospital. The second man, who seemed to Jessie to be the leader of the three, emerged from their room with a tool kit, and headed toward the elevators. Meanwhile, Arlette, her weapon at the ready, assisted Claude Malloche as he directed the shift nurses, Jessie, Gilbride, and Catherine Purcell to move over to the nurses' station.

Physically, Claude Malloche still looked like Eastman Tolliver, but there the similarity to the man he had portrayed ended. His facial expressions, the set of his jaw, his posture, demeanor, and even his English were completely changed. The kindness and patience in his eyes were gone, replaced by the kinetic alertness of a tiger.

"Down, right now!" he ordered to Jessie and the others. "Sit on the floor against that counter."

Four nurses, two aides, a lab tech, and Jessie did as they were ordered. As she slid to the floor, not far from Lisa's body, Jessie realized that thirteen-year-old Tamika Bing—the girl so traumatized by her loss of speech that she had been virtually catatonic since awakening from anesthesia—had witnessed the killing. The girl remained motionless, propped up in bed as usual, staring straight ahead. But Jessie could tell she was riveted on the scene evolving outside her room. She wondered what the grand total of Malloche's victims would be if all the witnesses like Tamika Bing and relatives like Alex Bishop were counted as well.

It was that notion that made Jessie suddenly appreciate how clearly she was thinking—how calm she was, given their situation and the unspeakable violence she had just witnessed. Perhaps her clarity reflected the realization that she, of all of the captives, was in no danger—at least not for the time being. Malloche did have a brain tumor, and he had chosen her to be his surgeon. She was safe. But soon, very soon she suspected, demands were going to be made of her. When that time came, she had to be ready with a few demands of her own.

"What in the hell is going on here?"

Carl Gilbride had not taken his place with the others.

Instead, he had stepped forward, hands on hips, to confront Malloche.

"Let's see," Malloche said with syrupy sarcasm. "To the best of my recollection, the woman lying over there identified herself as an FBI agent, pulled a pistol from her leg holster, and ordered my wife not to move. Then I shot her. I do not believe a medical degree is required to determine that she is dead."

Jessie was in position to see Carl's expression—a strange mix of defiance and utter befuddlement.

"You're not Eastman Tolliver," he said, clearly unable to put the pieces together.

"Brilliant deduction, Dr. Gilbride. If you must know, I borrowed Eastman Tolliver from among the correspondences I found in your office. His secretary in California was kind enough to inform me he was out of the country for several weeks. Now, I'm telling you one last time to get down on the floor with the others."

"Carl, please do as he says," Jessie urged softly.

"I . . . I will do no such thing," Gilbride blustered. "I simply will not tolerate someone coming onto *my* service, in *my* hospital, and pushing people around and shooting them. We have patients to care for here."

Moving like a striking snake, Malloche whipped the barrel of his pistol across Gilbride's cheek. The neurosurgical chief lurched backward, clutching his already hemorrhaging wound, and dropped heavily to his backside just a foot or so from Jessie.

"That wasn't necessary!" Jessie snapped at Malloche.

She grabbed a box of tissues from the counter above her and pried Gilbride's hand away from his cheek. The gash was only about an inch and a half long, but deep— just below the cheekbone, and almost through to his mouth. It would be no problem to sew, but even sutured

by a crackerjack plastic surgeon, the resulting scar would
be a reminder every time Carl looked in the mirror—
provided he survived long enough to do that. She placed
a wad of tissue on the wound and set Gilbride's hand
against it with the whispered instruction to press hard.

"Oh, it *was* necessary, and it *was* deserved," Malloche
replied. "I hope you can all see that your health, your
pain, your very survival mean nothing to me. Nor do
your precious egos. So keep quiet unless you are asked to
speak, and do as we say, and you have every reason to expect that you will not end up either like our FBI friend
over there, or even like our esteemed neurosurgical
chief." He stepped forward and looked down at Carl
with disdain. "Dr. Gilbride, you are a hollow, fatuous ass
of a man. It was you who was responsible for Rolf
Hermann's death, not any mechanical failure of your
robot. That device functioned perfectly, but you didn't.
Your arrogance, greed, and surgical incompetence killed
that man as surely as if you had put a gun to his head and
pulled the trigger. I want you to hear that. I want them
to hear it." He gestured to the group huddled on the
floor and continued the sweep of his arm to include the
rest of Surgical Seven.

"Excuse me," Jessie said calmly, "but could you please
tell us exactly who Rolf Hermann was?"

Malloche's expression was smug.

"He was a count, actually, although a rather penniless
one. He was delivered to me by the neurologist—I
should say the *late* neurologist—whom I went to see in
consultation. I asked about patients whose tumors were
similar to mine. Count Hermann was beginning to develop neurologic weakness. I still had no signs except for
my seizures. Hermann was told by the man, as was I,
that his tumor was virtually inoperable. If we did insist

on surgery and could find a neurosurgeon who would attempt it, there was a very high, if not certain, risk of serious neurological impairment."

"So the Count was a stalking horse for you—a test case."

"I am nothing, dear Doctor, if not careful," Malloche replied. "I assured Rolf that whatever happened here in America, his family would be well cared for. That was far more than his so-called doctors in Germany were able to offer. At worst, he knew his wife and children were provided for, and he would get the services of one of the finest neurosurgeons in America. At best, he would have a cure from his brain tumor, and financial security for the rest of his life. Not a bad deal, if I do say so. Not a bad deal for me either, considering the outcome of poor Rolf's operation."

Ten minutes passed, then twenty. No one moved. The buzz of patient calls for assistance echoed down the hallway, but went unanswered. One by one, the three young killers returned, each whispering a report that clearly pleased Malloche. The five terrorists huddled, while Arlette continued to keep her weapon aimed at the group on the floor—specifically at Carl Gilbride. Finally, Malloche turned and spoke to the captives.

"The doors onto Surgical Seven have been sealed and wired with enough explosives to blow the top off of this building." He nodded toward the younger of the two men. "Armand, here, was personally trained by me, so I can assure you he has done an expert job. And Derrick, over there, has seen to it that only one of the elevators will stop at this floor, and then only when I wish it to." The other man, broad shouldered and Aryan, with a blond crew cut, did a half-bow for the captives. "And finally, you should meet Grace, who left a girls' finishing school right here in

Boston to seek adventure in Europe, and found it with our merry band. She has disconnected all the phones, except the one here in the conference room. No one, but no one, will make contact with the outside unless I allow it. Is that clear? . . . Dr. Gilbride?"

"C—Clear," he managed.

"Dr. Copeland?"

"I want that poor woman's body moved into the back room, where the patients can't see it," Jessie said.

Malloche's expression remained unchanged, except for his eyes, which narrowed as he studied her. She had no doubt he understood the significance of her demand. The battle of their wills had begun.

"Derrick," he said finally, in English, "would you please do as Dr. Copeland requests."

"Very well," Derrick replied, his English heavily accented.

"There," Malloche said. "I've shown my good faith. Now, I think you and I must speak in private. The rest of you will be allowed one by one to get a chair to place right here. Armand will accompany you. From now on, no one will leave this spot unaccompanied whether it is to go to the bathroom or to see one of the patients. Dr. Copeland?"

He motioned her toward the small conference room to the left of the nurses' station.

"Before we speak," Jessie said, "I want to go in and talk to the child who has witnessed all this."

"Another demand. My, my. Very well, then. Grace?"

Grace, her gun hanging at the ready from its shoulder strap, walked Jessie into Tamika Bing's room and stood by the doorway, a respectful distance away. Jessie pulled a chair over to the bedside and sat.

"Tamika, I'm sorry for what you have just seen. I know it was awful for you," she whispered. Not surprisingly, the girl continued staring straight ahead. "Some very bad people have taken over up here. One of them needs an operation just like you had. After the operation is done, they'll leave. Meanwhile, I don't think anyone is going to be allowed up here, including your mother. Do you understand? . . . Tamika?" Jessie stood, then bent down and kissed the girl on the side of her forehead. "Hang in there," she whispered.

By the time Jessie emerged from Tamika's room, each of the staff was seated on a chair in front of the counter, and one of the nurses had pulled a chair over for Carl and was helping him into it. Humiliated and physically beaten, his authority stripped away, he seemed to have aged twenty years in just an hour.

"Carl," Jessie said softly, "I'll sew that cut up as soon as I can. Meanwhile just stay right here and keep pressure on it."

Gilbride nodded vacantly.

"So," Malloche said to her, "I have honored two of your requests. Now we should talk."

He unscrewed the silencer, slipped it into his pocket, and holstered his gun. Then he followed her into the conference room and motioned her to a seat across from him.

"Sit, please, Doctor," he said. "We have some business to discuss."

"Your tumor."

"I would like you to take it out as soon as possible."

"If I refuse?"

Malloche gauged her resolve, then retrieved a phone, plugged it in, and dialed a local number.

"Put her on," he said.

Malloche passed the receiver over.

Jessie listened to a few seconds of silence, then a tentative "Hello?"

Emily!

"Em, it's me. Oh, God, are you okay?"

"He hasn't hurt me, but he won't tell me anything. What's going on?"

Malloche took the phone away before Jessie could reply.

"She's safe for the moment," he said, setting the receiver down. "But I will not hesitate to order her killed if you fail to cooperate. I believe you are a very capable surgeon with a special piece of equipment. I want this tumor out of my head."

"ARTIE's not ready for this."

"I believe it is. I want the surgery done by you, with MRI guidance and robotic assistance, tomorrow."

"I need time to check the system. We'll have to get your lab work done, and you need to be examined by an internist and an anesthesiologist. I also need to speak to people about adjusting the schedule. . . . I'm not in charge of the OR."

"Tomorrow."

"If there're problems with the operation, do I end up like poor Sylvan Mays?"

Malloche looked genuinely impressed.

"I assume our FBI friend had you looking for me?"

"She had me on the alert, yes. She didn't want anyone else to know who she was." Jessie forced herself to back up the lie with a steady gaze. "Later, when I thought Rolf Hermann was you, I tried to tell Carl, but he didn't believe a word of what I said."

"Good old Carl."

"So, answer my question. Do I have any assurances you'll let me live?"

"If you do your job and do it well, you have nothing to fear. You also have my promise of what will happen if you refuse to do this operation. As to what will happen if there are complications, I cannot say. My family is very devoted to me."

"The day after tomorrow," Jessie said. "You'll be seriously affecting your chances if we have to do this as a semiemergency."

Malloche weighed the demand.

"You're going to cause a large number of people great inconvenience," he said. "Tomorrow afternoon."

"Only if everything is ready. And one more thing."

"Yes?"

"I want Emily DelGreco to assist me in the OR."

"I can't allow that. Carl Gilbride will assist you."

"Please. Carl's incompetent. You said so yourself. And right now, he's a doddering wreck. Emily's the very best I have ever worked with. Keep her away and you only hurt yourself."

Again, Malloche took time before replying.

"You win again," he said. "But I promise you, if there is a problem with any phase of this procedure—any problem at all—not one patient or staff member on Surgical Seven will leave this hospital alive. Is that clear?"

Jessie took a deep breath.

"Clear," she said.

She had gotten Emily back and had given Alex added time to act, once he discovered Hermann was not Malloche. That was the best she could do.

"Could you tell me one thing?" she asked.

"Perhaps."

"How are you going to keep an entire hospital floor sealed off without a massive response from the outside?"

For the first time since their discussion began, Claude Malloche smiled.

"It's a bit like bridge," he said. "As long as you play as if the cards most dangerous to you are in the hand of the opponent who is positioned to do you the most harm, you will generally be a step ahead." He slid the phone across to her. "Call Richard Marcus and tell him it is essential that he meet us just outside the pathology office in ten minutes."

"But what if he—"

"Just call him!"

Jessie snatched up the phone and was patched through to the hospital CEO's office immediately. Malloche watched and listened intently until she set the receiver down.

"Ten minutes," she said.

CHAPTER 28

RICHARD MARCUS, ROTUND, BALDING, AND NOT much taller than Jessie, had been the CEO of Eastern Mass Medical Center for six years. A physician with an MBA, he was a decent and intelligent man whom Jessie had always liked and respected. Under his guidance, the hospital had evolved from mediocrity to a place of rising prestige and public confidence. His main failing had always seemed to Jessie to be that he would rather listen to himself than to others. But unlike with Carl Gilbride, who suffered from the same malady, persistence usually succeeded in getting Marcus's attention.

Marcus was waiting outside the pathology office when the elevator doors opened and Jessie emerged with Malloche and Derrick. Both of her companions, she knew, carried weapons—Malloche's concealed beneath his sports coat, and Derrick's beneath a black wind-

breaker with an elastic waist. Marcus had met with
Eastman Tolliver previously and recognized him immediately.

"Mr. Tolliver," he said heartily, "good to see you
again."

Malloche simply grinned and took Marcus's prof-
fered hand. Marcus looked as if he expected an introduction to Derrick, but when none was forthcoming, he
extended his hand and introduced himself. The terrorist
held his grip as briefly as possible and said nothing.
Nonplussed, Marcus turned to Jessie inquiringly.

"Richard," she said, "I think we should go down the
hallway, to where we can talk."

Marcus scanned from one to another of the three and
then did as she had requested.

"So, what's this all about?" he asked.

Malloche nodded that Jessie could do the honors.

"Well, Richard," she said, "it's all about that this man
is not Eastman Tolliver."

"But—"

"His name is Claude Malloche. Have you heard of
him?"

"No, I haven't, but—"

"Mr. Malloche kills people for a living, Richard. And
right now he and his people are holding all the patients
and staff on Surgical Seven hostage. The doors to the
neurosurgical ward are closed off and wired with explosives. The elevators can't be taken to the floor unless Mr.
Malloche brings one there. The reason for all this is that
Malloche has a brain tumor that he wants me to operate
on. Apparently the FBI knew he was sick, and after all
the publicity over Marci Sheprow, they thought he might
be coming here. They had an agent on Surgical Seven
working undercover as a volunteer. Malloche just shot

her to death. Until he has recovered successfully from his surgery, he intends to keep everyone up there prisoner."

The color had drained from Richard Marcus's face. He pulled a handkerchief from his pocket and dabbed at the sheen of sweat that had materialized across his forehead and upper lip.

"I . . . I don't believe this," he managed.

"Believe it, Dr. Marcus," Malloche said. "It is very important that you believe it. I had hoped to have my surgery and return to my home without incident. Fortunately, we were prepared for other possibilities. But we need your help."

"My help?"

"Would you please take us over to the microbiology laboratory."

Marcus hesitated.

"Richard, please," Jessie said. "They're both armed. Just do as he says. Malloche, please don't hurt anyone."

The killer looked at her placidly and gestured Marcus toward the lab. They stopped outside the door—heavy oak with a rubber seal around it. A pane of glass filled the upper half, with MICROBIOLOGY stenciled across it in gold. The room beyond the door was largely Corian counters, sophisticated glassware, stainless steel refrigeration units, and incubators. Two men and two women in lab coats were busily working with agar culture dishes, viral tissue culture bottles, and microscopes.

Jessie knew one of the four, Rachel Sheridan, fairly well from a ski trip to New Hampshire and some other hospital-sponsored social activities. Rachel, divorced with a school-aged daughter, was athletic, fun-loving, and popular. Sound from the room was somewhat muffled by the door and seal, but Jessie could still make out that one of the men—she thought his name might be

Ron—was asking for help identifying the microorganism beneath his scope. Music, maybe Mozart, was playing in the background.

Viewed this way, Jessie almost felt as if she were watching the four technicians on television. *Almost*. A dreadful apprehension was building in her gut. Malloche looked chillingly calm, almost dreamy. His lips bowed in a half-smile, and he nodded to Derrick, who extracted a small transmitter from his jacket pocket and pulled up the antenna.

"NO!"

Before Jessie could even scream the word, Derrick depressed a button on the face of the transmitter. From inside the room, they heard a muffled pop and the sound of breaking glass. A small puff of grayish smoke billowed up from beneath a counter. The technicians spun toward the noise. Jessie cried out and lunged for the door, but Malloche grabbed her lab coat and scrub shirt firmly at the neck and pulled her back.

"Opening that door at this moment would be a foolish mistake," he said.

"Oh, God," Jessie murmured.

Beyond the glass, a hideous dance of death had already begun. Rachel Sheridan, standing closest to the gas, lurched backward as if she'd been kicked in the chest by a mule. At almost the same instant, she began retching violently, setting the counter awash in vomit and splattering two of the others. Her head had twisted abnormally to one side. Her face, frighteningly contorted, had turned the color of gentian violet.

Seconds later, two of the others were staggering about as well, vomiting uncontrollably with projectile force, and sending glasswork, incubators, and stacks of culture dishes crashing to the floor as they thrashed about. The grotesque discoloration of their faces and almost inhuman torsion of their necks mimicked Rachel's. The three of them were collapsing to the floor when the fourth, perhaps having held her breath, began to twitch and clutch at her belly. As she stumbled to one side, she looked through the glass and saw the group standing there, transfixed. With overwhelming panic distorting her face, she stretched an unsteady, clawed hand in their direction.

Help me! came her silent scream. *Help me.*

Then she, too, began retching.

In less than two nightmarish minutes it was over. The four technicians, grotesquely discolored, soaked in vomit, lay dead on the floor, limbs splayed, faces violet, necks twisted almost ninety degrees to one side.

Richard Marcus turned away and braced himself against a wall. Jessie, who had been standing shoulder to shoulder with him, also looked away.

"You monster," she said, her back still to Malloche. "You fucking monster!"

She whirled and threw a closed-fisted punch at his face. Malloche caught her fist as calmly as if it were a tennis ball she had lobbed to him, and squeezed it just hard enough to warn against any repeat.

"Easy, now," he said. "We don't want anything happening to that hand of yours. Perhaps we'd better head back up to Surgical Seven before someone has the misfortune to come along and see us. With the ventilating hoods in that room, the gas should be dissipated in just a minute or two. Come along."

Jessie supported Richard Marcus, who was ghastly pale and perspiring heavily. Once in the elevator, she lowered him to the floor. Gradually, his color began to return. Derrick made a call on a two-way radio, and they headed upward. Somewhere between the third and fourth floors, Malloche threw the emergency switch, stopping the car.

"I'm sorry if our little demonstration upset you both. But I need your complete cooperation as well as your confidence that my threats are not idle ones. Dr. Marcus, do you hear me?"

"I . . . I hear you."

"Then look at me, please. You have a very important role to play in all of this, and you have precious little time to prepare."

Marcus struggled to his feet.

"Bastard," he muttered.

"There, that's much better," Malloche said. "The gas whose power you just witnessed is called soman. You may have heard of it as GD, currently the most virulent neurotoxin known to man—far more potent than sarin. Some friends of ours in Baghdad have made a generous supply available to us. But I assure you that, depending on placement, population density, and the prevailing wind, a generous supply of soman is not needed to cause a massive amount of damage. We have placed radio-detonated vials, much larger than the one whose effects you just witnessed, in well-camouflaged spots in heavily trafficked areas throughout the city. If anything should happen to prevent my surgery, or if I should not wake up promptly after leaving the operating room, not only will all those on Surgical Seven pay the price, but a significant proportion of the city as well. Is that clear? . . . Dr. Marcus?"

"Oh, God. Yes, it's clear, it's clear."

"I will be cured of this tumor in my head, and I will make it safely out of the hospital. Is that clear, Dr. Copeland?"

Jessie sighed.

"Clear," she said.

"Okay. I'm glad we're on the same page. Now, Dr. Marcus, you have about two days to keep the public at bay, maybe three, depending on my recovery time. In the process of so doing, you will save the lives of a great many people. First, I want you to empty the pathology department and seal it off. Then announce to the media that there has been a biological disaster here at the hospital—a deadly viral exposure of some as yet unknown sort, requiring that the microbiology lab and the neurosurgical service on Surgical Seven be sealed off. Inform the public that the rest of the hospital is perfectly safe, but as a precaution it is being closed to all but essential personnel. All other hospital employees should be told to stay away until the crisis has passed. Go to minimal staffing. Double or triple all pay for those who come in. Discharge as many patients as possible at once. Chain off all entryways except through the main lobby. Divert all emergencies to other hospitals. Clear?"

"Yes, but—"

"Then you are to do whatever is necessary to muddle efforts to get to the bottom of the problem. If one agency wants to investigate, tell them another already is. Create as much confusion and dissension as you can. Whatever you need to do to buy time you must do. Derrick, here, or one of my other people, will be with you at all times seeing to it that you perform the way I know you're capable of. Another of my people will be out in the city, connected to us by radio, and never far from the vials of soman. Please do not do anything that will force me to conduct another, more extensive demonstration of its virulence."

"I—I'll try my best," Marcus replied.

Malloche threw the switch and returned Marcus and Derrick to the basement. Then he took Jessie back up to Surgical Seven.

"Dr. Copeland, I have decided that my surgery will take place tomorrow afternoon no matter what. Offer whatever assurances and financial inducements necessary to assemble the essential operating room personnel. Fail in this regard, and I promise you a quite sizable group of people will suddenly be on intimate terms with soman."

"I don't see how—"

"Dr. Copeland, my patience is thin, and my demands are not up for debate. Now mobilize whomever you have to and get this goddamn tumor out of my brain."

CHAPTER 29

OVER THE SEVENTEEN YEARS SINCE THE CIA HAD recruited him, Alex Bishop had become used to dealing with informants. Most were no less criminal than those on whom they were informing. Jorge Cardoza was no different. A scarred, rodent-faced little man, he had made it up the ranks in Claude Malloche's organization simply because he was quite proficient at the one skill Malloche demanded—killing.

As Alex inched back from the airport into Boston through the Sumner Tunnel, he assessed the man who he knew was responsible for the deaths of many. Cardoza, dressed in worn jeans and a stained polo shirt, sat slumped in the passenger seat, head pressed against the side window, staring out at the exhaust-stained concrete and tile. He had traded information on Malloche for his own freedom and had paid dearly for that decision. Now, with his wife and child dead, and a hefty price on his head throughout Malloche's organization, information was all that was keeping him from being thrown to the wolves. With no money and no support whatsoever as far as Alex could tell, he was attempting to start his life over again in Uruguay—the one place outside of Europe where he had relatives.

"You promise I can have my money and my plane tickets out of here as soon as I have done what you want?" Cardoza asked in Spanish.

"You identify this body and I will keep my side of the bargain," Alex replied, his Castilian Spanish fluent and with little accent.

"What if the man you have is not Malloche?"

"Then I will have made a very serious misjudgment, and you will still be free to go."

"With the money."

"Yes."

"And the tickets."

"Yes. But I am certain the man I have *is* Malloche."

Alex used his cell phone to call the FBI answering service that was functioning essentially as his office. No word from Jessie, no word from Lisa Brandon. Both were good signs. Arlette Malloche was still at Eastern Mass Medical, apparently willing to accept as necessary the delays in allowing her to claim her husband's body. It would not be long now. Once Malloche was positively identified, he was sure the Boston FBI would cooperate fully and move in on Arlette and her people.

"It has been hard on me," Cardoza said.

"I know, I know."

Ratting on your cohorts often is.

"Malloche has forced me to do this."

"Yes, he has."

"You are a good man, Bishop."

"That means a lot coming from you, Jorge."

The Bowker and Hammersmith Funeral Parlor, in the city's Dorchester section, was straight out of *The Twilight Zone*—weathered sign, gray, peeling clapboard siding, front steps that creaked and groaned on the way up to a porch that couldn't possibly have supported an oak casket and full complement of pallbearers.

"I need a funeral parlor that will rent me a hearse and store a body, and not ask any questions," Alex had asked his FBI contact.

Bowker and Hammersmith's number was given to him without hesitation.

Alex pulled the rental car into the driveway on the side and motioned Cardoza to bring along his luggage—a single black nylon gym bag, small enough to carry onto the plane. They entered the funeral parlor through a service door and went directly to the basement room that held the refrigerated walk-in storage unit.

The man Alex had dealt with at the funeral home had identified himself as Richard Jones. He had gladly taken five hundred dollars, along with another thousand that would be returned when the hearse was. Now, as Jones put it, he was out of the loop and would be gone until the body had been identified and someone from the coroner's office had come by to pick it up.

Alex flipped on the light and directed Cardoza to wait while he went to get Malloche.

This is it, he was thinking. *Five years.*

He wheeled out the body and pulled the sheet down to the nipples. The lips had pulled back in a gaping, toothy rictus so that it looked as if Malloche were grinning at him. Unsettling.

Jorge Cardoza approached the corpse cautiously, then bent over and studied the face.

"You have my money and my ticket?" he asked.

"Right here." Alex patted his pocket.

"And I get them no matter what?"

"No matter what." Alex felt suddenly cold. There was no reason for Cardoza to be stalling like this unless—

"It's not him."

"What?"

"I don't know who this is, but it is not Claude Malloche."

Alex braced himself on the stretcher and stared down at the corpse.

"Could he have had plastic surgery?"

"I saw him just three or four months ago," Cardoza replied. "There is no resemblance."

Alex grabbed the man by his shirt and pulled him up onto his tiptoes.

"Look at me, Jorge! Look me in the eyes and say this isn't Malloche!"

"Bishop, I want the man to be dead as much as you do. He killed my wife and child, and he wants to kill me! But this is not Malloche."

Slowly, Alex released his grip.

"I don't believe this," he said. "I . . . I was so certain. What about Arlette? Have you ever seen her?"

Cardoza shook his head.

"I only know that she is said to be a very beautiful woman," he said. "Now, please. . . ."

Bishop replaced the sheet, wheeled Rolf Hermann's body back into the refrigerator, and closed the door. There was no sense trying to keep Cardoza around to identify a man who might already be back in Europe after having been operated on at some other medical center. He had lost, and that was that. With luck, Malloche would die from his goddamn tumor. But it was doubtful Alex Bishop would ever hear about it.

Numbly, he walked the Spaniard back to the car, gave him his tickets and money, and dropped him off at a T station.

CHAPTER 30

THROUGH LATE AFTERNOON AND INTO THE EVENING
the moans of Surgical Seven patients begging for services
or explanations was constant. The beepers of Carl, Jessie,
nursing supervisor Catherine Purcell, and the lab tech
were sounding so persistently that Malloche finally had
them confiscated and turned off. Worsening the situation, Malloche's headache had returned with force,
causing him to be increasingly irritable and uncommu-
nicative. Finally, he ordered some painkiller from one of
the nurses and returned to his bed.

Arlette readily took over, controlling the siege with
even more dispassion than had her husband. Nurses
were sent to aid patients only one at a time, and never
unaccompanied. One guard was constantly watching the
staff seated along the nurses' station counter, while another was positioned by the doors and elevator, wiring

more explosives in place. Arlette herself spent much of the time at the doorway to her room, watching as news reports of the biological disaster at Eastern Mass Medical Center unfolded on television. At other times, she patrolled the corridors, her semiautomatic slung at loose readiness over her shoulder.

Carl Gilbride was still in near shock. Except for the thirty minutes it took Jessie to guide him to the treatment room and sew up the gash in his face, he sat slumped in his chair, showing no particular interest in his surroundings, at times even dozing off. At five, his patient Lena Levin lapsed into a coma from the bacterial infection that was building rapidly where he had recently removed her tumor. Jessie was allowed to examine her and then confronted Arlette.

"She needs to have a spinal tap and be moved into the unit," she said.

"The unit is closed. The patients and the staff have all been moved in here."

"I want to call an infectious disease consult to discuss her therapy and order some antibiotics."

"No calls. Use what medicine you already have here."

At that moment, one of the nurses came racing up to Arlette in a panic, with Grace a few steps behind.

"I need to call home," she said breathlessly.

"No calls," Arlette responded.

"It's my son. He has a seizure problem and he needs medicine I give him, that my sitter doesn't know about."

"I said no calls and I mean it. We let you, and everyone will have a reason to need a phone. We have more important things to attend to."

"Please," Jessie said.

Arlette shot her a withering look and demanded, with a jerk of the muzzle of her machine gun, that the nurse get back to her seat. After the woman had settled down, Arlette motioned Jessie over to a spot away from the others.

"My husband's headache is worsening," she said.

"I'm not surprised."

"I want his surgery done first thing in the morning, not tomorrow afternoon."

"A pediatric neurosurgeon has the OR booked. There's a very sick child who needs his tumor out."

"Get the case postponed."

"I can try, but I want you to let that nurse call home."

"What I'll do instead," Arlette said, "is to kill her."

Jessie sized up the threat and realized that Arlette wasn't bluffing. She saw beyond the woman to where Tamika Bing lay propped up in bed as usual, watching and listening.

"I'll do what I can," Jessie said.

Calling from the treatment room, with Arlette monitoring, she succeeded in convincing the surgeon that with the burgeoning crisis in the hospital, it was prudent to forget about using the MRI operating room at all, and instead arrange to do his case at the Hospital for Infants and Children. Then, with Armand following her, she went to check in on some of the patients, beginning with Sara. Her friend was lying on her back, eyes closed. She looked peaceful enough, but her breathing seemed slightly rapid.

"Hi, pal," Jessie said ". . . . Sara?"

She had expected a quick response. Instead, Sara remained as she was. Anxious, Jessie took her by the shoulders and rousted her gently. Sara's eyes blinked open, and she forced a smile. But she seemed to be having trouble focusing.

"Hey . . . ," was all she managed to say.

"You okay?"

"I . . . okay."

"Sara?"

Sara's reply was slow in coming—too slow, Jessie thought. She did a rapid neuro check, including a careful examination through her ophthalmoscope. Everything seemed okay . . . everything except the patient. Gradually, Sara became more able to answer questions appropriately, but she still appeared marginally less aware and more sluggish than she had been. Jessie mentally scrolled through half a dozen diagnostic possibilities, including medication toxicity and simple exhaustion. But the one diagnosis that worried her most was a slow pressure buildup from a blockage to the flow of spinal fluid in and around the brain. The obstruction, if there was one, was most likely caused by scar tissue, a blood clot, or local tissue swelling. And if it became a total blockade, it would result in acute hydrocephalus— a true neurosurgical emergency. But right now, without access to the scanners in radiology, Jessie could do nothing but watch her closely.

Damn you, she thought as Armand followed her around to Tamika Bing's room. *Damn you all.*

The thirteen-year-old appeared as she always did— stiff and motionless, gazing out at the spot in the hall where, just a few hours ago, a woman had been shot to death. Jessie wondered if there was anything at all she could say to the child that would blunt the impact of having witnessed such brutality. She pulled up a chair.

"Hi, Tamika," she said. "Here I am, back again. . . . Everyone is very upset about what happened to that poor woman. She worked for the FBI, and she was trying to help us all when she was shot. . . . When this is all over, I'm going to find her family and tell them how

brave she was. . . . Tamika? . . . Please look at me, baby.
I want so much to know how you are feeling and to help
in any way I can."

Suddenly, almost imperceptibly, Tamika Bing's hands
moved from where they were folded in her lap up to the
edge of her tray table. Her eyes remained fixed straight
ahead, her posture rigid. Aside from chewing food that
was placed in her mouth, it was the most purposeful
movement Jessie had seen her make since the surgery.
Again the girl's hands moved. Now her fingertips were
touching the edge of her laptop. The computer was always open and ready on her tray table, but as far as Jessie
or Tamika's mother knew, it had never been used.

Jessie risked a peek at Armand, who stood at attention by the doorway, peering over to check on them from
time to time, but without much interest. Mostly his focus
was out in the hall. Tamika's fingers were now on the
keyboard. Jessie shifted her chair just enough to be able
to read the screen. The girl struck the keys softly, with
the economical movements of a skilled typist.

Give me a phone connection and I can get outside, she wrote.

Stunned, Jessie stared first at the screen, then at Tamika.
The girl continued looking straight ahead. But Jessie noticed the corners of her mouth were drawn up ever so
slightly.

Fooled you, the expression was saying.

Bless you, child.

"So, dear," Jessie said with clarity, careful to avoid
any change in tone that might alert Armand. "It's so nice
that you're practicing your typing again. Let me see what
else you can do."

My friend Ricky checks his e-mail all the time.
I can get a message to him.

Jessie's pulse was racing. The phone cable lay on the
floor, still connected to the wall. She checked the back of
the laptop to establish where the modem port was. With
luck, lots of luck, they might have a connection to
Alex—a connection Arlette and her crew would know
nothing about.

"Yes, of course," Jessie said. "I can get that for you,
Tamika. I'll be back in just a little while with that medicine you need. Meanwhile, you just rest. You're doing
terrific. Absolutely terrific."

With Armand not far behind, Jessie went to the
nurses' station and retrieved the red loose-leaf notebook
that was Tamika Bing's chart. Now, both Armand
and Arlette were watching her, but neither of
them seemed particularly interested as she opened the
record and began writing a message to Alex on a
progress note sheet. She said a silent prayer of thanks
that she had jotted the number of his answering service in her pocket-sized clinical notebook. The book,
hers since medical school, was tattered and swollen
to the point where an elastic band was required to
hold it closed. It was packed with normal lab values,
medication doses, diagnostic tables, and other reference
cards. For a decade now, when she was in the hospital and not in the OR or showering, the little black
book was never out of her possession. Her message completed, she wrote Alex's answering service number at
the top of the progress report sheet, then slowly slid
the paper free from the binder rings. Moments later,
the weeping of the distraught nurse diverted Arlette
and Armand long enough for her to fold the sheet and

drop it into her pocket. Their response also gave her an idea.

Broad-shouldered linebacker Dave Scolari was up in a chair by his bed, wrapped in a blanket, his head immobilized inside his steel cervical halo. He was still unable to bear enough weight to walk, but the therapists had fitted him for braces and were glowing about his future prospects. Quadriplegic less than two weeks ago, he now had excellent movement and strength in his arms, and improving coordination in his hands. As Jessie anticipated, Armand took his post by the door. She took her stethoscope from her lab coat, placed it around her neck, and positioned herself so that she could converse with Scolari without being easily overheard.

"What in the hell is going on here, Doc?" Scolari asked. "Who took my phone? I've been ringing the call button like crazy. Nobody answers. Who in the hell is he?"

"That's Armand. Armand, this is Dave."

The killer looked over at them disdainfully and locked his hand on the stock of his weapon.

"Armand and some others have taken over Surgical Seven and sealed us off from the rest of the hospital," Jessie went on. "They plan to be here for a couple of days."

"Did they hurt you?" Dave asked.

"No. They've killed five people so far and are threatening everyone else, but I'm immune. They want me to operate on their leader."

"Enough!" Armand barked in heavily accented English. "Finish what you have to do and move on."

Jessie set her stethoscope in her ears, but kept the earpieces pressed just outside her auditory canal opening.

"I need a diversion, Dave," she whispered as she pretended to examine him, her back to Armand.

"Something loud that will bring all these people running in here."

"I'll try."

"It's got to be convincing."

"I understand."

"In ten minutes. Do it at exactly five past."

"Got it," Dave said, looking up at the wall clock.

Armand was moving toward them when she pocketed her stethoscope and stepped back.

"You're coming along fine, Dave," she said. "That little wheeze in your chest is nothing to worry about."

The clock ticking, she led Armand back to the room next to Tamika Bing's. With a minute to go, she reentered Tamika's room and again fixed her stethoscope in place. At precisely five after the hour, there was a loud crash from Scolari's room, followed by eerie, animal-like, bellowing cries of pain. Another crash. Armand turned and raced toward the sound. A moment later, Arlette hurried past the door without looking in.

Jessie quickly tucked the note she had written under Tamika's thigh, then picked up the phone cord and ran it under the tray table before inserting the connector into the back of the laptop. Finally, she pulled the sheet over the cord, covering as much of it as possible. She had just set a towel on the tray table to shield the rest of the cord when Armand reappeared at the door.

"Come quick," he commanded.

Jessie kissed Tamika on the cheek.

"Remember to dial nine first for an outside line," she whispered.

I knew that! the girl typed.

Dave Scolari was thrashing about in what was probably his attempt at feigning a seizure. He had somehow managed to knock over his sturdy bedside table and his tray table. Saliva was bubbling from his mouth, mixing with blood from where he had actually bitten through his lip. Jessie was relieved to see that the cervical halo was intact.

"He's having a seizure," she said. "I need medicine to stop it. Tell the nurses to bring me a syringe with ten of Valium in it."

Arlette hesitated, then nodded to Armand that he could carry out the order. A minute later, he handed Jessie a loaded syringe. She jammed the needle just beneath Dave's thigh, and injected his robe with tranquilizer. Then she bent over and put her lips by his ear.

"You did good, Dave," she whispered. "You did real good."

CHAPTER 31

CORRIGAN'S TAVERN WAS A DARK, MUSTY CORNER saloon not far from the Bowker and Hammersmith Funeral Parlor. Alex sat on a stool at one end of the bar, working on a tumbler of scotch—the second of what he planned to be a series of twenty or so. The evening crowd was drifting in, and the level of smoke in the place was actually starting to get to him.

Well, so be it, he thought. The deal he had made with himself about no cigarettes until Malloche was dead or in prison never mentioned secondhand smoke. And if the shit gave him lung cancer, so what. He had blown everything that mattered to him, and blown it all big-time. Along the way, he had called in enough markers from the agency, the FBI, and certain politicians to finish forever any chance of ever getting more help in catching Malloche. Then there were all the ways he had lied to Jessie, and the risks he had convinced her to take in helping him with Hermann's body. And for what? Now, he had no place to go and no one who cared. After this fiasco, it was likely that even the people at the academy would want nothing to do with him.

There was also the slight matter of the body he had stolen from the hospital—another gem. He had called and left a message for Richard Jones at the funeral parlor to contact Orlis Hermann on Surgical Seven. That was the best he could do at the moment.

What difference does it make anyhow?

Alex sipped at his scotch and tried to remember the last time he had been certifiably, gut-tearing, bury-me-before-you-wake-me drunk. It wasn't anything he was especially looking forward to, but then again, what was? Okay, he acknowledged, Jessie Copeland would have been something to look forward to. Every single day. He cared about her—more than for any woman he could remember. He cringed at the thought of calling her with the details of the monumental failure of his life. She had just begun to trust him. Now, she'd never believe anything he ever had to say.

What did he have to show for his forty-three years on earth? A one-room flat in Paris that he could barely afford, a future at the agency that he could probably measure in weeks, and a résumé that was one prolonged blank spot. His bank accounts were woefully thin, and his connections to friends and family had long ago been sacrificed on the altar of destroying Claude Malloche. What more could a good-looking, brilliant woman like Jessie Copeland possibly want in a man?

He drained the last of the scotch and was about to order a third when he caught a fragment of conversation from a man standing behind him. Actually, what he overheard were three words: Eastern Mass Medical. He spun around on his stool.

"What about Eastern Mass Medical?" he asked a group of four.

"Where the fuck have *you* been all afternoon?" a lumberjack-sized construction worker, his speech beginning to thicken, roared at him.

The others laughed. Alex blew past them, grabbed the larger man by his shirt, and hoisted him up onto his tiptoes. This is what he *really* needed at this moment, he was thinking. A huge wise-ass to bring down to size, not a self-destructive bender. The bender could come after.

"I asked you a question," he said.

The giant stumbled back, brushing Alex's hand aside in the same motion. The talk throughout the tavern abruptly ceased with anticipation. For several seconds, no one around them moved or spoke. There was the scraping of chairs as others in the place stood to watch. Then the man, perhaps sensing from Alex's expression and stance that he was some sort of psycho, put his hands up, palms out.

"Hey, pal, easy does it," he said. "Cool your jets. This is a friendly place. If you don't like the way we do things here, go somewhere else."

"I asked you about the hospital."

"Okay, okay. They had some kinda outbreak there. A virus, I guess. I don't know for sure. A bunch of people are dead, though. I do know that much."

"The hospital's closed down," someone else chimed in.

"It was four," another offered. "Four people are dead."

With the crisis in the bar over as quickly as it had begun, the patrons now seemed to be talking all at once about the developments at EMMC. Alex pushed a twenty toward the bartender, found a relatively quiet corner, and called the hospital. He got a recorded message saying that all hospital lines were tied up, that the hospital was temporarily closed to new patients, and that all emergencies should be taken to Eastern Mass Medical's associate institution, White Memorial, or to one of the other Boston hospitals.

A previous page to Jessie had gone unanswered. Now, he tried her again. The recorded electronic hospital page operator answered, and promised his message had been sent.

Four people dead. The hospital sealed up. Alex dialed his answering service.

"Oh, yes, Mr. Bishop," the FBI operator said. "We were about to try to reach you. A call just came in for you a few minutes ago. Someone named Ricky Barnett."

"Never heard of him."

"It was very strange. He sounded like a little boy, and he was very shy. He said that he had a message for you from a friend of his."

"A friend? Who?"

"He didn't say except that she was in the hospital."

```
Call  Alex  Bishop  at  4269444.  Message  from
Jessie.  Tolliver  is  Malloche.  Lisa  dead.  Five  of
them  have  wired  Surgical  7  to  explode.  Soman  gas
hidden  all  over  Boston.  Will  be  released  if
there  is  any  trouble  for  Malloche.  Four  killed
in  lab  as  a  demonstration.  Be  careful.
```

Alex sped toward EMMC with Ricky Barnett's e-mail message propped against the steering wheel.

Tolliver is Malloche.

Bishop felt a dreadful spasm in his gut at the news. Not only had he completely missed his target, but because of his incompetence, agent Lisa Brandon was dead, and Jessie—and it appeared many others—was in serious danger. The irony was almost more than he could bear. Claude Malloche was right there on Surgical Seven, all right. But he was most certainly not there for the taking.

Thirteen-year-old Ricky Barnett told him that he had formed a secret computer club with Tamika Bing and two other kids. The e-mail message from Tamika, which Alex had the boy spell out for him letter by letter as he transcribed it onto a blank bar tab, had been sent from the hospital earlier in the afternoon, but wasn't retrieved until Ricky came home. Alex had him send a message back to Tamika, telling Jessie he understood and would do what he could. Now, he was trying to learn about soman. He was about a mile from the hospital when his cell phone rang.

"Agent Bishop?"

"That's right."

"Abdul Fareed, here. I'm a toxicologist at Georgetown. I do some contract work for the agency. They said you wanted information on soman."

"I do."

"If you're dealing with soman, you've got trouble. It's also called GD. It's an inhaled neurotoxin—the most powerful stuff of its kind. Works three or four times as fast as sarin, the gas those fanatics used in the Tokyo subway. Respiratory and central nervous system collapse all at once. One hundred percent fatal from a single decent breath."

"Any antidote?"

"The only antidote I know of, carbamate physostigmine, is almost as toxic as the gas, and has to be taken *before* exposure. I've got a call in to a friend of mine in Jerusalem who is one of the world's experts on neurotoxic gases. If she has anything to add to what I've said, I'll call you."

"Okay. If I don't answer, call my service and insist on speaking to someone from the agency or the FBI. Tell them all you know."

"One other piece of information I can pass on is that the half-life of soman is pretty short. If you're at ground zero, and there's decent ventilation, and you can hold your breath for two or three minutes, you've got a chance."

"Thanks, that's very reassuring."

Alex hung up and dialed a number in Virginia.

"Seven-eight-two-eight," a woman answered. "May I help you?"

"This is Alex Bishop calling back."

"Oh, yes, sir."

"Were you able to get any of the information I wanted?"

"Yes, sir. Eastman Tolliver is the executive director of the MacIntosh Foundation in Valencia, California. They fund research projects, mostly in the medical field. Mr. Tolliver has been on a trip to China for over two weeks. He's not expected back for another ten days. That's all we have right now. Is there anything else we can do?"

"No, no thank you."

Police had cordoned off the area a block away from the hospital. Filling the streets outside the blockade were mobile broadcasting vans and enough police cruisers to suggest that the rest of the city might be ripe for the picking. From what he could tell, no one seemed anxious to get any closer to EMMC than they were. With no CIA

ID, it took fifteen minutes and two phone calls before
Alex was waved past the wooden barriers.

He pulled onto a side street just across from the main
hospital entrance and waited. Ten minutes later, an un-
marked, windowless van pulled up behind him. He
waited until the lights had been cut, then scanned the
area for anyone who might be watching them. Finally,
he gathered up his security guard uniform from the back
seat, left the rental, and approached the van on the driver's side. The two FBI agents inside introduced themselves as Stan Moyer and Vicki Holcroft. Moyer was a
slightly built, balding man in his forties, whose heavy-
lidded eyes and wire-rims made him look more like a
classics professor than a Fed. Vicki was young, though
not as young as Lisa Brandon. Her blond hair was pulled
back in a ponytail, and her features, while undeniably
pretty, were also sharp and businesslike.

"Back door's open," Stan said. He waited until Alex
was inside, then asked, "Is it true that Lisa's dead?"

"I believe so."

"She was a terrific kid."

"I know."

The van was equipped with three TV monitors, several telephones, and banks of instruments on both sides.
Alex freed up a chair from its tie-down straps and
scanned the consoles. Then he brought the two agents up
to date on what he knew. Vicki worked her way into the
back and took a seat beside him.

"I'm glad we were around," she said. "Stan and I
helped design this van. There are others who can handle
most of this equipment, but not like us."

"The problem spot is the seventh floor of the Surgical
Tower, right over there."

Vicki peered at the tower through the front windshield and shook her head.

"Too high to pick up anything through our parabolics. We've got fiber-optic cameras, though, and some pretty awesome little microphones. If we can slip them up through the floor, or down through the ceiling, we should be able to see and hear a heck of a lot. Stanley's a master at doing it if you can get him up there."

"I don't know. Maybe. They've got about forty hostages up there right now, and a million hostages out here. That gas could be hidden anywhere."

"And what's your connection on the floor?"

"Believe it or not, it's a thirteen-year-old kid named Tamika Bing, with a laptop. She's a patient on Surgical Seven. Somehow she's been able to get an e-mail message out to a friend of hers named Ricky Barnett. He called me."

Vicki brightened.

"How much into computers are they, do you know?" she asked.

"I can find out by calling the kid in Roxbury. He and Tamika formed some kind of computer club. I know that much."

"That sounds promising. We'll call and ask him if Tamika has an ICQ number."

"ICQ?"

"It's an instant messaging system. If she's got one, I can download the ICQ software from our office in just a few minutes so that we can hold a give-and-take conversation with her from right here."

"Here's the boy's number," Alex said. "He's waiting to hear from us. I need to change back into my security guard uniform so I can get into the hospital. Vicki, if you haven't had a cardiogram lately, you may want to look the other way."

The woman smiled, picked up the phone, and turned her back to him.

"What are you going to do once you're in there?" Stan asked.

"I'm not sure. First, maybe, I'll try to speak with someone in maintenance, or else the hospital CEO, to see if I can get blueprints of the place."

"The CEO is otherwise occupied," Stan said. "He's supposed to be holding a press conference right now. No, wait, it's not as late as I thought. It should start in a minute or two."

He clambered into the back, electronically raised a satellite dish that had been concealed in the van's roof, and switched on one of the monitors. All the local channels were getting pictures from the same single feed—an unadorned podium in the main foyer of the hospital, fitted with several microphones. For a time, there was only a technician, readying some cables. Then, a drawn and clearly troubled Richard Marcus approached the podium. Behind him stood a scientist in a lab coat, and a man from security.

"I am Dr. Richard Marcus. For more than six years I have been the CEO of the Eastern Massachusetts Medical Center. My specialties are internal medicine and, ironically, infectious disease. I am here to give you all a briefing on the situation in our microbiology lab and on Surgical Seven, our neurosurgery floor. To this moment, there have been five deaths, four in the lab and one on Surgical Seven. We strongly believe the deaths are due to a very rapidly acting microorganism—most likely some sort of virus, which causes a brain infection called encephalitis, characterized by massive brain swelling and in most cases, rapid death. There is evidence of several more cases still evolving on Surgical Seven, so we have shut the floor down, and effectively sealed off the hospital as well. We currently have a team of microbiologists at work. That is all the information I can share with you at this time. However, we will bring you updates every hour on the hour, and immediately if there are any major developments. Hopefully, next hour there will be some telephone hookups here at this podium so reporters can phone in questions. Meanwhile, I beg your patience as we try our best to contain this outbreak. Thank you."

Marcus left the podium without calling on the scientist to speak.

"Impressive man," Stan said. "Maybe there *is* no gas. Maybe it *is* a virus."

"Highly doubtful," Alex replied.

"Why?" Vicki asked.

"Well, for one thing, that security guard standing behind Marcus was one of Malloche's men."

CHAPTER 32

FROM THE WINDOWS OF SURGICAL SEVEN, JESSIE could see the phalanx of news vehicles and police cruisers lined up along the streets a block away from the hospital, like strobe-lit spokes on a wheel. It was after eleven. The surgery on Claude Malloche was less than seven hours away.

Scrub nurse . . . circulating nurse . . . console technician . . . Hans Pfeffer and one of his computer people . . . Skip Porter . . . Jessie decided to involve only a skeleton crew in the operation. One by one, she had contacted the team to notify each that the case they would be working on first thing in the morning was a matter of great urgency, and could only be done with MRI assistance. She guaranteed them a sizable bonus and assured them that there was no danger from exposure to Eastman Tolliver, who was in the ICU, isolated from the rest of the patients on Surgical Seven. Of the group, only the scrub nurse balked at the idea of coming in. Jessie actually resorted to having Richard Marcus call to assure the man that he would be placing himself in no danger. Finally, the team was set. Only Emily was missing, but Arlette had promised that she would be brought to the floor sometime during the night.

Jessie didn't even bother to point out the obvious— that the way they were doing things, both surgeon and assistant would be operating with major sleep deprivation. Except for delaying the case so they could rest, which was simply not going to happen, there was nothing anyone could do about it.

Determined to have as few people as possible involved with Malloche, Jessie elected to forgo the standard pre-op medical clearance and instead had Malloche's man Derrick help her wheel him down for a chest X ray and EKG, which she then had the appropriate on-call residents review.

Next came choosing an anesthesiologist. Jessie was pleased that Michelle Booker was available and willing to do the case. Booker, a descendant of slaves and the daughter of an uneducated single mother in Alabama, had finished first in her class at Tuskegee Institute, then first again at Harvard Med. She was already a full professor in her department, though she was only Jessie's age. She was also intuitive enough, Jessie believed, to pick up on some of what was going on without asking too many questions. Jessie felt bad at having to involve anyone in such a potentially perilous situation, let alone someone as essential to the medical community as Michelle. But a great many lives hinged on Malloche's surviving his surgery. The pre-op anesthesia evaluation was conducted in the recovery room on Surgical Eight.

"So, Mr. Tolliver," Michelle said after she had completed her history and physical, "our plan is to put you to sleep initially so that the tiny robot can be worked into place. Then we will wake you for most of the remainder of the procedure so that Dr. Copeland can monitor your neurologic function while she resects your tumor. Do you have any questions regarding that or any other aspect of tomorrow's procedure?"

"No," Malloche said. "You've explained things well. Several days ago I was in the operating room, observing the robot at work on a case. I know what to expect."

"That's excellent. Still, I'm told that the sensation of being awake during one's own brain surgery almost defies description. I plan to keep you sedated as much as possible, even though you won't actually be asleep."

"You're the doctor," Malloche said.

"Correction," Michelle said. "I'm the anesthesiologist. That woman over there by the window is The Doctor, capital T, capital D. And you couldn't do any better. Jess, do you have anything to add to what I've said? . . . Jessie? . . ."

Jessie was gazing out the window at nothing in particular. Booker's description of the procedure had sent an idea flashing through her mind—something important, she was almost certain. But the notion had vanished before she could get a fix on it.

Now, an hour later, back on Surgical Seven, Jessie was still struggling to reconnect with the thought. Something Michelle Booker had said to Malloche had triggered an idea . . . something . . .

With Grace dogging her step for step, Jessie wandered around the Track, carefully pausing at each patient's doorway. Although she tried to show interest in all of them, only two of the patients really concerned her at this moment: Sara Devereau, who continued to seem just a bit more sluggish than she had been, and Tamika Bing.

Tamika had made contact with Alex, and in fact was on-line continuously now with someone named Vicki. Jessie had risked going into her room twice during the evening and managed to come out each time with a message from Alex. The first, which she had read right off the screen, said simply:

```
I am with you. Please be careful. When is
Malloche's operation? A.
```

The second was more detailed.

```
We are working on penetrating the hospital.
Understand that Orlis Hermann is Arlette
Malloche and that there are three plus her and
Malloche on Surgical Seven. Any more? Probable
contact point will be the MRI-OR. Any idea where
the soman might be hidden? Tamika, good job.
Jessie, hang in. Be careful. We're going to win.
A.
```

With her captor standing so close, Jessie felt reluctant to speak to Tamika of anything but how she was doing. She did risk another pass with her stethoscope and some whispered words of encouragement. Then she remembered that all Malloche's people she knew of were accounted for when she spoke by phone to Emily.

"Tamika, you're doing great," she whispered. "Tell Vicki there is at least one more of Malloche's men outside the hospital."

While Jessie continued listening to her chest, Tamika

silently typed out the message. Moments later, Jessie was walking the halls again, frantically trying to reconnect with the thought that had eluded her on Surgical Eight. As she passed Claude Malloche's room, she paused. Through the semidarkness, she could see the monster, asleep on his back, the sheet over his chest rising and falling with each easy breath. Jessie had never encountered anyone so depraved.

Aside from his wife and perhaps his cadre of trusted followers, there was no one in the hospital—hell, probably in the world—whose life meant anything to Malloche except as it served him. To assure a successful operation and subsequent escape, he would think nothing of killing every person on Surgical Seven, or possibly even hundreds more on the streets of the city. It was easy now for her to understand Alex's hatred of the man and the obsession with bringing him down. If only there were some way she could enter Malloche's room, crouch down by his bed, and make some sort of subliminal suggestion that he—

The thought was never completed. It yielded instead to the evanescent idea that had been tormenting her so. This time, though, the notion stuck in her mind like a well-thrown dart, and quickly grew in clarity. Afraid that something in her expression might betray her to the young terrorist Grace, Jessie turned from Malloche's room and headed, as nonchalantly as she could manage, down the hallway. Her heart was racing. The logistics of her plan would be tricky, but there was a possibility, however remote, that it might work. And with so many lives at stake, she had to try. The first step might actually be the most dangerous. She had to chance going back into Tamika Bing's room with one more message for Alex.

With Grace several paces behind, Jessie followed the Track back to the nurses' station and slid Sara's record from its holder. As before, she block-printed the message for Alex on a progress note sheet and waited until Grace's attention was momentarily diverted before tearing the paper free from the binder rings and folding it in her pocket. Now, all she needed was some excuse to reenter Tamika's room. Absently, she put her hand in her lab coat pocket. Her Game Boy was there. Sharing it with the girl wasn't the strongest motivation for a return visit, but it was at least something. She pulled it out and approached Grace, yawning.

"Well, I think I'm going to turn in down the hall there," she said.

"Good idea," the woman replied coolly. "You need to be at your best tomorrow."

"Before I do, though, I want to stop in seven-ten again just for a minute."

"What for? You were just there."

"The kid in there had a brain tumor taken out by me. The cancer had eaten away her speech center, and now she can only communicate by her computer. She has no games on it and she's getting very bored. I promised her a go at my Game Boy."

"You stay here. I'll bring it into her."

"I . . . I need to show her how to work it. It won't take but a couple of minutes."

For an interminable few seconds, Grace mulled over the request. Then she shrugged.

"Okay. But make it quick. You need to get some rest."

Jessie reentered Tamika's room. The girl, still propped in bed, was dozing.

"See her in the morning," Grace whispered.

The sound was enough. Tamika awoke and instantly tapped on her tray table to get Jessie's attention.

No new messages, she typed.

Jessie shielded her from Grace and passed the progress sheet over.

> ### FIND DR. MARK NAEHRING. URGENT HE MEET ME IN MRI-OR AT 6 A.M. BRING MAGICAL MEDS HE DEMONSTRATED AT RECENT GRAND ROUNDS. MATTER OF LIFE OR DEATH. JESSIE

"So, Tamika," she said in a strong voice, "here's that Game Boy I promised you. Let me show you how to run it. This switch right here . . ."

While Jessie droned on, Tamika glanced down at the note and quickly typed it. Then, as Jessie handed over the electronic toy, she retrieved the paper and stuffed it deep into her lab coat pocket.

"Just what in the hell is going on here?" Arlette Malloche stormed into the room.

As Jessie leaped back from the bed, she noted that Tamika had instantly broken off contact with Vicki.

Good baby! she cheered. *Send the message later.*

"Everything's fine," Grace said.

"Is it? It seems like the doctor's been in here all night."

"Just twice before this. She's been in several rooms that much. This time, she was just dropping off a toy."

"Well, she's finished going into any patient's room until Claude's surgery is done. Dr. Copeland, a room has been prepared for you. Get to bed at once."

"I want to see Sara Devereau," Jessie said. "She may be in some trouble."

"I said you're going to bed, and that's it."

Suddenly, Arlette's eyes widened. Jessie followed her line of sight to the telephone cord snaking from the wall outlet up under the bedsheet. Muttering a curse, Arlette pushed the tray table back from the bed. The cord straightened, then pulled the computer off the tray table and onto Tamika's lap. Furious, Arlette slapped Tamika across the face, then, in almost the same motion, slapped Jessie as well.

"What is going on here?" she demanded. "Who connected this?"

Tamika, who never even flinched at being hit, tapped on the computer to bring Arlette around to see the screen. She typed

I DID IT. I WANTED TO E-MAIL MY BOYFRIEND.

"She's mute from her tumor surgery," Jessie tried to explain. "The computer is the only way she can communicate with—"

"Shut up!" Arlette snarled. "Grace, did she send any e-mails while Dr. Copeland was here?"

"None," Grace said, clearly frightened.

"You checked?"

"Yes . . . yes, I checked everything she did."

"For your sake, I hope that's true."

She snatched up the laptop, tore it away from the phone line, and lifted it above her head.

"Please don't," Jessie said. "It's her only—"

Arlette slammed the computer on the floor. The cover flew off, the casing split, and the screen shattered.

"Get to bed," she said. "Now!"

CHAPTER 33

THE VENTILATION SYSTEM TO THE SURGICAL tower was a series of aluminum tubes about the size of the opening in an MRI machine. Arms extended, Alex inched his way through the maze, using raised toeholds to move up from the entry port on Surgical Five. He wore a miner's helmet with a spotlight above the brim and carried a blueprint of the system in one hand. In the other he clutched a tape measure with which he was keeping track of his progress and location. Strapped to his back was a small knapsack containing a slender video camera and a transmitter, as well as metal shears, drills, bits, and other tools for boring. His pistol was jammed into a shoulder holster tucked beneath one arm.

The circular shape of the Surgical Seven hallway made positioning the camera and microphone a problem. The ceiling over the nurses' station was the ideal location, but it was unlikely he could get the setup in place there without one of Malloche's people hearing him or noticing the tip of the fiber-optic camera. He had instead chosen a location just around the bend from the nurses' station as the spot least likely to be detected and most likely to help monitor the situation on the floor. Now, to the best of his calculations, he was there.

He had always had difficulty being in tight quarters. Now, he had been negotiating the two-foot tube for over an hour. Each heartbeat seemed to echo through the cramped space. He was drenched in sweat and finding it hard to breathe. For increasing stretches of time, all he could think about was standing up. But there was no room to stand, and no place to go but forward.

He extended the tape measure and once again checked his position on the blueprint. As best as he could figure, he was twenty feet from the center of the nurses' station. Off to both sides of him, narrow ducts snaked away to the patients' rooms and core service area. The ducts helped to relieve some of the dreadful feeling of being unable to straighten up or even turn over, but the anxiety was still there every second. He worked the backpack off his shoulders and removed the metal shears and powerful drill. Two drill holes in the aluminum and he would be able to cut an opening large enough for him to work on a panel of the drop ceiling.

Easy does it, he urged. He could do it and get out. He just had to stay calm.

It took a while, but finally the eight-inch-square opening in the ventilation pipe was complete. Alex shut off his headlamp for a time and lay in the darkness, regaining his breath and his composure. Silence was crucial now—absolute quiet and skill in handling the drill. Slowly, carefully, he set the bit in place and squeezed the trigger on the housing. The pressboard of the ceiling panel gradually gave way as flakes of the material spun off.

Slowly . . . slowly.

Almost directly below where he was working, Jessie walked along the corridor toward the room that had been designated by Arlette as her sleeping quarters. Behind her followed the ever-present Grace, accompanied by Arlette herself. Suddenly, just as Jessie was precisely beneath the place where Alex was working, no more than a few feet from him, his drill bit caught on something in the ceiling panel. Before Alex could adjust and react, the drill housing spun out of his hand and dropped onto the panel with a thud that might as well have been the impact of a wrecking ball. The panel gave way at one end. Instantly, weapon ready, Grace leaped up and pulled the entire piece down. Alex, exposed above the opening in the aluminum, was fumbling for his weapon. But Arlette and Grace were way ahead of him.

"No!" Jessie screamed as they opened fire. "Noooo!"

Several shots caught Alex flush in the face, while a dozen or more slammed through the aluminum and into his body. A thick, heavy rain of blood fell from the ceiling, splattering on the floor and pocking Jessie's white lab coat with crimson. Alex's face, a red mask of death, pressed grotesquely through the opening in the aluminum.

"Oh God," Jessie moaned. "Oh God . . . Oh God . . . Oh—"

"Jessie?"

Gentle hands pressed down on her shoulders.

"Jess, wake up."

Soft, reassuring whisper . . . warm breath on her ear. The horror of the nightmare began to fade, and with it the almost painful rigidity in Jessie's body. She was facedown, clutching her pillow in a near death grip, jaws clenched. Her scrubs were damp with perspiration. Slowly, she turned and blinked herself awake. Emily looked down at her, her face shadowed with concern.

"You must have been having a real bad one," she said.

Jessie sat up, still trying to shake off the startlingly vivid dream. Then she threw her arms around her friend.

"Oh, Em. I'm so glad you're here. I was worried to death about you. Are you okay?"

"Nothing that a week in the Caribbean won't take care of."

Jessie managed to stand. Leaning in the doorway, dressed in scrubs, his gun over his shoulder, was Derrick.

"What time is it?" Jessie asked, still less than fully awake.

"Five-thirty."

"The OR. We're due in the OR at six."

"I know. There's still time for you to shower and change. I brought a clean set of scrubs for you."

"Have you had any sleep?"

"I'm okay. I understand from Mrs. Hermann that I'll be assisting you and ARTIE in the OR."

"She's not Mrs. Hermann. Her name's Arlette Malloche. Eastman Tolliver is actually her husband, Claude. They kill people for money."

"The guy who had me tied up never said anything about who he worked for," Emily replied, "but I'm not surprised. My, my. I guess this means Carl won't be getting that big grant."

Jessie grinned momentarily.

"Guess not," she said. Her expression darkened. "Lisa Brandon, the candy striper who was so kind to

Sara, was actually an FBI undercover agent. Carl got her killed by losing his temper and forcing her to disclose who she was. Since then he's come damn close to getting himself killed as well."

"He's bunked in the room next to yours and—"

"Sara!" Jessie exclaimed.

"What?"

"Sara—I've got to get in to see her. Arlette wouldn't let me last night. She was starting to seem, I don't know, sort of sluggish."

"Jess, she's been sluggish since she woke up."

"I know, but she seemed more so to me."

"Okay, I'll go check on her. You shower. Here are the scrubs."

Jessie took the clothes and turned to Derrick.

"Can my nurse, here, go to check the woman in seven thirty-seven?"

"If Arlette says it's okay."

Derrick radioed down the hall, and in a minute, Grace appeared at the door.

"Tell her I'll be down as soon as I've changed," Jessie said.

As Derrick followed Emily down the hall, Jessie checked the ceiling, half expecting to see it stained with Alex's blood. How much prophecy was there in her dream? She also wondered if Tamika had managed to send the message about Mark Naehring before her laptop was destroyed. If so, they had a chance. If not, there was really nothing else she could think of to do. She would just have to perform the best surgery she could and pray that ARTIE functioned to its potential, and that Malloche recovered and made it out of the country without any more killing. Deep inside, though, she knew that praying for no more killing was wishful thinking. Claude and Arlette Malloche were animals—animals with their teeth on the throat of the hospital and, indeed, of the city.

Grace closed the door to the hallway and stood by the open bathroom doorway while Jessie undressed and stepped into the shower. Hot water, soap, and shampoo did good things for her flagging morale. Alex and Emily were still alive, and even Carl had survived. Tamika Bing had broken through her horrible depression, and had helped put a long-shot plan in motion. Jessie closed her eyes for a time and let the hot water beat against her face. She was toweling off when Emily came bursting into the room.

"Jess, come quick," she said, breathlessly. "It's Sara. She's in big trouble. I think she may be going out."

Jessie grabbed her glasses, pulled on the fresh scrubs, and bolted past Grace and down the hall. Sara indeed was *in extremis*. She lay motionless in bed, unconscious and unresponsive to voice or touch. Her respirations were labored. Her pupils were dilated and barely reactive to light—a sign that there was massive brain swelling, which was pressing a portion of her brain stem up against a bony ridge on the floor of her skull.

"Acute hydrocephalus," Jessie said. "I'd bet the ranch on it."

Something—possibly a small clot or piece of scar tissue—was obstructing the flow and drainage of Sara's spinal fluid. The fluid, which was formed in the choroid plexus organ in the brain, was now blocked from flowing throughout the central nervous system and down around the spinal cord. But production of fluid by the plexus was continuing, and the resulting buildup of pressure within the rigid containment of her skull was about to become lethal. Jessie cursed herself for not being more aggressive last night when she had sensed that something in her friend's condition might be changing.

"I'll call the OR," Emily said. "The team should all be in by now."

"You'll do no such thing!"

Arlette Malloche barged into the room and confronted Jessie.

"This woman must have an immediate drainage procedure to relieve the pressure that's building up in her brain," Jessie said. "She needs to be brought to the OR right now."

"The only person who will be brought to any OR right now is my husband," Arlette said.

Jessie was about to beg for her friend's life, but she stopped abruptly. To people like Arlette Malloche and her husband, begging was nothing but a sign of weakness—certainly nothing to be respected. Instead, Jessie confronted the woman with all the hatred, all the fire, that had been building inside her.

"Arlette," she said, "I'm drawing the line here. Claude's operation can wait until I perform the drainage procedure on this woman. I swear that if you allow her to die, there is no way I will operate on your husband, no matter what you do to me."

Arlette gave her the haughty look of an Olympian goddess confronted by the demands of a mere mortal. Then she calmly took her weapon from her shoulder and forced the barrel of it between Sara's teeth and deep into her throat. Sara's reaction to the violent insult was a faint, impotent gag and some involuntary movement of her arms.

"My husband is due to head down to the operating room in fifteen minutes," Arlette said. "If you are not there with him, I will begin killing one person on this floor every minute until you are, beginning with this woman right here. Do you understand?"

Jessie and Emily exchanged looks.

Is it worth calling her bluff? they asked one another. *Right here—right now, simply refuse to operate on the man.*

Jessie was well aware of the answer. The price of that hollow victory was hardly one she was willing to pay. She cared about the lives of others, and Arlette knew that as well as she did, just as she knew that Arlette cared not at all. The clash of wills, at this moment at least, on this battleground, was no contest.

"I understand," Jessie said quickly. "Now please, take that out of Sara's mouth."

"Fifteen minutes," Arlette said, withdrawing the muzzle. "Don't test me on this."

She turned toward the door.

"Wait!" Jessie cried. "There is something I can try right here."

Arlette made a regal turn and assessed the faces around her. It was as if she saw the chance to become something of a benevolent despot in the eyes of the staff and her people. There was everything for her to gain by relenting here and nothing to lose.

"You have ten minutes," she said. "At five of six, I want you out of here, accompanying my husband to the operating room."

"One thing."

"Yes?"

"Your people took a piece of equipment from me that I need right now—a twist drill. It looks like a big screwdriver with a black handle and a drill bit at the other end."

"It looked like a dagger to us."

"I'll need some other equipment, too."

Arlette nodded to Grace, who motioned Jessie out of the room and followed her off down the hall.

"Don't do anything stupid," Arlette called after them.

By the time Jessie returned with her twist drill, a scissors, a prep razor, a hemostat, and a Silastic catheter, three minutes of her ten had elapsed. Even worse, one of Sara's pupils had become larger than the other and no longer constricted in response to the beam from Jessie's penlight. The lethal brain-stem herniation and compression was happening. Perhaps sensing that death was in the offing, Arlette had chosen to remain in the room to monitor the procedure.

"I should have made this diagnosis last night," Jessie muttered as she and Emily shaved away some fine new hair from the top of Sara's scalp, an inch back from her front hairline, and just to the right side of the midline. "I could have taken her to the OR and done this right. Now it's too late. It . . . it was just crazy here last night. I should have taken a stand then."

"Just do what you can do, Jess," Emily said. "We both know she still has a chance."

They pulled Sara down in the bed. Jessie gloved, then climbed up on the mattress, beside Sara's head. Next she squirted some russet-colored Betadine antiseptic on the spot and on her drill, and began manually twisting a hole into Sara's skull. There were less than five minutes left. The procedure did not go quickly. The twist drill was as much standard equipment to a neurosurgeon as a stethoscope was to an internist. But it was used infrequently and only in the most dire emergencies. Jessie began to wonder if she had the arm strength to complete the procedure.

Across the room, Arlette, positioning herself so that

Jessie could hardly miss the movement, brought her weapon off her shoulder, and cradled it in front of her.

"Two minutes," she said.

"Hand me that catheter and a hemostat, Em, please. I'm through the dural membrane."

Jessie snapped one end of the catheter into the hemostat, tunneled for an inch beneath Sara's scalp, and pushed it through the skin to the outside. Then she grasped the other end and worked it through the hole she had just made in the skull and dura, and down toward the ventricle chamber, where the mounting pressure was greatest.

"One more minute and you're done here," Arlette said. "And I mean it. I gave you your chance."

"Go for it, Jess," Emily said.

Jessie gripped the catheter and with a twisting motion forced it into the ventricle. Instantly, spinal fluid under high pressure shot through the catheter, actually hitting Emily on the sleeve.

"Yes!" she exclaimed. "Oh, yes!"

Quickly, Emily fixed the catheter to a drainage system.

"Time's up!" Arlette announced. "Let's go, Doctor."

"I can't leave her yet," Jessie implored.

Arlette readied her weapon and strode to the bedside, clearly ready to finish Sara off.

"I'll stay with her," Emily said quickly.

Arlette glared at her.

"You'll do nothing of the sort. I want you both out of here and on your way to the operating room."

Her voice was strident now. Jessie was certain that at any moment she would simply raise her weapon to Sara's head and blow it apart. But the drainage catheter hadn't even been sutured down yet. What if it got pulled out, or plugged? What about antibiotic coverage for what was hardly a sterile procedure? What about steroids or other treatment for brain swelling?

"Okay, okay," she pleaded. "Don't shoot her. Please. We're going. We're going."

"I'll take care of her."

Carl Gilbride spoke from the doorway, then stepped into the room, with Armand right behind him. His cheek was bandaged, and he looked disheveled in his bloodstained designer shirt and lab coat. But his eyes were clear, and the purpose in them unmistakable. For several seconds there was only silence.

"Thank you, Carl," Jessie said softly, pushing herself off the bed to make room for him. "Thank you."

"Now!" Arlette barked. "Let's go." She turned to Armand. "Let Dr. Gilbride do whatever he needs to her."

"Jessie," Gilbride said as she reached the door, "what antibiotics do you want her on?"

Jessie turned back to him and, for the first time in longer than she could remember, liked what she saw of the man.

"You decide," she said. "I trust your judgment."

CHAPTER **34**

THE TRANSPORT TEAM CONSISTED OF JESSIE AND
Emily, Grace and Derrick. Armand and Arlette were to
remain on Surgical Seven. Another terrorist—the one
who had held Emily captive in a room somewhere in the
subbasement of the hospital—was not accounted for.
Jessie strongly suspected he was either keeping an eye on
Richard Marcus, or was outside, somewhere in the city,
positioning himself to detonate one or more of the vials of
soman should anything go wrong.

Just having Emily there with her made the entire or-
deal more bearable, although since her arrival back on
Surgical Seven, there hadn't been one moment when the
two of them could talk in private. Once they were in the
OR, though, there would be a chance, thanks to the relative privacy of the space between the MRI tori.

Although ARTIE was scheduled to perform the en-

tire operation, Malloche's head had been shaved as a precaution should Jessie have to go to a full craniotomy. He
lay calmly on the stretcher, holding hands with Arlette.
His headache had responded reasonably well to the nar-
cotic injections, but he had needed to be kept almost constantly medicated throughout the night.

"You've done a good job holding everything together,"
he said to his wife in French. "I'm lucky to have you."

"No," she replied, "we're all lucky to have you."

Jessie refrained from letting them know her French
was passable.

Sweet monster love, she thought. *Spare me!*

The elevator doors opened and Claude Malloche was
wheeled inside.

"Grace, you have the gun?" he asked.

"Right here," she replied, tapping the shoulder holster beneath her lab coat.

"Wait a minute," Jessie said. "If she's planning on
coming into the operating room, everything metal must
be left outside. The electromagnet would pull that gun
right through someone's body."

"Correction," Malloche said. "Everything *magnetic*
must be left outside. Grace's little thirty-eight is a custom
order cast especially for our visit here. Titanium, I think,
and goodness knows what else, but nothing magnetic.
And trust me, Grace knows how to use that pistol well.
I forget, Grace, how many people have you sanctioned
since you came to work with us?"

The slender American shrugged matter-of-factly.

"I don't know," she said. "Nineteen? Twenty? I don't
keep count exactly. I just do what I'm told."

"Please let that serve as a warning to you, Dr.
Copeland. Do my operation well—no, do it perfectly—
and get me back up here to recover. If there is anything

that seems the least bit out of place or subversive of our goals, Grace, here, has instructions to shoot Mrs. DelGreco. We will then send Dr. Gilbride down to help you finish my case. Is that clear?"

"Clear."

"Good."

Jessie flashed a look of hatred down at Malloche, but his eyes had closed and his mellow half-smile suggested that he had allowed himself to yield to the euphoria of his pre-op medications.

"Dr. Copeland," Arlette said, "Derrick will be stationed outside the operating room. He is to be introduced to the others as being from hospital security, sent by Richard Marcus and his infection control team to ensure that no unauthorized personnel enter the operating room. Claude and I have reviewed this list you gave us of participants in his surgery. It will be Derrick's responsibility to see that nobody who is not on the list is allowed in the operating room."

"I understand."

"There is one name in the group that we are concerned about. Dr. Mark Naehring. Exactly who is he, and what will he be doing?"

It was not the actual question that caught Jessie off guard, so much as the timing. She wasn't at all certain Naehring would even show up in the OR, but she had decided it would be foolish to leave him off the list of participants that Malloche had demanded from her. As they were wheeling Malloche to the elevators, Jessie had allowed herself to believe that Naehring's name had simply slipped past them. She should have known better. Now, she wondered how much truth should be laced into her response. If Malloche or Arlette had looked up Naehring in the annotated directory of EMMC physicians, they would know something of the man. Any contradiction now between what Jessie told them and what they had learned would be a red flag, and would almost certainly put an end to her already shaky plan.

"Dr. Naehring is a psychopharmacologist," she said carefully. "I intend to do a great deal of surgery with your husband awake and responsive. Dr. Naehring is more experienced and expert at administering medications that allow patients to be maintained at that level than anyone in anesthesia, including Dr. Booker."

Several frightening seconds passed during which Arlette assessed the information. Finally, she handed the list over to Derrick.

The elevator doors closed, and the five of them—Malloche, Grace, Jessie, Emily, and Derrick—began the descent to the subbasement of the Surgical Tower. Ordinarily, before a difficult case, Jessie would have spent an hour, often more, in her office, poring over MRIs and neuroanatomy textbooks, setting up her plan for the surgery, and reviewing the anatomy she would encounter. Never before this moment had the elevator ride down to the OR doubled as her pre-op preparation.

Random snatches of thought passed through her mind like a meteor shower, making it difficult to concentrate on ARTIE and on Claude Malloche's meningioma. This was hardly the state of mind she wanted to be in for a major case—much less one that could have such grave consequences. Throughout the operation, her ability to stay focused would determine the outcome as much as her surgical skill.

The elevator doors opened, depositing them just down the hall from the MRI-OR.

"I will be with you every inch of the way," Grace said to Jessie as they pushed the stretcher toward the OR.

Jessie could see Michelle Booker waiting for them in the prep area, but there was no sign of Mark Naehring.

Damn.

It might well be academic now, Jessie realized, but Emily had no idea that Naehring had even been called in. She also reminded herself that at the moment, Michelle Booker might be sensing that this case was unusual, but she wouldn't have a clue as to why. It was going to be essential to find ways to communicate the situation to each woman without endangering anyone. Fortunately, they were among the sharpest people she knew.

What if the psychopharmacologist didn't show up? she asked herself now. Was there any way she could handle the drugs? He used some sort of mixture of three hypnotics—or was it four? Clearly, the answer to her question was a resounding no. If she tried using drugs to interrogate Claude Malloche and somehow screwed up, there was no doubt in her mind that a great many people would die.

Jessie introduced Grace to Michelle Booker as a biomechanics student from Chicago who had written her some time ago expressing an interest in ARTIE. Then, as instructed, she introduced Derrick to the console tech Holly as a hospital security officer, who was not going to allow anyone into the operating room other than those on the list she had provided for him. Neither of the lies would survive much conversation, but Holly and Michelle were usually all business anyhow, and the seriousness of the procedure was certain to keep them zeroed in on the patient.

The first real opportunity Jessie had to pass any information to Emily was in the scrub room. With her identity as a biomechanics student established, Grace had to remain several paces away from them. Jessie began her scrub by turning up the water full force so that it splashed noisily in the stainless steel sink. Emily quickly followed suit.

"I wish I knew how Sara was doing," Jessie said, looking straight ahead as she spoke.

"Me, too. Jess, I know you're feeling guilty about not insisting on going in to see her last night, but you really had no choice. And you did a helluva job at getting that catheter in."

"Thanks. I don't mind telling you now that I was scared stiff. Em, listen. I tried to get word to Alex last night to have Mark Naehring come down here."

"The drug doc who called you the other day?"

"Exactly."

"What for?"

"Come on, you two," Grace called in over her shoulder. "You said four minutes."

"To use his stuff on Malloche so I can question him about the soman," Jessie said. "Naehring may not show up at all, but if he does, just follow my lead and do what you can to help me replace you with him."

"Does Michelle know what's going on?"

"Not yet. You'll have to help me out there, too."

"Keep Grace with you outside the OR for a few seconds, and I'll see if I can at least tell Michelle that there's some weird stuff going on around this case and she should be on her toes."

"Just be careful. The microphones are on. Everything you say will be broadcast out here."

Emily shook the excess water from her hands. "Okay, it's show time," she said. "Give me a minute or so in there to get gowned, then you can make a grand entrance like Gilbride always does."

"I don't know if I can pull it off without the scepter, crown, and cape."

Thirty seconds of stalling was the best Jessie could do before Grace ordered her into the OR. Skip Porter, masked, gloved, and gowned, was just finishing preparations on ARTIE. Outside the window, she could see the console tech and radiologist Hans Pfeffer, preparing their equipment and checking communication with the computer lab upstairs. Behind them, standing almost at attention, was Derrick. He was posing as a security guard but he was inside the area where only scrubs and lab coats were allowed. His loose white coat, buttoned once in the front, completely hid the deadly machine gun that was slung over his shoulder. It was just past six-thirty. By eleven—noon at the latest—the resection of Claude Malloche's tumor would be over.

What then? Jessie asked herself. *What then?*

She accepted a towel from the scrub nurse and thanked him for coming in.

"No problem," he said. "Why the big deal about this case?"

"Eastman Tolliver is the administrator of a fund that is about to give the hospital several million dollars in research money."

"That's why Richard Marcus is so anxious to get his operation done?"

"Exactly."

"Well, I'm sorry I made a big deal about coming in, but I've got two little kids, and this virus thing really has me spooked."

"I understand. Believe me, I don't want to die any more than you do. Trust me that it's safe. There have been no new deaths on Surgical Seven, and Mr. Tolliver's been kept well away from the floor since the outbreak."

Jessie slid her arms into the sterile gown he opened for her and then thrust her hands down into her gloves.

Spooked by the virus thing, she was thinking. *Nice going, Claude. You don't miss a trick, do you.*

"Emily, I'm all set," Michelle Booker called out. "He's under and intubated. I'm going to slide him through."

Jessie stood back and watched as the padded platform bearing Malloche was eased along its track through the opening in the magnet to her right.

"Ready . . . and . . . stop," Emily said when his head was positioned in the two-foot separation between the massive tori—the tightly contained universe where, for the next five hours or so, she and Jessie would work.

Emily began by prepping the area around Malloche's nose, and another at the hairline. The second site was for backup in case ARTIE could not be inserted through the right nostril as planned. Jessie remained outside the magnet. It was time to get Michelle Booker into the act.

"Michelle," she said, "there's a possibility that Dr. Naehring may be coming down to assist with part of this case."

The anesthesiologist looked up quickly.

Stay cool, Jessie's eyes begged. *Stay cool.*

What on earth are you talking about, woman? From above the top of her mask, Booker's wise, dark eyes asked the question.

"Mark Naehring," she said matter-of-factly. "I admire his work."

Tell me more.

"When we get to doing the functional MRI, he'll take over for you. But he'll be working across from me at the table, where Emily is now."

"That's an interesting approach. I've never done a case like this with him before."

Are you crazy?

"I hope he gets here. If, by any chance, he doesn't make

it down, would you be able to handle the meds the way he did at grand rounds?"

Michelle made the faintest gesture toward Grace. *Does she have something to do with this craziness?*

Jessie nodded. Beneath her mask, she was smiling. Michelle Booker had no idea just what the ship was or where it was headed, but she was on board.

"I suppose I could try some of my own combinations," Michelle said, "but Naehring's the pro."

"If we have to do it that way, I'll send Emily over to you for a quick in-service on monitoring the anesthesia equipment, and you'll get gloved and gowned and work with me."

I sure hope you know what you're doing, Michelle's eyes were saying now. "Hey, no problem," she said. "I like to teach."

Jessie moved into her spot across from Emily, and together they draped Malloche's head and fixed his skull to the titanium immobilization frame. Grace was now screened from them by Jessie's back, although she was just a few feet away. She would have been able to observe more and hear more by standing on a riser, but Jessie had thought to nudge the two risers they had out of sight under an equipment table. Now she switched off her microphone and motioned to Emily to do the same.

"We can't keep these off for too long or Derrick will get suspicious," she whispered. "You keep yours turned off. We'll just use mine." She switched her microphone on again. "Okay, everyone, on your toes because we're ready to roll. Jared?"

"Ready," the scrub nurse said.

"Sylvia?"

"All set," replied the circulator.

"Skip?"

"All systems are go."

"Hans?"

"We are ready."

"Holly?"

"No problems."

"Well, okay. Holly, how about popping in that Bob Marley CD?"

"You got it," Holly said. "It *is* a reggae kind of morning at that."

"Come on, robot," Jessie cooed. "Please don't fail me now. Skip, we're going in."

Jessie made a half-inch hole through the back wall of Malloche's nostril, cauterized the bleeding, and guided ARTIE through the opening and into the cranial cavity.

"Hans, are you ready to show me some views of this tumor?"

"It's on the screen right now. Quite an impressive lesion. Manipulate the orientation with your foot control as you wish."

The views were perfect. And, as Pfeffer had observed, the tumor was extensive. Thanks to the transnasal entry, ARTIE was already just a centimeter and a half from it. A standard, non-robot approach would have presented a hideous technical problem, and would have undoubtedly destroyed some—maybe a good deal—of the uninvolved brain tissue. Once again, Malloche had justified his reputation for genius. There was no way Sylvan Mays could have promised a total excision with no residual neurologic deficits. Malloche must have gotten him to admit that before he killed him. With ARTIE, there was a very good chance.

The guidance system for the tiny robot was as smooth and responsive as Jessie could ever remember. Still, she held back, progressing much slower than she needed to, stalling in hopes that Mark Naehring might still show up. But with each passing minute, that hope diminished. Maybe Tamika had never gotten that final message through before the laptop was destroyed. Maybe Naehring couldn't be located. Whatever the reason, Jessie knew she was going to have to find another way, or else give up on her plan and simply pray that Malloche would recover from his surgery intact and head home, sparing the hospital and the city.

"Skip, ARTIE's working beautifully," she said as she manipulated the unit until it was positioned at the very edge of the meningioma.

"I did some tinkerin'," the scientist said. "Besides, ARTIE likes you. It always performs well for people it likes."

Just then, through the intercom, Jessie heard an exchange of voices.

"Naehring. I'm Dr. Mark Naehring. I'm here to—"

"I know why you're here," Derrick said. "Go on in."

Jessie rose on tiptoe to see over Emily. Naehring, who looked taller than she remembered, went directly to the scrub nurse's area, opened a Ziploc plastic bag, and dropped several vials out.

"They're sterile," he said.

"Do you want gloves and a gown?" the nurse asked. "Yes."

There was something about Naehring's voice . . .

Jessie was straining to get a better look, when the man, now in his surgical gown, turned toward her.

Alex!

CHAPTER 35

JESSIE CONTINUED HER ULTRASOUND DISSECTION
and aspiration of Claude Malloche's tumor as Alex took
Emily's place at the table.

"I'm glad you could make it, Dr. Naehring," Jessie
said, her eyes asking a dozen questions at once.

"Mark'll do fine," Alex replied.

"Okay, Mark. I'm glad you could make it. Holly, is
everything okay out there?"

Jessie used the question to be certain Alex knew they
were being monitored.

"Everything's fine," the tech said. "Why?"

"The MRI image seems a little grainy, that's all."

"I'll check on it."

Jessie switched off the microphone.

"The microphone's off," she whispered, still working
ARTIE through Malloche's tumor. "But I can't keep it

that way for long. The woman behind me is one of them."

"I know."

Jessie turned the microphone back on, straightened up, and worked some of the stiffness from her neck. In addition to the tightness in her muscles, she felt her touch on ARTIE's controls was getting a bit heavy. And although the Marley album might be making it easier for them to talk, it was also beginning to grate on her.

Easy, she warned herself. *Relax, stay focused. No screwups.*

"Holly, we're getting down to the nitty-gritty here," she said. "How about switching to *Rhapsody in Blue*?"

"*Rhapsody in Blue* coming up."

Jessie waited for the music change, then switched off the mike again. "Now, what on earth are you doing?"

"Naehring's at a conference in Maui. It took most of the night for us to track him down. Once I learned what he did, I realized how brilliant your idea was."

"What good does that do?"

"He told me where to find his potion and how to use it."

"Over the phone?!"

"I've—um—had a little training in the area."

Out of the corner of her eye, Jessie became aware of Grace, who had shifted over a few inches.

"Michelle," she called out, switching the sound back on, "everything looks great. Any problems?"

"None. I'm here elucidating some of the finer points of anesthesia to Nurse DelGreco."

Finer points of anesthesia. Hardly likely, Jessie thought. *The notion made no more sense than her elucidating some of the finer points of neurosurgery.* Michelle was telling her that Emily had found some way to communicate more of the situation to her without calling attention to them. *Excellent.*

"Well, Mark," Jessie said, "the dissection is going fine so far. Hans, can you put up the pre-op screen? . . . Great. Mark, the yellow is his meningioma before we began. Back to the current screen now, Hans. . . . And this is what's left of the tumor as of this moment."

"Nice job," Alex said. "Very nice. This is one lucky guy."

He patted Malloche on the head as if he were a puppy. Jessie's eyes flashed a warning and directed him up to the overhead camera that was monitoring the operative field for Derrick and the others.

"Michelle," she said, "maybe seven more minutes and we're going to wake him up."

"We're ready, Doc. This Gershwin's great. I never remember you playing it before."

Mike off.

"Grace, the woman behind me, and Derrick, the guy outside, are both armed," Jessie murmured. "Malloche had a nonmagnetic gun made for her."

"Well, isn't he something," Alex replied. "Tamika went off-line. Is she okay?"

"For now. They smashed her computer, though."

Mike on.

Jessie continued to guide ARTIE flawlessly, liquefying Malloche's tumor with ultrasound, then aspirating the melted cells and debris through the robot's suction port. The heavy core of the tumor—60, maybe even 70 percent of it—was gone. They were in uncharted waters now. Gilbride's success with Marci Sheprow's uncomplicated, superficial tumor notwithstanding, they were clearly beyond where Jessie had taken ARTIE on the cadaver of Pete Roslanski, or where Carl had come apart in the ill-fated operation on Rolf Hermann. The complexity of the dissection ARTIE was accomplishing here was justification for the hundreds of hours she had spent at the drawing board and in the lab. If only the patient were someone she wanted to cure.

"Well, gang," she said, "it's time to get ready for the hard part. Michelle, please go ahead and start waking Mr. Tolliver up. We've got this thing about seventy percent gone. The next thirty will take us a while. Mark, let's take our time."

Mike off.

"You sure about this?" she asked.

"Of course not. But Naehring spent almost an hour on the phone with me. The stuff I'll be using came from his office. It's all mixed—four drugs in just the right proportion."

"What are they?"

"Scopolamine, *Pentothal,* I think. . . . I can't remember the other two. Jessie, I've been screwing up right and left ever since I learned about Gilbride using this robot, here. I'm not going to mess this up."

"Good luck, Alex."

Mike on.

"Michelle," Alex said, "if it's all right with you, I'd like to handle the meds myself, from right here."

"There's an IV port under the drape just next to your right hand, Doctor," the anesthesiologist replied. "It's sterile. If there's anything I can do, just say the word."

Jessie took a step back—out from between the tori—and turned to Grace.

"Things are going very well so far," she said.

"I can tell," Grace said. "That's good. That's very good."

Jessie stepped forward, once again positioning herself to block the young killer from Malloche and Alex.

"Doctor Naehring, he's all yours," she said. "For the time being, ARTIE and I will be dissecting around the left motor cortex. I need the patient to keep working his right hand and foot. Michelle, you can see his feet, yes?"

"They're right here."

"Perfect. Mark, would you prefer music or none?"

"Music, most definitely. What you have on is fine. I want him wide awake, Michelle. Then I'll bring him back down again myself."

Jessie's eyes smiled across at him. Claude Malloche, mythologized as the Mist, killer of so many, wide awake with his head screwed to an immobilization frame, a half-inch tube up his nose, through his skull, and into his brain. Not the full payback Alex wanted, but certainly a sweet, sweet ante.

"Mr. Tolliver," Jessie said, "it's Dr. Copeland. Can you hear me?"

"I can," Malloche rasped.

"The operation is about three-quarters done, and everything is going perfectly."

"Good."

"As I told you, we've got you immobilized so you can't move your head. But you can move your hands and feet. Shake your right hand for me, please. . . . Good, good. Now your left . . . excellent. Your right foot?"

"These little piggies went to market," Michelle called out.

"Now your left foot."

"These little piggies had roast beef."

"Terrific. Now, the tube you feel in your nose is ARTIE, the tiny robot. Do you understand?"

"Yes."

"You may feel some movement or vibration as I guide ARTIE further into the tumor. We're going to medicate you a bit more so that we can keep working without causing you too much discomfort. You'll hear commands from me or from Dr. Mark Naehring, who's right there on the other side of you. Just do whatever it is we ask. Some commands will be given in a loud voice, some will be softer. Sometimes we'll ask you over and over to do the same thing. That's how I'll be able to monitor things if I'm working close to a vital area."

"Understand," Malloche said.

"Good. You're doing great, Mr. Tolliver. Just great. Ready, Mark?"

"Ready. Could I have five ccs of the mixture in vial number one, please?"

"Five ccs," the scrub nurse said, passing the syringe over.

"Half a cc, then wait one minute," Alex said. "Mr. Tolliver, lift your right hand. Good. Do it again. Once more." He bent down closer to Malloche's ear and nodded for Jessie to cut the mike. "What's your name?" he whispered harshly. ". . . *Your name!*"

"Claude . . . Paul . . . Malloche."

Jessie glanced behind her to see if Grace had heard. She was nodding her head to the Gershwin piece.

"Move your right foot," Jessie ordered after keying the mike again.

"Okay," Michelle called out.

Jessie cut the mike and nodded to Alex. He tested the dose level with several inane questions about Malloche's birthplace and parents. On the fourth go-round with the mike off, he was ready.

"Soman," he said. "Do you know what I'm talking about, Claude?"

"I . . . do."

"How many vials are there hidden in Boston?"

"Three . . . four . . ."

"Which? Three or four?"

"Three . . . four."

Jessie raised her hand for Alex to stop and once again checked on Grace.

"We're still doing terrific," Jessie said over her shoulder.

"Keep it up," Grace replied.

You bet! You bet we will!

"Take your time, Mark," Jessie said.

She continued her dissection and nodded that the mike was off once more.

"Where are the vials of soman, Claude?" Alex asked. "Where are they?"

"Quincy . . . Market . . . rotunda . . ."

One.

"Go on. Where else?" Alex injected more hypnotic. "Claude?"

Malloche looked to be unconscious.

Too much! Jessie's eyes cried out. *You gave him too much!*

"Government . . . Center . . . green . . . subway . . . ," Malloche murmured suddenly.

Two.

Jessie turned the mike on and held a conversation with Hans Pfeffer that must have struck the radiologist as strange for its vapidness. Anything to keep the rhythm going and Grace and Derrick distracted. The dissection was more than 80 percent complete now. Only fragments of the tumor remained to be melted. It appeared Malloche was going to get his cure.

Just then Alex did, in fact, inject too much hypnotic. Malloche's breathing slowed and he slipped into unconsciousness. Jessie feared she might have to stop the operation to try to put a breathing tube in him. But just as she was about to make a move, Malloche coughed and muttered something unintelligible. A minute later, he had rasped out the third location—Filene's Basement.

"That may be it," Alex said as Jessie flipped the mike back on.

She held up three fingers on one hand and four on the other.

Which is it? her eyes asked.

Alex shrugged and shook his head.

Frightened of having questioned Malloche too often, Jessie took him through some unnecessary maneuvers with his feet.

"Right foot up . . . now down . . . now left . . . now down."

Finally, it was time. Alex got another 5 cc of hypnotic and injected some.

"Claude, the last vial. Quincy Market, Government Center subway, Filene's, and . . . and where?"

"Don't know . . . ," Malloche responded dreamily.

"Is there another vial of soman?"

Jessie anxiously put a finger to her lips and motioned for Alex to lower his voice. Again, through the corner of her eye, she sensed Grace shifting to get a better angle. Clearly they were running out of time.

"Don't know . . . ," Malloche said again. "Don't know . . . don't know . . ."

"He seems confused," Jessie whispered. "Maybe if there was a fourth vial, it was the one here in the lab. We've got to stop."

"Naehring said to give him one shot of two ccs at the end. Supposedly, once I do that, he won't remember any of this."

"Just don't kill him."

Jessie turned the microphone on once more and again issued some orders to Malloche until it was clear he was unable to respond anymore. Across the room, over Alex's shoulder, she could see Derrick. He had moved to one end of the console and was leaning forward, peering intently through the observation window. He was suspicious. She felt certain of it. Thank goodness they had ended the interrogation.

"Well, Mark," she said, "that was a terrific job. Michelle, Emily, we're almost ninety percent done. We could stop here, and I doubt the tumor would have enough blood supply left to survive. But I want this to be perfect, so we're going to keep working. Michelle, if you can keep him on the way to never-never land, we should be able to wrap this up in forty-five minutes or so. Em, do you want to come back and replace this genius, here?"

"Your wish is my command."

"Thank you, Dr. Naehring."

"I look forward to working with you again, Dr. Copeland," Alex said.

As he turned to move past Emily, Jessie saw her suddenly thrust a piece of paper into his hand. He reacted to the surprise not at all. Instead, without even the slightest hesitation, he slipped the paper beneath his surgical gown and deposited it into his scrub pants pocket. Then he removed his gown and gloves and dropped them where the circulating nurse indicated.

Jessie held her breath as he approached the OR door. Half a minute more. No more than thirty seconds and he would be on his way out of the hospital with more information than she had even dared to hope for. As he opened the door, he checked back over his shoulder at her. The triumphant spark in his eyes was unmistakable.

Just then, through the observation window, Jessie saw Derrick stride up to Alex.

"You, Doctor," he ordered, "pull down your mask."

KILL OR BE KILLED. WHEN ALEX ARRIVED AT THE operating room, he had been approached and asked his identity by Malloche's man Derrick, who introduced himself as a security guard assigned to monitor this section of the hospital. Now, as the man strode up and confronted him, Alex sensed that this was it. One of them was going to die.

"You, Doctor," Derrick demanded, "pull down your mask."

His knee-length lab coat barely concealed the weapon that was slung over his right shoulder—a semi-automatic of some sort, Alex guessed. He probably had a pistol concealed somewhere as well. He was about Alex's height, but much broader across the shoulders and ten or fifteen years younger. The hardness in his pale eyes said that he would kill without hesitation.

Slowly, Alex untied the upper strings of his cloth mask and let it flop over onto his chest. Derrick studied his face. Then Alex saw recognition spark in the man's eyes.

"I believe I have seen you before, Doctor," Derrick said, easing his right hand inside his lab coat toward his lower back. "Where could that have been?"

Kill or be killed.

Derrick was reaching for a handgun. Alex was certain of that. He also knew that surprise, his only advantage, was fading fast, and would be completely gone in another second or so. He viciously brought his foot up between Derrick's legs, catching him firmly in the groin. The killer's knees buckled, but he stayed on his feet and reacted with the quickness of a professional, spinning away from the looping right hook Alex threw at his chin.

The console tech shrieked as Derrick pulled the pistol from his waistband and fired. But Alex was already sprinting away through the anesthesia prep area, staying low and weaving from side to side like a running back. A bullet pinged off the cement column by his ear. A second grazed his scalp. Over his years in the CIA, he had been shot at several times, but never at this close range, and never without a weapon with which to defend himself. The only choice he had right now was to run—try to put some distance between himself and the younger, stronger man who was intent on killing him.

He pulled several rolling carts into the path behind him as he reached one of the many tunnels connecting the various EMMC buildings. This tunnel, to the main hospital, was too long and too straight for him to chance making it to the end. Instead, Alex bolted one flight up a staircase and cut to his right. He was in the basement corridor of the Kellogg Building—the largest building in the hospital. The brightly lit hallway was almost deserted. But again, it was long and straight. Alex charged across the polished tile and dove through a doorway and into the computer lab. Alex knew that at best, he had bought himself a few seconds. Even if Derrick hadn't actually seen the computer lab door close behind him, he would know that Alex couldn't possibly have made it down the hall. Alex hit the light switches as he passed, throwing this end of the lab into relative darkness.

"Hey," an accented voice called, "what are you doing?"

"Shhhh."

Alex raced toward the voice and found a bookish, rail-thin young man, interpreting the MRI data and monitoring the progress of the case he had just left in the MRI-OR.

"What the—?"

"Get down and stay flat," Alex ordered, shoving the man face first to the floor just as a prolonged burst of machine-gun fire shattered the computers and video screens over their heads.

An Uzi, he guessed from the sound.

He forged ahead on his knees, casting about for a weapon—any kind of weapon. There was nothing— nothing except the computers themselves. He crawled around the corner of a row of instruments and screens just in time to see the edge of Derrick's lab coat as he crept around to where the computer geek lay.

"Please. Please don't hurt me!" the man begged.

Instantly, there was a brief burst of gunfire, an unearthly cry, then silence. Alex cringed and angrily clenched his fists, but he kept crawling. Derrick was exactly opposite him now, separated by the bank of workstations and instruments. Alex slid himself up and placed his hands on either side of a seventeen-inch video monitor screen. Slowly, noiselessly, he lifted the heavy screen off its base. Then, certain the soft scraping sound beyond the workstations localized Derrick, he stood up quickly, raising the monitor at arm's length over his head. The killer whirled, but not in time. Alex hurled the monitor down on him, striking him in the forehead. The picture tube shattered with the sound of a shell burst. Derrick cried out as he was knocked backward, but he was firing even before he hit the floor. Alex, up on the counter, preparing to leap at him, was hit in the shoulder and grazed alongside his chin. The shots spun him around and hurled him into the instruments across the aisle. He fell heavily, blood instantly staining the sleeve of his scrub shirt.

Forcing himself not to panic, Alex righted himself. Derrick had absorbed his best shot, and it hadn't been enough. The man was hurt, though—he had to be. From the other side of the workstations came the angry bellow of a wounded animal and another wild burst of gunfire, most of which ripped through the wooden shelves and snapped into the ceiling. Malloche's man was still on the floor, Alex reasoned, firing upward. But any moment he would be back on his feet. At that point, if Alex wasn't out the door, he was dead.

He crawled to the door and pulled it open. Light from the corridor flooded the darkened area of the lab. Instantly, a volley of shots slammed off the wall above his head.

Alex plunged out into the eerily deserted corridor, scrambled to his feet, and bolted to his right, toward the pathology department, twenty yards away.

·   ·   ·

"WHOEVER HE IS," Grace whispered to Jessie, "he's a dead man."

Jessie could only look across at Emily and shake her head. Their counterattack against Malloche and his people had gone so well. Then, in seconds, everything had come apart. She felt ill, and very frightened for Alex.

"Jessie, what on earth is going on here?" Hans Pfeffer asked. "Who were those men?"

"Hans, I'll have to explain it all to you later. For now, it would probably be best for us just to get through this case. I have very little left to do."

Jessie guided ARTIE into the last remaining portion of Malloche's tumor. The dissection—clean and complete with virtually no damage to intervening vital neurologic structures—was exceeding anything she could have done by hand. Now, though, she was working with far less composure and concentration than she had been, coupled with an overwhelming sense of foreboding.

"How much longer?" Grace asked, no longer bothering to lower her voice or even pretend to be a graduate student.

"Ten, fifteen minutes," Jessie replied.

"I don't see any more tumor."

"Well, there's just a tiny bit right at the tip of where the robot is now. It's yellow on the screen."

"I'm still not sure I see it."

"I don't care whether you do or not. It's there."

At that moment, the feed from the computer lab to the OR viewing screens went dark. Pfeffer tried calling his associate for an explanation. There was no answer. Bewildered and angry, he raced upstairs to the lab. A few minutes later, he was back, pale, and shaken to the point where he was barely able to speak.

"Jessie," he called into the OR, "Eli Rogoff is . . . is dead. He's been shot . . . many times. There's blood all over. . . . My . . . my lab has been destroyed."

Jessie whirled and confronted Grace, but the young killer could only shrug and shake her head.

"Well, your friend has really messed things up for us," Jessie said. "As far as I'm concerned, this is it for this case."

"But you said you weren't done. Will this hurt Claude?"

"I don't know. We may not know for years. What little tumor remains may not have enough blood supply to regrow. Or it might. It doesn't matter now. We can't get at whatever is left, and that's that. Even if I did a craniotomy and open procedure, I doubt I'd be able to find it."

"I'm going to call the police," Pfeffer said.

"Hans, just wait a little while! Let me finish this case and get this man out of here, or a great many people could be killed. I'll explain to you and everyone else after I've gotten ARTIE out of his head."

"And just how are you going to do that without an MRI," Pfeffer cried shrilly, "put your foot on his face and pull?"

"Emily and I will just have to back it out."

"Do it now," Grace said. "I want to get Claude back upstairs as quickly as possible."

"Who in the hell is she?" Pfeffer demanded.

"Hans, please," Jessie begged. "Em, you take over the controls. I'm going to put some gentle tension on ARTIE's cord. We'll bring him out together. Each time I say *now*, hit straight back reverse for like two seconds, then stop. With any luck and the right touch, I think I might be able to guide it back along the track it made going in. If we can't do this, we may have to open him up and go in after it."

"You'll do nothing of the sort until Arlette approves it," Grace said.

"Oh, just shut the fuck up!" Jessie snapped.

THE GLASS DOORS to the pathology unit were closed, and behind them all was dark. There were stretches of yellow plastic ribbon across the entry, and above them a DANGER KEEP OUT sign, along with a red skull symbolizing lethal biologic activity. Alex charged toward the door, expecting to hear the staccato volley of shots at the instant a cluster of bullets slammed into his back. The shots came just as he reached the doors, but miraculously, none of them hit home. Instead, the heavy glass door to his right suddenly spiderwebbed from top to bottom. Without breaking stride, he lowered his uninjured shoulder and rammed into it. The weakened glass shattered inward. As Alex barreled through the opening, he stumbled to one knee and rolled, sending a dagger thrust of pain from the gunshot wound up into his neck. Then he struggled to his feet and pounded on, deeper and deeper into the windowless darkness of the pathology department, away from the glow of the corridor lights.

Ahead of him, just to the left, was another door marked with plastic yellow ribbons and a warning sign. Through the dimming light, he could still make out the gold-leaf lettering on the glass half of the door: MICROBIOLOGY. Over his shoulder he could see Derrick nearing the shattered main door. He had, at best, a few seconds. Sensing what awaited him inside, Alex raced over to the microbiology door, carefully turned the knob, slipped in under the warning ribbon, and closed the door behind him.

The stench of death in the room was overpowering. Crouching low, he retied his surgical mask over his mouth and nose, making breathing a bit easier, and perhaps giving him the first tiny advantage over his pursuer since they left the OR. Remaining in a crouch, he duck-walked away from the door, then suddenly hit against a body and fell over it. His eyes had adjusted enough to see the face of a woman awash in drying vomit. Her mouth was agape and her eyes open. He shuddered and scrambled off her, then backed farther into the lab.

Six years ago, he and a badly wounded friend had spent the night huddled on the brink of a shallow, open death pit in Angola just a foot or so above at least a hundred decaying corpses. If that was the most sickening, repugnant situation in which he had ever found himself, this place was a close second.

Derrick's silhouette appeared at the door. Alex got up on his knees and ran his hands along the countertop, feeling for something that he could use as a weapon. He tripped over a second body, lost his balance, and inadvertently set his hand down on the face of a third. As he quickly moved his hand away, it hit against a small cardboard box. *Stick matches!*

He crawled with the matches to the end of the lab, where the fourth body lay spread-eagled amid shards of glass from equipment that the man's death throes had swept off the countertop. Cautiously, Alex raised his head above the counter and peered across at the door. Derrick's silhouette was gone, although certainly not for long. Assuming he was outside the microbiology lab when Malloche released the soman, and that he didn't see Alex enter the room, it would be the last place he would want to search. His eyes still fixed on the door, Alex struck one of the matches and cupped it in his hand.

The corpse next to him was a grotesque shade of violet. Its wide-open mouth held a pool of vomit. Alex gasped for a breath and shook out the match. Then he checked the door once more. Nothing yet. He tried another match. This time, his eyes were drawn immediately to the one intact piece of glassware on the floor, an opaque, glass-stoppered bottle, nestled in the crook of the corpse's rigid right arm. "Hydrochloric Acid—1m," the label read.

Now we're talking, Alex thought, shaking out the match.

He had no idea what the "1m" signified, but if it meant strong, he had his weapon. Another check of the door, and he lit a third match. Then he carefully removed the top from the nearly filled bottle and poured some of the contents on the chest of the corpse. Instantly, amid a swirl of smoke and even more stench, the concentrated acid ate through the dead man's shirt and into his skin.

Bingo!

Now, all he had to do was get close.

He dropped down once more and worked his way through the debris toward the door. He was on the other side of the central lab bench from where he came in. It had been three minutes, maybe even four. Had the killer given up and left?

At that precise moment, Derrick's silhouette reappeared at the glass. The door slowly opened, and he stepped inside the room. From where he was crouching, Alex could just make out the man's form as he looked about, no doubt trying to adjust to the heavy, fetid air.

Then he turned to the wall by the door. *The lights!* His first move was going to be to turn on the lights. Alex pressed against some cabinets and steeled himself as he heard the switches being thrown.

Nothing.

Of course. At Malloche's orders, Richard Marcus had sealed off the area, and had probably done everything he could to delay intervention by investigators from state or federal agencies. It appeared as if no one had been in the lab since the disaster, so the lights had to have been shut off at the fuse box—probably for the whole pathology unit—to discourage anyone who might have made it past security. Another break. Alex inched his way along the base of the lab bench. Then he stopped and slowly set aside the stopper from the bottle of concentrated acid.

Derrick, wounded from the monitor screen, irritated by losing his quarry, and now distressed at having to be in the center of such an unpleasant stench, had to be off balance, as ripe for taking as he ever would be. The muted sound of his footsteps said that he was just on the other side of the lab bench now—not five feet away.

Alex held his breath and could hear Derrick's panting, possibly as he tried hyperventilating through his shirt.

Are you feeling ill, bastard? Close to puking? Well, with any luck you're going to feel a hell of a lot worse in just another few seconds.

Alex shifted his weight for better leverage, grasped the bottle tightly, and tried to imagine how Derrick was positioned—where he was facing. Slowly . . . slowly, he began to straighten up. Derrick was just three feet away, facing toward the far wall, searching for him in the carnage he and his employer had created. Alex raised the bottle over his head. Then, barely audibly, he cleared his throat. As Derrick swung around, Alex whipped his arm down, sending a full splash of the acid directly into the man's eyes. In the same motion, he ducked back behind the counter for safety. Piteous screaming erupted instantly from the terrorist, who managed to fire a short burst before his weapon clattered to the floor.

Alex shook his hand against the intense burning where several drops of the acid had hit him. He stayed low until the uncontrolled wailing had given way to whimpering. Then he rounded the lab bench and struck a match. The killer's eyes, brows, and much of his nose were already eaten away. Smoke was still rising from his flesh. His moans were unintelligible.

The semiautomatic was, in fact, an Uzi. Alex cradled the gun and headed for the door. Then he turned back.

"My brother's name was Andy Bishop," he said.

And he emptied a burst from the Uzi into Derrick's skull.

CHAPTER 37

"ATTA GIRL, JESS," EMILY WHISPERED AS JESSIE turned back to the table. "I've been itching to tell her to fuck off, too."

Cursing at Grace had been a great release for Jessie, but otherwise didn't seem to have had much effect, except to shock the scrub nurse, Jared, into dropping a hemostat.

"Em," she said, "I don't think Alex could have gotten away from that guy. I just can't believe this is happening. What do we do now?"

"First we finish," Emily said. "Then we worry."

Jessie nodded across at her friend. The right advice at the right time, as always. First things first. When in doubt, just do what you can do. Simple wisdom until you try and give it to yourself.

"Thanks, pal," she said. "You're the ultimate friend in need."

Friend in need. For almost the first time since the surgery on Malloche had begun, Jessie's focus shifted to Sara. The diagnosis of acute hydrocephalus and the treatment she had begun with the twist drill were right; she felt certain of that. But had she been in time? It was possible that at this moment Sara was already dead. Sara and Alex. Was there any way she could just wake up from this day and discover it had never happened?

Jessie looked down at the monster, sleeping so peacefully, secure in the knowledge that he had covered all the bases. For Claude Malloche, it was all about manipulation—his surgeon would perform a perfect operation because she wanted to keep her patients alive. Richard Marcus would lie and cover up murder to protect masses of people outside the hospital. If Sara Devereau died, so what? To Malloche she was worth keeping alive only so long as she added to their leverage. Jessie made a claw of her hand and, shielded from Grace, set it down over Malloche's face.

"I want to kill him, Em," she whispered fiercely. "For as long as I can remember, I've gotten guilt pangs from just swatting a mosquito. But right here, right now, I want to dig my fingers into his eyes, and rip his evil face right off."

"You were thinking about Sara?"

"How did—?" Jessie laughed ruefully. "Yeah," she said. "I was."

"You did everything you could up there. I pray she's okay. But either way, you did everything you could. Just hang in there, Jess. What goes around comes around. Our turn will come."

Emily's words unlocked the dam of Jessie's emotions.

Tears of sadness, anger, and intense strain began to blur her vision. Ignoring her sterile field, she reached up a gloved hand, lifted her glasses, and wiped her eyes dry on the sleeve of her surgical gown.

"What's going on there?" Grace demanded, moving in close.

"Oh, nothing," Jessie replied. "We're just getting ready to bring our little friend ARTIE the robot back from Brainland. You're absolutely right, Em," she added without bothering to lower her voice. "What goes around comes around. Let's do it. I'm putting just a little bit of tension on the cord. Please put all six pods in reverse for a short burst right . . . now. Good. I got about an eighth of an inch back. And . . . again."

The extraction of the tiny robot took most of twenty minutes, during which Jessie's voice and the soft gurgle of flowing oxygen were the only sounds to penetrate the tension and fear in the OR. The final move in the recovery was simply a gentle, blind tug. ARTIE, bloodied but intact, popped out through Malloche's nostril, still firmly connected to its polystyrene umbilical cord.

"Yes!" Jessie said softly. "Welcome back, little fella. You were immense." She sutured the insertion hole closed, then called out, "Michelle, *we . . . are . . . finished*. Could you wake up our patient, please?"

"One awake patient comin' up," the anesthesiologist said.

Jessie packed Malloche's nose with gauze, then stripped off her gloves and stepped back from the table. She could tell that Grace had a grip on the pistol that was tucked into the waistband beneath her scrub shirt. It might be possible to overpower the woman and then try to make some sort of deal with Arlette—a trade involving Grace and Malloche for the hostages on Surgical

Seven. But there were too many ifs and too many potential casualties to chance it. And if Grace was as competent as Malloche had boasted she was, disarming her
might be extremely costly.

No, Jessie decided. For the moment, this one was
simply going to have to play itself out.

"Now, what about my explanation?" Pfeffer demanded petulantly. "My lab tech is dead up there."

"*I'll* give you the explanation," Grace said.

She marched quickly out of the operating room and
straight over to where Pfeffer was standing beside the
console. Then she pulled the snub-nosed revolver from
beneath her shirt and jammed the barrel up under his
chin.

"What—?"

"Not another sound from any of you, or I'll blow this
man's brains out," she said. "And after I've done that,
then I'll move over and do her."

She motioned toward Holly, the console tech. Then,
without moving her gun from beneath the radiologist's
jaw, Grace picked up a phone, tucked it between her
chin and shoulder, and called up to Surgical Seven.

"Arlette, the operation's over," she said. "Everything
went well in that regard. The tumor has been removed
and Claude is waking up. But there has been some trouble. I need Armand down here right away. . . . Derrick?
He's—um—he's not here. He fired at a man who was
down here, and then chased him. It's been about an hour
since he left. But the other man wasn't armed. I think it's
just taken Derrick a while to catch up with him. Now,
please, send Armand down. I'll explain everything that
happened when we get back upstairs."

There was nothing Jessie could think of to do at this
point but cooperate and wait. It *had* been an hour since

Derrick took off after Alex, and now she knew that Malloche's right-hand man hadn't returned to Surgical Seven either. He was heavily armed and wasn't that far behind his unarmed prey when he took off. Could Alex's hatred and determination possibly have been enough to overcome such odds?

One thing was certain. If Derrick didn't return with Alex or an account of his death, there was going to be hell to pay on Surgical Seven.

ALEX SMASHED THE window to the chemistry lab and found a flashlight and a first aid kit. He used gauze pads and tape from the kit to stem the bleeding from his shoulder, and ointment to ease the burning on his hand and arm. The concentrated acid that had plashed on him had left a dozen or more deep sores along his right forearm and across his hand. Finally, covering Derrick's Uzi with a towel, but keeping it at the ready, he left the hospital by a staircase in the back of the pathology department. In five years, he hadn't so much as bruised Malloche or his tightly knit, suicidally loyal organization. Now, at last, he had done some damage.

This is just the beginning, Claude, he was thinking. *Just the beginning.*

After the death-cave horror of the micro lab and the darkness of the pathology department, the bright noontime sunshine hit him like a slap. It took time to get his bearings. He was on a largely deserted street, behind the main building of the hospital. The van, with Stan Moyer and Vicki Holcroft, was a block and a half to his left. They had stayed up with him all night, chasing down first Mark Naehring in Hawaii, then the hypnotic truth concoction in his office. Now, with more than four hours gone since he left for the OR, he felt certain they were beginning to get antsy.

Alex carefully made his way out to the street. He had no doubt that once Malloche and his wife realized their man wasn't coming back, there would be trouble for Jessie and the others. Having reduced the opposition on Surgical Seven by 20 percent—40 with Malloche now out of commission—he even gave thought to putting a force together, heading up to the floor, and attempting to end matters then and there. But according to what he had learned from Jessie, it was a good bet the neurosurgical unit was sealed off with Malloche's notorious thoroughness and skill.

There would doubtless be reprisals for his showing up in the OR as he did, and also for Derrick. As long as Malloche needed medical care, it seemed likely that Jessie was reasonably safe. But it was also clear that as long as one of Malloche's crew was roaming about with the trigger to three or four vials of soman, the people of Boston weren't. As things stood, an assault of any kind just didn't make sense—at least not yet. But whether they stormed Surgical Seven or found another way, one thing was sure—Derrick was not the last of the body count.

Stan and Vicki were struggling to come up with a Plan B when Alex knocked twice, then once on the rear door of the van. He fell as much as climbed inside, and lay on the floor for a while. He was mentally and physically exhausted, and much more battered than even he had appreciated. Vicki redressed his wounds from an elaborate first aid kit, as he filled in the two FBI agents on the events in the OR, and later, in the microbiology lab.

"Remind me not to get on your bad side," Moyer said

when he had finished. "Hydrochloric acid. Nasty. Tasteful, but extremely nasty."

"It wasn't Derrick's best day," Alex replied.

"So," Vicki asked, "where do we go from here?"

"You know Boston better than I do. What do you think of the three places Malloche gave to us?"

Holcroft and Moyer decided with their eyes who should respond. Vicki won.

"The way I see it, they may have made a big mistake."

"Tell me."

"Assuming the information you got from Malloche is the truth, all three places they chose to hide the soman can be sealed off from the public and searched. The search crew is standing by."

"How many?" Alex asked.

"As many as we can get. The number's probably growing by the minute."

"But they're going to need time and some sort of serious exposure suits," Moyer added. "And if Malloche's man on the outside realizes what we're doing, and there is a fourth or even a fifth vial of the gas, all hell's gonna break loose."

"Wait, tell me again," Alex said. "All three locations—the rotunda at Quincy Market, the Green Line at Government Center, and Filene's Basement, are normally locked for the night?"

"I'm not sure what time," Vicki answered, "but yes. Probably by one A.M. they'll all three be closed off. Filene's a lot earlier."

"The break we have is that Malloche doesn't have a clue that we know anything."

"What about the people who were with you in the OR?" Moyer asked.

"Jessie's the only one who knows why I was there. I don't think they'd hurt her."

"The question may not be whether or not they hurt *her*. The question may be how well she can stand up to watching someone *else* get hurt."

Alex was silent. Of course they wouldn't touch Jessie. With Malloche just recovering from surgery, they couldn't afford to—and they wouldn't have to. They could get at her through Emily, or Sara, or little Tamika, or any of the others she cared so deeply about. And if she broke before the soman locations could be sealed off, the vials could easily be moved to new locations . . . or even detonated.

It was all up to Jessie. Somehow, regardless of the pain Malloche's people inflicted on her patients, she had to keep herself from giving them any information until they were no longer suspicious that she had caved in too easily. Then, smoothly and convincingly, she had to come up with some believable explanation for who Dr. Mark Naehring was, and what he was doing in the operating room—some explanation other than the truth.

Too much, Alex thought. It was too much to ask of anyone.

"We've got to assume Jessie will eventually tell them what Malloche disclosed to us," he said.

"Would she do that?"

"It depends on how they try to break her down. They'll probably go after her patients. I don't know how she's going to respond, but we've got to assume the worst."

"If we seal off those places now, we'll be tipping our hand just as surely as if she *did* tell them everything."

"What time is it?" Alex asked.

"One," Vicki said. "A little after."

"Do you think we could get teams mobilized at all three places by midnight with the suits—or at least with gas masks?"

"Assuming the Boston police continue to cooperate, and I have no reason to think they won't."

"Everything's got to look perfectly ordinary until the teams are inside the gates. I want them brought in gradually from directions where Malloche's man out there wouldn't notice. Damn! I wish we had some clue as to what he looked like."

As Alex was speaking, he almost inadvertently slipped his hand into the rear pocket of his scrub pants. The folded paper Emily had given to him in the OR was still there. The sheet was an anesthesia record. At the top of the page, in pencil, was a decently done three-inch sketch of a man's face. Below the picture, Emily had printed:

white male, 6'2", slim, 160–170, short light-brown hair, blue eyes, nose looks like it was broken and poorly set, name may be Stefan

Alex studied the page, then handed it over to Moyer. Emily had done the drawing in the OR while she was pretending to work with the anesthesiologist. If she had been caught by either Grace or Derrick, it would have gone very poorly for her.

"Jessie's nurse risked dying for this," he said. "It's got to be Malloche's man on the outside. It gives me an idea."

"I think we're already right with you on this one," Holcroft said.

━━━━━━━━━━━━━━━━━ CHAPTER 38

THEY WERE HERDED AT GUNPOINT UP TO SURGICAL
Seven in two groups. First, Grace took the console tech
Holly, radiologist Hans Pfeffer, Skip Porter, the scrub and
circulating nurses, and Emily. After the elevator was
brought back down, Jessie and Michelle Booker made the
trip with Malloche, on a gurney, and Armand. The young
killer seemed high-strung and edgy, and never lowered his
pistol.

"How is my patient in seven thirty-seven doing?"
Jessie asked him as they approached the elevator.

Armand looked at her blankly and motioned her
with his gun barrel to move ahead.

"Jesus," Jessie exclaimed. "I just saved your boss's life.
The least you can do is answer my question. Do you understand me?"

"He speaks English," Malloche said hoarsely, but

with surprising force and clarity. "He just doesn't like to."

Since waking up from anesthesia, his responses had been groggy and monosyllabic. Clearly his condition was rapidly improving. He rattled at Armand in French and got a terse reply.

"Armand says your patient is alive," Malloche reported. "But he cannot vouch for her condition. The fact that I am this awake and alert and we have yet to return to the floor suggests that things have gone well for me, yes?"

"I suppose you could conclude that," Jessie said. "Believe it or not, I told you just a few minutes ago that the operation was a complete success. It may be a while before information hits your memory bank and gets deposited. You were actually awake quite a bit during your surgery." Then, heart hammering, she added, "Do you remember anything of that?"

"Remember anything? Not really. I remember getting wheeled onto an elevator and heading down the corridor to the operating room. Then the next thing I remember, I am being wheeled back."

Jessie silently sighed her relief. It appeared that neither Malloche nor Grace had any idea who Dr. Mark Naehring was, why he was in the operating room, or, in Grace's case, why Derrick confronted, then chased him. Jessie suspected that soon, though, very soon, they were going to be looking to her for answers. And whatever those answers were, they had better have the ring of truth.

Michelle Booker had been silently watching and listening. Jessie reached over and squeezed her hand.

"Hang in there, Michelle," she said. "I'll explain everything to you when I can."

"You mean when we allow you to," Malloche corrected.

"You just treat this woman well," Booker said boldly. "She just performed an operation on you that maybe no neurosurgeon anyplace could have done better."

"I was counting on that."

Arlette was there when the elevator arrived. She took her husband's hand and kissed him on the lips. Then she looked up at Jessie.

"He looks quite good. I understand the surgery went well."

"As of this moment, it has. But post-op, much can happen. My patient Sara Devereau is a perfect example. How is she doing?"

"What do we do for my husband now?" Arlette responded, pointedly ignoring the question.

The battle of wills between the two of them had begun anew. After nearly seven hours in the operating room, Jessie was in no mood to back down.

"I asked you a simple question," she said.

"And I—"

"Tell her, Arlette," Malloche said with a weak wave. "Tell her what she wants to know."

"Very well. Dr. Gilbride has been in with your patient since you left. She is awake and seems to be responding to commands, and the doctor seems quite pleased with himself."

"Oh, thank God! I want to see her."

"My husband . . . ," Arlette said stonily.

"Okay. The surgery was, I would have to say, an unqualified success. We were able to remove about ninety-five percent of the tumor."

"You left some in?"

Jessie hesitated, wondering what the immediate fallout would be of explaining that the reason she couldn't get all the growth out was that Arlette's man Derrick had murdered the computer expert and destroyed his equipment. She decided now was not the time.

"The little I left in will probably never cause a problem. In fact, the blood supply to that fragment may have been disrupted enough to kill what cells remain."

"Go on. What can we expect now?"

"Well, seizures may be a problem. We've medicated him for that with a drug he has taken before. My nurse practitioner, the one your people kidnapped, should stay with him continuously for a while to administer medications and monitor his vital signs. Infection is always a concern post-op. There is also the chance of a pressure buildup like the one that happened to my patient."

"That could happen this soon?"

"Oh, yes, or up to several days after surgery. There's no way to predict whether this particular complication is going to happen, or when. Now, may I go in and see Sara Devereau?"

"First, get Claude settled in with his nurse. Then you may go and check on the Devereau woman. After that, Doctor, you and I have some very serious matters to discuss."

"What matters?" Malloche asked dreamily.

Arlette kissed him on the forehead and spoke reassuringly to him in German. Apparently satisfied with whatever she said, Claude smiled feebly and closed his eyes, obviously exhausted.

Under Arlette's watchful gaze, Jessie and Booker wheeled Malloche into the deserted ICU. Then, while he was being transferred to a bed and hooked up to a monitor, Arlette and Grace huddled in the hallway. Jessie had no doubt whatsoever about the subject of their conversation. She was running out of time to prepare some believable explanation.

A fairly extensive neurologic exam on Malloche verified what Jessie already suspected—that ARTIE had excised nearly all of a very extensive, hard-to-reach meningioma without causing any gross neurologic damage. Sadly, ironically, she acknowledged that the tiny robot and the MRI guidance system may have come of age working within the skull of a demon. She was just finishing when Emily came in.

"Sara's wide awake," she said excitedly.

"Talking?"

"She's not ready for the debating society, but she's certainly making her needs understood. You're on a helluva roll today, Jess."

"Carl's still there with her?"

"A man on a mission."

"Maybe someone should have smashed him across the face with a gun a long time ago."

"Amen to that," Emily said.

Jessie went over Malloche's up-to-the-minute condition and medications.

"Between you, me, Michelle, and the nurses, we should be able to provide him with continuous coverage."

Arlette and Grace reentered the room. Neither looked too pleased. Until that moment, Michelle Booker had remained silent. But now her exasperation broke through.

"Would somebody please tell me what in the hell is going on?" she pleaded. "I went off coverage half an hour ago, and my kids are expecting me home. I need to get out of here."

"I don't believe that's going to happen," Jessie said.

She received an assenting nod from Arlette and gave a capsule summary of their predicament. Michelle's expression—increasingly astonished and fearful—suggested that the reality of the situation on Surgical Seven was far more bizarre and dangerous than whatever her imagination had conjured up.

A muttered "Dear God" was all she could manage when Jessie had finished.

Arlette motioned the two of them out into the hall, then down to the small conference room. She was wearing her machine gun over her shoulder and had a thick-barreled pistol stuck in her belt. For the first time Jessie could remember, the woman wore no makeup. Her porcelain skin was unlined, but her lips looked bloodless, and her eyes had an unsettling hollowness about them.

Exhaustion? Tension? Anger? Jessie wondered. All three, perhaps. It certainly seemed as if the strain of running such a show by herself was beginning to take its toll.

"Dr. Booker," Arlette asked when they reached the conference room, "do you have any knowledge of what transpired downstairs in the operating room?"

"Nothing other than what I saw," Booker replied.

"Well, I'd like you to tell me exactly what that was. But first, Dr. Copeland, why don't you go on down the hall and see how your patient is doing. I'll send for you when I'm ready. It won't be long."

Jessie knew that Arlette would have Booker go through the surgery on her husband step by step until she reached the part when Mark Naehring entered the OR. Then the questions would become more and more detailed until Arlette had a crystal-clear image of what the anesthesiologist had seen. And later, the details of Booker's story would be used to check off on Jessie's account.

Just don't lie, Michelle, Jessie begged silently. *Don't take any chances with this woman. Tell her what you saw.*

"I'll be down the hall," she said, her eyes urging Booker to be strong.

With Armand in tow, Jessie hurried to Sara's room. Her friend and patient was indeed awake and alert, sitting up and sipping some juice. The shunt Jessie had placed through the twist-drill hole had been carefully sutured down and hooked up to a drainage system. Carl Gilbride was adjusting the valve that controlled the flow rate.

"Hey," Jessie said, "an island of sanity in the sea of madness. How're you doing, Sar?"

"Nah . . . sobad. Tube . . . inma . . . head."

"I know. I know." Jessie hugged her. "Don't worry about it. If the tube needs to stay in to keep the pressure down, we'll hide it beneath your skin. Understand?"

"Yes."

"The drainage was dropping off, so I repositioned the tube," Gilbride said, sounding to Jessie like a four-year-old announcing he had picked up all his toys.

"You did great, Carl," Jessie replied. "She would have never made it without you."

"How'd the case go?"

"ARTIE did well. Malloche is awake with no apparent residual neurologic problems."

"Does that mean we're going to make it out of this?"

"You're asking the wrong person, Carl," she said. She lowered her voice, making it difficult, if not impossible, for Armand to hear. "Something happened during the operation that Arlette isn't too pleased about. One of

their people—the big guy with the blond crew cut—
took off after someone and hasn't returned."

"Took off after who?"

"I don't know. I'll speak to you about it all later.
Meanwhile, please just keep on doing what you can for
Sara. How's everyone else on the floor?"

"I . . . um . . . haven't been around to see them. It
seemed like this is what you wanted me to do."

With the power to dictate all the rules in effect
stripped from him, Gilbride seemed almost helpless.

"It was, Carl," she said.

"Dr. Copeland?"

Arlette Malloche stood by the doorway. Red smudges
of anger colored her cheeks.

"Yes?"

"Come with me now."

"I'd like to make rounds on the other patients."

Arlette grabbed the pistol in her belt, but didn't pull
it out.

"Now!" she demanded.

Jessie took a calming breath. This was the moment
she had been dreading since she realized that Derrick
hadn't returned to the floor. She had never been much of
an actress or much of a liar. But she knew she was going
to have to be both now. She had to believe that Alex had
somehow managed to get away from Derrick; he would
need time to locate the soman vials and disarm them. The
moment that Arlette suspected they had learned the locations, it seemed certain one or more of the setups would
be detonated. No matter what pressure Arlette brought
to bear, that was the one piece of information that had to
be kept from her.

"Hang in there, Sar," Jessie said. "You, too, Carl.
Keep up the great work."

Arlette motioned her to the conference room and into a chair, and closed the door.

"I assume you know what I wish to learn about," she said.

"The man who came into the OR."

"Precisely. I warn you in advance, Doctor, that I have a version of this story from your anesthesiologist friend. If your account differs in the slightest from hers, I'm going to let you watch while I kill her."

Jessie sucked in a jet of air, then moistened her lips.

This had better be damn good, Copeland, she was thinking. She had come up with the rough outline of a story that would jibe with anything Booker might have told Arlette. But there would be a major problem if Arlette went to Gilbride for confirmation. Somehow, he had to be kept out of the loop. Just as Jessie was preparing to ramble through the version she had created, something Alex had said about Gilbride gave her the answer she needed.

"I don't know as much as you might think," she began.

"I don't believe that."

"Well, you've got to. I don't want anyone to get hurt."

"Go on."

"The whole thing was set up some time ago by that woman Lisa from the FBI—the one that your husband shot. I don't know how, but somehow they knew Claude was in the States looking for a neurosurgeon. Eastern Mass Medical Center was just one of the hospitals they targeted. I don't know how many others there were. Lisa was the agent assigned here, and she was around almost all the time. She was certain Rolf Hermann was Claude, but she didn't trust Dr. Gilbride enough to tell him that. She said they had done some research on Carl, and felt there was a good possibility he had been paid off by you. So she spoke exclusively with me. When it was clear Hermann was going to die, she had people from the FBI lined up to storm the floor and capture you and the Count's so-called children."

"But then your Dr. Gilbride made a mess of things by losing his temper at the agent and forcing her to identify herself before she wanted to."

"Exactly. She had given me a number to call if there was trouble, but I never had a chance to use it until Dave Scolari, the man in seven-seventeen with the broken neck, had his seizure. During the commotion, I took a chance and slipped into the conference room to use the only phone you had left hooked up. The conversation with the FBI people who answered only lasted maybe a minute before I had to hang up. I was told to prepare the way for one of their people to come into the operating room. I said whoever it was should use the name Dr. Mark Naehring."

Arlette motioned for Jessie to stop so that she could mentally pick through the story for inconsistencies.

"All right," she said finally, "what happened next?"

Jessie released the death grip she had on the arm of her chair. She was improvising—flying almost blind. But so far at least, her account seemed to be holding up.

"I made up the story that Dr. Naehring might be coming into the OR to help me with part of the case. He's a psychopharmacologist—someone who works with the sort of medications we use when patients are kept awake during brain surgery—so I thought if you checked up on him, his helping me would make some sense, at least as long as you didn't try to call him."

"That was very clever. Go on."

"The night before the operation, I made it a point to say something to Dr. Booker about it when she was doing your husband's pre-op physical."

"I remember."

"I wasn't sure anyone was going to show up, but right in the middle of the case, someone from the FBI did. We were able to speak to one another by turning off our microphones and whispering. Because of the way the MRI magnets are set up, both Grace and Derrick were shielded by our backs."

"What did this agent want?"

"He wanted to kill your husband, and then kill both of your people, and then go up to Surgical Seven and kill you."

"And—"

"I had to tell him about the soman—that it was out there in the city someplace, and that you would have it released in a crowded area if anything happened to Claude. I also told him I had seen the way it killed the microbiology people."

"That was good. What did he do then?"

Jessie regripped the chair. This chapter, the most far-fetched of the fish tale, had to be totally believable—and diverting.

"He said he had a tiny transmitter in the locker room that he wanted me to insert into your husband's head."

"My, my," she said.

"I told him the transmitter couldn't be brought into the MRI room because of the magnets. They would destroy it and it might damage the machine. He argued with me that there must be a way to do it, but I assured him there wasn't."

"Then he left?"

"He did. He asked me how many people were being

held on Surgical Seven and if anyone had been harmed. He said the FBI would work something out, but that no one would be placed in any more danger than they were in right now. Then he left. A few seconds later, I heard Derrick demand that he pull down his mask. Next thing I heard was shooting. I saw them take off, so I just finished the operation."

For a full minute, Arlette studied her face, probing. Jessie forced herself to maintain eye contact.

"You're certain they know about the soman," Arlette said finally.

"I . . . I'm sorry. I couldn't think of anything else to tell them but the truth."

"You did right. I want them to know. In fact, I'm thinking about giving them a demonstration."

"No! . . . I mean, please don't. As long as it's only a threat, I think the FBI will keep their distance. Once the gas is used, I think they'll just do whatever is necessary to get at you. Ask your husband if you don't believe me. There's no need for a demonstration."

"We'll see," Arlette said.

But Jessie could tell she understood the point. Once again, her hands stopped compressing the oak armrests.

"Could I please go and check on the other patients now?" she asked.

Arlette brought her hand across and rested it on the gun.

"I don't believe you," she said.

A knot formed and tightened in Jessie's gut.

"Well, everything I said is just the way it happened."

"We shall see."

Please. Please don't hurt anyone.

"That woman Grace brought up from the operating room is an X-ray technician, is she not?" Arlette asked.

"She is," Jessie replied, suddenly terrified for Holly. "Why?"

"I'm going to send her off the floor with Grace to bring back a portable X-ray machine."

"For what?"

"I want a picture done of Claude's head, that's what. You knew that one of the first things I'd think of was that the FBI man wanted you to insert a tracer into Claude's head. That's just the sort of thing they do. So you thought that by telling me they had asked you to do it, I'd believe that you hadn't. Well, I think you underestimate me. You did it, didn't you?"

The knot loosened. Jessie actually had to keep her lips pressed tightly together to prevent a smile. She had almost rejected using the idea of the implanted transmitter because it sounded so far-out.

"Believe me," she said with genuine conviction, "I did nothing but remove his tumor."

"We'll see. I think between Grace, Claude, and me, we should be able to spot the device on an X ray. As things stand, I owe you some distress for calling the FBI the way you did. But you did a good job in the operating room, so I'm going to let that go—as long as I don't find out you are lying."

"I'm not," Jessie said, perhaps too quickly.

Again, Arlette searched her face for signs of deceit.

"When do you think Claude will be ready to travel?" she asked.

"Do you mean travel without risk?"

"No. I mean the soonest he could travel at all. He won't have to sit up. We can keep him on a stretcher."

"It's hard to say, because I've never done an operation with the robot before. I guess a day. Two or three would probably be better. As you saw with Sara Devereau, things can happen."

"That's why you're coming with us."

"What?"

"Armand will give you a large canvas bag. I want you to fill it with whatever medical supplies you are likely to need in any situation or emergency that might arise with my husband."

"When are we leaving?"

"When we leave, you'll know," Arlette said.

CHAPTER 39

Quincy Market Rotunda—RED TEAM
Green Line—Government Center—WHITE TEAM
Filene's Basement—BLUE TEAM
??

IT WAS NEARING TEN IN THE EVENING. ALEX was in the van, parked on Cambridge Street, just across from the entrance to the MBTA Government Center station. He was flipping through the pages in one of the three loose-leaf notebooks he, Stan Moyer, and Vicki Holcroft had put together. The notebooks contained as much information and as many maps as they could accumulate on each of the three soman locations Claude Malloche had disclosed. They also contained the list of team members assigned to find the vials of gas. The teams were a mix of FBI, local police, National Guard, and several Army specialists in biologic and toxic warfare flown in from D.C.

Moyer was coordinating the Red Team, assigned to the center rotunda in the tourist mecca Quincy Market. Less than a mile away, Holcroft was organizing her Blue Team people in Filene's Basement at busy Downtown Crossing. And in between them, Alex had taken responsibility for the largest team, with the daunting task of sweeping the sprawling Government Center T station.

The plan was straightforward enough, but did require the quiet cooperation of people in charge of each location. The teams would infiltrate their targets before they closed and hide out in various positions. Then, an hour or so after closing, they would seal off every window and systematically search until the gas had been found. Filene's had closed at eight-thirty, and there, the search was already under way.

The cavernous Government Center station would be the toughest nut. The plan was to have it first be inspected and cleared out by transit security people. Then, at 2 A.M., Alex's White Team would enter along the tracks through the tunnel from Haymarket station. The target would be divided into six-foot-square numbered grids and searched that way. A simple plan if ever there was one.

But there was one very major catch. Claude Malloche's drug-induced revelations had been fairly specific, but only up to a point.

How many vials are hidden in Boston?

Three . . . four.

Alex had mentally replayed the snippet of his conversation with the killer a hundred times.

Three . . . four.

What did that mean? Under heavy medication,

Malloche had given out only three locations. Was there another? Malloche was a control freak. Would he ever allow a strategy that purposely deprived him of information? But on the other hand, he was also obsessive about detail—about having backup plans to his backup plans. Could he have covered himself for the possibility that either he or one of the others might be captured and tortured by having the location of a fourth vial withheld from him?

Is there another vial of soman?

Don't know . . . don't know . . . don't know.

In the end, Alex felt that they had no choice but to go with what they had. But the existence of a fourth vial could by no means be discounted. The key to dealing with that possibility was finding Stefan—Malloche's man on the outside. And the key to doing *that* was to have everything look exactly as he expected it to look until the very moment he pushed the button to release the gas.

Alex set the notebooks aside and swung around toward the aging police demolitions expert who was laboring at a small bench top beneath two powerful lights. The best of the best, he had asked the captain for. This rumpled senior citizen was the man they had sent. But Alex had already been with Harry Laughlin long enough today to know the captain hadn't let him down.

"How's it going back there?" he asked.

"Ten or fifteen minutes, boyo," Laughlin said, with just a hint of a brogue. "I should know the deepest mysteries of this beastie in that time."

The beastie laid out before him was the detonation system that had been used to kill the four microbiology technicians. To obtain it had meant Alex had to return to the cave of death. Under the cover of evening darkness, he had slipped back into the hospital through the door in the rear of the pathology department. Laughlin, well into his sixties, had listened to Alex's description of what the lab would be like and, without batting an eye, had still insisted on going in with him.

"Once you've seen two buddies blown to bits tryin' to defuse a canister," he said, "nothin' affects you that much. I'm with you all the way."

"Tell me that afterward," Alex had replied.

They donned paper surgical masks, then Alex pulled away the yellow plastic tape and eased open the door to the lab. The wall of stench hit them like a blast furnace, with the pungent smell of chemically burned flesh even more repugnant than the other odors.

"Still with me?" he asked.

"When did I ever say that?"

The bodies, including Derrick's, were just as he had left them. But under the glare of their high-beam flashlights, the scene—the oddly positioned corpses, the rigor mortis, the blood, the vomit—looked even more eerie and repulsive. It took nearly half an hour, but they found the detonator still taped underneath an incubator stand—a neat package of circuits about five inches square. They carefully untaped it and set it in a plastic sack, along with shards of glass and what appeared to be a metal casing of some sort. Then, close to being overwhelmed by the hellish scene, they left.

"Nice place you took me to, there," Laughlin said as they headed back to the van.

"If we can't find and deactivate those other packages, Harry, we may get to see the scene again, only on a much grander scale."

Now, Alex made his way back to where Laughlin was working.

"Okay," the policeman said, "here's the pitch. A small charge is detonated by radio and blows a glass vial to bits. If the gas works the way you say it does, the circuitry and explosive in the three locations may be the same as here, but the gas containers must be larger—probably much larger. I would guess the total size of the package may be a foot or so long, and maybe half that wide and deep."

"Can you disable the system?"

"I believe I can, yes."

"And then put it back together again so it looks the same but just doesn't work?"

"With the gas?"

Alex thought about their need to draw Malloche's man as close as possible to the vials so that one of their observers might get a fix on him.

"I'll decide about that when we find one," he said.

AT THREE-THIRTY in the morning, the Blue Team scored. The twenty members of Vicki Holcroft's unit had drifted into the department store throughout the early evening, and had hidden on the upper floors until closing time. Then, after an hour's wait, they had assembled in the basement and set up their grids. The key to completing their search was Harry Laughlin's suggestion that the gas would not have been placed beneath clothes or inside of a cabinet where its diffusion would be restricted. Eliminating all cabinets, at least for the first pass through, made the search of the vast store basement at least manageable.

The deadly black glass cylinder, with its attached detonating device, was in plain sight, yet essentially invisible to any casual passerby. It was screwed in place beneath the customer side of a counter, not far from the escalator bringing shoppers up to the store from the Downtown Crossing MBTA station. The cylinder was shielded in front by a black metal plate drilled throughout with minute holes to allow diffusion of the poison.

Alex got word of the find at Filene's as his White Team of forty were halfway through a grid-by-grid search of the Government Center Green Line station. He had assumed that the gas would be placed in a spot likely to be densely populated, and so had the search begin with the central area of the terminal, and slowly fan out toward the more remote stretches of track. So far, nothing.

Reluctant to be seen entering the department store at this hour, Alex had the MBTA supervisor accompany him and Harry Laughlin down into Park Street station, then through the Red Line tunnel to Downtown Crossing, and up the dormant escalator to Filene's. Most of the Blue Team was sent back through the tunnels to join the White Team at Government Center. It was well after four and the station was due to be opened at five. A delay much later than six would certainly risk creating suspicion.

Alex donned a sealed antiexposure suit and ordered the transit authority supervisor, Vicki, and the two agents who would be left with her to try and spot Stefan, to wait for them at the base of the escalator. Laughlin set up a pair of powerful lights and lay down on the floor with his tools close at hand. He had refused the suit.

"The glass in them things fogs up too much for this kind of work," he explained. "Besides, after what I went through to get that beastie from the hospital, if I blow this one, I'd be too embarrassed to want to live."

"Obviously, you didn't get a close enough look at those stiffs in the lab," Alex replied. "I'm not afraid of biting the big one with a bullet or a blast, but I can't stand the thought of puking to death."

With Alex assisting, Laughlin took fifteen minutes to isolate the wire he wanted to cut.

"This cylinder's a big one," Laughlin said, "maybe ten times the content of the one that went off in the hospital. With any air movement at all, my guess is there's enough to reach every cranny of this place."

"At the moment, the only cranny I'm concerned about is this one."

"You want me to leave everything here except this connection, right?"

"Yeah. If he comes by and checks, I want it all to look normal. Then, if he tries to detonate the thing, he won't know whether the screwup is in the circuitry or the transmitter. Something he'll do at that point will call attention to himself. I'm sure of it."

"Actually, we can do better than that," Laughlin said. "Looking at the components of this receiver, I'm making an educated guess that the transmitter that will set it off is working somewhere on the VHF band. Once I get this thing deactivated, I have a scanner that should be able to isolate the frequency. Then all we have to do is give monitors to your people who are here, and they should know the instant someone tries to blow this thing."

"That's perfect. Will it be the same for all three setups?"

"Most likely, but we'll check just to be sure. First, though, we've got to neuter this beastie. Okay, then, here goes. Just like in the movies."

The click of the wire cutter was like a gunshot.

"Nothing," Alex said after finally exhaling.

"That's the idea, bucko. In my job, nothing is *very good*."

At that moment, Alex's cell phone went off. The Red Team had located the soman package bolted beneath a stool in the rotunda of the Quincy Market food court.

THE UNKNOWN KILLER virus at Eastern Mass Medical Center remained headline news—especially now that a team from the MRI operating room had been placed on isolation precautions. Sitting at Sara's bedside, Jessie had watched the bogus story unfold on the first news program of the morning, complete with clips of Michelle Booker's businessman husband complaining that, although he had been assured by hospital administrators that his wife was all right, he had not heard a word from her since she left for the hospital twenty-four hours ago.

Now, in the supply room, Jessie systematically loaded the black nylon gym bag with first aid supplies and life-saving equipment, recording the items on a pad so that nothing would be overlooked. Next, she would raid the med room and stock up on all manner of drugs. The charade on Surgical Seven was wearing thin to the outside world. Arlette knew that as well as she did. It was only a matter of time before antiterrorist rescue teams came calling. Arlette planned to be gone when they did.

Tracheotomy kit . . . laryngoscope . . . breathing bag . . . endotracheal tubes . . . hydrocephalus drainage system . . . urinary catheters . . . IV infusion sets . . . twist drill . . . blood pressure cuff . . . scalpel . . . sutures . . .

Arlette, Grace, and Malloche had studied the portable X ray of Claude's head. For the moment at least, Arlette seemed to believe Jessie's tall tale about Mark Naehring. It was almost six in the morning. Malloche had been sleeping most of the time since his surgery, but he was always easy to arouse, and appeared to be doing remarkably well. Still, moving him at this point carried some danger. Jessie knew that Arlette was weighing her options, just as Jessie was weighing the merits of encouraging them to leave, versus stalling to give Alex more time. Leaving might well remove the patients and staff from harm's way. Stalling for time might save lives on the outside, especially if Arlette planned to use the chaos of a massive toxic gas exposure to divert attention from the hospital.

If only there was a way to get word from Alex about the results of his search. But she knew there wasn't.

Jessie was in the med room, loading a box with antibiotics, antiseizure meds, injectable steroids, anticoagulants, and tranquilizers, when she made the decision to do whatever she could to maintain the status quo by keeping the Malloches from leaving. She had seen firsthand the horrors of soman, and she trusted that Alex wouldn't risk the carnage that would result from an assault on Surgical Seven. The longer she could stall their departure, the more chance he had of finding the three vials. All she needed was a plan.

Jessie looked down at the drug in her hand and realized the answer, the plan, was that close. Injectable diazepam—Valium. She filled several 5-cc syringes and carefully wrapped the empty vials in paper towels before throwing them into the trash.

You don't know it, Claude, she was thinking, *but you're about to take a little turn for the worse.*

SIX FORTY-FIVE. A mechanical breakdown in the Government Center station had forced a two-hour delay. At least, that was the story the media had been fed. Dozens of buses had been rolled into service to bypass the station. The Blue Line, which also used Government Center, was being delayed as well.

Alex knew that the massive interruption was a potential red flag. But it was early, and Malloche's man, assuming he was even awake yet, had three locations to keep track of—at least three. With the addition of the Red Team, the force searching the station was now almost eighty—an irony that was hardly lost on Alex. For five years he had toiled alone and in obscurity, tilting at a deadly windmill that some in power denied even existed. Now, here he was, commanding a small army.

After Harry Laughlin had disarmed the detonator in Quincy Market, Stan Moyer and two other agents had been outfitted as maintenance men, given copies of the sketch and description of Stefan as well as monitors set to the detonator's frequency, and left inside the building.

Two of the locations were now secured and under observation. The third had proven to be incredibly difficult. Alex stood beside Laughlin, halfway up one of the staircases in the Government Center station, overseeing the search. The demolitions expert had to be near retirement age, if not past it, yet he looked as fresh after nearly twenty-four tension-filled hours on the job as he had when they started.

"What are you going to do if we can't find it?" he asked.

Alex shrugged. "What do you do when you can't find a bomb?"

"It depends on how much we believe the tip we got."

"I believe this one hundred percent."

"Then we keep looking."

"We've gone over every inch of this place, Harry. Most of it twice."

"No, we haven't."

"What do you mean?"

"We haven't gone over the inch that includes the device. We need to try and think about what we're doing wrong."

For several minutes the two of them stood there, elbow to elbow, watching, thinking. Then Harry began nodding as if he had just realized something.

"What? What?" Alex asked.

"Look at them all down there."

"Yeah?"

"What do you see?"

"I see a huge number of men and women searching—some of them hunched over, some on their hands and knees."

"Where *aren't* they searching, bucko?"

"I don't understand."

"For hours we've been looking down—under benches, behind trash cans, alongside the tracks, in alcoves. That's where the other two cylinders were—down. But—"

"Hey, everyone!" Alex called out without waiting for Laughlin to finish. "I want all the spotlights and all your eyes focused up along the I-beams and across the ceiling. Start from your original grids. Those of you who don't have a grid, just pair up with someone and work the same area. Remember, what we're looking for is probably encased in black. It's not going to be easy to spot."

"I admire a man who can make a decision," Laughlin said.

Fifteen silent minutes passed. . . .

"We have about another half an hour, Harry," Alex said as they continued surveying the deeply shadowed areas overhead. "Then we're going to have to open those gates up there and let the passengers in. If there's a fourth location, sealing this one off much longer is going to be like asking them to set that one off. These people aren't stupid."

"Neither are we, boyo," Harry said suddenly, pointing upward and outward. "Neither are we."

Alex followed his line of sight for about fifty or sixty feet to the place where one of the dozens of support beams met the ceiling. There, virtually blending into the shadows, was the barely visible outline of a rectangular casing.

"Does the Boston Police Department appreciate how good you are?" Alex asked as they raced to the base of the beam.

"I think they might," Laughlin said. "I applied for retirement three years ago and haven't heard a word from them yet."

It took twenty minutes on a ladder before Harry announced that the package had been neutralized.

"Well, bucko," the policeman said after he had climbed down and most of the troops had been dispatched back through the tunnel to the Haymarket station, "that's three out of three. Are you going to go after the hostages?"

"Not yet, Harry. If I was certain it was three out of three and not three out of four I might try and think of some way. But as long as Malloche doesn't know how much we know, I think the hostages are reasonably safe. We've got to see if we can flush out this Stefan."

He gestured to the six undercover police who were now positioned around the area, waiting for the morning crush.

"I think I'll hang around until you do," Laughlin said.

"Hey, that's not necessary."

"Hell, this is all a movie, right? I want to see how it comes out."

CHAPTER **40**

IT HAD BEEN NEARLY TEN YEARS SINCE JESSIE
had adjusted the green felt doctoral cape over her shoulders and strode up onto the stage to accept the parchment that would forever make her a doctor of medicine. Over those years, over those countless hours in the hospital and the operating room, she had never knowingly done anything to injure a patient . . . until now. Throughout the day, every hour or two, she had been injecting Claude Malloche with Valium or with Haldol, another major tranquilizer—the former into his IV line, and the Haldol into a muscle. The combination of the drugs had resulted in a somnolence bordering on coma. Malloche could still be aroused, but only with a great deal of stimulation, and then only for a matter of seconds. The trick was to maintain him in that state without causing a life-threatening depression in his ability to breathe.

If Arlette had been planning to leave EMMC—and it certainly seemed as if she was—her husband's turn for the worse had delayed their departure. Throughout the day, she had maintained a nervous vigil near Claude's bed, leaving only to pace the hallways like a cat, checking in on the hostages and her people. At noon, Gilbride's post-op patient, Lena Levin, was found dead in bed from her infection. Arlette's only reaction was to have the door to her room closed. Otherwise, the hours crept on monotonously and without incident. Now, it was nearly seven.

Jessie knew she was flirting with disaster. Claude was breathing, but not deeply enough to keep his lungs fully expanded. Mucus was starting to pool in his alveolar sacs, and pneumonia was probably already beginning. He had been an operative marvel. Now, his surgeon was celebrating her success by slowly killing him. And if he died, there was no way any of them would survive Arlette Malloche's fury.

"What do you think?"

Arlette's question startled Jessie, who was wondering what was going on with Alex, assuming he and Derrick hadn't killed each other, and how he planned to approach rescuing forty-five hostages on a floor mined with explosives and controlled by three well-armed professionals.

"I don't know for sure," she lied. "I think it must be brain swelling."

"You're treating him for that?"

"I am."

"Can he travel?"

"I don't see how."

"Well, he's going to have to, and soon."

"Then it's on your head, whatever happens."

Arlette grabbed Jessie by the shirt and shoved her roughly against the wall with surprising strength.

"No, it will be on your head! Believe me, it will."

She stalked out of the room.

A few seconds after that, her husband stopped breathing.

"Jesus, Em," Jessie whispered, her heart pounding. "Quick, give me the Ambu bag. Michelle, there's a black gym bag in the med room filled with equipment and drugs. Bring back whatever equipment you need to intubate him, please."

"Here's the breathing bag," Em said.

Her expression left no doubt that she understood the gravity of the situation.

"Suction up, please."

Malloche's complexion was already beginning to darken. His oximeter reading on the monitor screen began to edge downward. His pulse immediately jumped from eighty to a hundred as his body commenced the frantic search for more oxygen. Jessie deep-suctioned his throat, pulled his chin up to straighten his airway, and with one hand tightened the triangular rubber seal over his nose and mouth. Then, with the other, she began rhythmic compressions of the breathing bag, monitoring that air was getting in by the rise and fall of his chest.

"What else can I do?" Em asked.

"What's your connection with the Almighty?"

"Decent enough."

"Talk to her, then."

At that instant, Malloche took a breath. Jessie suctioned him again. This time, he gagged and managed another, gurgling inhalation. Then another. Michelle Booker hurried in with the equipment to intubate.

When she saw the improved situation, she stopped and sighed audibly.

"Ka-ching!" she said. "The bullet is dodged."

"Not by much," Jessie replied.

She knew she had to stop. If Alex hadn't figured things out by now, he wasn't going to. She had to back off on the meds and let Malloche wake up.

"Exactly what is going on here?"

Arlette approached the bed and gestured at all the emergency equipment.

"He had a momentary slowdown in his breathing," Jessie said. "He's doing better now."

Arlette stroked his hair and moved the plastic oxygen mask aside to kiss his still-violet lips.

"He had better be," she said. She turned to Grace, who was standing by the doorway. "Call the chopper in," she ordered. "We're moving in an hour."

As Grace hurried off, Arlette stepped back and leveled her machine gun at Jessie and the others. Then she opened her cell phone and made a call. She spoke rapidly in French, but Jessie picked up the name *Stefan* and the phrase *il est le temps*: it is time.

"No," Jessie pleaded. "Please don't."

"Shut up!" Arlette snapped. "You just take care of my husband, and you may keep a lot of people you care about from getting hurt."

She disdainfully jabbed the barrel of her gun at Jessie, then hurried from the room.

"She's going to do it," Jessie said. "She's going to have the gas released to create enough chaos for them to escape by helicopter."

Emily put her arm around Jessie's shoulder.

"There's nothing you can do about it, Jess, except to pray that your friend Alex made it out of the hospital, and that he's been able to find where the gas was hidden. And also pray this guy keeps breathing."

In fact, not only was Malloche breathing more comfortably, but he had started to move his head and arms. Michelle listened to his lungs, gestured up at the improving oximeter reading, and made a thumbs-up sign.

"Jessie, that woman doesn't seem disposed to shooting anyone right now. But I'm upset she's going to take you when she goes."

"If she does, she does," Jessie said. "As long as Claude needs me, I'm safe enough. Once it's obvious he's recovered, I'm banking on them making me an honorary member of the gang."

"That certainly would be quite a tribute."

"I just wish I could have convinced them not to set off that gas. I watched what it does, and it's a horrible way to die."

"It was their plan the whole time. Malloche wasn't going to be talked out of it."

"I guess."

Helpless, the three of them worked on their patient, reversing the effects of nearly twelve hours of sedation.

"Do you think the police'll try and storm Surgical Seven?" Emily asked.

"I think the moment that gas goes off, they'll seal up this place and start negotiating with the Malloches for our release and the location of the other tanks of gas."

On the bed between them, Claude coughed, moistened his lips with his tongue, and began to blink.

"He's baaack," Michelle said.

"I liked it better when there was only one Malloche to worry about," Emily added.

"Maybe being deeply stoned has been an epiphany for him," Jessie whispered, "like Mr. Scrooge. He'll wake up ready to devote his life to the lepers of the world. Here, help me pull him up in bed."

Before anyone could move, Arlette burst into the room, breathless and agitated, her pistol in her hand. Behind her, machine gun ready, was Armand. She crossed to her husband.

"Claude? It's Arlette," she said in German. "Can you hear me?"

Claude groaned, then nodded. Her eyes flashing, Arlette whirled to face Jessie.

"You two, come with me," she said, motioning first at Jessie, then at Michelle. "You stay here with Armand and take care of my husband," she said to Emily.

She directed them down the hallway to the area by the nurses' station. Then suddenly, fiercely, she jammed the muzzle of her gun against Michelle's temple and forced her to her knees.

"You have ten seconds, Dr. Copeland, to tell me what went on in the operating room, and what they know."

"I don't—"

"Nine."

"Please."

"Eight."

"Stop! Stop! Okay."

Jessie looked around. They were at the exact spot where Lisa Brandon had been killed. At least a dozen patients and staff were watching, transfixed. Tamika Bing, with whom Michelle Booker had spent a good deal of time over the thirty hours since Malloche's surgery, was looking on in mute, wide-eyed terror.

"Quickly," Arlette demanded. "And no more lies. If you hesitate, if I even *think* you are lying, I will blow her brains out and start on someone else."

"Okay. Okay." Jessie was shaking. "The FBI agent

used a drug of some sort—a truth drug. He asked about the gas."

"And what did he learn?"

Arlette jammed the pistol in so hard that Michelle cried out.

"He . . . he learned there were three locations— Quincy Market, Filene's, and the subway at Government Center."

"Only three?"

Jessie felt herself go cold at the question.

"Only those three."

Arlette lowered the pistol.

"My husband is a genius," she said to no one in particular.

She dialed Stefan again on her cell phone. Jessie could pick out very little of her French this time, but she knew the essence of what Arlette was saying. There was a fourth soman site—a location that had been kept from Claude at his request—and she wanted the gas released.

"I saved your husband's life," Jessie said. "Please don't do this. You don't need to kill all those people to get away."

Arlette put the phone away and again brought her gun up to Michelle's head.

"You lied to me, Dr. Copeland. That cannot go unpunished."

"Please, you said you wouldn't hurt her."

"You are right, I did."

In one rattlesnake-quick motion, Arlette swung the pistol away from Michelle, pointed it into Dave Scolari's room, and fired. The big linebacker, propped up in his bed, never even had the chance to move. The bullet hole materialized just above the bridge of his nose and just below the steel halo frame that had been immobilizing his neck. The impact drove his upper body back several inches. His pillow instantly became spattered with blood. Then, with wide-eyed disbelief frozen on his face, Scolari toppled off the bed and fell heavily, face first, to the floor.

CHAPTER 41

ALEX WAS IN GOVERNMENT CENTER STATION WHEN the radio call came in from Stan Moyer at Quincy Market.

"Bishop, my monitor just started beeping! He's here someplace and he's tried to set the shit off! I have two people outside and me inside. We've all got the description you gave us and that little sketch. No sighting yet."

"Are you watching the package closely?"

"I'm staring at the seat it's under right now. A teenage girl is perched on it."

"Let's hope she doesn't knock it over. You and your people keep looking. I'll alert Vicki that our man's probably on the move."

Alex radioed Filene's.

"Vicki, he just tried and failed at Quincy Market, but no one spotted him. I think he'll write off the first failure as some sort of mechanical glitch, and go for one of the other two. That means there's a fifty-fifty chance between your spot and mine, but we're closer, right?"

"Much closer. Right across the street, really."

"Okay, make that seventy-thirty. Keep your eyes on the prize, though. It's possible this man isn't even the one we're looking for, but he's the only one we've got any description of."

Alex slipped the radio into his belt. He had been going nonstop for more than thirty-six hours, but he was still riding on adrenaline rapids. He flashed on Jessie. She, too, had gone a day and a half now with virtually no sleep.

Hang in there, Jessie, he urged. *It's almost over.*

He turned to Laughlin.

"He's coming here, Harry, I'm sure of it. The bastard's beginning to panic, and he's coming down here. Tell me again what you think the range of that transmitter is?"

"There's no way to say for sure, but it's got to be far enough away so he can escape before any gas reaches him. I would guess he's got to have a clear line of sight, though. So what—thirty yards? Forty at the outside."

Alex scanned the station. It was rush hour. There were probably two hundred students, shoppers, and commuters on their way home. Overhead, unseen in the shadow of the support beam, was enough poison gas to kill almost every one of them. And somewhere, approaching the area, was a man determined to release it. Alex made visual contact with two of the four men scanning the station, and pointed to his eyes. *Stay sharp!*

"Harry, how long would it take him to get from Quincy Market to here?"

"Five minutes. Not much more."

"Perfect. That gives me time."

"For what?"

"For this."

"A candy bar?"

"Not just a candy bar, an Almond Joy. I do them instead of cigarettes. Want one?"

Laughlin looked at him queerly, then said, "Well, yes, boyo. As a matter of fact, I do."

"Okay. But first you've got to let me show you the right way to eat it."

After the lesson, the two men ate in silence, waiting, watching. They had just finished when Alex's monitor began beeping. He could tell by the reaction of his men that theirs had gone off as well. He searched the crowd. Nothing. Then the stairs. A train came roaring into the station at the instant he spotted Stefan. The killer, if in fact it was he, stood out because he was motionless halfway down a flight of stairs on the opposite side of the tracks, maybe fifty yards away. It looked as if he was holding the transmitter or a cell phone. Alex slipped his radio from his belt.

"Leaning against the railing on the stairs across the track from where I am!" he said. "Move slowly. We don't want him to bolt."

But the man had probably reported the failure of his transmitter to Claude or Arlette and was already starting back up the stairs.

"Harry, help me. He's just reached the top of those stairs. There's got to be a fourth vial, and I think Malloche has just told him to go set it off."

"He has a lot of options in this area. We've got to pick him up before he leaves the station, or else risk losing him. Don't wait for me. I can still run, but I was no track star even when I was young. Go! I'll follow."

Amid screams, Alex leaped down onto the tracks and pulled himself up the other side. Then he charged up the stairs, scanning everywhere for a tall, brown-haired man in a tan jacket. At the last possible moment, he spotted him, moving quickly against the crowd up another stair-case to the street. Alex shoved his way up through the dense crowd of commuters, knocking many of them off balance. Curses were still echoing up the stairwell when he slammed through the exit door onto the street. Stefan was at least fifty yards ahead of him now, on the other side of a busy street, jogging slowly to the left.

Sprinting between cars, Alex narrowly avoided being hit by one and rolled across the hood of another. The curses from the subway were replaced by the blasts of auto horns. By the time Alex reached the sidewalk, badly in need of some extra air, the killer had disappeared up a steep hill to the right. BEACON STREET, the sign read.

"Go up Beacon!" Harry shouted from across the street. "He's headed for the State House—the capitol building!"

Pounding up the hill was agonizing on Alex's knees. A stiletto-like pain had developed under his ribs. Not far ahead, Stefan was running now, probably alerted by the blaring horns. But still, the gap between them was nar-rowing.

Ahead and to the right, early-evening sunlight glinted off the golden dome of the State House. Harry was right. Malloche's man had hidden the fourth canister of gas somewhere in the capitol! Defying the pain, Alex was sprinting now, fighting to keep his head up. A few yards ahead of him, Stefan was approaching a chanting crowd at the base of the capitol steps, many carrying pickets that urged the defeat of capital punishment. Near them, an equally large and noisy group was chanting in favor of it. The TV network vans were there, too.

As he reached the edge of the crowd, Stefan glanced back over his shoulder, tripped, and fell to one knee. He was stumbling to his feet when Alex launched himself in a flying tackle. The two of them hit the sidewalk heavily, already flailing at each other. Alex's fist connected firmly with the side of the killer's face—a blow that would have dazed most men. Nothing. Stefan was young, incredibly wiry, and strong in the way of men who worked at it. He landed one jackhammer punch to Alex's cheek, then another to his mouth. Alex was driven backward and down. His head struck the pavement, and for an instant, his consciousness vanished. He came to spitting blood from a cracked lip, blinking through waves of unfocused color, and expecting to be shot. Instead, he felt a hand on his shoulder and heard Harry Laughlin's voice.

"You okay?"

Alex rose shakily to one knee. "Where is he?" he asked.

"He charged off through the crowd."

"See what you can do to empty the building out. I'll go after him."

"You sure you can?"

"Just get going!"

Harry took off as someone came over and helped Alex to his feet. Battling a wave of nausea, he pushed his way through the pickets, catching enough snatches of conversation to realize that a vote on the death penalty must be imminent. Stefan was nowhere in sight, but there was only one place he could have gone. Begging his legs to cooperate, Alex pounded up the several dozen granite steps to the main entrance—single doors on each side of the stairs. Just as he reached them, he was driven back by a frightened mob of reporters, legislators, and lobbyists trying to escape an apparent bomb threat. Harry!

Alex forced his way through to the central rotunda beneath the dome—stolid and elegant with flags, statues, and marble. No Stefan. He approached a cameraman, who was moving slower than the rest and was actually photographing the panicked crowd.

"Where are they taking the vote?" he asked breathlessly.

The man gave him a queer look, but then shrugged and pointed up the grand, curving staircase.

"House chambers," he said. "One flight up."

Working off a new jet of adrenaline, Alex bolted up the stairs. Two guards, one an armed state policeman and the other a blue-uniformed court officer, lay on the floor by the open doors to the chamber, both wounded by gunshots. Inside, he could hear Harry Laughlin shouting that he was Boston police, that there was a bomb, and that people should leave immediately. The legislators were already clawing at one another to get out.

The wounded state cop groaned and looked up at him. Alex pulled his gun and motioned with his other hand for the man to stay calm.

"Alex Bishop. I'm CIA," he said. "Tall man, tan jacket? Quickly!"

Feebly, the policeman pointed up toward the fourth floor.

"Gallery," he managed to say.

"Help these two men!" Alex barked at the legislators. "Get them away from here!"

Then, he raced up the stairs toward the gallery.

Another court officer lay slumped like a rag doll by the open door to the gallery. He had been shot through the mouth. Inside, people were frantically climbing over the seats to get up to the doorways. Some were screaming. From below, he could hear Harry bellowing at the legislators to calm down but clear out. Gun drawn, Alex pushed through the doorway just as Stefan reached the gallery railing.

"Hold it, Stefan!" he shouted. "Hold it right there!"

Stefan froze.

Beyond and below him, Alex could see Harry, now near the front of the chamber, frantically trying to keep a large number of legislators from trampling their fallen comrades. All around Alex, observers in the gallery had responded to his gun by ducking beneath their seats. Slowly, the tall killer turned toward him. His silenced pistol was dangling loosely in his left hand. In his right, he held a transmitter.

"Don't move," Alex ordered. "Now, drop the gun. Drop it!"

Stefan grinned at him in a most uncomfortable way and then released his grip and let the gun clatter to the floor.

"Now that!" Alex demanded, approaching carefully. "Set it down."

The man's grin broadened and he shook his head. Then he whirled toward the speaker's podium. Alex fired three times, catching him in the head, neck, and back. But he knew it was too late. Stefan lurched forward and toppled over the balcony at the moment the large voting tote board to the right of the podium exploded. A rapidly expanding cloud of death billowed out.

"Get out! Harry, get out of there!" Alex yelled.

But his voice was lost in the screams from below, as the deadly gas began to take its toll. For a moment, he couldn't locate Laughlin. Then he spotted the aging policeman lying facedown in one of the aisles, being stumbled over by those escaping . . . and those dying.

CHAPTER 42

THE SCENE IN THE CHAMBERS BELOW ALEX WAS
from hell. The billowing gray-black cloud of death had
already reached the third or fourth row of seats. Several
legislators—those closest to the epicenter of the blast—
were already down. Others—perhaps twelve or fifteen of
them—were lurching about in a violent, ungainly death
dance, shrieking, vomiting, and collapsing. Still others
were clustered at the doors directly beneath Alex, shoving and tearing at one another in their efforts to escape.

It was clear that the number of dead and dying would
have been much higher had not Harry Laughlin raced to
the front of the hall with his warning and the order to
clear the place out. Now, the man who had just saved
hundreds of lives by his skill in demolitions, and dozens
more by his actions here, lay facedown and motionless,

midway up the center aisle, two or three rows from the leading edge of the smoke and gas.

There was no possibility of making it down the stairs and through the crowd in time. Instead, Alex grabbed the gallery railing just above the center aisle, took as deep a breath as he could, and dropped. Two of the representatives charging toward the door inadvertently broke his fall. Screaming at him and flailing at his face with their fists, they fought to their feet and battled on, pushing and hammering at those in front of them. Alex fended off their blows as best he could, then, still holding his breath, he crawled toward where Harry lay. A woman, staggering and vomiting, stumbled over him and fell. Another collapsed a few feet away. The cloud of smoke and soman enveloped Harry at the moment Alex, now on his feet, grabbed him by the neck of his jacket and one arm, and began dragging him toward the exit. He closed his eyes tightly against the possibility the gas could be absorbed through that route, and pulled with all his strength. Harry was deadweight. Ignoring pain in his shoulder and head, Alex hauled him up the aisle. The crush at the door was nearly gone now, but there were still several people blocking the way. The smoke had diffused so that it was impossible to tell how close the soman was. Alex kept his lips pressed tightly together. In just a few more seconds, though, he was going to have to inhale. He staggered and fell to one knee. His chest felt as if it were about to explode. Suddenly, one of the escaping legislators reached down and grabbed Harry's other arm. Together, they dragged him through the door, and then slammed it closed behind them just as air burst from Alex's lungs.

"Thank you," he gasped, as they continued hauling Harry's inert body toward the stairs.

The man, in his sixties like Laughlin, simply nodded.

"He saved us all," he said.

"Get the rescue squad up here!" Alex bellowed down the stairway. "Rescue squad!"

He rolled Laughlin to his back, preparing to begin mouth-to-mouth. The policeman's complexion was ruddy, not the violet Alex expected. His eyes were closed tightly, and his cheeks were puffed out like a squirrel's in autumn. Alex squeezed the tense skin, forcing a jet of air out between Laughlin's lips. It was only then that he realized the man had been holding his breath.

"Harry!" he shouted. "For crying out loud, Harry, open your eyes and breathe."

Laughlin's lids fluttered open, and he took a breath just as a rescue squad arrived with oxygen.

"I hear you, boyo," he said weakly. "Am I dead?"

Alex motioned the rescue people to get some oxygen on him and take over.

"I don't think so, Harry," he said. "I can't believe you held your breath so long."

"Boy Scouts . . . I was the underwater champion."

Harry closed his eyes again as the oxygen began to flow.

Alex patted the policeman on the shoulder and then headed down the stairs, anxious to get out of the way and to begin formulating some sort of plan to infiltrate Surgical Seven. He was on the capitol steps, watching the onslaught of police cruisers and rescue vehicles, when his radio sounded.

"Alex, it's Vicki. What happened?"

"He set off the gas in the State House. Thanks to Harry Laughlin, we got nearly everyone out in time, but about fifteen or so are down."

"Well, something's happening at the hospital. Ryder, the man we left in the van, radioed a few seconds ago that a helicopter has come up from the south and has just landed on the roof of the Surgical Tower."

"They're moving! How soon can we get a team onto the roof?"

"That depends on what they've done with explosives and what they've done to the elevators. I don't believe we'll be nearly in time to keep that chopper from taking off. Twenty minutes, maybe? I can't say for sure with all that's going to happen where you are."

"Then I need a helicopter. Where can we get one?"

"The state police handle that. Let me make a call."

"Hurry. If they take off, we've got problems. Whatever happens, no one should shoot the thing down. They'll have hostages."

For an anxious two minutes, all Alex could do was pace and call out to the police and rescue people that they were dealing with a highly toxic gas, but that it had a relatively short time of potency. The first of the casualties was being hauled out when Vicki called.

"The State Police Air Wing is on the way," she said.

"From where?"

"Norwood. Ten or twelve miles south and west of you. Go across the street to the open, flat part of Boston Common. They'll be there in ten minutes or less."

"Less would be good."

"They know that. These guys are the best, Alex. If anyone can pull this off, they can."

"Did you tell them I want the thing forced down, but not shot down?"

"Yes. Apparently they're bringing someone who can help do that."

"Keep in close touch with Ryder and get some other observers in the area of the hospital as well, if you can. If they take off, we've got to know exactly when and in what direction."

"Roger that. Now get over to the Common. The area you want is down the hill and over to your right. I'll try and get over there to meet you. Stan's on his way to the hospital."

Alex charged down the steps and across Beacon Street, pushing his way through the mob of protesters and legislators that was being herded in the same direction. There were already half a dozen cruisers and ambulances fighting for space on the sidewalk and street, and more strobes and sirens approaching from every direction—just the pandemonium Malloche had counted on.

Although night was settling in, the Common was still busy with couples, tourists, businesspeople, and groups of kids strolling the crisscrossing, tree-lined walkways. Many of them were now racing past Alex toward the commotion at the State House. He hurried past a tall monument and loped down a gentle slope to the broad, open field. Five minutes passed.

"Alex!"

Vicki Holcroft ran across to him, accompanied by a uniformed policeman.

"Ryder just called. They're lifting off right now," she said, panting. "Ryder says he knows helicopters. He thinks they're flying a Bell Jet Ranger. The State Air Wing should be here any minute."

"Keep him on. We need to know what direction they go in."

"I have two more men in the area watching," she said.

A minute or so later, the thumping of its rotor announced the arrival of the state police chopper. Vicki circled a flashlight over her head. The aircraft swooped in through the evening gloom, over the buildings from the southwest, stopped almost directly overhead, and sank neatly to the turf. Vicki held her radio tightly against her ear.

"Northeast," she said. "It looks like they're headed toward the ocean."

"You coming?" Alex asked.

"No. Less weight, more speed."

"Thanks."

Alex ducked down, sprinted to the open door, and was pulled inside by a man in short-sleeved fatigues, wearing a state police baseball cap.

"Agent Bishop, I'm Trooper Ken Barnes from STOP," he said as they lifted off. "Special Tactical Operations."

"Rick Randall," the pilot called out. "And this geeky-looking guy next to me is Dom Gareffa. You can call him Giraffe. We would have been here a few minutes sooner, but from what I was told, I thought we'd need someone from STOP—that's Ken, there."

"Boys' night out," Barnes said with just the touch of a twang. "I love it."

"Well, as of two minutes and twenty seconds ago, they're airborne," Alex said. "Possibly headed northeast from Eastern Mass Medical Center."

"Got it," Randall said as they lifted off and banked sharply to the right. "Keep talking."

"It's a terrorist, his wife, and maybe some killers from his organization. He also almost certainly has a female neurosurgeon from the hospital along with them."

"Any idea what they're flying?"

"The police spotter who's been watching the hospital thinks it's a Bell Jet Ranger."

"That would be good news. The BJR is fine to look at, but she's slow. This Aerospatiale of ours can fly circles around any Ranger ever made, especially with them carrying a load of people."

"Provided we can find them. Will they be on radar?"

"Not if they fly map-of-the-earth low and keep their transponder off, they won't."

Alex looked out into the deepening blackness. Ahead of them, sky and ocean were almost one.

"Then how?" he asked.

Rick Randall turned around.

"We have our ways," he said. He patted the control panel lovingly. "FLIR. Forward Looking Infrared Radar."

"Heat?"

"Exactly. Any engine for several miles, we'll know about. Right now we're moving at a hundred and forty-five knots. The Bell maxes out at one thirty, but with a full load she'll be going a hell of a lot slower than that. We'll assume your information is right, and keep on sweeping low and to the northeast."

"Unless they're going to land on a boat, I would bet they swing more to the north," Alex said.

"Maine?"

"Maybe."

"You got it."

The powerful airship nosed a few degrees west.

"These people are from Europe," Alex said. "How do you suppose they got a helicopter like that?"

"Probably corporate transport," Randall replied. "They could have bribed a corporate pilot to borrow the company's Ranger for a fun run. Everyone has his price."

"If that's so, that's good news."

"Why?"

"The terrorists are fanatically loyal to their boss,

Claude Malloche. One of them just died so that he could make this escape. I doubt that any corporate jock would have that kind of zeal. If we can put some pressure on them, I'm willing to bet he'll fold."

"You want this guy Malloche bad, eh?"

"I've been after him for five years," Alex said. "He's responsible for about five hundred deaths over his career. One of them was my brother. So yeah, I want him real bad. I have no desire to die bringing him down, though . . . unless that's what it takes."

"Then let's hope it doesn't come to that," Randall said. "And remind me to stay on your good side."

"Rick?" Gareffa said. "Check it out."

"Bishop, come see," Randall called back. "This dot right here. Altitude three hundred and fifty feet, moving to the northwest at a hundred and ten knots. Range almost five miles. Do we go after him?"

Alex barely hesitated. The sky they had to search was already vast, and getting bigger. And now, night had fallen completely.

"We do," he said.

"Okay. Trooper Ken, you may want to get your toys ready."

"You don't have to ask twice," Barnes said.

He unwrapped a machine gun for himself and one for Alex.

"MP5s," he said. "Heckler and Koch from Germany. Best weapons makers in the world. You ever fire one?"

"As a matter of fact, they're sort of standard with the agency. I never set the world on end with my shooting, but I know the gun."

"Good enough. We'll only use you if we have to."

"Two and a half miles and closing," Randall said.

"Can you raise them on the radio?" Alex asked.

"We can try, but I wouldn't recommend it until we're looking up their bunghole."

"I agree. I'm really worried about the doctor they have with them. We've got to find a way to force them down without having them land in pieces."

"Enter Heckler and Koch," Barnes said.

"You know how to miss with that thing?"

"It goes against my grain, but I can try."

"One mile," Randall called back. "Half a mile," he announced a minute later. "Let's hope it's them. They're sure not behaving like they know we're here. I'm going to wait until we have a visual, and then call them up. If it's not them, we may have shot our wad."

They were over sparsely populated land now, knifing along at 145 knots. Another minute and they made visual contact. The totally dark shape was silhouetted against the blue-black sky and blotted out lights on the ground as it passed over them.

"Looks like a Ranger," Gareffa said. "No running lights, no cabin lights. That's got to be a good sign that it's them."

Less than a hundred yards separated them now. Randall made several attempts to raise them by radio.

"Another good sign," he said. "I think we got 'em."

"Not until we have them on the ground in one piece," Alex said. "We may be in for a firefight then. Is it worth alerting the Maine state police?"

"Can do."

"I can't imagine they'd be interested in waltzin' with these MP5s," Barnes said.

"Don't kid yourself. They may be better armed than we are."

They were no more than twenty or thirty yards away now—behind the Ranger and just to the right.

"Giraffe, let's put a spot on them," Randall ordered.

The spot hit the passenger-side window. Randall had been dead-on about the pilot and helicopter being bought. The chopper had the name and logo of Saito Industries painted on the side. He made yet another attempt to hail the pilot by radio. Less than twenty feet separated the two choppers now, as they careened through the night sky at 125 knots. Randall was handling the Aerospatiale with the deftness of a symphony conductor, inching slowly ahead of the Ranger. Alex strained to see inside as they passed. There was a woman in the forward passenger seat. Grace!

"The woman in the seat right here is one of them," he said. "I think she has a gun on the pilot."

Ken Barnes settled in with his submachine gun.

"I can miss in front of them or I can miss through her head," he said.

"No!" Alex said. "I know you're good, but I don't want anything happening to that pilot. Let's send them a message."

He could see both Grace and the pilot now, but none of those in the rear of the aircraft. She definitely was holding a gun.

"Anytime, trooper," Randall said.

"How about now?"

The submachine gun rattled off a five-second burst. Reflexively, the Ranger veered off to the left.

"Put her down right now!" Randall demanded over the hailing frequency.

Then he nudged the Aero next to the Ranger's new position and repeated the order over a loudspeaker that had enough volume to awaken half the state. Barnes punctuated the order with another five-second barrage. Alex could see that there was discord in the Ranger's cabin. The pilot was shaking his head. Grace was waving her gun at him.

"We can't keep doing this indefinitely," Randall said. "I trust myself to be able to fly this close, but I don't trust him. Can you put a few rounds through the windshield without doing any other damage?"

"Probably not," Barnes said. "But I can certainly plant a few around the door."

"Just stay away from the passenger and the pilot," Alex insisted.

Barnes was more than up to the task. The H & K rattled off another burst. Sparks flared from just above the door, and the Ranger lurched to the left. For the Saito Industries pilot, the shots were clearly the last straw. The Ranger slowed, then began to descend.

"Way to go," Alex said.

"Get your weapon ready, friend," Barnes said. "Rick, Giraffe, there's an MP5 for each of you back here."

"Their leader just had a brain tumor removed," Alex said. "I don't think he'll be in any condition to mix it up or run. Just the same, keep some distance away and let me and Barnes here jump out. Don't follow us until you're absolutely certain they're not going to take off again."

The Ranger touched down in a hay field. Randall brought the Aero in about twenty yards away and kept the spotlight drilled on the corporate chopper's side door. Alex and Barnes dove out, rolled, and came up low, sprinting across the grass. They split up as they reached the tail of the Ranger and flattened out on the ground on either side. The rotors slowed, then stopped. As soon as they had, Randall and Gareffa raced across and dove into place, one beside each of them.

"Come out with your hands high!" Alex called out. "Quickly now."

His heart seemed close to pumping right through his chest. Five years and it was about to end—this time for real.

"Get ready," he said to Randall. "They may come out trying to use the neurosurgeon as a shield."

"What do you want to do then?"

"Remember what I said about my being willing to die if necessary to get Malloche?"

"Yeah."

"Well, that goes double for saving the doctor. Hurry up!" he yelled at the helicopter. "One at a time."

The Ranger's door opened. The pilot quickly jumped down, his hands in the air. Then Grace appeared and meekly tossed her gun out before stepping onto the grass.

"Stay over there, Barnes," Alex called out, rising to his feet.

He readied the MP5 and approached the chopper. The Malloches and Jessie were still inside.

If you hurt her, you bastards . . .

Alex was several feet away when Carl Gilbride appeared at the doorway, looking dazed. He reached a hand out for help, but Alex motioned him down. Another shadow, another person silhouetted in the cabin doorway. Emily DelGreco.

"Emily, where is she?" Alex asked. "Where's Malloche?"

"They're not here," she said grimly. "I'm afraid we're it."

CHAPTER 43

UNNOTICED IN THE PANIC AND PANDEMONIUM
that had gripped the city, an ambulance pulled up to the
deserted bay behind the closed emergency ward of the
Eastern Mass Medical Center and waited. Minutes later,
Armand, Jessie, and Arlette Malloche emerged, wheeling Claude on a stretcher. With the help of the driver, a
muscular Arab who was clearly another member of
Malloche's gang, the stretcher was hoisted into the back
of the ambulance and secured. Armand then climbed
onto the passenger seat, and the large van eased away
from the hospital.

Jessie set her bag of instruments and pharmaceuticals
aside and sank onto the padded bench next to the
stretcher. The Malloches hadn't said as much, but she
could tell from snatches of conversation and the sounds
of sirens audible even seven stories up, that they had or-

dered soman to be set off someplace in the city. And now, God only knew how many people were being sacrificed on the altar of their escape.

For an hour, Jessie had watched Armand, Grace, and Arlette gathering their weapons and packing their things. She knew they would be going momentarily, and she knew they would be taking her with them. Armand left the floor briefly and returned with the sort of stretcher used by ambulances and life-flight helicopters. Jessie made a final check of the supplies she had gathered and stopped to say good-bye to Sara and Tamika. Then, to her surprise and bewilderment, Carl and Emily were led off before she was, directed by Grace at gunpoint into the elevator.

"Where are they being taken?" Jessie had asked.

"Away," was Arlette's annoyed reply. "Now, let's get Claude onto this stretcher. We have to get going."

Cardboard had been taped over the windows in the back of the ambulance, but Jessie could still monitor their progress through the windshield. As they were pulling away from the hospital, she heard the distinctive thrum of a helicopter, lifting off from directly overhead.

"Very clever," she said sardonically.

"Actually, it is," Arlette said. "Don't you think so, dear?"

Claude, still somewhat groggy from what remained of the sedatives Jessie had been giving him, nodded and smiled.

"I do, my love," he replied. "I do, indeed."

"The day we decided on your hospital," Arlette boasted, "we borrowed this ambulance and arranged for that helicopter and pilot up there, without even knowing we were going to have to use them. Now, I wouldn't just call that clever. I'd call it brilliant."

"Brilliant," Malloche echoed.

Arlette seemed displeased that Jessie hadn't commented on their genius.

"Maybe you should be doing something besides scowling, Doctor," she said. "Check my husband's blood pressure."

"Whatever," Jessie replied, rummaging through the nylon gym bag for her stethoscope and BP cuff.

"You'd best continue to do your job enthusiastically and well," Arlette said. "Your nurse friend is being brought along to ensure your cooperation. And Dr. Gilbride's presence up above us should assure you that once we all meet up again, you are no longer indispensable."

"In that case, why don't you just let me out right here. I'll call a cab."

Jessie peered ahead through the windshield. Half an hour ago, they had crossed the Tobin Bridge, cruising north. In another fifteen or twenty minutes they would be entering New Hampshire. Then what? Maine? Maybe even Canada. Arlette was right. Their preparations for the contingencies surrounding her husband's surgery *had* been brilliant. And now, it actually seemed they were going to make it.

Aside from Arlette's steely anger at the betrayal in the OR, there had been few threats directed toward Jessie. Still, she sensed that no matter how good a job she had done and would do in treating Claude Malloche, there was a very good chance that neither she nor her two colleagues in the helicopter would be allowed to remain alive. They were the only ones who would know where the killers had gone after leaving Boston.

Jessie was fearful for the others on Surgical Seven who knew what Malloche and his wife looked like, par-

ticularly Michelle Booker and the team from the OR.
From the moment Arlette ordered her away to the ambulance, she had been terrified that they would set the
timers on the explosives and kill everyone remaining on
the floor. Now, she asked once more if that had been
their plan, and once more Arlette gave her reassurance
that the telephones had all been removed, the elevator
disabled, and the doors rigged to detonate if they were
opened, but that no timers had been set to destroy the
neurosurgical floor and its patients.

"You had better be telling me the truth," Jessie said.

Arlette looked at her dispassionately.

"I will say this one more time. You are no longer indispensable to us. I would suggest you take care how you
speak to me."

The smugness in the woman's expression and words,
the unbridled arrogance, had Jessie on the brink of lung-
ing at her to gouge away her eyes. If Armand turned and
shot her to death, so what? She was as good as dead anyway. At least by maiming Arlette, she would be hurting
both of the Malloches before she died.

Hurting both of the Malloches . . .

The words resonated in Jessie's head.

Hurting both of the Malloches . . .

For a time, the notion swirled about without focus.
But there was something there . . . something. Suddenly,
Jessie knew. There was a chance, the smallest chance, for
her to take control—to put her captors to the ultimate
test. The plan was shaky, but it was still a plan. It required careful movement on her part, plus an unerring
insight into Claude and Arlette. Which of them was the
crueler? Which the more devoted to the other? Which
the less likely to sit by and watch the other die? And to
succeed, the plan required two other elements as well—

the absolute devotion to the Malloches of both Armand and the driver, and an inordinate amount of luck.

They had just passed the sign welcoming them to New Hampshire when Jessie put her plan in motion. She knelt beside the stretcher and, under Arlette's watchful eye, examined Claude carefully. Then she went back and reexamined his eyes with her ophthalmoscope.

"Any headache at all?" she asked.

"Not really," he replied. "Why?"

"Squeeze my hand, please. . . . Now with your other hand. Spread your fingers and don't let me push them together. Harder. Is that the hardest you can push against me?"

"Yes."

"Is something wrong?" Arlette asked.

"I don't think so. I don't know."

"What are you talking about? He seems fine to me."

"Mr. Malloche, repeat this phrase after me: Methodist Episcopal."

"Methodist Episcopal," Claude said, with the tiniest hitch.

Jessie shook her head just enough for the gesture to be noticed. Saying the two words, used by many physicians as part of their neurologic exam, was awkward enough to have tested even Demosthenes.

"There are some neurologic signs that haven't been present before," she said. "Very soft signs—a slight thickness in his speech as you just heard, a slight weakness in his right hand—but I think both signs are real."

"What does that mean?" Arlette asked.

"Maybe the early signs of a buildup in intracranial pressure."

"Like the Devereau woman?"

"Yes, exactly."

"What do you want to do about it?"

"I'm going to increase the steroids he's been getting, and add another medicine to reduce swelling."

"Do whatever you have to."

Jessie drew up some steroid and injected it into Claude's IV line. Then she drew up a second medicine and left the syringe just on the surface of her supplies, close at hand.

Claude or Arlette?

Another twenty minutes passed. They had traversed the narrow southeast corner of New Hampshire, entered Maine, and then left the highway. Nightfall was complete now. They were rolling along darkened country roads and through small villages. Jessie sensed the driver had taken the route before—probably on a practice run. As best as she could figure, they were still headed north, maybe northwest. Claude had drifted off to sleep. Arlette seemed heavy-lidded, but she remained vigilant, her stubby machine gun in her lap, her finger on the trigger.

"Where are we headed?" Jessie asked, loudly enough to wake Claude up.

"To a quiet place where my husband can finish his recovery. I don't believe we'll be on the road too much longer."

Jessie knew she had to act soon. Once Carl, Emily, and the others met up with them, the chance would be gone. She was willing to risk her own life, but there was no way she could stand firm while someone threatened to kill her closest friend. And under pressure, there was every reason to believe Carl would crack. It had to be now. First, though, she had a decision to make.

Claude or Arlette?

She examined Claude once more and asked him all

the same questions as before, ensuring that he was awake and alert. Then she motioned Arlette over. The decision had been made. She was the indispensable one. She was the one to fear.

"I think the swelling may still be increasing," Jessie lied. "Look. Look at what happens to the corner of his mouth when he shows his teeth."

As Arlette moved forward, Jessie leaned back and slipped her fingers around the loaded syringe. She had chosen an exposed spot just at the base of the woman's neck.

"I don't see—"

Arlette Malloche never finished her sentence. In one motion, Jessie straightened up, drove the needle to the hilt into the trapezius muscle, and depressed the plunger. Arlette cried out and whirled, her gun leveled at Jessie's face.

"Kill me and you're dead," Jessie said quickly. "Claude, I've just injected your wife with a lethal dose of a medicine called Anectine. It's just like curare. In a minute or so, every muscle in her body will be paralyzed. She will be unable to breathe. But until the very moment she asphyxiates to death, she will be wide awake and aware of everything. Tell them to stop the ambulance. I can save her, but I won't unless you do as I say."

"Don't believe her!" Arlette cried.

But her gun hand had already begun to shake. Claude forced himself up onto one elbow.

"Four minutes," Jessie said. "If I don't get a breathing tube in her within four minutes, her brain will be irreparably damaged. After that, you would not want her to be saved."

Jessie made a theatrical point of looking at her watch. Claude Malloche's eyes met his wife's, and in that moment, Jessie knew she had chosen her victim well. Whether or not Arlette would have reacted as her husband was about to, she would never know. But Jessie had her doubts. Arlette, stunned and undergoing massive chemical change in her muscles, could no longer hold the gun up at all, and in fact, was having difficulty holding herself up as well. Still, she would not ask for help.

"Stop the ambulance immediately, Faoud!" Claude barked.

Without a word, the driver pulled over. Jessie took two rolls of adhesive tape from her bag and had Claude order the two men out of the cab and onto their faces on the ground. Faoud quickly did as he was ordered. Armand hesitated.

"A minute's gone," Jessie said.

She gestured at Arlette, who was bracing herself on the seat but was no longer capable of speaking.

"You'll regret this," the Mist growled. "Armand, just do as she says or Arlette will die. We will get our chance. I promise you that."

Slowly, shielded from Armand's line of sight by Malloche's stretcher, Jessie slid her hand over and wrapped it around Arlette's gun, adjusting her finger onto the trigger.

"Armand!" Malloche snapped. "Quickly! Do as she says."

Twisted around in his seat, the thin, ferret-eyed man looked at Jessie with hatred. But he didn't move.

"Armand!" Malloche barked again.

Jessie could see the indecision on the young killer's face. The muscles by his jaws twitched. His lips tightened. *Prison!* Jessie could almost hear the thought in his mind. She tightened her grip on the gun.

Suddenly Armand's pistol was up and firing. Jessie

dove to the floor, knocking Arlette over as two shots ricocheted off the rear door. Then she shot back, a prolonged burst of machine-gun fire up under the stretcher
into the back of Armand's seat. The killer screamed once
as he was slammed backward into the dashboard.
Behind Jessie, the rear doors were thrown open. But before Faoud could even get a shot off, Jessie ripped him
across the chest with another volley. Blood erupted from
half a dozen wounds. The heavyset man spun around
nearly full circle, and dropped to the ground.

Jessie, who had never handled anything more lethal
than an air rifle, was astonished at how easy it had been
to kill with a weapon built for that purpose. Her heart
was pounding, but she was surprised at how little shock
or remorse she was feeling. She took some time to catch
her breath, and assured herself that both of the killers
were dead. Then she set the machine gun aside and
quickly taped Malloche's wrists and ankles to the
stretcher.

"Help her," Malloche said hoarsely, gesturing to his
wife, who was now on her back on the ambulance floor,
totally awake, but unable to breathe, staring wide-eyed
at the ceiling, her paralyzed limbs in an odd, awkward
position.

No tube! Jessie's mind screamed. *Just lie there! For
Lisa and Scolari, and those people in the lab, and all the others you have killed, just lie there and die!*

"I wish I could do what I want to, Arlette," she said
as she taped the woman's ankles together, then her
wrists. "I really do."

She retrieved the laryngoscope, endotracheal tube,
and Ambu breathing bag from her kit. Then she pulled
Arlette until her head hung backward out the rear door
of the ambulance—a position that straightened her tra-

chea. Finally, she hunched down beside where Faoud lay to get a good view along the lighted arm of the laryngoscope into Arlette's throat. The breathing tube slipped easily between the woman's vocal cords. Jessie inflated the balloon around it to seal it in place.

Finally, she dragged Arlette back into the van next to her husband and began ventilating her with the black latex bag. In just a few minutes, she would be breathing on her own. Even then, Jessie had no intention of removing the thick tube. It would be a perverse pleasure leaving it in Arlette's throat, but a pleasure nonetheless.

As expected, in five minutes or so, Arlette Malloche was breathing on her own, shaking her head against the profound discomfort of the tube, and piercing Jessie with a look so intense that it was unsettling even though the woman's wrists and ankles were tightly bound. Jessie responded with a bland grin and a thumbs-up sign.

Thanks to a med school rotation riding on the ambulances, she had little trouble working the radio. In just seconds, the C-Med operator had patched her through to the Maine State Police.

"We've got an awful lot of people looking for you," the officer said. "One in particular. Wait a minute."

There was some static, then Alex's voice.

"Jessie?"

"Alex, where are you?"

"In the sky, headed your way."

"They've got Emily."

"Not anymore, they don't. She's okay. So is Gilbride. The pilot of the helicopter told us where they were headed in Maine, so we've been looking for you along the way. Where's Malloche?"

"Right here, Alex. He and Arlette are right here, but they can't come to the phone."

"How did—?"

"I'll tell you when I see you. Can you find me?"

"We think so. Listen, turn on the headlights and every other light and flasher you can find. It shouldn't be long."

"Were many people killed by the soman?"

"It was bad, but it could have been much worse. Hang on, we'll be there soon. I'll tell you about it then."

"It's almost over, Alex."

Jessie switched on the ambulance lights and flashers. Then she checked on her prisoners and walked across the road to a small field. The night air was chilly and sweet. Overhead, the pitch black rural Maine sky was radiant with stars. Exhausted and drained, she sank onto the cool unmown grass and waited.

Ten silent minutes later, she realized that one of the thousands of stars was growing larger and moving steadily in her direction.

AUTHOR'S NOTE

While a flexible robot such as ARTIE remains a thing of our future, many of the neurosurgical innovations described in this novel, including intraoperative MRI, are available today. The remarkable evolution of computer technology that has revolutionized much of our world over the last three decades has advanced our surgical capabilities beyond what even the visionaries of medicine could have predicted. High-speed graphic computers are radically changing the face of surgery and information exchange. Virtual reality, the assembly of realistic realms within the computer environment, now enables a surgeon to see and experience in advance the intricate, physiological relationships and anatomical problems he or she will encounter during an operation.

Minimally invasive surgery using thin, flexible endoscopes is being applied to more and more clinical disorders, and the use of lasers and precisely guided radiation as alternatives to the scalpel is growing daily. Telesurgery, with the surgeon operating through robotic hands that may be hundreds of miles away, is being pioneered by the United States military. In the not-too-distant future, a surgeon may be able to perform simultaneous operations on patients in locations across the globe from one another, or even in outer space.

In fact, ARTIE's day may not be that far off. Currently, the use of robotic arms for performing tumor biopsies and placing counterstimulating electrodes in the brains of epileptics is nearly routine. And one team of neurosurgeons is experimenting with a small, intraoperative robot that is steered through the brain to its target using strong magnetic fields.

Michael Palmer, M.D.

References

Grimson, W. E. L., Kikinis, R., Jolesz, F. A., Black, P. M. "Image-guided surgery." *Scientific American,* June 1999; pp. 62–69.

MIT Medical Vision Group. http://www.ai.mit.edu/projects /medicalvision/surgery/surgical_navigation.html.

Textbook on computer workstation–guided neurosurgery. Alexander, E., III, and Maciunas, R. J. *Advanced Neurosurgical Navigation.* Stuttgart, New York: Thieme Medical Publishers, Inc., 1999. (See http://www.thieme.com/onGJHFFAEHKIEFM/ display/590.)

ABOUT THE AUTHOR

MICHAEL PALMER, M.D., is the author of *Miracle Cure, Critical Judgment, Silent Treatment, Natural Causes, Extreme Measures, Flashback, Side Effects,* and *The Sisterhood*. His books have been translated into thirty languages. He trained in internal medicine at Boston City and Massachusetts General Hospitals, spent twenty years as a full-time practitioner of internal and emergency medicine, and is now an associate director of the Massachusetts Medical Society's physician health program.

Look for Michael Palmer's
next hardcover . . .

available in summer 2002
from Bantam Books